THE UNBEKNOWN

BY SHEILA MUGHAL

THE PROPHESY OF TAMAR SERIES

BOOK   2

Published February 2017

AspireINation

www.sheilamughal.com

Twitter - @LinesTamar   Facebook @theunbeknown

THE LINES OF TAMAR

'I am enough of an artist to draw freely upon my imagination.
Imagination is more important than knowledge. Knowledge is limited.
Imagination encircles the world.' – Albert Einstein

Dedicated to some important people in my life

To my enduring second father
Frank Green 1929
A man who stepped into my life when I was about 5 years old, following on from the sudden death of my first father. He rescued my mother and he rescued me on many occasions – mostly in the middle of the night from a broken-down vehicle on the M62. As he became old and frail, I then had the privilege of rescuing him. What goes around – comes around. Such is life; cycles and balance. Thank you, Dad, #2…

Also, my first father
David Norris 1918–1962
A man I never really knew, but a loving spirit who has never left my side or my heart.

Last but not least – my husband
Sohail Mughal
From time to time we all need that one special person who believes in us and gives us confidence, Sohail was that person for me. Thank you for your inspiration.

The dedication would not be complete without mentioning my three precious children,
Martin, Liana and Zarah

And my energetic grandchildren,
Esmee, Elijah, Isaac, Oliver

and my new granddaughter
Talia Ivy Rose Egan – 2016

'Our elders are our inspiration, but our children are our reasons'
Sheila Mughal 2016

Sheila Mughal

Acknowledgements

As a first-time author I was delighted with the five-star reviews for my first book, *The Lines of Tamar*. It is a nail-biting moment liberating precious words into the stark light of critical appraisal. You hold your breath and hope for the best. I completely understand that science fiction may not be a genre favoured by everybody, but those who enjoyed reading my first book informed me that they didn't want it to end. Yet more pleasing was the way in which some readers identified so closely with the characters, that they wanted me to bring them back again.

With the formation of a small, yet enthusiastic fan club, I bowed to the demands of my public and created a sequel. Originally called *The Descent of Sheol*, I later changed the book title to *The Unbeknown* – mainly because the word perfectly described the mysterious nature of many of the new characters. In this strange otherworldly tale, not everything or everyone are as they seem to be.

If I assumed that writing my first book was going to be a challenge, then delivering a sequel conveyed a whole new set of issues. The first one being that I wanted *The Unbeknown* to stand as a book in its own right and sit proudly independent of its older sibling. The aspiration for my second book being that the reader wouldn't need to have read *The Lines of Tamar* to understand the twists and turns of a whole new narrative. Neither did I want Chapter 1 of Book 2 to be a continuation of Chapter 36 of Book 1. As such, and to mix things up a bit, I begin to tell the story of *The Unbeknown* by going back in time – initially to the year 1365 and then to 1793. We do eventually catch up with the 21st century, but as with life – tomorrow only exits because of yesterday.

As for the loyal disciples of *The Lines of Tamar*, you will not be disappointed. As requested, some of the original characters resurface, and any loose strings of unexplained riddles will finally be tied together and resolved. For example, you will find out who killed Katya Beselovaya and learn exactly what became of the formidable Mercy De Vede and Eenayah's twin sons. We will even journey back to the gothic Welsh mansion of Darwydden – a mythical place many of you told me that you would love to visit – should it ever exist. However, *The Unbeknown* will also lay bare an extraordinary new storyline along with a series of new characters to support it. The twists and turns of the plot will continue to unravel throughout.

Sheila Mughal

About 'The Lines of Tamar'

The Unbeknown is a sequel to my first book *The Lines of Tamar* – so it seemed fitting to make an introduction.

Who was Tamar? Well … she was a woman who made history and was a real person as far as we can tell. She lived over 4,000 years ago, in ancient Palestine and her story is told in Genesis 38.

Tamar believed that she was very special, yet she lived in a bygone era; existing in a culture where females were seldom considered to be special. She was so keen to reproduce, that in the biblical story she tricked her own father-in-law into impregnating her. Tamar had something important that she wanted to pass into the future – her genes. Time would prove that Tamar's instinct about her own DNA would turn out to be correct. But, how did she know?

She had twin boys, Pharez and Zarah. Pharez produced a lineage which included King David, King Solomon and even Mary and Joseph. Zarah and his children disappeared from the scriptures, but Celtic hieroglyphics in Ireland revealed that they travelled to Northern Europe. Many royal houses consider themselves to be direct descendants of Zarah, and therefore of Tamar herself.

The Unbeknown

The Lines of Tamar tells of other twins who were later
born to Tamar; on this occasion, they were girls. A biblical
prophecy relating to these children was rumoured to have been
torn from the Old Testament and hidden. The scripts were
concealed for the girls' own protection. The eldest twin 'Leda'
was a pure genetical copy of her mother; she was the clone of
Tamar. Leda was the carrier of the unusual mutant gene and as
such she would also give birth to a clone, who would then give
birth to a clone and so on throughout history. At a time in the
future when it was deemed appropriate and astrologically
significant, Pharez and Zarah would be reincarnated and
reborn from Tamar's clone. It was foretold that the sacred
lineage would begin yet again, as would the biblical scripts
destined to be recreated in a modern world. The name of the
future clone chosen to be the re-embodiment of Tamar, was
that of 'Eenayah Baratolli' – a modern woman living a
privileged and pampered life in Miami. Yet a woman beset
with tragedy.

The youngest of Tamar's female twins was Sheol.
Although not a clone, Sheol was bestowed with supernatural
powers so that she, and all her descendants, would have the
magical ability to protect the line of clones. Throughout
history, many renowned soothsayers, psychics and magicians
were alleged to have descended from Sheol.

Sheila Mughal

A secret cult, known as the 'Ledanites', moved mysteriously in and out of people's lives – controlling and influencing the 21st-century twins (Eenayah and Ruby), who were totally ignorant of their connection to the ancient prophecy.

The Lines of Tamar tells the modern-day story of Eenayah and Ruby. What becomes of them is the direct result of both the Ledanites who are determined to conserve the lines of Tamar, and demonic forces who want to destroy it. Yet all of this happens in the background of a modern narrative which tells of the strife's and struggles of two 38-year-old women in the summer of 2013.

The sequel *The Unbeknown* is a different story, but does explore the strange mystical world of the Sheol descendants and also exposes the true origins of Tamar's unusual genes.

Introduction

5th August 1365 – It was not an easy place to find and
those not local to the area would not know of its existence. It
was just an ordinary sort of a wood; a small scattering of trees
that made up little more than an overgrown coppice. However,
the nettles, the dandelions and the freshly sprouting saplings
hid a colossal secret. Tucked away in a corner of North West
England was a place of universal importance. Not that anyone
would ever know, and that is the way it should have remained.
Surely all great secrets should sleep in peace, perhaps veiled
beneath the guise of mundane normality. However, the secret
slumber of the woodland was about to be disturbed.

It was over 600 years ago, when the hidden mysteries of
Crank were first laid bare. It was told that three pilgrims were
making their way from Burscough, in Lancashire, to a place
known as Hermitage Green near Winwick. The pilgrims went
in search of the Holy Well of St Oswald's, as was common
religious practice of the time.

In times past, there was a vicious clashing of armies,
known as 'the battle of Maserfield'. The Christian King,
'Oswald of Northumbria', was killed and dismembered by the

army of the Pagan King, 'Penda of Mercia'. After Oswald was slain, his devotees carried the soil away from the spot, creating a hole as deep as a horse's height. A spring later emerged from the ground. As was a common rumour surrounding such Holy Wells, pure crystal water gushed from the torn earth, water which was reputed to have magical healing properties. As such, it was an acknowledged tradition in the medieval era to walk to this revered Holy Well on St Oswald's feast day – 5th August.

The three pilgrims gathered their provisions and started their journey shortly after sunrise. Halfway along their journey, in a wooded area near Rainhill, the men stopped to find shade and rest. It was a hot, sticky summer's day and the travellers were wearing heavy, waterproof, woollen cloaks. They heard water trickling from within the copse of a wood, and so made their way through the birch thickets to locate its source. They came across the entrance to a vast cave, and noted fresh spring water cascading down from the rocks. The area where they had found themselves was known as the Crank caverns. Within the cooling shade of the cavern, they quenched their thirst and ate venison pie. They laughed and made merry, full of anticipation of their pilgrimage. According to local folklore, it is then told that the men heard strange unearthly noises coming from within the myriad of tunnels. They had inadvertently stumbled upon a resting place used by others – others not of this world.

Curiosity got the better of them. Somewhat imprudently, they followed the sound of hushed whispers and shuffling of feet. What then befell them became lodged within the chapters of local mythology for centuries. Their eyes met with strange macabre creatures, small timid beings with a peculiar appearance and pale translucent skin. The pilgrims had never seen such a sight before. Terrified, they ran screeching from the caves. The three fellows didn't stop running until they reached a nearby coaching house. Exhausted and breathless, they tried to describe what they had seen to the innkeeper and his wife. Deeply shocked, all they could utter were the words, 'We saw strange beings – creatures unbeknown to us.'

From that moment onwards, the locals referred to this area as 'that of the unbeknown'.

The natural cave system was later quarried for sandstone, and eventually the sprawling acres of underground tunnels became treacherous and unsafe to navigate. Many miners became curiously disorientated in the darkness and lost within the numerous sub-terrarium passageways. The unbeknown, whatever they were – went into hiding and avoided the mortals – the solitude of their hiding place now destroyed.

Sheila Mughal

In order to keep curious children at bay, mothers warned their youngsters about the unbeknown. However, sometimes children do not listen to their parents. Sometimes even adults choose not to listen. There are some mysteries that remain forever unbeknown to those who choose not to pay attention.

CHAPTER 1

27th March 1793

John Anderton's little body shook and shivered as he crouched down behind a large sandstone boulder positioned close to the cave entrance. Sorrowful tears meandered down his dimpled cheeks, whilst his heart silently called out for his mother. His whimpering prayers for rescue and solace destined to be unanswered and unheard.

The porthole to the outside world – although tempting – was equally as menacing as the sanctuary of his undercover hidey-hole. March storms had whipped up a frenzy of turmoil in the wooded valley outside the cave entrance. Sycamore branches, agitated by the vortex of air, participated in an angry orchestra of noise. Like drum sticks, bark clashed with bark. The wind, sucked into the mouth of the cavern, gyrated off the stony walls and spewed out an eerie animalistic howl. The clatter of rain, the clash of thunder, the howling gust, the percussion of angry tree branches; it was all too much for a terrified little boy.

John considered a dash to the stormy world outside, but the cave floor was littered with a lethal ambush that could ensnare, trip and maim. A silky green slime carpeted the rain-splattered pebbles layering the ground. Their slippery surface could easily throw tiny legs towards sharp jagged rocks with razor-edged knives. Knees could be gashed, tendons torn and bones easily broken.

The stench inside the cavern entrance was musty and tinged with decaying human excrement. The ether was chokingly stagnant and oppressive. More than anything he had ever wanted in his short life, John wanted to move. His legs longed to rush towards the outside tempest and his heart craved to be back at home in the arms of his mother – but he was paralysed with fear. After days lost and trapped in a myriad of black endless tunnels, his hollow stomach groaned from its emptiness.

Yet in the stillness of his bleak surroundings, he could still hear the faint echo of commotion. These were not the vocals of his giddy young friends, the pals he had long since become separated from. Neither were they the bellowing yells of those frantically searching for their children, calling out in desperation for their missing sons. These were the sounds of strange, alien movements. He recognised their sinister whispers and knew them to be the muted mumblings of the bearded ones. Whatever they were, they had captured and mutilated his three best friends. In this moment of distress, he dare not dwell too long on the awful memory his infantile eyes had witnessed. Survival had little regard for the past, and cared only for a gateway to a future.

It had been little more than a childish jaunt. Four young pals went out to play and boys being boys, they decided to explore the nearby caverns at Crank. They recognised that they were being foolish, as they knew the tunnels to be dangerous. They had all grown up in the nearby town of Billinge, and often overheard whispers of the horrific legends surrounding the area. Their parents had warned them time and time again to keep away from the mining excavations at Crank. Many local folk had previously explored the extensive network of caverns, never to be seen again. The tunnels were dark, long and spread out on many levels for many miles. It was all too easy to become disorientated and lost. Lancashire folklore had become rife with illustrious stories of cannibals, witches and demons, apparently manifest in equal proportions within this malevolent sub-terrarium network. It was the domain of the unbeknown, and the boys should have known better.

John Anderton and his cousin, along with their best mates from the neighbouring village, were nothing more than bored, restless children. With the fearlessness and presumed immortality of youth, they had plucked up the courage to disobey their parents. It had seemed like a good idea at the time; however, it was to become a moment of tomfoolery that became a tragic mistake.

The storm passed over and the air became still. The silence suddenly became more intimidating than the commotion of the wind. As the sun sunk towards the west, darkness fell upon the wooded glade. For such a young boy, nightfall became even more threatening and eerie.

As the malevolent shuffling moved closer, John spotted a ray of light beaming down from the sky. It illuminated the profile of a narrow ledge. It was a full moon, and with all the clouds blown asunder to reveal a clear sky, the moon came to his rescue. The lunar beams shone through the smallest of gaps, a tiny tunnel leading directly up to the surface. Only a small boy would be able to snake his way through the narrow inlet. He was uncertain, the gap looked too tight. What if he became stuck in the hole? It was a risk, but – as the shuffling feet of the strange bearded beings moved towards him – it was his only hope of escape. John Anderton was only 8 years old, but even for one so young he understood that he had reached the point of no return. Escape and possibly live or stay and most certainly die.

With his heart pounding and adrenaline injecting his brain with courage, young John Anderton made a dash for the ledge – trampling upon a human skull as he sprinted and gasping in horror as the bones cracked beneath his clogs.

Heaving himself up into the tunnel, he felt something grasp at his ankles as he clung on to the perimeters of the sandstone ridge. He was being pulled back into what he knew could soon become his grave. Despite his tiredness, his hunger and stomach-churning fear – he had a resolve to stay alive. With what little energy he had left, he pulled his foot free from the clutching clasp that gripped his tiny ankle. His clogs fell from his feet, but he was beyond caring.

With his cold, tiny fingers grasping at little more than damp bare earth, he pulled his body upwards and worked his way free from the shaft. Barefoot, he ran like he had never run before in his life. It was as though he had wings on his legs. He cared not about the nettles stinging his calves or the grit cutting into his feet. All he could focus upon was his mother. It was as though an invisible cord of maternal love was guiding him home and reeling him in. The child made his way back through the hedgerows and thorny thickets with speed, determination and precision. He wanted to cry, but was determined to hold back the tears until out of harm's way. Flight or fright – he felt and did both.

John Anderton would never run that fast in his life ever again, nor would he venture even remotely close to the caverns of Crank. He lived to tell the tale of his strange encounter and eventually died peacefully in his sleep in 1863 aged 78, surrounded by his numerous grandchildren. His cousin and his friends were never to be found and the sorry story of their demise joined the ranks of multiple other strange myths and legends surrounding this deepest, darkest and most unusual of places. A place hidden away in the North West of England. A place that should have remained hidden.

CHAPTER 2

3rd March 2011

Soul was a young man who was just starting out in his career on a cabaret circuit. His manager promoted him to booking agents as a stage magician, but Soul knew there was no slip of the hand or conjured illusion with his particular stage act. Everything he put on show, was via his inherent natural ability. From the age he could walk and talk, he understood he had a rare ability known as clairsentience. Once he had gained the maturity to control his gift, he was then left with the dilemma of how best to use it.

Working the cabaret circuit seemed an attractive prospect for one with the self-assured foolishness of youth. Work was inconsistent, but slowly he was beginning to gain a reputation and bookings were on the increase. One day, quite out of the blue, he received a phone call from a young woman who called herself Saskia. The gauntlet thrown at his feet was too big a challenge to ignore, and for once involved him using his born-given gift for a serious purpose. He had been asked to contribute to a most peculiar historical detective project and driven by intense inquisitiveness and a financial offer too good to refuse; he rescheduled some tour dates to basically connect with a cave. It was an odd request, but it came with a signed cheque and besides that, his rent payment was overdue.

Little more than a fortnight after Saskia's phone call, Soul found himself in one of the most unnerving places he had ever visited. Descending into a densely overgrown valley, he could feel an unusual vibration in the atmosphere. Soul had a heightened sensitivity to magnetic fields and sometimes felt a dizzy sensation when two ley lines intersected with each other. He wondered if a spiritual portal was active in the valley and made a mental note to investigate the electrical vortex later.

Moving into the cave entrance, his hand felt ablaze as he touched the craggy rock John Anderton had once hidden behind 226 years earlier. Blowing on his fingers to cool down the heat still radiating from his palms, he witnessed the scene play out before him with discomforting clarity. He could see the events unfold before him as clearly as watching a play at the theatre. He could smell the boy's fear, feel the boy's hunger and hear the distant shuffling of feet as strange beings attempted to locate the escapee.

The sandstone cavern was now littered with empty beer cans, discarded hypodermic needles, glue-sniffing paraphernalia and unsightly graffiti. Soul considered the place to be a defiled and ugly ruination. He could feel that the local teenagers had often camped out here in a daredevil show of macho daring. For some reason beyond his understanding, the caverns of Crank seemed to have an ability to suck curious young males into its ravenous domain, as indeed it had done to John Anderton, his friends and the pilgrims centuries earlier. Crank called and they came running. It was nothing more than an inanimate structure of sandstone chasms; some man-made and some natural – but nonetheless it appeared to have an organic temperament and Crank seemed to enjoy throwing out a sporting challenge to overzealous males.

Standing nearby, several men in luminous yellow jackets and hard safety helmets watched Soul with a mixture of inquisitiveness and stifled amusement. Mike, the eldest of the engineering surveyors, mouthed to his two younger colleagues, 'What the heck is he doing?' He looked on bemused as Soul touched the walls of the cave with closed eyes, as though drinking in the energy.

The three engineers watched transfixed as Soul looked up towards a small slither of light exposing the tapered channel which ran up to the surface. In 2011, this was now mostly occluded by climbing ivy and two centuries of gravel that had tumbled down from above. However, touching the sides of the outlet, Soul could see the tunnel as it had looked back in 1793. In his mind's eye, he saw John's clogs discarded on the ground below, as indeed they must have tumbled upon over a century earlier. He squatted down to touch the spot where the skull had been trampled underfoot. Sensing the vibrations left within the ground, he could feel that the skull of a fox had once lay here and not the human skull as presumed by the frightened child. He wondered how much else of John Anderton's tales were the wild imagination of a lost and starving child. However, his job was not to wonder and the story was not his to judge. He was merely the conduit and his ability was restricted to seeing the past as the reality it had been deemed to be at the time. The past was little else but a fingerprint, an impression of former activity.

Rob nudged his two colleagues, 'I think I know this guy. He is some sort of a stage magician. A mate of mine saw him perform at the Parr Hall, Warrington last Christmas. I believe he can read into the history of objects just by touching them or something like that. My mate said he was very good. The bloke has an unusual name; that's how I remembered him. I am sure it must be the same chap.' Rob was unusually animated being in the presence of a performer with a most unusual talent.

Soul was indeed a young man not to be forgotten. With long white-blonde shoulder-length hair, intense steely turquoise eyes, and with a tall thin frame adorned with a black leather ankle-length coat; he looked every inch of the persona he was trying to portray in his stage image. The young Icelandic magician was truly mysterious, unusual and enigmatic. Soul was anything but average-looking, as indeed his name was anything but average-sounding. His birth certificate gave his name as being Saul, but when his manager screwed up the vowels on a press release, the unintentional alteration to his name seemed most fitting. So, Saul became Soul, a young man gifted with a form of clairvoyance known as psychometry – an ability to pick up on the energy of non-living objects by touch and read into its history as easily as others would read a book. Although still only 21, his arrogant confidence was that of a man who was truly in touch with nature and the unseen world around him.

'What do you think he is doing here?' asked Ryan, the youngest of the engineers. Mike shrugged his shoulders, responding, 'All I have been told is that we are here to set up the lasers for the geological survey, while this Soul chap does the energy analysis … or something weirdly similar. That's about as much as the boss told me. Somebody somewhere has big plans for this place and as much as we have been employed to map out the underground tunnels and so on, I am guessing that this Soul chap is here to piece some history together. My wife told me this place is haunted. All very bizarre, but then again – I am not into this paranormal stuff so maybe I am not the right person to ask Ryan.'

Soul spun around and smiled at the watching engineers. He sensed their inquisitiveness. It was not a nice, engaging smile, but more of a polite 'I know what you have been talking about' sort of sarcastic grimace. His icy stare froze them into immediate silence. Soul could be quite intimidating when he set his mind to it. However, for the moment, he needed to vacate this oppressive place before it drained him of verve. He turned to the engineers and asked, 'I need access to the centre of the cave system, could this be arranged?' The men shrugged their shoulders. They were new to this particular job and were not sure how best to answer. Without the guidance of expert cavers and potholers, even they wouldn't attempt to venture into the blackened maze.

Soul walked over to the main tunnel entrance and grasped the metal grate which secured its entry. The thick, rusty iron grills looked more like prison doors, as though they had been designed to keep something in, rather than keep something out. He noticed the effort that had been made to secure the posts firmly into the ground. The sturdy thickness of the metal seemed somewhat of an overkill if just designed to keep curious children from entering. He could smell the fear of the men who had constructing the gates, yes indeed – they had been deployed for containment purposes. The year 1968 came to mind. Soul touched the metal frame lightly and closed his eyes with tight intensity. He could see men in military uniform. He couldn't identify the khaki green/brown outfit, but he felt a sense of urgency. He could smell dynamite. Before they had closed down the entrances, they had blocked some of the other tunnels using explosives. Soul noticed an industrial-sized lock on the gate. He resolved to ask Saskia about the owner of the keys. Images flew into his head. He could see body bags being passed through one of the tunnels. He sensed the relief of those who had been lost inside the tunnels, when they finally made their way back to the safety of the main entrance.

'Have you any idea when you will be able to blast a hole in the surface so we can get into the core?' The engineers gazed upon Soul with a vacant and stunned stare. It was as though he had asked them to stop the orbit of the moon. It was a strange thing for him to think, and a thought that would revisit him in years to come.

Mike answered the question as best he could. 'Just like you, sir, we have been commissioned to do a job. We are here to do a full geological and engineering survey of these tunnels and – in all honesty – I don't suspect we will be igniting any fuses anytime soon. Until we know what we are dealing with, we certainly won't be blowing any holes into anything. Anyway, it's our job to map out what exists and not alter it by dynamiting new holes to change the construction. If you are willing to take a risk, I think there are guides who could take you into the central structure. Saskia may know who they are, so it's best if you talk to her about it. She seems to be the one in control.'

Soul appeared unimpressed by this non-reply. Without making any response, he turned to leave, allowing the puzzled engineers to get on with whatever it was they intended to do with the numerous scientific instruments littering the cavern. For now, Soul had seen enough and would report back to Saskia later that afternoon. He hated this awful, evil, nasty place. It had taken many lives – he was sure of that. He wished his psychic sister could be with him, as maybe she would have sensed something more. He was sure that there must be many other oddities waiting to be told within the rocks of the inner chambers, but for now he had seen and heard enough. Crank was sapping his energy; he simply had to get away.

Before making a hasty retreat, he reminded himself that he had made a mental note to check out if any ley lines surrounded the area. Soul did not require the assistance of any dowsing tools or other divination paraphernalia to locate ley lines. For one with an amplified connectivity to the Earth's cryptic forces, he simply had to stand still, hold out his hands and concentrate. He had predicted the results even before commencing his investigation. The conclusions were as he had presumed them to be. A spider's web of ley lines appeared to converge somewhere deep inside the caverns. He was well aware that ley lines could exacerbate the nature of the energy they flowed through. If the energy was negative, this could have a devastating effect on any people frequenting the area. He was sure that there must be a portal within the cave system; however, as he couldn't get much further than the main entrance, there was little else he could do to confirm his suspicions.

Standing in the wooded valley outside, he then located the oldest tree in the vicinity and lay his hand upon its mighty trunk. He liked trees; they were naturally friendly and chatty. An abundance of human activity had passed by the tree, from it being a tiny sapling to a mighty oak. All he could see were flashing images of transitory humans, as though being fast-forwarded on a video. This little-known sunken valley had indeed been a busy place. From miners quarrying the sandstone, to hunters using the woods as a game reserve, to soldier's hand-lifting anti-aircraft ammunition for storage in World War II to … to what the hell? He took a sharp intake of breath.

Soul jerked his hand away from the tree as though an electric shock had passed through his fingers. He was accustomed to reading history, but was not as familiar with reading the present. Now the present-day was flooding his mind and tapping him on the shoulder. He was being watched. Whatever was watching him was in the here and now. This was not a flashback into a former time, as with the monk who had occasionally caught the corner of his eye as he drifted past in his long, dark robes. The monk was harmless in that he was little more than an imprinted memory. By contrast, whatever had just sent shockwaves through Soul's body was current and real. This was something more than capable of invading flesh, but whatever it was, it was not human.

Not one to usually be intimidated by anything, Soul made a dash out of the valley, along the footpath and to his awaiting car. He recalled John Anderton making that same dash along that same route – as though his legs had wings. He was reliving a former moment from someone else's past, as he now ran down the same winding path. This was unusual; something that he had never experienced before. His world, and the world as was before, normally never collided. In his rushed exit, he resolved to stick to stage shows.

Soul was relieved to reach his car. Tumbling into the front seat, he locked the doors and simply sat for a moment as he struggled to catch his breath. His nerve endings still tingled. Could something have given chase? He started the engine and endeavoured to drive away as quickly as he could. He would call the boss lady once he was safely back at his hotel.

A few therapeutic Brennivín shots later, he gave Saskia a call. He kept the conversation brief. Trying to remain calm and professional, he told her, 'Yes, I can conclude that Crank caverns carry a lot of historical activity and the story about the four boys appears to be true. I saw just one boy escape and something did try to capture him.' Saskia responded,

'Have you any names for me Soul?' He replied, 'John Anderton was the boy who escaped, he was 8 in 1793 and I can confirm that he died in 1863. His grandson came to visit the cave after his funeral. It was a sort of memorial pilgrimage to help him cope with his grief. I can be fairly accurate about that date. I am very good with dates, so hopefully that may give you something to work on.'

Saskia scribbled down the details. Her employers would require this level of information. She continued with her questioning. 'And what about the other three boys, John's friends who were supposed to have been murdered in the cavern – are the stories true, did this really happen?' Soul could not be sure. 'I cannot tell simply by touching the rock in the outer cavern to confirm if this was the case. If the boys had been murdered deep inside the cavern, then you need to get me deep inside the cavern. I can only pick up the energy as it existed at the time and in the place when it occurred. I do know that in John's mind, he believed he had witnessed his friends being slaughtered; however, he also thought a fox's skull was a human skull. He was a frightened little boy who had been lost in the darkness for several days and his imagination was in overdrive. I connected to what was in his thoughts at the time, but I cannot conclude how demented or accurate his thoughts were. You must remember that at the moment I connected with his energy, he felt he was about to die. His energy was catastrophically distorted by fear.'

Saskia felt slightly disappointed. She had been hoping for a greater level of detail. Needing to dig further, she asked, 'And what about the small, bearded creatures who allegedly grabbed at the boy's foot? They searched for the boy within the large cavern at the entrance, so if they were there then you must have picked up on their vibrations – surely?'

Soul shivered. It was a cold, unnerving quiver that descended down his spine. He knew that whatever had been hunting down the boy had not been mortal, and – more so – it had the ability to disguise itself or even transfer its energy elsewhere. Most unusually, he had not felt it whilst in the cave; however, it had watched him as he left. It was observing him as he linked with the large oak tree. Over 200 years later, and it was still alive – whatever alive was to such a thing. How could something remain alive for so long? He was confused. Soul could have offered up more detail, but did not want to give Saskia any reason to send him back to the area, and so he kept this information to himself. He responded with a vague, 'No, I felt nothing more. The boy's distress was so intense that his energy drowned out any other vibrations.'

Not wanting to revisit the caves he concluded, 'I trust that the tunnels are unsafe and so, until they can be made secure enough for me to venture inside and all entrances opened up, there is little I can do to assist you for now.' Soul felt a sense of relief in that he had conjured up a way to exit from the immediate project. With that statement, Soul paused. He felt guilty. He didn't enjoy lying, but he knew that if he mentioned the strange presence, he would risk enflaming her curiosity further. Saskia did not respond. Soul sensed her disappointment. He had no idea why she was so determined to find out what happened to some schoolboys who got lost inside the caves over 200 years ago, but, then again, he had been hired to help and not hired to question.

Saskia eventually responded with a sigh. 'So be it, Soul. I understand what you are saying. Just email me your full report as soon as you are able. No doubt I will be in touch once we have surveyed the full tunnel system.' With that, she hung up without so much as a friendly 'bye'.

After concluding the conversation, Soul felt more determined than ever that his unusual ability should be reserved purely for entertainment purposes. He was not cut out for paranormal detective work.

As for Saskia, she was someone he had never met in person. Their only interaction thus far was by phone or email. Given the nature of his recent experience, he silently hoped he would never hear from her ever again.

CHAPTER 3

3rd August 2011

Don Morris had been a TV Historical Researcher since leaving university. He had taken early retirement from the BBC almost a year ago, and apart from a part time job in the local library, had been looking forward to a life of relaxation, golf and days out hill walking with the rambling club. Of course, all his future plans had included the woman he loved – his wife Patsy.

Although still in his early 50s, Don had been a prudent saver since his student days, and had accumulated enough financial security to swap his life of international travel for cosy slippers by the fire. It seemed to be a cruel blow of fate that all his lifelong aspirations had been cut short, when Patsy was given a diagnosis of pancreatic cancer. Maybe the timing was wrong, maybe it was right. Who could say? In many ways, the time away from the demands of work gave him precious moments with Patsy. Time he could never reclaim. Trying to be philosophical in difficult circumstances, he was at least grateful that he could be there for her in her final moments. The disease was cruel and inconsiderate. It did not care about timing. It did not care about Patsy. It did not care about him. Cancer simply did not care.

The cut ran deep and the wound was still very raw. Don had a need to get back to work so he could vanquish the clutter that tormented his thoughts. His desire for new employment was less to do with money and more to do with keeping busy and falling exhausted into a sleep undisturbed by melancholy. Fatigue seemed like a welcome but temporary panacea, until the stark light of sunrise nudged him awake to live yet another lonely day. Mornings only served to remind him that the loss of his wife hadn't been a brutal nightmare. It was real, it had happened. He would open his eyes and pinch himself. Yes, Patsy was still gone and he would spend yet another day home alone. He resolved to find something – a job, a hobby – just something … anything to shut out the vacuum of a future without his soulmate.

He had not been on an actual job interview in maybe 20 or so years. He recognised that he was rough around the edges and had no idea what to expect. Miss Saskia Usov had requested to meet him at the Inglenook Lavender Farm near Rainford at precisely 1 p.m. He had no idea what this was, but was keen to find out. His interview for his previous job was at White City in West London at the former BBC Television centre. He recalled it as being formal and stuffy. The Lavender farm - he didn't know what to expect from such an unusual-sounding venue.

Should Don have envisaged a business centre or boutique restaurant, then his assumptions would have rescinded the moment he drove down the dirt track and into the farmyard. Indeed, this really was a lavender farm, complete with petting donkey, goat and home-made ice cream. It was a sunny English day and the front garden was packed with people enjoying afternoon tea and scones; yummingly layered with jam and clotted cream. The main clientele appeared to be mothers with young children or pensioners with no particular schedule of importance. Geese and hens wandered freely around the ankles of those consuming calories in the warm sunshine.

Don scanned the vista of picnic tables. Only one played host to a solitary woman, smartly dressed and working on a laptop. He approached her cautiously, not wanting to be too assuming. 'I am so sorry to disturb you, but are you Miss Saskia Usov?' A young, petite woman in a tight brown pencil skirt rose to her feet. 'Indeed I am, and I am guessing that you are Mr Donald Morris.'

Saskia was much younger than he had imagined. He had already been through a preliminary phone interview with her and her professional, enquiring tone had portrayed the image of a much older woman. However, the petite girlish frame facing him, with golden kiss-curls that naturally coiled around her face like bouncing springs, was not an image he could have predicted. She had the appearance of a grown-up Shirley Temple or perhaps Goldilocks as often read to children as a bedtime story. Transfixed by her golden tresses cascading against the backdrop of the lavender fields, Don was finding it difficult to take this interview seriously. Saskia was less than half his age, but nonetheless she came with the authority to offer him a much-desired job.

She commanded the waitress with a commendable degree of assertiveness and began her introductions. 'Don, thank you for meeting me at such short notice. This place is fairly close to the Crank Caverns and if we offer you this research job, we would expect you to become quite familiar with this area and the people who live here. This café offers the best tea and cake in the locality in my humble opinion, and so I thought I would introduce you to it.' Don concluded that Saskia was talking as though he had already got the job, but then again … maybe she just flirted with all the candidates. Perhaps that was part of her interview technique. He guessed that she had sensed his nervousness and was probably trying to put him at ease.

During the phone interview, Saskia had taken the driving seat and all the questions had come from her direction. However, now Don was keen to know more about the job in hand, especially as it meant taking time away from home. As soon as that thought trickled into his head, he remembered that home wasn't home anymore. Time away – from what and from whom? A hotel room in a strange town would be no less lonely and forlorn than home.

'Saskia, can you give me more detail as to what the work entails?' enquired Don. The young interviewer flicked her gilded ringlets back off her face, as though by way of a reflex response. 'Yes, of course Don. Basically, I represent a group of people who have an interest in the caverns and tunnel network at Crank. They are considering buying it and possibly may wish to develop it for other purposes; however, before they make any decisions they need to know what they are up against.'

'Hmm,' thought Don, 'odd turn of phrase.' His puzzled facial expression encouraged her to resume her synopsis. She continued, 'As far as the disused mining shafts are concerned, they are numerous in quantity and are supposed to stretch for many miles. There are some peculiar local yarns surrounding the Rainford Delph Quarry – note that this is its official name. There are tunnels which are rumoured to have existed long before the quarry was operational and it is alleged that there are many secret entrances and exits that open up into the cellars of local pubs and trapdoors of old manor houses. God forbid, it is even said that one of the crypts in St Aidan's cemetery is supposed to be a false grave and, instead of housing a coffin, leads to steps descending down into the tunnels. Sounds all very Hammer Horror!' Saskia gave a mock shiver, seemingly appalled at the thought of using a tomb as a portal to some dark underworld. She continued, 'There has been so much local gossip that has passed down through the ages, that nobody really knows how many fabrications of the truth exist. Don, we require the successful applicant to interview all the local folk and then find out if any of this mythology actually has any basis in historical fact or is merely the result of overactive imaginings. Whatever tales are unearthed need to be verified, evidenced by fact and of course documented. I am looking for a researcher who has the appropriate experience and your CV seemed quite fitting.'

Don liked the idea of mingling with the locals. It was probably the distraction he needed after months of isolation. The young woman had caught his attention. 'Fascinating, please continue Saskia.' Don was intrigued. Saskia obliged accordingly. 'As I have just mentioned Don, there are many myths about this place – some of them quite extraordinary. The group I represent want to know the truth. I am assured that there is an underground cathedral within the Crank cave complex, complete with altar carved into the stone, and obligatory gargoyles. They want to know if this exists and, if so, who worshipped there and why.' Don was quite speechless and so he simply sat and listened. Saskia continued, 'Numerous people are supposed to have died in the cave network. If that is the case, then there should be official reports that exist about them – newspaper cuttings, death certificates, burial records. We want dates, names and as much detail as available. Do you think you can do this, Don?'

Of course, Don knew that he could more than take on this strange project. It was totally in scope. He recognised that, as a former BBC researcher, he was made for this task. Plus, the subject matter sounded totally captivating. He knew himself well enough to know, that if a mission caught his attention, he was bound to do a good job. However, he was curious. 'If you were to offer me this assignment, Saskia, I would say yes. All you have described so far meets with all I can offer. I am a widower – not a term I thought I would ever use, but basically, I have nothing else left but to completely throw myself into research such as this. I have just one question, however, and it is a question the local people I interview will ask of me, so I need an answer – why do you and the group you represent want to know any of this, why should rumours of events from long ago matter to anyone? I haven't actually worked with any land developers in the past, but I would suspect that the majority of them probably have little regard for history.'

For the first time since they had met, Saskia looked on edge and fidgety. She knew she had to give him some sort of an answer. Don had worded it in such a way that he himself would be required to give the locals an explanation. She considered her words wisely, taking just a few seconds longer than required. The lack of an immediate response told Don that she was about to embellish the truth with a sweet sugar coating. Such was the wisdom of age and a career in the media of misshapen truths.

Eventually she replied, 'Good question, Don. By trade I am a solicitor. As well as doing a zillion other admin jobs, I also help pull the legalities of a deal together. The group I represent are cash rich investors and wish to develop the area. There are many possibilities as to what Crank could become, but as yet they seem undecided about future plans. The tunnels could be a great asset and maybe the legends exploited commercially – for instance as the ultimate spooky theme park … by way of an example. On the other hand, the alleged vast underground lake may have some therapeutic uses and if, for example, the group wanted to convert this into a classy health spa, such rumours about cannibals and demons may have the opposite effect and revolt a possible pampered clientele. Either way, the myths could be viewed as a positive or a negative. Before making a major investment, the board just need to know which direction to take. As to what you tell the locals – I am sure that any financial venture that could bring money into the area would benefit the native community, plus the tunnels are unsafe, so they cannot stay as they are. Surely any use that makes them purposeful as well as harmless would be most welcome. As reasons go, does that sound okay Mr Morris?'

Don wasn't sure if she was asking if her version of the truth sounded plausible or not, but it certainly came across that way. Somehow, he didn't totally believe her, but he wanted the job. It was a most curious story, and time away from a house that was no longer a home would be most welcome.

She didn't ask him if he wanted the job – she didn't need to. He simply said the words, 'I'll take it.'

Saskia was shocked by the swiftness of his reaction, especially as she hadn't yet made him a formal offer. She was quite taken aback. 'Err, well – okay. You caught me off balance for a moment, Don; but indeed, I would like to offer you the job, although I would have liked to have asked before you accepted. Do you not want to know about the salary before taking the position?' In truth, money was not the issue, but Don felt it best that he played along. Saskia continued, 'We can offer you £800 a day minus expenses. It is only a 6-month contract at minimum, maybe less. Do you think this would be acceptable to you?' Don would have accepted a quarter of this offer, but indeed it was generous and it would help ease his shrinking bank balance somewhat. 'Yes, thank you, Saskia – I am happy to accept. Six months should be more than long enough to uncover the creepy Crank cave myths.'

Saskia was delighted. She had already pre-prepared a contract in advance as she knew Don was ideal for this assignment even before meeting him. Once he had made his mark on the appropriate lines, Saskia deposited a large file on the picnic table. 'That's brilliant, Don. I will book into a local hotel from next Sunday night if that works for you, and in the meantime, here is a stack of geological reports for light bedtime reading. It will give you a good feel for the tunnel network. The other historical stuff is for you to uncover.' Don was quietly impressed by how organised and prepared his youthful new boss seemed to be.

'Okay, so now business has been concluded Mr Morris, how about we order some afternoon tea and you can ask me more questions about the caverns if you like, or not as the case may be.' She giggled at what she presumed to be a humorous quip.

As Saskia jumped up with girlish energy to track down a menu, Don uttered a silent prayer. He felt rescued. He had been given a purpose and, for now, it was a small step closer to healing and closure. He gazed out at the endless lines of lavender plants in the field ahead, and noted how they contrasted against the beautiful azure sky. Patsy would have loved this place. Lavender was amongst her favourite fragrances. The setting for his reinvention was most fitting. For the first time in a long time, he felt at peace. He doubted he would ever be truly happy without his lifelong partner, but in the absence of happiness, peace of mind was a good enough bed mate.

CHAPTER 4

17th January 2012

Saskia Usov was working from home today. She did rent an office in Central London; a place she kept mainly by way of an impressive mailing address and occasional meeting place, but looking out at the cars skidding on the iced roads of the village High Street, she decided home was by far the safer option this morning. Victorious in managing to light the lounge fire to ward off the January chill, she hurriedly drank down her cereal, forever mindful of the time. She had a video link conference call in less than ten minutes, yet she was still adorned in her PJs and oversized granny-like dressing gown.

As homes go, this was a chocolate-box cottage in the middle of the English Cotswolds. Built around 1640, her Grade II-listed abode came with a thatched roof, English elm beams and adorned with the honey-coloured limestone typical of the area. Ambrose cottage was picture postcard perfect, and it was almost all hers. Still only in her early twenties and nearly mortgage free, Saskia had done well in life – somewhat of a rarity for one so young. She appreciated her good fortune, but she also recognised the price she had to pay for such providence. Luck had not come without a cost.

With its low ceilings and protruding beams, the lounge could not play host to the huge gigantean plasma screen hooked up to her PC, so with her bare feet hopping along the cold stone floors, she made her way into the conservatory which doubled up as her home office. She made a mental note to invest in some slippers. As lovely as her cottage was, it lacked modern-day insulation and could become hideously cold in winter.

She had been awaiting this video call with anticipation for many months. She knew that members of the Ouroboros Board would also be eagerly watching. Saskia was in the bizarre position of not actually knowing who her employers were, in as much as she had never met them. She had graduated from the London School of Economics with a top-notch law degree back in 2008, and shortly after graduating was hired after her first and only interview. Her appointment seemed like an unbelievable stroke of luck, but she accepted the job without question. She had never met any of her elite and secretive employers, but was paid handsomely for her obedience and lack of curiosity. Business was conducted on a 'need to know basis' and she knew not to pry beyond that. Team Ouroboros had obviously profiled their young candidate well.

From what she could gather, they were a group of exceptionally wealthy property investors. As their solicitor, a greater proportion of her job involved her sourcing unusual historical properties and then handling the conveyancing legalities of purchase. However, the estates she was tasked with finding were somewhat unusual. Typically sprawling old manor houses, listed barns, crumbling castle ruins or ancient antiquities, they all had one common characteristic – an underground feature of one sort or another. Be they tunnels leading to coastal caves once frequented by pirates, or the covert hideaways used by priests and monks during the Protestant Reformation, it mattered not. The Ouroboros seemed to be obsessed by subterranean hideaways. They would invest to investigate and then either convert their portfolio to hotels, restore them for some other use, sell them on to other investors, or simply leave them alone to perish into ruination. As business plans went, it didn't always stack up financially, but she had learned not to challenge her enigmatic employers.

Today, the surveying company (some of them being from the same team that had mapped out the catacombs of Rome in 2009) had finally made their three-dimensional images available for preview. Using the same laser-scanning technology, the caverns at Crank would be exposed in multi-layer detail. Saskia had been the one to transfer payment into their account, and so she knew how much this had cost. She had no idea why the Ouroboros would go to such trouble and spend so much money on a few mining shafts, but she sensed she was about to find out.

She switched on her PC, hooked up the plasma screen, and then scrunched herself up on her wicker settee, as though settling in for a night at the movies. She had been looking forward to this screening for what seemed like far too long. It was all very exciting.

The Chief Engineer, Clive Andrews, began with an explanation of the science surrounding this ground-breaking 3D-surveying technique. 'Basically, we set up scanners in as many locations we could gain access to and keep in mind the fact that we couldn't get into some of the blocked tunnel systems, so sadly this cannot be a totally complete picture. However, what we did get will impress you. The scanners are programmed to turn very slowly, and in so doing send out millions of light pulses that bounce off every surface they make contact with. The light pulses ricochet back into the scanner and from there are recorded on a computer as a series of white dots, known as a "point cloud". Gradually, every rock face, ceiling and floor is bombarded with the dots, enabling the computer to build up a representation of each of the tunnels and caverns.' With that he paused for questions, but hearing only the silence of a stunned audience he continued.

'Okay, so no questions so far? Great, then let's continue. What I am going to play for you now will look as though it's actual video footage of the tunnels we gained access to – but that isn't actually the case. What happens is that the computer completes a 360-degree, three-dimensional, moving image of the tunnels and caverns, with every surface looking like it is made up of small white dots. As all of this is being processed, a camera on the scanner takes a picture of each surface. The data is then fed into the computer software, enabling colour to be added to basically join up and fill in the dots. We also considered the fact that the tunnel system is multi-layered and some of the mining shafts come quite close to the surface. So, to compliment the underground laser work, we also used a technique called GPR or ground-penetrating radar. Over ground we used radar pulses to detect the reflected signals from subsurface structures. All in all, the combination of both techniques brings an interesting 21st-century twist to the art of subterranean map making.'

Once again, he paused for a vocal reaction, but meeting with yet more silence Mr Andrews began to worry that the video link was broken. 'Can I ask everyone to just confirm their attendance please?' It was an illuminating question which was met with a multitude of responses in several languages. Saskia herself was shocked by just how many people had tuned into this presentation. These were the voices of her secret and mostly silent employers, and by the mumbled multilingual response, there was lots of them. The Ouroboros were global – this was a revelation!

Assured by the fact he wasn't alone on the call, Clive continued, 'I think you will be amazed and captivated by what we have found at Crank, so if everybody is ready, I will hit play. This will take about 30 minutes as it's only really a preview, but I will send Saskia the master tape for her to distribute. When you all have this installed on your own computers, it will be like playing a video game. You can zoom in and out, turn corners, jump over ledges, swim through water and go wherever you want in the cave system without even leaving your office, or getting shot with a laser gun for that matter.' Clive Andrews's feeble attempt to be amusing obviously failed, but nonetheless his extreme pride and delight of what his team had achieved was obvious from his voice.

With that Saskia relaxed, took a swig of coffee and waited to see what the merging of these ultramodern technologies could deliver. Indeed, an unusual tale was about to unfold. She felt a mix of elation, with a confusing sprinkling of fear. What would the caverns of Crank reveal?

Her eyes were transfixed on the images being played on her plasma screen. It was as though she had stepped inside a game of Minecraft. In this truly extraordinary 3D world, tunnels lost to darkness had been opened up into a light so detailed, that each grain of quartz and orthoclase seemed to sparkle and stand proud. On some of the tunnel walls, man-made chisel marks were clearly visible. Underfoot, debris from explosive blasts could be evidenced so lucidly, that one could almost smell the dynamite. Stacks of thin slate like stone had been placed one upon another to form huge columns, presumably to give some stability to the rock above. Panning around the chambers, Clive then tilted the angle upwards to reveal a multitude of hanging stalactites –

some with a drip of water still hovering from their tips as though captured in mid-air. Pulling back to reveal a bigger area, layers upon layers of structures could be seen stacking up, one upon the other like a house of cards. Clive explained that on the 3D map, they had identified at least six layers of tunnels; some were deep underground, whilst others were dangerously close to the surface. Like a spider's web, this mesh of subterranean labyrinths connected with other quarry works from neighbouring sites. It was as though the miners had unintentionally created a myriad of interconnecting worlds.

Clive began to explain, 'What we can see here, folks, almost resembles a rabbit warren. The mine shafts of Rainford Delph Quarry extend for an estimated radius of just under 3 miles. However, because the miners tended to follow the seams, they often met up with excavations from other quarries, linking up with neighbouring miners, also hacking away at the same seam. We haven't explored beyond Rainford, but we can clearly see where tunnels converge. Taking that into consideration, the complexity of the multiple layers of passageways and underpasses – what we are left with is a very dangerous killer maze. It is no wonder that some people entered this structure and remained lost for eternity. This whole underground system could easily have an expanse of over 10 miles ... maybe more. Once in there, and confused by the darkness, it is entirely probable that a person would never find their way out again.'

A voice raised a question. Saskia recognised the familiar tones of the one and only person she communicated with by phone – the enigmatic Mr Smith. His soft voice had a distinguished Scottish lilt that was unmistakable. She had often wondered if the commonality of his name meant it was an alias; however, she knew not to probe. AKA Mr Smith made a handsome monthly deposit into her bank account and that was all she needed to know. Mr Smith enquired, 'Clive, what you have shown us so far is technologically mesmerising and of geological interest; however, we are more concerned with the unusual legends surrounding Crank and are also curious to know about the rumours surrounding the secret exits and entrances. Can you show us anything pertaining to this?'

Clive had been playing with his audience. He had recognised that the myths surrounding Crank had always been their real interest, but first wanted to captivate his spectators with the magnitude of his team's achievements. Responding more like a showman than a scientist, he replied, 'Buckle up your seatbelts, we are going for a ride.'

Clive zoomed in on one particular tunnel as it terminated. As it reached its end point, a set of stairs could clearly be seen leading up to a trapdoor. Clive zoomed out and then back in again, to view another tunnel which had been clearly blocked by concrete sometime in the last seventy years or so. Clive explained, 'As you can see, some of the surface tunnels have been deliberately blockaded. Given how hazardous this entire underground area is and how many people have allegedly been killed down here, I guess that's hardly a surprise. With regards to the surface tunnels, some of these don't appear to have anything to do with the original quarry. Many of these run through the subsoil and clay, so it seems they were used mainly to gain access to the caverns, rather than for the purpose of mining. At least six of these surface exits lead up to the outside world via carefully constructed steps. Not a job for us, but if you get a map expert on the job, they may be able to locate these hidden entrances for you. All very fascinating I am sure you will agree. Now hang on to your hats, because you will enjoy where I am about to take you next.'

Clive flipped into another area of the caverns and continued with his narration. 'Not all of the underground systems at Crank are man-made. In fact, the caverns at the entrance have probably been in use since the Stone Age. I understand that fossilised animal bones, still bearing marks from stone tools, were once found in the area. Maybe we can date habitation here back to before the Bronze Age. However, there are other geological items of interest I would like to show you.' With that Clive pulled a virtual rabbit from out of his wide-screened hat.

A vast underground lake filled Saskia's plasma screen with its majesty and immensity. With a computer-generated blue tint, and filled by several waterfalls plummeting from higher river systems, the main cavern was bejewelled with garlands of crystal. Beguiling sparkling anthodites, stalactites and stalagmites decorated its shores. Clive spoke with delight and animation. 'We could not measure the lake with absolute accuracy as we couldn't get laser cameras around its total circumference, but we are talking about a measurement of at least 2 to 3 acres. This is a full-on lake. In fact, there is a complete underground water system at Crank. We also located a "blue lagoon" which is probably about 50 metres across, plus many miles of various rivers, streams and weirs. We even traced the source of an artesian well, and it could be that there are more than one. So somewhere within the woods and fields of the overlying area, there must be a bore hole pushing up water. Maybe one of the surrounding houses used this as a source of spring water, but whatever and wherever – it does exist. Sandstone is very porous, so it lends itself to invading water. This area has some interesting geology.'

Clive waited for a reaction, but yet again he was met with stunned silence. He looked at his watch. He had been talking for a good twenty minutes now, but he had left his final and best revelation until last. Flipping over to a different view, he zoomed into another screen. His audience would be in for a treat. In his line of work, he seldom had the theatrical opportunity to build up to a crescendo, but right here and now this was his moment. What they were about to see would blow their minds, and Clive knew it.

CHAPTER 5

25th January 2012

Saskia was in deep thought. With her face cupped in her hands, she looked out of her kitchen window at the strange orange and pink winter sky. She paid little attention to the water cascading out of her Belfast sink and covertly tumbling like a waterfall onto the stone floors. Her mind was over the hills and far away. With sodden feet suddenly shaking her back into reality, she turned off the taps, cursed her own carelessness and then went to check the time. She hated goodbyes.

Don had become something of a friend over the past five months. Every week they had a regular Friday catch-up, which although conducted in the capacity of a professional relationship, had a tendency to become side-tracked into personal issues. In different ways and for different reasons, they were both lost and lonely souls. It is possible that they recognised themselves in each other. Don was a widower and Saskia was Saskia – an independent woman, living in a tiny village and new to an area where even second-generation families were still just about tolerated as strangers. Saskia was very much alone in middle England.

She heard the creaking of her front gate and felt the dread of confrontation lying heavy on her shoulders. She had deemed it best to meet Don in a neutral place. It would be an easy train ride back home for him afterwards. She considered it cruel to drag him all the way into her London office, simply to terminate his contract and then have him battle his way home on crowded city tubes. Every so often, she was thoughtful like that.

Don gingerly picked his way along Saskia's slippery front path – still frozen despite a handful of grit intended to provide traction. Wrapped up warmly, and wearing his favoured Ushanka hat, Don still felt a chill in his heart. He had relished and appreciated his time with Saskia, as well as the villagers of Rainford and Billinge. The research project he had been tasked with was both enlightening and fascinating, plus as a regular of the local pub, he had made many new friends. But all good things must come to an end at some stage, and alas this particular project was nearing its completion. Saskia had invited him to her home and then offered to take him out to lunch afterwards. Don was too long in the tooth not to realise what this meant.

Saskia opened the door, cheeks flushed deep pink from sitting too close to the lounge fire. She gave Don a warm embrace. 'Don, so lovely to see you again. Wow, you have changed. You look so much better than when we last met.' Don appreciated the compliment and yes – he did feel much better. Months of healthy eating, followed by a daily swim and sauna in the hotel spa, had done wonders for his complexion and his waistline. He responded accordingly, 'Thank you for noticing, boss, and yes – I am feeling a million times better. Sleep, food and exercise.'

Don felt sorry for the young woman, the unwilling assassin who welcomed him into her cottage.

He knew she was inexperienced in such matters and he felt obliged to make this process easier for her. He decided to cut to the chase. He hung up his coat and made himself comfortable on her floral Laura Ashley settee. Accepting a china teacup gingerly playing host to a ginger biscuit, he then took a deep breath. He always preferred the position of attack as opposed to defence.

'Saskia, I have been working for you for five months now and although I have a six-month contract, we both understand that I have done about as much as I can with regards to the Crank assignment. When you asked me to come over and meet with you, I suspected that this was by way of us concluding our business. Am I right or am I right?'

Saskia was stunned by his forthright, upfront manner, but she also appreciated his 'cards on the table' approach. She replied, 'My goodness, Don, you don't mince your words do you? However, since you have thrust this conversation upon me, I can confirm that you are correct. You have already emailed me all your files, and from what I can tell we do seem to be approaching the end of this project. I am sorry, Don.'

Don put his teacup down and leant forward to give her a reassuring hug. 'Please don't apologise Saskia. You may not know it, but you have saved my life lass. Plus, you have made my bank manager a very happy man. I have savoured every minute of this assignment, and by way of a bonus I have found a new friend.' He gave Saskia a cheeky, yet reassuring wink.

Saskia resolved to remain professional; however, despite her best efforts, her eyes glistened with the tears she was trying not to release. 'I am pleased you have enjoyed working with me, Don, and you seem to be rebuilding your life after Patsy. Where will you go from here?'

Don remained composed, feeling slightly more concerned about Saskia and her secretive employers than he did about his own future. 'Bless you for asking. I appreciate your concern. Since I have been living in a hotel for the last few months, I have rented my house to a lovely family and in all honesty, I don't feel like evicting Mr and Mrs MacDonald any time soon. Their teenage son went missing in Greece.

He went on holiday last summer and never came home. They are out of their minds with worry. The last thing they need right now would be me playing the part of the evil landlord. Anyway – my home is full of too many memories and I don't want to be burdened with constant reminders of the past. So, dearest Saskia, I have decided to leave my tenants where they are and I am going to rent out an apartment in Oxford instead. Start a new life … if I can.'

It wasn't exactly what Saskia expected to hear, but nonetheless she was delighted that Don had turned his life around. She enquired, 'Oxford – lovely city, but why Oxford?'

Don smiled knowingly and replied, 'I have an old friend who lives there. Well actually he was my former history professor, back in my university days. Good old Roland De Vede – lovely man and exceptionally intelligent. We keep in touch from time to time, and he gave me the heads up that his daughter Mercy was looking for a research assistant to join her company. I went for an interview, got the job and I can start as soon as I am ready.'

Saskia was slightly shocked by how swiftly she had been replaced as his employer, but nonetheless was relieved that Don had found his feet again. Yet she was curious and so asked, 'What type of company is it, Don?'

Don scratched his head. He wasn't overly sure himself. 'Hmm, some sort of detective or investigative agency I think. Actually, I could have a word with them about the missing MacDonald boy now I think on it. Perhaps they can be of help. I also believe that the Prof wants me to assist him with some of his genealogy work, so I am sure they will have more than enough research projects to keep me out of trouble; I hope so anyway. I feel positive about the future. Gee, I never thought I would ever say that.'

The mood in the room lightened. Now that Saskia was assured of Don's well-being, she felt they were ready to move along and discuss his research activities.

'Don, the heat of the fire in this lounge is killing me. Let us move into the conservatory and discuss your findings. A pub lunch awaits us when we have finished. Before we delve into local legends, I have something to show you which will blow you away. Mr Morris, you are in for a treat.'

Taking his hand and guiding him towards her plasma screen, Saskia was keen to conclude their business with haste. The sooner they could wrap up their professional relationship, the sooner they could slip into the domain of friendship.

Saskia had been enthralled by the ridiculously expensive multi-dimensional underground video map, as commissioned by her rich employers. She had not stopped playing with her new game since the file had been delivered safely into her hands. She knew exactly where she was going as she guided the mouse to the one location she knew would amaze and delight. One simple click and a vast natural cavern opened up within the confines of her glassy screen. Entering into a once hidden spectral realm, a vast subterranean cathedral revealed itself. Ugly, wizened gargoyles had been carved into the rock face. Judging by obvious evidence of their erosion, they had evidently been sculptured hundreds of years ago, yet their eyes still seemed to watch. They had been purposely displayed along the entrance chamber, seeming to depict a line of security guards. Moving the virtual camera upwards, one could see that the gargoyles also looked down from above; suspended from the ceiling, as though mocking a hellish Michelangelo canvas.

Large candelabrums fashioned from the same rock, still evidenced former trails of dripping beeswax and tallow. With clear signs of human activity, it was obvious that this mysterious place was far from an idle folly. This was a place that had a purpose and indeed had been used – but for what reason? Moving the mouse in a different direction, a large rectangular altar could be clearly seen at the far end of this most peculiar ecclesiastical cavern.

Saskia gave Don a sideward glance to check on his facial expression, and was pleased to note his wide-eyed bewilderment. He was captivated like a moth drawn into a flame.

Finally breaking the silence, she explained, 'This place is amazing, isn't it Don? The geologist took a sample from the far altar; I guess because the stone looked different to that seen elsewhere. It turns out that indeed, it has been made from some boulder that cannot be found anywhere within the local area. I was told that it is called Cosheston sandstone. Quite superbly beautiful; a sort of a pale green/blue-grey stone studded with miniscule garnets. I understand that Cosheston is frequently referred to as "The Altar Stone". Some believe it to be the same as the Preseli Bluestones found in South Wales. Whoever made the effort to transport this here went to a lot of trouble. People don't break sweat for no good reason.'

Don interjected, 'I have heard about Preseli Bluestones. Isn't this the rock that makes up the inner circle of Stonehenge?' Saskia shook her head in agreement. 'Yes, I believe so, Don. I have also read that these were magical stones and, as such, were of immense importance to the

Druids. I believe that they possess an almost primordial vibration from an ancient energy, or something like that.' She pulled one from out of her pocket and smiled. 'I ordered one for myself on line... just in case.' As she held her carefully crafted talisman she remembered Soul – a most unusual man. She had never met him in person, but his reputation was as one who could connect to such stones. As she held the rock in her hand, she thought of him and considered that maybe she should get back in touch. She didn't know it at the time, but the stone heard her! A stone is but a stone – but this was not just a stone. It had ears.

Jolting herself back into the moment, she turned to Don. 'So, Mr Morris, this has been my contribution to the morning's conversation. Now, what can you tell me about the legends of Crank and do you know what this weird chamber could have been used for?'

Don had researched the religious history of the area in great detail and had much to contribute; however, before doing so he had noticed something in the corner of the cavern that had captured his attention. 'Saskia, can you just pan out and zoom into the shadowy corner to the left please.' Saskia did as was requested. She gasped, 'Crikey, I hadn't noticed that before. How peculiar.'

On the floor, tiny pebbles had been strategically placed to represent what appeared to be a witch's face. Above it and engraved within the cavern wall was a five-pointed star, apex pointing in a downwards direction. Encircling it was a snake, the mouth devouring its own tail. The outer area had been eroded with the passing of time, but displayed traces of what appeared to be wings. Dan muttered to himself as though deep in thought. 'How very curious, it almost looks like the image of the Ouroboros – the great Serpent of Eternity, in this instance embracing a pentagram. I have seen something similar to this in the village, with the wings but minus the pentagram. In the local version, the snake encircles a skull. To quote a local author, "curiouser and curiouser" me thinks.'

Saskia heard only one word, 'Ouroboros'! She shuddered with a sudden disquiet.

Her employers occasionally referred to themselves by this name. It seemed to be more of a code name rather than a limited company title. She had often silently wondered why a group of wealthy investors had been so keen to dig up old ruins and explore deep beneath the earth. What had they been searching for? Had they now found it? Could it be here? So far, she had not dared to allow herself to consider their motivations. It had been a strict condition of her employment that she displayed no outwards signs of curiosity. After all, had this not killed the cat? She did not want to wonder, but against her better judgement she was wondering. She flicked off the screen. It had become too great a distraction.

Don understood the signal. He was on the last day of his employment and he had work to deliver. As Saskia refreshed his teacup, he launched into the results of his research project.

'Where do I begin, Saskia? Let me start with simple. When I was a young boy, my mother told me that the old woman who lived on the hill made clothes pegs from children's fingers. Sure enough, Gertrude did sell wooden pegs, but none of them looked anything like skeletal phalanges. The old lady was an eccentric and so was often taunted by the local children. As I grew up, I finally began to understand that our parents told us this macabre story to keep us away from her. This was not so much to protect us. Gertrude was just an eccentric old lady. It was to prevent a bunch of mischievous kids from making her life a misery. It worked; none of us ventured up that hill towards what we thought was a child killer's dungeon. I believe that the same scenario was played out at Crank. The mines were unsafe and inquisitive youngsters could easily become lost in the endless miles of tunnels. We have seen them for ourselves on your humongous plasma screen. That place is treacherous. I have interviewed countless locals who grew up in the area, and most of them tend to believe that the stories about cannibals and of the like, were deliberately propagated to keep children away. I have emailed you a full list of all my interviews and you will find many reoccurring themes, but sadly there is little in the way of supporting evidence.'

Saskia had little intention of reading through these innumerable interviews. All she required was a top line brief from Don. She would email Mr Smith details of the interviews, and it was for him to filter through centuries of hearsay. Not her job!

Don continued, 'However, the story of the three missing boys and the lad that escaped appears to have some basis in truth. I did uncover a name for the boy that got away. The locals believe he was a lad called John Anderton. I also found a baptism for a boy by this name in 1785 at St Aidan's. This would make him around 8 years old in 1793, the same date this incident was supposed to have occurred. According to local folklore, the boys were supposed to be around 8 at the time and so this fits in with the dates.'

Saskia's waning attention was suddenly stimulated. She frantically flicked back through her notepad. 3rd March 2011; it had been almost a year ago. She read Soul's notes. How odd for her to think of him after all this time. He had suddenly come into her mind as she held her mysterious talisman. Remarkable; Soul had given the child the same name, 'John Anderton'. She asked, 'Don, do you know anything more about the Anderton boy?'

Don flicked through his own notes and responded, 'I uncovered a few interesting snippets. It seems that young John was connected to the Anderton printing press dynasty. Just to bring you up to speed with some local history, Saskia, this area was engrained in staunch Catholicism during a period in time when it was very dangerous to be a Catholic. The boys' ancestor was a chap called James Anderton, who was born circa 1557 and was raised in a religiously conservative household. As a practising Catholic, James wrote a number of works defending and justifying his faith. After his death, his younger brother, Roger Anderton, operated a secret Catholic press in the nearby hall at Billinge. Roger was taking a huge risk as he only did this in order to publish his brother's books. Can you imagine how dangerous this act would have been during the Reformation? Locals have informed me that the hall did have hidden escape tunnels which ran to the Crank caverns, and it is entirely possible that the underground church we both witnessed was used by the former Catholic Anderton family.'

Don had caught Saskia's attention. She knew this information would be of interest to her employers. She asked, 'Well if young John Anderton knew of these tunnels, why and how did he get lost?'

Don tapped on his keyboard and opened up a spreadsheet. It was a document which contained many names against years of baptism and burials. He continued to explain, 'You must keep in mind the timelines we are referring to Saskia. There are two centuries between John Anderton and the earlier Catholic Anderton family. The boy may not have known about the tunnels. He may not have even known much about the great hall. The Andertons' eventually lost ownership of the hall. One ancestor became a Benedictine monk. Another became part of the Jacobite rising in 1745, and was later convicted of high treason and sentenced to death. Although later pardoned, his estates were sequestered and basically confiscated. So, although the young lad who escaped was connected with the earlier Anderton family, and although it is highly likely it was his family who constructed some of the tunnels – and maybe even created the underground cathedral as a secret place to worship – the fact remains that this little boy and his friend still lost their way. Unless, of course, three of them really were murdered by strange little people with long beards.'

Saskia thought for a moment. She wasn't sure she agreed. 'Accept that the Anderton boy didn't get lost. John Anderton made his way out. He escaped. He sounds to me like a little boy who knew the cave system very well. As you concluded, it is probable that it was his ancestors who excavated some of these tunnels by way of secret passageways. This is fascinating. So, what else happened down there? What of his friends? Do you know who they were?'

Don shrugged in a resigned manner. He explained, 'Early 18th-century life for commoners was mostly recorded by baptism and burials, rather than proof of existence via a birth and death certificate. If the bodies of the three boys allegedly murdered in the caves were never recovered, then quite simply they could not have been buried. If the only way we can prove death is by a burial, then we cannot prove their deaths. There is nothing in any of the records I have reviewed that indicates three little boys were ever buried on or around the same date. However, what I have done is search for boys baptised within the local area circa 1785. I have then matched this against future burials. Although I have found the names of three boys who were baptised between 1784 and 1786, they were never shown as being buried. Of course, they may have all moved area, grown up and been buried somewhere else, but I have searched every record in England and cannot find any matches. I cannot say with certainty that these are the missing boys, but they seem to be the only probabilities. I have used a sort of fuzzy logic to reach these conclusions.'

Saskia beamed with delight. She had no concept of why her employers had gone to so much trouble, time, energy and expense to investigate these local myths, but she had recognised that one of the most important items of information that they had required was the names of the three boys supposedly murdered in the caverns of Crank. For some reason, their identities mattered. She was impatient and she knew her employers were also growing inpatient. She enquired, 'So, using your fuzzy logic of baptisms with no matching burials, who do you think the other children could have been, Don?'

Don deliberated so as to stretch out the moment. 'John Anderton had a cousin called William Chaddock, who was of a similar age and for whom I can find no evidence of a burial. I have also found twin boys who lived in the village at the same time and so they could easily have been John's playmates. They were called Samuel and Benjamin Smith. These boys have very interesting family histories if you care to hear them.'

Saskia concluded that to be a silly question. Of course, she wanted to hear about Don's little genealogical fairy stories. Don had a soft bedtime reading voice, and was a good storyteller.

Sipping his tepid tea, Don located the pink sticker in his thick notebook. Saskia smiled; she found his rainbow-coloured method of note-keeping quite endearing. He began to read his notes aloud, 'William Chaddock is the descendent of a chap called Peter Chaddock, who was directly responsible for having a local woman accused of being a witch and who was subsequently hanged to death. The poor lady in question was called Isabel Robey and she lived in nearby Windle. She was associated with the Pendle witches. Have you heard of the Pendle witches, Saskia?' She responded, 'Of course – they are famous, but I had no idea that Crank had an association with them. Please go on, Don. You have my full attention.' Don continued as requested. 'Isabel Robey lived in a very traitorous era, during the reign of Queen Elizabeth I and King James I. This was a period of extreme religious unrest and distrust. Peter was married to Isabel's god-daughter and it was said that Isabel didn't approve of Peter, and so the accusation was his vengeance upon her. So goes the story. However, if Isabel had been a typical Lancashire woman of the time, she was probably quite curt with her tongue and spoke the truth as she saw it to be.' Saskia nodded, commenting, 'Indeed, my mother always told me that a word from a woman's mouth could be like a stone from a sling.' 'Quite true,' continued Don, 'it seems that old Isabel hated Peter Chaddock, and accusing her of witchcraft could have been his way of making her pay.' Saskia gulped, feeling saddened by the whole witch-finder era and the general ignorance of people from that strange period in history. 'What happened next?' she asked.

Don continued to read from his notes. 'The trial took place at
Lancaster Castle in August 1612. At the end of the three-day inquest, ten
women were found guilty of witchcraft and sentenced to death by
hanging. I believe that Peter later retracted his statement about Isabel.
However, many local people did believe Isabel was genuinely guilty of
bewitchment and that Peter Chaddock and his family would be cursed.
Five generations later, and it is likely that if and when William Chaddock
went missing in Crank, that the local population would still connect that
event to witchcraft. Folklore can run in the veins for many centuries. All
in all, the episode of the missing boys could have easily taken on a
supernatural connotation, thus increasing its mystery. Note, that we have
just seen an effigy of a witch made from pebbles. Could this have once
been a lair for a witch's coven? The history from the area hints at this
possibility.' 'Or maybe, 'added Saskia, 'the effigy was also part of the
plot in keeping children away.'

Saskia continued to listen with wide-eyed interest. She added,
'Maybe there is a connection … and we did see that upside-down
pentacle engraved into the cavern walls.' Don looked back to his hand-
scribbled notes and concurred, 'I agree. The thing is, that William's
father was a descendent of Peter Chaddock, but his mother was also the
descendent of Isabel Robey and there are those in the village who did
believe her to be a witch. Should this be true, it could be possible that the
other young boy, William Chaddock, may also have known secret ways
to gain access to the Crank tunnel system. These boys grew up in the
area and with its history. It seems implausible that they would simply
have become lost.'

Saskia nodded in agreement. She enquired, 'And what of the twin Smith boys? Do they have any unusual histories?' Don continued with his stories, 'Beyond their baptism, I can find no other accounts of the Smith twins – however they could be the descendants of Kitty and George Smith, whose story you may find quite interesting. As we are aware, the caverns are natural; however, they have been mined from around the 18th century. A chap known as George Smith was supposed to have been a wealthy mine owner from Scotland. It seems he was in the area with a view to acquire the mines and some surrounding land. It was alleged that he died in the tunnels in 1720 in undocumented, strange circumstances. Again, this could be local tongues adding mystery to the story to keep their children away from the area. However, George and later his wife Kitty were buried in a most unusual grave. The tombstone lies in St Aidan's church cemetery and it is shaped like a coffin, but bares the mark of a skull with bat-like wings, encircled by a snake – not that unlike the Ouroboros symbol we have just seen on your plasma screen. The grave at St Aidans, is one of only a handful of headstones with the status of being registered as a listed monument.'

Saskia was deep in thought. She paced up and down the room, clicking her fingers – an irritating habit she had acquired from her feisty mother. She thought silently to herself, 'Smith, Smith, Ouroboros, Smith – could there be a connection?' Don broke the silence, by adding more mystery to this particular story. 'Saskia, this may not have any relevance, but I have searched the parish records for the burial details of George and Kitty Smith. The records go from 1699 to 1714. There is then a gap of seven years before the next records, which go from 1721 to 1760. George and Kitty were buried in 1720, and yet all burial records for 1720 appear to have vanished into thin air. Maybe a coincidence, but if so … an unusual coincidence.'

After at least five minutes of hushed contemplation, she turned to face Don. 'And what of the small, bearded ones, the creatures that eat little boys for breakfast?'

Don suppressed a giggle. 'This sounds to me like the Gertrude peg story from my youth, Saskia. Unless someone can dig up small, adult skeletons with white beards, then this is just a rumour. My mission was to report and not to judge. Local folk tell stories of Boggarts that hide within the caves. Some of the older locals have even given them the names of Churn Milk Peg & Melch Dick, who I understand to be female and male dwarf faeries. Peg must be fairly ugly if she could churn milk. There are those who take on board a more scientific anthropological view, and argue that in times of yore, dwarves were probably teased and mocked. Perhaps they took to the caves to keep themselves out of harm's way. If folks died in the tunnel system, why waste good protein? It was a long time ago, Saskia, and any evidence to back the folklore up is lacking. We can only deal with facts. Until you tear down the blockades which have prevented us entering the greater majority of this underground maze, and then find skeletons, anything I report on is merely conjecture.'

Saskia was still deep in thought and silently questioned herself, 'Why underground? What was the Ouroboros fascination with such places?' She asked Don, 'Why do people hide underground, Don? I don't understand what the attraction would be?'

Don had also pondered this same question so was quick to respond. 'Should we want to be secretive, unseen, unheard, unnoticed, then think about where best to go. Deep within the earth, lies somewhere silent, dark, safe and hidden. Let me give you one example; the UK government have so-called COBRA meetings – the acronym commonly used in the press for Cabinet Office Briefing Room. These are an underground collection of secure, reinforced meeting rooms used in times of national crisis. Did you know that there is a large bunker complex underneath Whitehall? We may be in the 21st century, Saskia, but we still go underground when we want to feel safe. Maybe it is like a primordial instinct – back to the womb, or back to the caves. Who knows?'

Saskia had private thoughts she could not share with Don. She was mentally trying to tie up many loose strings. The Mr Smith who employed her; the Ouroboros group he represented; their obsession with finding old places with underground chambers; the identity of the missing boys from 1793 – it was all starting to make some sort of distorted sense. She considered the strange stories of the Crank cave system; its connection with the witches of Pendle; the clandestine Catholic prayer meetings; the shadowy Boggarts; the Pentacle and Ouroboros carved into the wall of the underground cathedral and also on the coffin of a couple known as George and Kitty Smith. Could they be connected to the missing twins, also called Smith? Could they be connected with her boss, also called Smith? It's a common enough name, so maybe just a coincidence. With answers came more questions.

Unintentionally, she held on to her blue altar stone talisman as she considered her thoughts. Instinctually she held the cold stone to her hot forehead to help unjumble her mental deliberations. Unbeknown to Saskia, holding the stone to her third-eye chakra gave it lobes and indeed the stone was listening. In a momentary rush of dread, she wondered how she had been profiled to represent the Ouroboros. She knew the truth! Firing off a sequence of neuron synapsis from some ancient extrasensory part of her brain – she understood. It was a truth she didn't want to face, so she would often dismiss it before the thought took form. Saskia had been highly trained in the art of circumvention. Her mother had passed that truth avoidance gene onto her.

'Before we go for lunch, is there anything else about the area which you have failed to tell me, Don?' Don licked his forefinger and flicked through his notes until he came to the blue page divider. 'Only that about 150 years prior to the incident with the boys, the area was also associated with a martyr known as Saint Edmund Arrowsmith. He was tried at Lancaster in 1628, and was found guilty of high treason for being a Jesuit priest. In this area, a lot of the history seems to be connected to the turbulence of religious reformation. Locals tell of a monk who haunts the area and many believe this to be Arrowsmith. Again, there are more suggestions pointing to the underground cathedral being associated with secret worship. Even hundreds of years later, this area is still rife with suspicion, folklore, legends and fear...mostly fear.'

Saskia seemed to be getting the picture. She observed, 'It's a bit of a strange combo isn't it, Don? From the clandestine Catholic worship of God, to the covert gatherings of a witches' coven, to the subterranean child-murdering dwarf cannibals; is Crank a holy place or a place of malevolent evil? I am confused.'

Even after five months of research, Don felt equally confused. He nodded in agreement and added, 'I forgot to mention to you, that some locals even described Crank as being one of many gates to Hell itself ... a portal from one world into another. They call it the place of the

Unbeknown. From what we have seen on your plasma screen with regards to the multiple levels of chambers, perhaps it is all of those things and more.'

Saskia shrugged. 'You know what, Don, it isn't my problem and it isn't your problem. You have delivered your research ahead of time and under budget. I have delivered a geological survey of the tunnel system, late and over budget. My employers will either have an interest in Crank or not, and if they have an interest they will probably dynamite the place apart anyway. If it is a portal to the underworld, then we could be in for some interesting times to come, because that portal may about to be blown open to the heavens, Are you thirsty?'

She teased him, 'Grab your coat Don – you have pulled. The Falkland Arms, lunch and a pint of Cotswold Cider awaits us. Let's go celebrate your new life and the long overdue holiday I am about to take.'

It was a sudden and dramatic change of subject. She was good at doing that. Saskia had a way of being able to pull a curtain around all the untidy mess in her mind, and make everything just go away. She had deflected her negative thoughts with relative ease, and she understood that this was why she had been chosen for her overly paid job. She could just close the door and shut everything down; a most unusual ability.

The Ouroboros knew it, Don knew it, Saskia knew it. None spoke of it, but the blue stone would not be quite so discreet.

Don linked her arm as they picked their way cautiously down the icy high street of the village. He wanted to ask Saskia so many questions about her past and wondered if the conclusion of their professional relationship would open doors to a more affable dialogue. Unable to chisel his way beyond the cement fascia she had constructed around herself, all he could figure out was that Saskia was educated in Roedean private school for girls as a full-time border. From threads of past conversations, he had assumed that she was the only child of a single mother – a woman with alternative social agendas. From what Saskia had told him, it became obvious that she was the most woeful of borders – a girl who seldom went home at the weekend. Her expensive private education had been funded by her estranged rich father, a man whom she had only met a handful of times in her life. She had a variety of half-brothers and a sister, most of whom despised her, aside from just one – a much older half-sister with a rebellious streak. She only had one true friend as far as Don could make out. Somebody by the name of Florence. Don knew very little of Saskia, but what he had discovered so far perturbed him. With no close family to speak of, no boyfriend and an admirable disposition for total discretion, she was the ideal legal representative of a deeply secretive society. Don was concerned about the people who had profiled her so judiciously, and was suspicious of what possible motivations would steer them towards a solitary soul such as Saskia.

As they entered into the warm charcoal-infused air of the Falkland Arms, Don understood it was now time to be light-hearted and sociable. As a lover of all things historical, Don appreciated the ambience of the pubs original leaded windows, flagstone floors, rustic furniture, smouldering log Inglenook fireplace and the low ceilings supported by great oak beams. He was determined to enjoy this final lunch with his ex-employer in the most perfect of settings. After all, he had no notion if he would ever meet with Saskia ever again. His mind wandered to thoughts of his beloved Patsy. He so hated 'last times'. He knew more than most, that sometimes these things cannot always be predicted, and that the appropriate degree of respect was not always awarded to a final meeting. The closing handshake, the goodbye kiss and the holding back of unspoken words as one walks away. He sighed long and hard at that sobering thought, determined that this luncheon with Saskia be respected as though it was to be a parting of friends.

Outside it was starting to snow. He gazed out of the window as Saskia was ordering more drinks at the bar. The snow was sticking to the hedgerows, painting the Cotswold vista like a Christmas card. Now that the weather was turning more inclement, he considered booking a room in the inn. Don was not keen to hurry along this final moment. He was old enough to recognise the conveyor belt of life that wants to move us along before we are ready. All too soon a new future would whisk him away from what was now, smug and comfortable. An Oxford apartment and a job with MeDeVe Ltd was awaiting patiently outside the door. However, just for the moment – a pint of cider, a toasty fire and dinner with a wonderful friend captured his attention. Now was for now – tomorrow can wait.

CHAPTER 6

2ⁿᵈ February 2012

Two surgeons, one trauma consultant, four nurses and an anaesthetist couldn't save the girl. The bullet had penetrated her spleen and as fast as they delivered blood into her veins, it gushed back out again. After the final shock to her heart delivered little more than an ominous flatline, the lead trauma surgeon at Duke University Medical Center in North Carolina called the time of death – 3.46 p.m.

As the clinical team left the room, the junior nurse stayed behind to remove all the various tubes and monitoring equipment from the girl's lifeless body. It was within the nurse's job description; she was paid to do this, but she wasn't totally immune to the tragedy of the situation. A young girl, a cheating boyfriend and a bullet that was meant for somebody else. As the nurse covered the girl with a white linen cloth, she exhaled. It was a deep, rueful sigh as she considered the waste of a young life. It was a sight she had seen all too often in her young career, but one she never became complacent about.

Unbeknown to her, she was not alone. She was being watched.

The nurse sensed a shadow in the corner of the operating theatre and even let out an alarmist gasp. Something moved – she was sure of it. She wondered what was making her so jumpy and entertained the thought that maybe she wasn't cut out for this line of work. As the hairs on her arm visibly rose, the nurse didn't stay much longer. Almost at the end of her shift, she couldn't wait to sign off duty. Just a call to the mortuary and then she was going to hotfoot it out of the hospital and try to forget whatever it was that had spooked her. Pizza and wine seemed like a decent remedy for young Nurse Jackson.

Just fifteen minutes earlier the operating room had been a hive of activity and organised panic. Shouts rang out commanding, 'Blood now; clamp and swabs; adrenaline quickly; isotonic sodium chloride; pulse feeble; BP falling; clear; shock; nothing; clear; shock; let's call it.'

Just words … lots of words. Words that could not save the young victim of a shooting incident. The hectic room now fell silent and empty; aside from the clicking of a clock that counted the passing of time and life.

A silhouette emerged from the shadowy corner. Black mist slowly pixelated into a female form. A thin pale hand with long, scarlet-painted fingernails caressed the linen sheet. The hand pulled the sheet back slowly to expose the sallow white face of a female corpse. Softly touching the girl's face – as yet still warm – a woman murmured into the girl's ear. In hushed tones, she whispered 'Venite ad me.' Within seconds, the girl's dead eyes shot wide open, the colour returning to her cheeks instantaneously. The woman was pleased with herself. 'Welcome back, my Little Bell.'

Arabella sat bolt upright, confused and shocked. As her vision adjusted to the light, she slowly came to realise where she was. Confused, she put her hands down to her stomach and toyed with the clumped blood clots on her gown. As blood returned to her veins, painful pins and needles, stabbed at her limbs. The memories came flooding back. She gasped, 'Oh my God – I shot myself.' Her newly flushed face, was a mixture of disbelief and horror.

The strange female manifestation cupped the girl's chin, fervently pulling her jaw upwards to face her own face. She looked deeply into her eyes and asked, 'Do you remember me, Little Bell?' The face was familiar, the voice was familiar and then … the circumstances of their introduction soon dawned upon the one mockingly referred to as 'Little Bell'.

Arabella's newly restored eyes began to shed tears. She cried, 'Shit – what have I done, what have I done? Did I die? Are you Emmanuelle? Holy crap – you are Emmanuelle, aren't you? Emmanuelle- High priestess of the bloody underworld. I didn't believe in you. I thought I was being cool messing with all that occult crap. I didn't think you were real.'

She recollected the night she first saw the nebulous image of the entity now holding her head in a stern upright position. The whole ritual thing was not something she had done with any serious intent. After all, Arabella was an atheist and didn't believe in the paranormal. It hadn't quite been a joke, after all her heart had been torn to shreds. However, never in a million years did she expect a result. It was just a spell she had downloaded from the Internet. Just a chant and a thimbleful of blood. Surely such things could not be real? She had drunk too much Bourbon and her emotions had overruled any sense of logic.

Indeed, it was real, and now Emmanuelle had come to collect her payment. She smiled at her young quarry, not so much in a kindly way, but in a victorious way. She towered over the girl with a commanding stance. 'You should never play with things you don't understand, Little Bell. Your poor pathetic broken heart wanted me to bring your ex-boyfriend back and you invoked me. I was summoned and I came. What

a silly girl. Things happen for a reason, Arabella, and when you mess
with your destiny then you create catastrophe. That lowlife scum of a
guy had vacated your life, but only to make room for a good guy to enter
it. A nice caring boy who would have loved you – a boy you will now
never meet, and children you will now never raise together as a sweet
little family. What a pity. When will you silly young girls ever learn?
Nope – you had to win the idiot back and you didn't care how you did it.
Why do so many female humans fall in love with the bad boys? Still – it
keeps me busy. I delivered him to you and now you have to pay me for
my favours. Did you really think a few drops of blood would suffice?
Really? It didn't work for the Incas or generations of Pagans and neither
is it sufficient disbursement in this instance. I came up with the goods,
and now I need imbursement.' She mockingly held out her hand as
though asking for money.

Emmanuelle sneered at the bewildered young woman, who by now
was shaking uncontrollably with fear. Some demons could be stupid and
as ugly as hell itself. However, Emmanuelle knew that her many
triumphs lay in her ability to softly reassure, cunningly manipulate and
then ultimately command her victims accordingly. Unlike her bestial
peers, she had a ruthless intelligence and the exquisite good looks to
captivate her prey, both male and female alike. Gender mattered not. To
Emmanuelle all meat tasted the same.

Arabella sobbed. The memories of the evening, and the events
running up to it, were replaying in her head like a nightmare video. She
had been desperate. She had loved Dean so much and despaired of losing
him. She had researched the rituals required and had called out for help.
An attractive female demoness with an alluring soft voice made an

appearance. She simply took hold of Arabella's hand, stroked her wrist and then vanished. Arabella trusted her. She looked gentle and sympathetic. Her eyes were the clearest of blue and her long platinum hair blew in a gentle ethereal breeze. She looked more like a fairy Godmother out of a children's book, than a demon. She didn't even look vaguely evil.

Within hours, Arabella's phone rang. It was Dean, begging for another chance. The black magic had worked and worked with haste. The lovers were reunited. However, several months later, Arabella was to discover that Dean had been cheating on her and in fact his secretive lover was heavily pregnant with his baby. Overcome with jealousy and rage, Arabella had taken her father's gun and went to hunt down the couple. Angry, broken-hearted, confused – she had lost all self-control. She approached them outside Dean's home. She pointed the gun at her boyfriend's lover with every intention of pulling the trigger. It was a moment of madness and rage. Then, one look at the swelling belly of her love rival caused a sudden change of heart. The baby kicked beneath its mother's floral dress. It was an obvious movement – maybe a well-timed plea for clemency. It was a little human – an innocent victim hanging on to life by a cord. Arabella turned the gun on herself. That was as much as she could remember. After that, complete blackness. She remembered nothing more, until the moment Emmanuelle breathed life into her lifeless body.

Arabella shook her head in denial and disbelief. She hoped to wake up in her bed and realise it had all been one awful, cruel nightmare. The moment was surreal, yet sadly … real. She pinched her skin – it hurt. She was many things to many people, but dead was not one of them.

Sheila Mughal

Finally gathering her courage, she asked, 'What happens to me now, Emmanuelle? Am I alive? Am I dead? Shit, am I the walking dead?' Emmanuelle stifled a laugh and teased her victim. 'You have been watching far too many horror movies, Little Bell. There are no such things as vampires, zombies and what you refer to as the walking dead. These are fictional fancies. One has a heartbeat or not, there is no halfway house. You are alive, but only because I keep you alive. Your organs had already started the process of decay before I rescued you. Fortunately, you were still warm, so the damage could be repaired. But know this – I can click my fingers and stop your heartbeat in an instant – your life belongs to me now. If you are not happy with this arrangement, please let me know asap and I will put everything back as it was and send flowers to your funeral. Any preference? Personally, I love white lilies.'

Arabella understood the austere seriousness of the situation. She pensively asked, 'And if I do go back to being dead, will I go to heaven or hell?' Emmanuelle was becoming bored and running out of patience. She responded sharply, 'You are asking the wrong entity, Arabella. I don't do the whole judgement thing, although it does sound like fun and I wouldn't mind giving it a go sometime. I consider myself to be a good judge of character.'

Arabella rephrased the question. 'I don't know who or what you are, Emmanuelle, but in a very short time I have come to learn that with you there is always a price tag. I am scared of death, but I think I am more scared of you. So, give it to me straight, if you keep me alive, what is the deal?'

Emmanuelle grinned and flicked her long golden strands of hair away from her face. She answered, 'If you choose to stay alive, I will give you the best job in the world. Indirectly you will work for me, but to the rest of the world you will be employed by a rich and famous man. You will be well paid, you will travel the globe, you will mix with good-looking celebrities, be invited to the best parties on the biggest yachts and drink the most expensive champagne. All I require from you Arabella, is little over ten years of employment, after which your contract will be terminated and you will be free. Remember this time and date – 02/02/2022 at 2.02 a.m. I have tried to keep the date nice and simple so you can remember it. I am considerate like that. When you have a shower, and wash all the blood away – you will also find that date tattooed on your stomach – just in case you forget. Can you believe that some humans deliberately brand themselves with ink? I honestly thought that after we introduced the concept in the Belsen concentration camp in the 1940s that it would never catch on. But hey – there you go. Hitler spotted a trend. Anyway, back to the subject at hand. After that date, you can come and join me and the rest of my devilish team, or simply be a human and hope you can gain a free pass into heaven. The kind of life you live will depict where your soul ends up. Be warned, if you should die within your ten-year contract, then you will also become a demon and will be my slave for eternity. If you don't like that option, you will need to look after yourself. Get a gym membership, become a vegetarian, watch your alcohol intake or something.' Emmanuelle giggled. She found pleasure in her own distorted sense of humour.

Arabella's former vagueness was now replaced by the awareness that she now had to make a life or death decision. She paused as she mentally deliberated. Emmanuelle grew inpatient. She attempted to hurry her prey along. 'Arabella, two men from the mortuary are making their way along the corridor with a trolley and a body bag as we speak. Your next destination is a fridge in the morgue. I can try to detain them, but not for long. You need to think quickly. You have a reasonable chance to win your soul back after a mere ten-year contract concludes, but in the meantime, you will live a full and entertaining life. Even God can't promise you that. I need your decision and I need it now.' Arabella sobbed like a child, 'I want my mother. I don't know what to do.' Emmanuelle squeezed her prey's hand so tightly that the girl's fingers went white. 'I am losing patience, Bell. You can have your mother or you can have a mortuary fridge and white lilies, but pick one or the other and do it now.'

'Yes, err … yes. I choose to live … Please let me live Emmanuelle.'

The demoness had won yet again. Victory had come with relative ease. Emmanuelle softly kissed the girl's sunken cheek. 'Congratulations, Arabella, and welcome to my team. Your first task is an act of supreme acting. You need to let these good folks know that by some miracle, you are still alive. You can scare the wits out of the porters and do the sitting bolt upright joke, or you can be subtle and make a few groans. Sure, the clinician who called time on you will get sacked, but he has another destiny I need to pick up on. I always have one eye open for my next opportunity. It's your call – dramatic or understated. Your choice, but I know what I would do in your position.' Emmanuelle laughed, flicking her long blond locks behind her as an evil snigger left her red painted mouth. She had an evil, vicious laugh.

Arabella was quivering. Her eyes appeared glazed and fearful. Emmanuelle instantly understood that her jovial mockery of the situation had been ill-judged. She added, 'Actually, thinking about it, you are not looking so great, Arabella. You are weak and have lost a lot of blood. I think your body needs time to recover. Here is the deal. I am going to send you into a long, deep sleep. You are frightfully anaemic and your organs are frail. I need you to be strong and you are useless to me in your present condition. I am also going to give you a very special gift. This is a little present from me to you – one that many women would have loved to have received at least once in their life. I am going to erase that loser Dean from your mind. Not only will you forget that you ever loved him – you won't even recall knowing him. With just a click of my fingers, your broken heart will be healed. So very simple. You humans constantly boast about your ability to love, and how powerful and all-consuming it is. Yet love is such a fickle emotion, so weak that it can be easily lost with a memory.'

Arabella finally found the strength to look up at her redeemer without the assistance of having her chin lifted. She knew exactly what Emmanuelle was. Her face so beautiful, her voice so comforting, her touch so gentle; yet she knew the creature that stood boldly before her had the soul of a beast. Intelligent, devious and in total control of her fate. Yet the agonising pain of a broken heart was indeed something she could not live with; something she had been prepared to kill or die for. She would do anything to fall out of love with Dean and she cared not for the price tag. Barely able to breathe she gasped, 'Just do what you need to do, Emmanuelle. Take of me what you want.'

Emmanuelle smiled; for the moment, her ravenous hunger satiated. 'Good decision, Little Bell. When I touch your forehead, you will slip into a coma. When you regain consciousness, you will not remember this conversation. Neither will you know who Dean is or what he was to you. Of course, your family will remind you of the details, but their words will not mean anything to you. All emotion associated with this sorry phase of your life will have vanished. When you are well enough, I will come and collect you, or maybe I will send one of my underdogs, we shall see. When you see me or one of my employees, you will know what is happening and will remember this conversation, but not until we are ready for you.'

Emmanuelle licked her long, manicured finger, and as her damp fingertip touched Arabella's forehead, the young woman collapsed back onto the hard rubber operating table. Emmanuelle reconnected the ECG cables so that her beating heartbeat would be clearly visible and audible to the mortuary porters. Glancing over towards the theatre doors, Emmanuelle mentally released the locks she had sealed earlier. The frustrated hospital porters – confused as to why their security fobs had been faulty – finally gained entrance to Theatre 5, and on so doing, were due for an almighty shock.

Emmanuelle was laughing to herself as she whipped her red cloak into the air and vanished back into the shadowy corner from whence she came. The hunt had been victorious; this was reason to celebrate. She would stay just a little longer, long enough to enjoy the dazed expressions on the porters faces. She took enjoyment from such cruel moments.

CHAPTER 7

10th February 2012

Tall, stone buildings stood proudly against narrow, pebbled alleyways, whilst endless flights of steps ascended the hill towards George Smith's Edinburgh office. The afternoon light was growing dim, and as the sun fell, casting its dying rays against the castle, the subtle yellow light of the streetlamps illuminated the close and its towering turrets. The wind howled up the tapering passageways like a rabid animal, making an eerie whistling noise as it dashed through the city's medieval streets. The thrashing and howling of the wind and rain eventually awoke George from his impromptu catnap. Still sleepy, he tugged at the unyielding sashed window. Desperate to keep the inclement Scottish weather at bay, he waged a war with the stubborn lower sash. In so doing, he cut his finger on a sharp nail protruding from the muntin grille. It was a deep cut, and the aggrieved gent cursed as droplets of blood dripped onto his rare Kashan carpet. Swearing as he searched his office for something to wipe up the blood stain, George Smith failed to notice a dark mist slowly forming in the far easterly corner of the room. The darkness developed slowly and silently; the menacing manifestation easing itself unnoticed into the shadowy angle of the walls.

Mr George Smith, Esquire, was a smartly dressed gentleman in his mid-forties. Not entirely unattractive, he possessed a discernible hint of nobility and arrogance. With more than a scattering of blue blood, he could trace his lineage back to the first titled Baron Strange. Yet the wealth of his family, came less from noble titles, and more from the many coal mines they owned in Scotland, along with diamond mines in

South Africa. Yet as the only son of a family disseminated by geography and financially debilitated by death duties and crumbling mansions, his heritage meant little more than an aristocratic veneer. Some had often considered that his passion for rescuing ancient places could be an ancestral throwback or perhaps some deeply entrenched sympathy for any type of ruination. Nonetheless, Mr Smith was a most intelligent and judicious chap. As Chief Executive, it was his job to ensure that the numbers on a spreadsheet played like musical notes to the ears of the secretive Ouroboros investors.

As darkness fell upon the city streets, George poured himself a wee dram of vintage single malt scotch whisky. Still uttering profanities at the bloodstain he had so far struggled to completely eradicate, he sunk into his antique leather captain's chair; gyrating it back and forth as though in deep thought. Inhaling his crystal glass, and savouring the briny spices and peaty citrus aroma from his Isle of Islay beverage, his thoughts wandered over to Ardbeg, and many happy moments spent on the westerly Scottish island. Before long his halcyon moment was to be disturbed by a clash of thunder – so close that it sent a synapse of vibrations along the rooftops of old-town Edinburgh. He moved over to the troublesome sashed windows, momentarily enthralled by flashes of forked lightening in the tempestuous skies above the castle. For several minutes, he simply stood and watched, quite hypnotised by the tentacles of light cascading from the heavens. Indeed, Earth was an interesting planet.

A strange smell pervaded the room. He couldn't quite establish what it was or where it came from, but the name formaldehyde came to mind. It was harsh and clinical, with a hint of disinfectant. It irritated his throat, causing him to cough. As he searched for his pocket handkerchief, cold thin fingers clasped his pin-striped shoulders. George yelped, quite literally jumping out of his skin. Spinning around aggressively and pumped up for a fight, George was astonished to find an attractive young woman standing beside him. With her long blonde ponytail pulled harshly back from her face, he failed to recognise her. Cool and collected, she stood perfectly still and smiled coyly. George stepped backwards, a puzzled look planted on his face. The woman was dressed in a designer tweed suit with matching red tartan gloves. Her crimson lipstick glistened as it reflected the lightening streaks from outside the window.

No words were spoken initially. George was confused. It was 6 p.m. on a Friday evening and he had no meetings booked in his diary, in fact he had been ready to vacate the office and make his way home. Not that the word home had any meaning for George Smith. He had no family. Home was just a house – be it a very large house on a former baronial estate which catered for archery, falconry and game shooting. With the River Leith running through its woodlands, George and a few selected friends often entertained themselves by fishing for salmon and trout – later cooked to perfection by George himself. He considered himself to be an accomplished chief and few would disagree. Be it that home was little more than a vast bachelor pad, it was one that George longed to get back to on a stormy Friday evening. Still mystified and startled by the striking intruder who had disrupted his plans, he sternly enquired, 'Who are you and how did you get into my office?'

The woman moved over to the bloodstain on George's precious rug and then, crouching down, dipped her index finger on the stain, rolling it around until her fingertip was coloured ruby red. Almost seductively she licked her finger clean with wanton deliberation. She looked up at the bewildered George, and flashing him a mischievous wink, she placed her damp finger back on the stain. Steam rose from the carpet as the crackling sound of heat exited her fingertip. The stain had completely vanished. The woman stood upright again, face cocked childlike to one side as she sweetly smiled. It was a misplaced look of innocence.

As soon as he witnessed this sorcery, George knew what and who the woman was. He sighed, 'Emmanuelle – long time – no see. A really long time actually. I have lost count of the passing centuries. Do you not believe in knocking, my dear?' Emmanuelle laughed dismissively, responding, 'I never need to knock once invited in. By the way, you are looking good for your age old chap – quite dapper.' George was not seduced by the comment – he knew the enchantress only too well. He also understood the rules of demonology. He rushed over to the sashed windows, only to find that they opened with the greatest of ease. He had been tricked. He looked over his shoulder towards Emmanuelle, whose face was now plastered with a gratified smirk. 'I see what you have done Emmanuelle. You can only be invited in by an incantation or a drop of blood. Quite ingenious! No storms had been forecast for this evening and there was nothing wrong with my windows, but hey – you got your drop of blood. Isn't that cheating?' Emmanuelle responded flippantly, 'George, you accuse a demoness of cheating? How awfully rude!'

George had not encountered Emmanuelle in many a year, but he instinctively disliked her. He could tell she was playing with him and he just wished her gone from his office, his city and his earthly existence.

'Interesting to see you dressed so demure Emmanuelle. Not your usual style. Where is your trademark scarlet cloak?' Emmanuelle responded sharply, 'I am off to a funeral, George, I need to blend.'

'Someone you put in the ground by any chance?'

Emmanuelle shrugged, 'Dean Waters – cheating boyfriend with pregnant whore. I wiped him from the memory of my latest employee, but I couldn't risk him coming back into her life again, so he had to go.' George took a swig of Scotch and then went to pour a glass for his female companion, hoping it would dissolve her as quickly as it would one's liver. He looked Emmanuelle directly in the eyes as he handed her a glass. 'You always were a disruptive entity, Emmanuelle. It is one of many reasons why the Ouroboros never quite liked you. By your actions, an unborn child now has no father. What gives you the right to be judge and jury?' The demoness yawned. Being challenged on grounds of ethics did not deserve the effort of her even contemplating a response. George continued with his cross-examination. 'Why go to a victim's funeral anyway. Do you like to gloat?' Emmanuelle responded curtly. 'Do not presume to know me, Mr Smith. I need to make sure that Dean Waters is in the ground and no other demons…or other entities, are around to try and take his body. He was a bad boy, but his body is ripe for snatching. Plus, I have an earthly daughter to acquire and my new child is next on the funeral list. Do you like the name Océane? I quite fancy a French name for her.' She noted the revulsion on George's face. 'What,' she yelled, 'do you expect me to give birth like human women? How much more revolting is that? I have done that…terrible procedure, but once in the last century and I am not opening my legs for the passage of any human thing ever again. Once was enough for me.'

George's glass was now empty and he was in need of more Scotch. This was a new depraved level of information he had not requested or expected. He was also dumbfounded by how Emmanuelle had switched around the grossness scale, to make body-snatching the lesser ordeal than childbirth.

He was curious as to why she had now picked this moment to visit him, and was dying to probe. 'What is that awful smell you have brought into the room with you? Certainly, not your usual trademark Shalini dear Emmanuelle.'

'Oh, the hospital disinfectant smell,' she responded. George finally recognised the clinical aroma; however, he had no compulsion to find out what Emmanuelle had been doing in a hospital and could only assume it was associated with more human body acquisitions. He did feel slightly two-faced by finding such body-pilfering disgusting, but he preferred that Emmanuelle should not know too much about him and his kind. He looked at his watch. He was keen to bring this meeting to a close.

'What do you want with me, Emmanuelle? You are here for a reason I take it?'

Straight talk! The demoness liked this approach. She replied, 'It appears, Mr Smith, that you and I are involved with opposite sides of the same coin. I have been observing your activities with some interest. I cannot pretend to understand why those old fogies you work with want to keep tearing up the ground, but I believe that what they are looking for has a connection with what I am looking for. Our worlds are destined to collide. So, I just want you to know that when that happens, we may be able to collaborate and even pool our resources.'

George was dismissive of the absurd suggestion. 'I have told you once before, Emmanuelle, the Ouroboros find you too disruptive. They have not forgotten the 1560 Siege of Leith or the 983 Great Slav Rising. Yes, in some vague respects, we may have some common ground – but they would never trust you enough to strike up a partnership. Whatever it is that you are suggesting, just forget involving us. A collaboration simply won't work.'

George put on his coat and hat. He knew that since Emmanuelle had invited herself in, she could equally see herself out. His patience was growing thin. He opened his office door, and by way of an old-fashioned gesture, tipped his hat to bid her farewell. 'Goodbye, Emmanuelle. It is Friday night and I am expecting guests. I have no wish to continue this conversation.'

Emmanuelle responded with a childlike wave. 'Oh, but you will. Georgie Porgie, pudding and pie, whether you like it or not, you will. You kissed the girls and made them cry, so our fate is linked. I will be in touch.'

With that, George slammed his office door shut. Descending the steps of the shiny damp alleyway, a sudden mist descended, therefore occluding his vision. As his feet met with a puddle, he almost went flying. Maybe just a coincidence, but from now on George suspected that rightly or wrongly, he would blame Emmanuelle for everything and anything. She was the most powerful type of demon and held a high chain of command. Not only did she possess implausible magical abilities and was gifted with a superior intellect, but she also had the appearance of a normal human being and could walk among them unnoticed. He did not – he dare not, underestimate her. As human as she looked, she was far from flesh and blood. She knew too much about him. The Ouroboros would not be pleased. He would need to take care.

CHAPTER 8

2nd March 2012

Soul's head was in the clouds, quite literally. At an altitude of 3,400 metres, and winding down 'La Grande Motte glacier' in the French Alps resort of Tignes, the snow offered a soft, silent escape. Absorbing all noise, the young psychometry wizard finally found a fleeting solace. Only the resonance of his thoughts disturbed him, whilst his skies swished and whooshed through the mountains' newly laid powder. Against the backdrop of the clearest cerulean sky and glistening iced peaks, Soul had absconded into his own personal wonderland. However, the serenity of the moment was not destined to last long.

Somewhere in the distance, he could hear the elated shrieks of his sister Eve and the notable grandiose chuckles of her husband Gérard. He had been feeling quite sorry for Gérard's situation and was pleased to hear the couple having so much fun. He had good reason to be empathetic. Soul had recently endured his own dark moments of foreboding regarding his peculiar career. He was equally aware that Gérard had also suffered his own setbacks of late. Soul was sympathetic to his brother-in-law's situation. This alpine holiday retreat was a much-needed getaway for all concerned. The timing could not have been better.

Gérard's parents owned a sprawling mountain chalet in Tignes-les-Brévières. Boasting twelve double bedrooms and with an expansive ultra-modern living space, this was soon to become a party home for Eve and Gérard's après-ski guests. The entire chalet was enveloped in a wraparound terrace, with steps leading down to an outside heated pool, hot tub and unusually with an opulent hammam built into the caves. The patio area (which frequently doubled up as a dance floor) was warmed by swinging overhead heaters and bordered by mosaic fire pits and Mexican chiminea's. Further steps descended to a cedar-covered BBQ area with obligatory bread and pizza oven. Not overlooked and with uninterrupted views of the mountains, the isolated abode was wired up to a 'state of the art' surround sound system. Tonight, was party night and Soul knew that Gérard's annual snow shindig was the best in Tignes … or perhaps even the entire French Pyrenees.

Finally catching up with the giggling couple, Soul discovered that his sister's attempt to take a toilet break behind a random boulder had resulted in an impromptu slippage down the slopes. With Eve's salopettes still at knee level, she was unable to dress herself due to fits of manic laughter. Gérard was equally incapacitated by the hysterics of the moment. Soul could do little else but smile at the ridiculous situation and knew this would become the main topic of conversation at tonight's party. Skiing over to rescue his sister and by now joining in with the mirth, Soul shouted out, 'Don't worry, Sis. I will close my eyes. Just grab my hand so I can pull you to your feet.' Looking over to Gérard he called out, 'Stop laughing and get over here to rescue your wife, Dr Bouvier.'

As Eve attempted to balance herself, still in a state of partial undress, the gravity of the situation was exacerbated by the gravity of the slopes. Losing her footing and landing on her back, she slipped further down the ski run with legs akimbo and resembling an overturned turtle. Gérard and Soul could do little else but focus on breathing whilst choking with laughter.

Despite being acutely embarrassing, it was also one of those memorable moments that would be told and told, again and again. Laughter was indeed the best medicine. It was a much-needed prescription for two chaps who had both reached a crisis point in their working lives. That was then and this was now, and right now, all their troubles had been swept away by a moment of pure hilarity.

Soul reached into the pocket of his ski jacket to recover something to wipe the tears of mirth from his eyes. Rarely had he seen a sight so hilarious as his partially undressed sister accelerating down a black run on her back. Fumbling around for a hanky or tissue, his fingers made contact with a hard, smooth rock, expertly carved into a half-moon talisman. He hadn't worn this jacket since he was last in Tignes a year ago, and had quite forgotten what he had left behind in the concealed inner pocket. Pulling out a delightfully presented blue meditation stone, his fingers began to tingle. No longer able to hear the shrieks and shrills ascending from further down the slope, the focus of his attention was now on the stone. It was no ordinary amulet. Made from the same Preseli blue rock as found in the Stonehenge inner circle, this was a most exceptional lump of mystical geology.

He suspected that the Stonehenge archaeologist probably had little concept of the functionality of the blue stones within the sarsen megaliths. As a reader of innominate energy, Soul had a superior understanding to that of the historians.

He knew that mounted in a circle of large boulders, the blue stones could act in much the same way as a soundproof insulating wall, not dissimilar to what would be employed in a recording studio. The crystallised fragments within its core would soak up sound waves, therefore preventing any external distractions (such as echoes and reverberations) from disturbing the sacred rites. Within the confines of a small, hallowed place, the physical properties of the rock prevented sound from moving from one space to another. This gave the inner chambers an eerie and otherworldly calm. Sometimes used in ancient courts, the stone also compelled truth.

Unlike the megalithic ancient civilisations, Soul had another purpose for his blue stone. As well as keeping sound from leaking out, the amulet also prevented unwanted sound from entering in and therefore was the perfect meditation stone. Soul lived in a world that was seldom silent. For one who could hear the energy from events stored like a tape recording from long ago, Soul often craved the hushed world of nothingness. His brain was constantly bombarded with electromagnetic radiation, and he often struggled to dull the unseen clutter that invaded his senses. He was pleased to have recovered his stone. He hoped it would bring a temporary peace and stillness to his life, whilst he had time alone with his thoughts. Time away from the jumble sale of self-doubt. Time to consider the uncertainty of his future.

Placing it carefully back in his pocket, he had a sudden visualisation. As a quiet stone, Soul did not expect the rock to talk to him. This impromptu communication was most unexpected. He sensed that another talisman had been carved from the same Preseli boulder, and one of these was nearby. His stone had a sibling. What a peculiar message. It had some greater significance, but he knew not what. Time would tell, as it always did.

Skiing to catch up with Gérard and Eve, Soul couldn't help but consider that he was ever so slightly weird. He had been given a gift that seemed to be more of a nuisance than a blessing. A strange ability which he thought he could turn into a livelihood, but now he was harbouring doubts about his chosen profession. 'Stuff it,' he thought, 'I'm a young guy stuck in some paranormal paradigm. I need to get out more and start having fun with the living.' Soul was a young man with a rare talent; however, right now he was a confused young man who was nearing the end of his tether.

***

The chalet girls and resident chef had done a marvellous job as per expectation. Lying in wait for tonight's guest was a large outside grill gently warming a variety of fondues. From piping hot Gruyère and Emmental cheese, to bubbling creamy wild mushrooms dashed with garlic croissants, followed by a tempting combination of Fontina and Butterkäse cheeses, spinach, artichoke hearts and paprika. The cheesy aromas from the grill seductively pervaded the outside patio area. Forever the perfect hostess, Eve scrutinised every last detail. Taking a forbidden lick from the caramel and chocolate fondue, she gave an audible satisfied sigh.

Eve could see that her husband was in deep conversation with the DJ regarding tonight's repertoire of music, so made her way over to the charcoal rack area. The smell of the smoky meat and the crackling of the burning skin welcomed her senses long before she had reached her destination. Picking her way down the recently gritted steps, she was delighted to find wild boar was slowly turning on a spit roast. Nico, their Italian chef, was attentively basting the meat with his favourite lemon marinade, whilst ostentatiously singing along to *'non è l'inferno'* by Emma Marrone. Eve smiled as she removed his earplugs and shouted,

'Ciao Nico, hai una voce molto buona.' They both laughed back at each other with friendly affection. 'I believe some of your family are joining us tonight, Nico?' Looking slightly alarmed, he replied, 'Oh I hope that is okay with you, Miss Eve. I asked Mr Gérard about it and he didn't seem to mind. They are here on vacation in the neighbouring village.' Eve hadn't meant to sound as though she was interrogating her favourite Italian chef. 'No, no, no, of course I don't mind,' she responded, 'your families are most welcome. I am just curious to know who is coming, that's all.' Nico looked relieved. He didn't want his family to be viewed as random gate crashers. 'Thank you, Miss Eve. I do appreciate this. It will be my brother Amedeo, his wife Becky and her younger sister … who I think is called Florence, and she is bringing her friend. Just four of them in total. Are you sure this will be okay, Miss Eve?' Eve smiled at him and patted his shoulder to assure him that it wasn't a problem. 'No, that's perfectly fine Nico. The more the merrier, but please stop calling me "Miss Eve". My name is Eve-just Eve. Anyway. I am just going back inside now to inspect your fudgy chocolate and orange gateaux chilling in the refrigerator. Gérard won't stop raving on about it, so I wouldn't be at all surprised to find some of it is already missing.' With that she gave Nico a playful pat on his gluteus muscles. After all, it was a party and Eve was in a playful mood.

As she started to walk away, she had a random thought. Eve suddenly turned back to address Nico. 'By the way, how old is this Florence girl and her friend?' Nico shrugged, 'Early twenties I guess. Why do you ask?' 'Hmm, no big reason,' replied Eve, 'it's just that most of our friends are middle-aged and I thought it would be nice for my brother Soul if there were other people at the party around his own age group – especially if they were girl people.' She winked at Nico and turned to walk back up the steps. In his youth, Nico was quite an Italian stallion. He understood. No other explanation was required. He smiled to himself, replaced his ear pieces and continued to sing loudly in a bold, baritone pitch whilst merrily basting his feast.

In the meantime, Nico's guests were already in the taxi, and making their way along a long winding road which coiled itself discreetly around the iced, mountainous terrain. Aside from the whiteness of the snow and a scattering of stars peeping through the clouds, it was the blackest of darkness. The chef's guests tried to remain jovial, but were secretly fearful that their driver was totally lost in the dusky contorted landscape. Disorientated and becoming increasingly concerned, it was therefore with much relief when they finally located the driveway to Gérard's parents' winter holiday home. The driveway to the mammoth chalet was illuminated by welcoming flaming torches, and the boom of a base beat sent out an audible assurance. Indeed – they had arrived at the party location. Lit up like a Christmas tree, the sight of the chalet created a communal sigh of gratitude within the taxi.

Soul tried his best to get into the swing of things. Bordering on being an OCD control freak, and not normally a big drinker, he had partaken in a few glasses of hot spiced buttered rum. He mentally argued that it was for therapeutic reasons since it abetted his resolve to become slightly sociable. Taking stock of the vast array of food and drink, Soul had to concede that Eve and Gérard's annual snow festivities must surely be the best party in the valley.

Neither actively participating and yet not totally aloof, Soul perched on the end of a chair and enjoyed a moment of people watching. He could hear the story of his sister's ungainly and undressed descent from the slopes being repeated several times throughout the evening – on each occasion resulting in a wave of laughter. Soul delighted in being on the outside looking in; however, he also felt strangely isolated. He decided to locate the pizza oven, grab something to eat and then inconspicuously disappear back to his bedroom and vanish within the pages of a good book. Parties were not really his scene, as wonderful as this particular party may be.

Queuing up behind other hungry revellers with plate in hand, Soul couldn't help but notice two young ladies toying with the chef's young assistant, Lazzero. He hadn't seen these girls at any of his sister's former parties, and so was curious. The girl with the stunning long red hair knew she was attractive and seemed totally adept with the art of flirtation. She struck a perfect pose, flicked back her luscious orange mane and gazed attentively into the eyes of Lazzero, the young pizza maker. The other girl looked ever so slightly embarrassed by her friend's overtly sexual behaviour. She covered her face in mock embarrassment as her flirty friend continued with her relentless inappropriate wooing.

Suddenly realising that they were being watched and had become a source of amusement, the girl's blonde friend addressed Soul. 'I am sorry about Florence', she said. 'She is just having a bit of fun. I hope nobody takes offence. I think Lazzero is enjoying the attention.'

With the deepest indigo eyes, a flawless porcelain complexion and cascading golden ringlets, the young woman's pure wholesome beauty quite took Soul's breath away. In that instance, he was completely captivated by her presence, and for once in his life was almost speechless. He stuttered almost incoherently, 'Err … Who the hell is

Florence?' He couldn't think what else to say. The blonde woman giggled. 'Oh, so you want to know about Florence ah? Well, she is the flame-haired cougar over there. She is the sister of the woman married to the brother of the chef. It's kinda complicated. Anyway, for all my sins, I am her friend. Rather, she is my friend. My only friend actually, and dear sir, who the heck are you?' She then hiccupped whilst almost losing her balance. A day of skiing followed by too many hot toddies had taken their toll. Soul caught her arm to steady her. His pulse was racing. This was most unusual. His heartbeat was normally a steady 60bpm. It was as steady as he was constant. He hated to admit it, but he found the tipsy young blonde with Shirley Temple locks quite captivating. As for Florence, indeed, she was cosmetically striking, but way too overly confident for a shy bloke such as Soul. He normally read stone walls better than he could people, but even from a distance he could determine that Florence was a 'Black Widow' amongst women. Not wanting to be devoured whole, he would keep his distance from the effervescent all-consuming spider woman.

Bringing his attention back to her friend, he fumbled to find the right words. Soul didn't know what to say or do next. He hadn't dated since leaving school and certainly hadn't trifled with a woman's affections in as many years. Of course, he realised that he was a well-built, fine-looking man. He possessed a mirror and he could appreciate his own reflection. His romantic reticence wasn't due to any lack of confidence on his part. He was simply an introvert who had somehow become lost in his own strange world of unseen forces. Most humans only had conversations with other humans; however, Soul's vocabulary ventured into the realm of strange silent energies. As such, human conversation sometimes defeated him. He tried his best to chit-chat with the blonde woman, but predictably kept stumbling over his words. Fortunately, she was a tad tipsy and so didn't notice Soul's malfunctioning flirtation techniques. However, his sister Eve was hovering on the overhead terrace and she did notice her brother's pathetic attempts at seduction. It was time for big sister to save the day.

She strode resolutely towards the blonde woman who had captivated her hopeless younger sibling. She held out her hand, 'Hi, I am Eve and I am your hostess. Lovely to meet you … and you are?' 'Saskia,' came the reply. 'I am Saskia,' she repeated. 'I am here with my uncontrollable friend Florence and her older sister Becky and her new husband … whatever his name is. It begins with the letter A. Am … err … Amar – name of a song. Give me a moment.' Saskia then started to sing the 1985 song by Falco. 'Sorry, I have drunk too much. We were invited by Nico and I do remember that much. This is a wonderful party, Eve. I have never been to anything quite like this before. You have made so much effort. Thank you for allowing Nico to bring us along. Wow, this place is pretty awesome.'

With a slight wobble and a few more hiccups, Saskia finally stopped talking. Eve instantly recognised that Saskia was a well-educated woman. She had a refined upper-class English accent, with a vague hint of an Eastern European dialect. She had also established that Saskia probably couldn't hold her liquor too well and black coffee was probably the most sensible prescription. Eve tried to manage the situation without being overly condescending. 'It is lovely to meet you Saskia, and I am so glad that Nico invited you. But hey, it is really cold out here and alcohol mixed with freezing temperatures can be a lethal combination. Let me take you inside and get you something to warm you up.' Saskia looked over at her friend Florence, who by now had all but crawled into the skin of the young pizza maker. She understood what Eve had suggested and why. She was in agreement. 'Yes, sure,' she responded, 'heat and coffee. Lead the way Eve. Let's go get sober.'

Eve held on to the arm of the young woman as she guided her up the potentially lethal icy steps and back towards the chalet. She looked over her shoulder at her bewildered brother and gestured for him to follow. In her own mind, she was trying to help the situation. Eve was unaware that Soul already knew the tipsy partygoer hanging off her elbow. He had overheard the introductions.

Soul was disheartened. He knew of Saskia. It wasn't just her unusual name, but with the benefit of hindsight he now recognised her unusual accent. How was he to know? All their prior conversations had been conducted by email or phone. He had never actually met her in person before tonight. Saskia would soon know exactly who he was and what he did for a living. He silently cursed the situation. For most of his life he had longed to be normal, and to meet a woman who would treat him as just an average bloke. He was tired of being categorised as some circus act. He couldn't believe it. On the one occasion, he actually got to meet someone he actually felt attracted towards, she would know him for the freak he believed himself to be. 'Give up Soul,' he muttered to himself, 'go back to your cage.'

Using the seldom-used rear stairs to his balcony, Soul quietly wandered back up to his room to collect his swimwear, towel and gown. He had decided to retreat to the quiet seclusion of the hammam, and let the boisterous party continue without him.

He hadn't expected to meet Saskia tonight, and worse than that, he hadn't expected to find her divinely attractive. Right now, he needed solitude and time away from the noise and the crowds. A childhood memory of being taunted at school was a scar that ran deep, but a scar that could be easily opened. For one who had been bullied many times, escape was a familiar remedy.

Aside from his love of skiing … essentially because it was a solitary sport, Soul loved to visit his brother-in-law's family chalet because of one very special place – the hammam. Carved into the rock, the Turkish bath consisted of clearly defined areas. From a relaxation room scented with Damask rose, to a hotter room vaporised with steam and then on to a cooler resting area. This ritualistic cleansing process suited someone such as Soul, who felt secure with the consistency of routines.

A pool area had also been added to the original hammam. It was dimly lit, with just the haziest suggestion of an opaque blue light and refreshed with a zesty hint of Bergamot. Almost like a hidden temple, the pool had been designed to offer meditative healing. The subdued lighting was only slightly enhanced by a few flickering candles. Surrounded by illuminated Grecian-style archways, the rectangular pool was steaming hot and yet fed by cascading snow water from an alpine spring. Both cool and hot at the same time, it was a tranquil, divine and surreal retreat.

Soul lay back under the spring and closed his eyes. The cold mountain water spurted forth from the wall, refreshingly cleansing the grime from his long blonde mane. Lost in the moment, he failed to notice that he was not alone, until a tide of rippled water pounded like waves upon his chest. Slightly alarmed, he opened his eyes and tried to focus on the person creating the ripples. The light was dim and misty. He couldn't make out who it was. As the body swam closer, a young nubile female stood upright. Her blonde ringlets were now dark and straightened by the weight of water; however, he still recognised her. Soul did not know what to say.

It was Saskia. She began by apologising. 'I am sorry to disturb you, Saul. You looked like you were in a world of your own then. I hope you don't mind. Your sister has allowed me to borrow one of her costumes and she told me I would find you in here. She marched me off so quickly before and I was actually enjoying talking to you before she ambushed me. I think she was trying to sober me up. To be honest, I am not really used to parties that much and I don't usually drink a lot. Now I am talking too much. Anyway, I wanted to catch up with you to say sorry for being so … so … drunk I think is the correct word. Anyway … this is me saying I am sorry, Saul.'

Soul was horrified. She had his name wrong – technically correct, but wrong. She had called him Saul. He knew that the moment he told her his acquired stage name – now his real name – she would know his identity. She would recall that he was that strange fellow whom she had once hired sometime last year. The bizarre chap who could listen to a cave talk. He felt mortified and deeply embarrassed.

She moved closer to him and it was more than obvious she was making her move in more ways than one. She was so close, that he felt her breasts make contact with his bare torso. He was mortified. Soul lifted himself up onto the side of the pool so as to give himself some distance. It was a mistake on his part. Now more than ever, Saskia had a full-blown view of his toned, muscular body. She considered him to be some sort of Nordic Demi-God. Unable to keep her thoughts to herself, she even exclaimed, 'Wow, you are in good shape, Saul. You work out I take it. Got a bit of a Viking look going on there.' Saskia bit her lip. Even she was surprised by how forward she was being. She concluded that she had been locked away in her Cotswold cottage for far too long.

Soul took a moment to consider. Yes, indeed, he could play along at being someone he wasn't and indeed the prize would be worth it. This exquisite young lady seemed to be putty in his hands. However, he was someone who was a seer of truth. How could he now become deceitful when it was in his nature to tell things exactly as they were? His mind was made up. He jumped back into the pool to face her directly. 'Saskia, you are lovelier than I ever imagined you to be. However, you already know me, although we have never met. You have my name wrong. Actually, I was called Saul once. However, I am now known as Soul. Do you now know who I am?'

Saskia moved backwards. It was an unintentional reflex action. Indeed, she knew of Soul. Soul was work. He was someone whom she had hired in her capacity of being employed by a secretive investment group. Her directive was clear. She was never, in any circumstances, to mix her private life with work. These words were etched into her contract and into her heart. Her mind tumbled around like a washing machine. Mentally her thoughts were just as jumbled and knotted as socks caught up in a duvet. She was here on vacation. Work was off limits and at work, pleasure was off limits. This was all too bewildering. Where did she draw the line?

Saskia simply turned around and swam away. She didn't even say goodbye. She lived with a fear that she could never share with anyone. Even by Soul's standards this U-turn seemed extreme … and harsh …

very harsh. He called after her, 'Saskia, please don't go. I would like to talk to you.' It was all too late. She swam off into the blue mist and soon she was gone. Soul blamed himself. Little did he know that this was nothing at all to do with him, but was more associated with Saskia's terms of employment.

As a child who grew up being persecuted for just being different, he still possessed a victim mentality. Victims mostly believe they are to blame. So, in his mind Saskia swimming away was his fault. He went back under the cold snow shower to cleanse away the negativity that had now suffused this sacred place. With emotions running as cold as the alpine shower, he could dismiss her with equal disregard. He was ever inch as good with dismissal as she could be.

When Eve finally caught up with her, Saskia was alone in the women's changing room, tucked up inside an oversized white dressing gown and shivering. Curled up in a foetal position, she looked pale and profoundly sad.

Eve was a psychic. This wasn't information she advertised to anyone outside her immediate circle and it wasn't a skill that she practised commercially. In differing ways, she was as gifted as her brother, but Eve's abilities mostly involved people, as opposed to Soul's connection with anything but. Eve sensed an aura around Saskia. It was an aura which had the dark tones of a deep-rooted primal fear. This was similar to the terror of a fox being chased in a hunt. It was a kill or be killed blind panic, which over the years had been well disguised and contained. Eve put a reassuring arm around the young woman and then held her cold, shaking hand to comfort her.

Eve closed her eyes. With soft, motherly tones she began, 'I see a little girl in a school dormitory looking out of a window. It's a very big building and she feels very small. All of the other children have gone home for the weekend. The child watches as cars pull up and parents take their children away. Tears are falling down her cheeks, but she wipes them away when the teachers walk into the room. She doesn't want anyone to think she is weak. So, month after month – the little girl remains alone while all her friends go home.' Saskia raised her head and looked up at Eve in disbelief. She uttered, 'Yes, that was me. How do you know all of this?' Eve didn't answer her, but continued, 'having a home became important to you, because of this experience. You like the idea of a lovely place to live Saskia. Somewhere you can hide away. To some a house is merely walls with a roof, but to you a home is sanctuary. Anyway, the child I can see has many siblings; nine or ten at least. I can see that they are mostly brothers. She hardly even knows them. In fact, I think she is hated and resented by her own family. She has only met her father a few times and her mother doesn't seem to want any part in her life. Her mother looks after her – yet she doesn't. She is a cold, nasty woman. I do not like the aura around the woman who is your mother – it is disturbing. There is a sister though, just one person she connects with. Am I correct Saskia?'

Saskia sat upright, her eyes dilated as she started to pay attention. She replied, 'Yes. How do you know all of this?' Eve responded, 'I am psychic, Saskia. However, I haven't practised in a long time so I could do with some feedback. How accurate have I been so far?' 'Very,' she responded. 'Great,' responded Eve, 'then if you are comfortable with all of this, I will continue, but please cut me some slack. I am an amateur.'

She closed her eyes again and breathed deeply as though in deep concentration. She continued, 'Your father has been married many times, but not to your mother. She was his mistress and yet more constant than any of his wives. They came and went, but she was always around, like a silent shadow in the background. I don't want to use the word concubine but this is the word that has floated into my mind. Is that why your siblings resented you?' Saskia was taken aback by the brutal honesty in Eve's words. Nobody had ever spoken to her like this before. Nobody had dared used that word to describe her mother before, although they all thought it.

Still shaken, Saskia replied, 'My father is a very wealthy man. He was married five times and had a couple of children with each wife. None of his wives lasted too long and yes, my mother was his mistress … a paid mistress. I think there is another and much cruder word that describes a woman like her. Not a word I care to repeat. They all knew about her and eventually they knew about me. They all blamed my mother for their own mother's demise. They thought of her as evil. Aside from one sister, they are all half-brothers, and to say they hate me is an understatement. What else do you see, Eve? You have caught my attention.' Eve was pleased she had gained Saskia's trust. 'Your mother was very attractive to your father, not only because she was outstandingly beautiful, but also because she wasn't possessive and didn't ask too many questions. Some could say she was paid to be tolerant. You are a lot like your mother, Saskia, and in a different way you are subconsciously following her path.' Saskia shrugged. She knew exactly what Eve was saying. Eve continued. 'Your conception was not a mistake, although your siblings were told that the pregnancy was unintentional. I think your mother may have told a few lies. Once she was pregnant, your father lost all interest. I guess a mistress with a bump and stretch marks may not be too appealing to a man like your father. He is a powerful man and very wealthy. Am I correct in saying this?' Saskia nodded in agreement. She added, 'I am told that when he found out, he paid for her to relocate to England, maybe to create space between them. He purchased a big house for my mother and gave her a generous monthly allowance. He paid for me to go to a top girls' private school and to acquire a privileged English education. However, I have only actually met him four times in my life, and – as you correctly mentioned before – aside from just one older sister, I am more or less hated by all my siblings. I do love my older sister though. She is brash and bold and an intrepid party warrior… a lot like my friend Florence and her sister Becky. Perhaps that is why I bond with audacious people.' Eve felt slightly disheartened on hearing this. She had been trying to play matchmaker, but recognised that her introverted, reclusive brother was nothing like the extrovert, bullish types Saskia indicated that she was drawn towards. She wondered if perhaps Saskia liked to be controlled, in which case a pairing with Soul may well be doomed. Eve sighed inwardly. She was sure that there was some spark between the couple, and was disappointed to be proven wrong, but she knew her brother well enough to know he wasn't the alpha-male controlling type at all. They were a total mismatch.

As Saskia's sorry story started to unfold further, Eve was beginning to feel deeply sympathetic for this stranger, a young woman whom she hadn't met prior to this evening. 'I am sorry, Saskia; do you want me to stop?' Saskia quickly responded, 'No, please carry on Eve. I am impressed by how much you have uncovered so far. You have an unusual gift. You should use it more.' As requested Eve continued. 'You seem to have had a very troubled childhood. Your mother also had her own issues and when your father sent her away to England, she was too busy rebuilding her own life to pay much attention to her little daughter. It can't have been easy for you. I can see that over the years she had many men-friends. On the few occasions, you were at home with her, you were pushed out of the way and sworn to secrecy. I can see you sitting on the top of the stairs trying to eavesdrop on conversations. Then one day, you simply stopped trying to listen. However, you are still good at keeping secrets, Saskia, very good. I don't see your mother around you anymore, but she is still alive. Does she live far away from you now?' Saskia was enthralled by the accuracy of Eve's words. She replied, 'She is having a wicked time being single. I cannot recall when I last saw her and I do not even know her present address.'

As Eve tried to focus in on Saskia's present life, a murky shroud descended. Eve instinctually knew she had pushed it as far as she could. The past was an open book for all to read. The past had been and gone. It could do no harm. But there were aspects to Saskia's present life and more worryingly her future, which were closely guarded and not open for Eve to view. She made her final psychic synopsis. 'You have had a tough life, Saskia, and yet strangely enough, you have also been given many advantages. I can see that you own your own house and few young people of your age could make that boast. You are proud of where you live. In my mind's eye, I can see a fairy-tale cottage with a typical English garden. There is an orchard at the rear.' Eve closed her eyes tightly. She was having to work hard to understand the Saskia of 2012.

She carried on, 'You gained a top law degree and presently have a well-paid job, one which you are rightfully protective of. I can sense that there is something about your job which worries you. I am sorry, but be this deliberate or not; you have shielded that part of your psyche. As such, I cannot tell you what it is. However, I don't have to tell you, as you already know. Something about secrecy – I cannot see anything beyond that. Given your upbringing, it is understandable that you may find it hard to trust people; however, if you care to listen, my brother has had his trials and tribulations as well. Do you care to listen?'

Saskia wasn't sure. She stood up and climbed back into her snug clothes, which had been warming up nicely by the radiator pipes. She realised that Eve was playing the part of matchmaker, but she felt incapable of explaining to her why Soul was off limits. Had he been anyone else, this would not be the case. Saskia had compartmentalised her life. There was work, and then there was personal and never the twain shall meet. Maybe there was no harm in just listening. She sat back down on the bench as she dried her hair with a heated towel. 'Okay, Eve, tell me about your brother Saul … I mean Soul?'

Eve looked up as though searching her mind for thoughts. How could she describe her brother in a few sentences? She began, 'Soul is a magician. He does this on stage for a living. You know, Saskia, from being a young boy, all Soul ever wanted to do was to find a constructive purpose for his gift. To some extent he is a recluse, but in a weird way, that also adds to the mystique of his stage image. Talking of the stage, that is the place where he is at his happiest. I often find it peculiar that some of the most reserved people come alive when performing, but it is as it is. Soul feeds off the veneration of an appreciative audience. I guess this is why recent events have come as a big blow to him.' Saskia was curious. She asked, 'Gosh, what happened?' Eve continued, 'He was doing a show a few weeks back and he was given a ring from someone in the front row. Soul struggles with discretion and he told them what he saw.' 'Which was?' asked Saskia. 'He said the ring was made from old Welsh gold – a rare metal mostly used for royalty. It was an unusual art deco-style engagement ring. He could see that the original owner of the ring had drowned in an accident and the ring had been cut from her lifeless, bloated body. I think he even said the word "bloated". He didn't mean to offend anyone; he just blurts out the truth sometimes. Anyway, he then said that the dead woman's fiancé was distraught and lost his job. The poor chap was broke and in need of money, so he pawned the ring. It was purchased by its second owner who gave it to his betrothed. It then seemed that his girlfriend was unfaithful to him and the relationship ended. So, it ended up back in the jeweller's window, where it was recently sold to its third owner at a greatly discounted price.' 'Phew,' gasped Saskia, 'what a story. Unlucky ring. I wouldn't want a ring with that history, that's for sure.' Eve sighed. 'That's the point. The man who handed him the ring did so because he was about to propose to his girlfriend on stage. Soul had been primed about this beforehand and should have remembered … but stupid boy – he had forgotten and came out with all that crazy poison about the ring's chequered history. You can imagine how the chap about to propose felt at that moment in time.'

Saskia began to feel vaguely sorry for Soul at that point. 'That's awful. What happened next, Eve?' Eve groaned. It was a deep, sorrowful exhalation of breath. 'The show came to a dramatic end and Soul's contract was immediately terminated. That performance had been a regular weekend gig for him and provided a constant stream of money. It's not just the money that was the issue; it dashed his confidence and self-belief. He is confused now and doesn't know which way to turn career-wise. He considers his gift to be a curse. So, you see, Saskia, my brother is here in the mountains to sweep the cobwebs out of his head and re-think his life. I have advised him to expand on his act to make it more visually appealing, maybe even develop his ability more. I am convinced he has other hidden talents he hasn't even begun to explore. So far, he has been resisting the whole conjuror scenario of illusions, such as being a trickster, hypnotist and a mentalist, but I think it would enhance his act. I don't know what else to suggest. I was hoping that maybe the company of a lovely lady would be a win/win, perhaps be a tonic for both of you.'

The suggestion fell on deaf ears. Saskia had already dismissed Soul as a work associate. Eve noted that she wasn't remotely curious about his past and made no effort to dig deeper. Eventually, and possibly out of politeness, Saskia asked, 'And how are you, Eve? I heard whisperings that your husband was also under some strain of late.' Eve shrugged. 'I guess so. My husband is a hospital doctor in North Carolina, or rather he was. He has been suspended at the moment, so we are all in the Pyrenees for a bit of escapism, I guess.' Saskia responded, 'Oh, I am sorry, Eve. If you don't mind me asking, what happened?' 'I am not really supposed to talk about it, Saskia, but I suspect that writing a death certificate for someone later found to be alive wasn't career enhancing.' Saskia was lost for words. 'Oh … okay,' was about as much as she could say. 'I hope it all sorts itself out.'

Eve wasn't technically a clairvoyant. She didn't possess a crystal ball and could rarely make predictions of what was to come; however, she did sense that Soul and Saskia were somehow connected in the future. Sadly, it seemed that for now, her hopes that this may be a romantic association were becoming a waning ambition. By this point, Saskia was brushing her hair and preparing to meet with the bitter chill she knew awaited outside the hammam.

Knowing her brother as she did, Eve suspected that he wouldn't emerge until after the party was over, if at all. That would be the end of that – romantic opportunity lost. Turning to leave, Saskia faced Eve. 'Thank you for the party, Eve; however, I am tired and cold so I will probably order a taxi back soon. Can you please convey a message to Soul? Just in case he mentions it to you, I did hire him a while back, so this message is work related. Can you tell him that we have now purchased the mine at Crank and pending planning permission, will soon be opening up some of the shafts. I would like to employ him to get back in there and take a look around. See what he can pick up on and all that supernatural stuff that he does. We will pay him well - should help out with his cash flow a bit. Please ask him to call me to arrange. He has my number.'

Eve was quite flabbergasted. Never before had she witnessed such a dramatic change of heart. From a woman who was slightly tipsy and overtly flirtatious, to one with a sad and tragic childhood, to a cold-hearted career woman who was now hiring him in a professional capacity. As that final thought came into her head, she wondered if perhaps Saskia had more in common with her absent father than maybe she realised. With an innate capacity to turn the charm on and then coldly switch it off again, Eve considered that her brother may have just had a lucky escape.

Just as that thought raised its head, a discreet three little taps knocked on the door of the female changing room. As Saskia was already behind the door and just about to leave, she opened it before the final knock had chance to materialise. 'Oh Saul, I mean Soul. I was just about to go,' gasped Saskia, looking slightly uncomfortable with the whole situation. Soul gazed at her décolletage. Saskia was confused. Eve was confused. 'What's the matter?' asked Saskia, touching her neck and feeling ill at ease with the direction of his glare. Soul pulled a talisman from out of his pocket. 'Snap,' he uttered, as he showed a half-moon amulet identical to that as worn around Saskia's neck. 'I knew the other half of this was somewhere in the resort,' continued Soul. 'I bet if we join these two stones together, they will be a perfect fit. They were cut from the same circular blue stone. Twin talismans! Who would have thought that you would have the other half? Where did you get it from?' Saskia was slightly dumbfounded. This was not a conversation she expected to be having. 'The Internet. I ordered it online,' was about as good a response as she could manage. 'Why did you order it, Saskia?' Soul was being unusually commanding and controlling, and as Eve had guessed earlier, this was an attitude that Saskia responded to. She stuttered slightly, 'I … err … erm … the altar stone at Crank was made out of the same sandstone. We gained entry to the underground cathedral a few months after you did your reading in the entrance cave. We had the altar stone analysed and we found it was Preseli bluestone. I was curious and did some research and I read it was good for healing … and maybe I thought I needed some healing.' Eve watched on with interest. Soul seemed to be leading this conversation with a degree of authority. Taking his eyes away from the Talisman she wore as a pendant, he gazed directly … even forcefully, into Saskia's eyes. The stare was deeper than that. He was gazing hypnotically into her essence and she was incapable of doing anything about it. 'I knew there had to be a reason for this,' commented Soul. 'These rocks never act by way of coincidence. What joins us together, Saskia, is not so much the twin talismans, but the caves at Crank. It wants to pull me back in there, and I don't understand why. By the way, be careful where and when you wear this thing. It isn't just a tame piece of New Age jewellery. I understand you are in the legal profession and this stone doesn't like its wearers to tell lies.' Ouch – Eve considered that comment a bit too condescending. Soul was clutching his own blue stone talisman, and was equally as bound by the requirement of brutal honestly.

He continued, 'Something in Crank is of immense importance and I need to know what you have found out since the time I did my initial reading. If you follow me, Saskia, we can go to my room where we will have some peace away from the party. Also, since I am holding my truth stone, I need to confess that I saw something at Crank which at the time I withheld from you. I apologise for this, but I was scared and didn't want to give you any excuses to send me back in there. I am sorry, Saskia, but I should tell you what happened to me. Now if you can follow me, we have things to discuss. This way - follow me, and just to cut through any crap – this is a work-related conversation.'

Soul took wide, confident strides out of the hammam cave exit, and without question Saskia obediently followed him. Eve was flabbergasted. She watched with astonishment as her brother walked up the balcony steps leading to his bedroom, with Saskia obediently walking a few steps behind him, subserviently tracking his steps through the snow. 'Well, I'll be …', was about as much as Eve could utter in profound disbelief.

As she stood outside in the cold and watched them disappearing towards Soul's bedroom, she also spotted the chief Nico watching the couple with interest. She caught a look in his eye. Eve knew that Nico was presently dating some famous celebrity whose name was a closely guarded secret – but now she could see another side to her friend Nico. He also had feelings for Saskia. She was sure of it.

Other eyes also watched. Eve felt a shiver run down her spine. She looked around in panic. Nothing was there. The partygoers were being loud and boisterous and the intensity of the bass beat threatened to cause an avalanche. Yet she knew something was hiding – something sinister and menacing.

She didn't see Emmanuelle as she turned to her minion and said, 'Things are becoming interesting, Tobiah, but you need to keep an eye on Nico.' The entities were not visible, but Eve knew that the coldness that fell upon her, had not just descended down from a frozen mountain. She shivered and quickly moved inside to find her husband's warm arms. She walked as quickly as the icy path would allow her to move. Something inherently unpleasant had just invaded the mountain resort. She was worried.

CHAPTER 9

3rd July 2012

It was late afternoon and despite the sinking sun, still a hot, sticky day in a small town somewhere in the middle of North Carolina. Home was a traditional colonial wooden-framed house. It was an older style two-storey detached, with a shingle roof and sat within a quarter acre of shaded, wooded garden. A young woman fed corn to the chickens near the shed, whilst her brother blasted out some anarchic heavy metal music from his open bedroom window. Around the property was an archetypal white picket fence, which was draped in stars and stripes in preparation for tomorrow's Independence Day party.

A strange man stood at the gate. He shouted over to the young woman, 'Hello there, can you let me in?' The gate wasn't locked. The man could easily have let himself him, but Arabella did not query his request and simply obeyed without question. She walked over to the man, a puzzled look etched on her face. As she did, she stepped on a fence nail and with a loud shriek hopped around in agony, whilst blood dripped onto the pink block-paving.

Finally hobbling over to the gate, she undid the latch. Again, he waited until the gate was fully opened and then – tipping his hat by way of a gesture of gratitude – he entered her domain. He conveniently pulled a plaster from out of his pocket, as though he had already known about her injury in advance. She accepted it and then scrutinised the stranger with a degree of apprehension.

Looking at him from top to toe, Arabella was quite bemused. His leather ankle-high shoes were buttoned up on the side. She had never seen that style before, aside from old black and white photographs. He wore tweed knee breeches with a distinct herringbone design. A hunting jacket matched his knickerbockers. A heavily starched Stanley collar was perfectly finished off with a silk neck scarf. His immaculate style was completed by a bowler hat and walking cane. He didn't look as though he came from this century. With a degree of reservation, she asked him his name. 'Who are you, do I know you?' Arabella did not know the oddly dressed stranger who stood before her, but she suspected she knew why he was here. He replied, 'Hello, Arabella, I am Tobiah. Charmed to meet you, madam.'

She looked down at the footprint traces of her blood on the floor. Combined with the fact that the unusual man needed to be invited in, the pieces of the jigsaw puzzle fell into place. 'I was expecting Emmanuelle,' stated Arabella. 'However, I guess you will do. I don't know if the heat troubles you, but it irritates the life out of me. Do you want to join me on the porch? I don't know if you creatures drink at all, but if you do can I tempt you with some chilled Sarsaparilla?'

The gent – dressed as though from some bygone era – smiled with a degree of amusement. Arabella could see that beneath the hat was the face of a young, handsome chap. He was not as old as his clothes portrayed him to be. He responded, 'Yes, indeed, I would most welcome a drink. Don't worry, I don't have holes in my feet. I won't leak all over your garden like a water sprinkler.' Arabella giggled at the unanticipated humour as she limped over to the porch with her strange guest.

After bringing out a jug of iced water and root beer, Arabella enquired, 'Do you work for Emmanuelle? I don't remember exactly what happened to me, but my family inform me that I was actually declared dead. I was even issued with a death certificate. Once I was well enough to come home, I have always known that someone or something would come to claim me one day. I am totally aware that I have cheated death, Tobiah, and I know that I now have to pay for my life. I must say, however, that I didn't expect someone like you to turn up. What am I? I need to know, what have I become?'

Tobiah sipped his cold Sarsaparilla with immense appreciation. Presently working in human form, he battled with thirst as much as any other living thing – plant or animal. He considered Arabella's question and responded with total honesty. 'Arabella, undead mythical beings belong to the work of fiction and the bizarre imagination of their authors. You were a fresh fatality. By that, I mean you were still warm. Emmanuelle was able to repair your organs. You are very much alive and you will grow old and die when it's your time to exit the planet. You will come home at Christmas, eat turkey with your family and still update your Facebook page. Not much has changed, not until your contract expires.' Arabella was confused. 'A deal was done, Tobiah. I may not remember anything about what led up to the incident. I cannot recall taking my father's gun and I can't even remember this Dean guy I was supposed to be in love with, but I do remember that a deal was done.'

Tobiah stood and took her arm. 'Let us walk over to the lake, Arabella. We need to go somewhere private. We cannot risk being overheard. What I am about to tell you may be difficult for you to take in. Call me old-fashioned, but these things need to be conveyed slowly. Some things in life, and in death and in the space in-between – cannot be rushed.'

They walked leisurely and in silence, until they reached the mangroves by a static, stagnant, swampy lake. By the shores of the lake, Tobiah squatted down and skimmed a pebble along the still water. It must have jumped five or six times. Arabella was impressed. As the sun began to sink beyond the horizon, Tobiah sat down amongst the yellow bittersweet nightshade. 'Be careful, they are poisonous,' warned Arabella, immediately realising that Tobiah was unlikely to be affected by such toxins.

She was inquisitive. 'What are you, exactly?' she asked. Tobiah took off his hat and smiled at her. Arabella couldn't help but admire his thick shock of black curls and deep russet eyes. He was indeed a fetching young fellow. 'I am a demon, but you know that already, Arabella.' It was an unembellished direct response. 'Should I be afraid of you?' asked Arabella. Tobiah responded with a question. 'How many murders would you guess are committed in the United States in a month?'

Arabella didn't have a clue. 'In a month, I don't know. Maybe 50 or 100 or even 500?' Tobiah skimmed another pebble on the lake. 'In 2012, so far around 8,024 people have been shot, knifed, strangled and so on. By the end of 2012, the total will be nearer to 14,827. That's well over 1,000 homicides per month.' Arabella was bemused. 'But we are only midway through 2012, Tobiah. That means there are another ... let me do some mental arithmetic ... err ... 6,800 yet to die. How can you know all of this? None of this has happened as yet.' Tobiah shook his head and laughed to himself. 'I can't be totally accurate, Arabella, but being a supernatural being, I do have a few powers that accompany my title. You were three deaths out, by the way. Anyway, how I know about this or that is of no concern. My second question to you is, out of all these murders, how many do you suppose were carried out by humans?' 'I guess all of them,' responded Arabella. Tobiah pushed further. 'And out of these 14,827 deaths, how many were carried out by demons?' Arabella got the point. 'I suppose you are going to tell me none of them … aren't you?' Tobiah nodded his head in agreement. 'Indeed I am. You guessed correctly. We are not always free of blame. Sometimes we can push the buttons that cause a person to pick up the gun, but it isn't me or my kind who pull the trigger. So, you asked if you should be afraid sitting by a lake with a demon, and I am saying back to you, that statistically you should be more afraid to be sat here … in this lonely, isolated place with another human. Do you understand what I am saying?'

Arabella was still confused. 'You are surely not going to tell me you are a Sunday school teacher, Tobiah. You may not do the whole killing thing, but after all you are a demon. By definition you are evil … aren't you? What are you, really?'

Tobiah picked a handful of yellow nightshade and proceeded to chew it. He sniggered at the look of horror on Arabella's face as he swallowed. It amused him. 'Okay, you asked me and so I will answer you as honestly as I can, and as a demon I don't often do the whole honesty thing, so don't expect me to repeat this cardinal sin too often. To begin with, we cannot kill humans directly. We have rules in our world as you have in yours. However, we can create the circumstances whereby people can become careless and accidents can happen, or we can employ humans or other entities to do our dirty work for us.'

He started to speak in hushed, creepy tones as he added, 'Sometimes, we can whisper bad thoughts into their ears and psychiatrists may think they are suffering from schizophrenia, and if it serves our purpose we will allow humans to believe this diagnosis. Sometimes the diagnosis is indeed a real illness caused by some chemical disturbance in the brain, but sometimes … just sometimes … the whisper will be mine.' Arabella shuddered at that thought, suddenly feeling quite uncomfortable. She asked, 'How many demons are there?'

'More than I can count,' responded Tobiah. 'Demons are diverse and multi-cultural; some originate from different species, others come from different galaxies and even other universes. Some were born demonic, whilst others became that way. We don't all look alike or act alike or even smell alike. Believe me when I tell you that some of those beasts are nose-shatteringly pungent. But just like human societies, we have laws and we have a hierarchy. Emmanuelle is a high-ranking demoness. You played a game of chicken with a hell of a potent lady.'

'What are you then? Where do you fit on the ladder, Tobiah?' 'I have never measured myself, Arabella. If I was to guess, I would hope about halfway up,' came his response. 'However, I was human once. I wasn't born like this.' Anabella was mesmerised. This was a subject close to her heart and one that held a fatal attraction. The same sinister fascination which disastrously caused her to summon Emmanuelle in the first place.

'When were you born, Tobiah? What were you like as a human?' Like many of his kind, Tobiah liked to boast about his former depravity and so was happy to comply with the teenager's desire for information.

'I was born in London in 1855. In demonic terms, that makes me very young. It was during the reign of Queen Victoria and at the time of the Crimean War. My father was a surgeon and even worked alongside Florence Nightingale.' Arabella detected a faint trace of pride in

Tobiah's voice as he spoke of his father's skills and attainments. He
continued, 'I became a surgeon like my father, but then I discovered I
had other abilities ... more profitable abilities, with bored ladies of a
certain class. This was before NHS healthcare was freely available in
England. People were very poor back in the 19th century. They would try
to pay me with what little money they had to spare and few had money to
spare. I would be lucky to earn a couple of shillings a week. However,
rich widows took a liking to me and they would spoil me – in return for
my attention.' Arabella was shocked and couldn't help but gasp, 'My oh
my Tobiah – you dirty man. You were a gigolo. How terribly naughty!'
He smiled and Arabella giggled. 'I am a demon, Arabella, and prior to
that a cad and a blaggard. By definition I am not supposed to be one of
the good guys.' Arabella was entranced. 'Please go on, Tobiah. I am
enjoying this, in some sick, curious way.' As requested, he continued. 'I
made a good living by deceit, by promising things I couldn't deliver, by
seducing and cajoling. I had no conscience, no regrets. I believe you
have a name for people like me these days.' Arabella was quick to
respond. 'Psychopath, I believe that is the word. Tell me, were you by
any chance a manipulative, shallow, charming, promiscuous parasite
with not a single ounce of remorse?' Tobiah smiled with smug
arrogance. 'Guilty as charged, Madam.' Arabella felt uncomfortable with
her enjoyment of the stranger's life story, yet wanted to know more. 'So
okay – you were a total shit. What happened next, Tobiah?' The demon
then became unusually coy and deliberated before answering. 'I don't
really want to say much more, Arabella. You will need to work with me
for some time to come and unlike this bittersweet nightshade, I don't
want to poison what you think about me. We have more important things

to discuss than my former life. Just know that very few humans make the transition into demons. You are born, you live and you die. So, for me to become what I am, you can deduce that I was guilty of some fairly vile crimes.'

Arabella's mind turned circles as she considered what she knew of Tobiah so far. Looking around, she realised that she was indeed sat in a lonely spot by a swamp, and in the company of an immoral entity that once lived in Victorian London. Here she was chitter-chattering with an actual real demon, and one who was a self-confessed psychopathic gigolo and a surgeon. The name 'Jack the Ripper' flashed into her mind, but then she bit her lip and said nothing of it. If it was true, she didn't want to know.

'Back then, when you were alive, did you see yourself as evil, Tobiah?' Tobiah rubbed his hands together, staring at them as though maybe looking back in time at what crimes they had helped him commit. To her shock, he responded, 'Nowhere near as evil as you are, Arabella.' The young teenager was aghast by his response. She demonstrated, 'What do you mean? I am not evil? I am stupid and hormonal and have made some bad decisions in life, but I have never cheated or stolen money or anything even slightly bad. I was rash. I am told that I was in love with someone called Dean and he made me do some crazy things and I guess in desperation I downloaded some dodgy rituals from the Internet. So here I am – alive and yet dead, plus I have just been informed that a demon thinks I am more evil than he … or it … assumes to be. Bizarre. Fucking off-the-scale bizarre.'

Tobiah skimmed yet another stone into the lake. It made a record seven bounces this time. Eventually he responded, 'Dear sweet Arabella, if I told you to cross a busy highway with earplugs stuffed in your ears, wearing a blindfold over your eyes, would you do it?'

'No, of course not,' came the stern yet certain reply.

'So, Arabella,' concluded Tobiah, 'why play with fire? Why dice with death? Why play with things of which you know nothing about? I know you have no recollection of what you did, but what you actually did was attract the attention of a high-ranking, powerful demoness. At the time, you knew who and what she was, so even though your memory has been erased, do be aware that you were totally sane, completely in control, and what you have now become is totally your fault.'

Not one to lose an argument, Arabella continued to protest. 'I still say I was stupid rather than evil.'

Tobiah had all the time in the world to challenge his new teenage underling. He debated, 'Mad, bad or sad – the three major reasons for crime. Was I sad? Well, yes. My father was a surgeon in the army and was never at home. My mother became an alcoholic and she beat me every night before I went to bed and often starved me for days as punishment for nothingness. Mostly she was so drunk she was unconscious, which was a plus as those were the days when I wasn't being whipped. Were you ever truly sad, Anabella? From what I have seen so far, you live in a nice house with loving parents and you have eaten well and been educated well. You have meat on your bones and I see no scars or bruises. If we were in a competition, I would say that I could plead sadness, but that you have little or no grounds to make the same plea. Do you accept this?' Arabella should have known better than to accept the words of a demon, especially one so eloquent and adept at trickery, but she made the mistake of agreeing with him. As accurate as he was, it was always a mistake to concur with a demon.

Tobiah continued, 'Could I claim madness? Well, to a degree, days on end of starvation and beatings were indeed enough to make any modern-day doctor diagnose me with having mental health issues, and as you mentioned before, I am a psychopath. My mind was wired slightly differently to yours, but that was not my fault. I was born that way. It was an accident of genetics. Can you look in the mirror, Arabella, and tell me that you are mad?' Arabella shook her head. The demon's defence was scarily making sense. He concluded, 'So where does that leave me, Arabella? Mad and sad, perhaps. More to the point, where does that leave you, however? Just bad! No other excuse other than sheer obnoxious badness. Wonderful, delightful depravity in all its North Carolina glory.

Since Emmanuelle had taken her memory of events away, Arabella couldn't even defend herself with any degree of competence. She argued, 'I dispute your version of the truth, Tobiah. My family inform me that I was torn apart by hurt and jealousy and then almost temporarily driven insane by rage.' Tobiah tutted under his breath. 'Oh dear, the human frailties of emotion! Demons feed on negative human emotions such as greed, envy, anger, jealousy and rage. Without your negativity, we would all have empty bellies. Can I remind you that you nearly killed an unborn baby, Arabella? Fortunately, little Clementina is now a healthy three-month-old little girl – one you would have killed had she not kicked out at the precise moment you were about to pull the trigger. Think upon it. Emmanuelle would never have wasted her time on some spotty teenage goth, chanting nonsensical blurb downloaded from the Internet. Such young humans are ten a penny – but you, Arabella, you must have had some potential. She saw your capacity for evil. So, now we are here and it is time for you to stop doing the whole "poor little me" act and accept who you are and embrace your forthcoming assignment. Rarely does Emmanuelle bestow such a fantastic future upon someone like you, so think yourself lucky. As for me, I just get the job of being a collector. For my sins, I am little more than a demonic taxi driver, just picking up and delivering. You will be far more blessed – you will get to have fun. I feel quite envious.'

The sun was beginning to set beyond the hills and despite the fact that the creeping dusk was still warm and humid, a shiver went down Arabella's spine. She was beginning to feel afraid. She asked, 'Can we walk back to the house, Tobiah? My parents may wonder where I am.' Forever the gentleman, Tobiah stood up and pulled Arabella to her feet. As they walked she asked, 'What becomes of me now?' Tobiah put a comforting arm around her shoulder. Given that she now suspected she knew who Tobiah may have been, once upon a gruesome time, the gesture was less than comforting. He handed her what looked to be a debit card. It was black and the numbers were embossed in pure gold – not like any card she had seen before. He informed her, 'In a month from now you will travel to Miami and meet with Reed Baratolli. I suspect you may have heard his name before.' Arabella's chin nearly dropped to the floor. 'No way – Reed B, the famous music mogul. You are kidding me – really?' 'Yes, really,' he responded. 'You are a very well-organised, intelligent young woman. Emmanuelle saw that in you. You are to become Reed's PA. Take this debit card and spend what you like. It isn't a bottomless pit, but the money mine runs deep. You need to change your look and become someone who fits in with the whole rock & roll scene. Get your hair styled.' He pulled a strand from her head with a mock look of disgust. 'Right now, it is a sort of mucky, mousy colour and looks a bit plain. Aim for something more… dramatic. Plus, lose the farmyard jean look and buy some expensive designer clothes. You have to look the part. We have an apartment waiting for you in Florida and the plane tickets and keys are already in the post.'

Arabella was beside herself. 'Wow, and you call this punishment. This is amazing. I am going to enjoy the shopping spree of my life. What is the PIN for the card?'

Tobiah laughed. She still really didn't get it. 'It's a magical card, Arabella. Whatever PIN you enter matters not, it will always work. However, it will also know if you are cheating it, so for instance if you try to give money to charity or to friends, do not expect the card to respond. This is solely for your selfish purpose, and so you can complete a very important project. The card expects your mercenary decadence. It is the servant, you are the master – but you are its only master.'

'Does Reed know who I am?' Tobiah responded accordingly. 'Yes, he knows you are part of our team. He is also part of our team. He isn't a demon, but let's just say he is assigned to the same project, for very different reasons. Look at your wrist, Arabella.' As she pulled up her sleeve, a purple band appeared to have been tattooed around her wrist with a golden knife seeming to cut the band. It was most unusual and exquisite. Arabella approved of her new ink. Tobiah then held up his wrist. A purple bracelet, broken on one side, appeared to be hanging from his arm – almost defying gravity. 'These are symbols, Arabella. In my world, we use symbols to communicate to each other. My bracelet signifies that I am a demon and my work is to break this purple line. It makes me and the nature of my mission recognisable to other demons. Your symbol is a tattoo on your skin. This makes you recognisable to other humans who work alongside us. Reed has the same markings. He will tell you more about this project when you meet him. What he doesn't know is that it is your job to monitor him. We have our concerns about Mr Baratolli. Even though you are going to work for him, never forget that you really work for Emmanuelle.'

As they finally reached the porch, it was time for Tobiah to bid his new human goodbye. However, before he went, Arabella had one major question to ask of him. 'Tell me, Tobiah, if I die will I go to heaven or hell?' Tobiah smiled knowingly. He had been asked this question many times before. It both amused and fascinated him. Why was it that audacious humans would be prepared to dabble into things of which they knew nothing, only later to become fearful at the mere threat of eternal damnation. Misplaced courage seemed like ice cream – sweet to the taste and attractive to the eye, but something that could easily melt. 'Dearest Arabella, only your God can be the judge of you. That is not my job. You have a ten-year contract. If you live a good life you will go to wherever you believe utopia to be, and if not – you will join me and become a demon. It really is that simple. Fret not. Prepare yourself for a new employment. I am convinced you will excel in what you are about to do, and Reed is excited to meet you.' Arabella went quiet for a moment. Something else seemed to be preying on her mind. 'Do you know that Dean is dead?' she asked. Tobiah nodded, 'I had heard, but as you can't even remember him, why should that concern you?' 'Just sad that he has left a baby without a father, that's all.' Tobiah smirked, 'and so now you suddenly start to care. Too little too late Arabella. Move on.' She had a look of genuine sadness on her face and responded, 'just glad that I didn't pull the trigger that's all. Do you know how he died Tobiah?' Tobiah shrugged, 'suicide. He danced the tango with a fast train. Look, you have a new life now. It will be varied, exciting and will take you around the world. Dean is history,' With that, he took her hand and kissed her farewell.

As he walked through the gate, she shouted after him. 'What do I do if I need to speak with you?' He replied, 'Just summon me. Say my name and then say "veni ad me". It's a bit old-school, but for some reason our rituals tend to be in Latin. It would do you good to learn it. Reed is quite fluent. He can teach you some commands if you ask him. In the meantime, "Te visurum."

With that, Tobiah simply faded away into the warm mist of the Carolina night.

Arabella sat on the porch steps, looking out at the ominous fog that had suddenly descended in front of the yard. She had never seen fog like this before. It crept along the path like a stalking cat. She had no memory of Dean – the deceitful ex-boyfriend who caused her to take such extreme actions. The police and her family had assumed that she had gone to his house to commit suicide. She turned the gun on herself, so there was no criminal charge to answer to. It was assumed that her memory loss was part of some kind of mental breakdown, even though the psychiatrist pronounced her to be sane.

Her family had informed her that Dean had recently died. They didn't tell her how, only that it was an accident. In their own way, they were still trying to protect her, even though she had no feelings for this stranger they called Dean. It was a shock to learn he had thrown himself onto a train track.

Her family had also told her that the hospital was still trying to determine how a death certificate had been issued for someone clearly still alive. She felt sympathy for the doctors and nurses who had been suspended pending an enquiry, but knew the legal teams and hospital internal reviews would draw a blank. Her resurrection was profoundly supernatural and no amount of investigations would ever come up with a logical explanation to explain something so otherworldly illogical.

Inside her house, she could hear familiar family noises. Her father snored loudly, her mother clanked pots and pans, and her brother yelled at the TV screen about the unfairness of some sort of decision by some sort of referee during some sort of game. Maybe she would miss this normality. But then again maybe not. She looked at her magical debit card. Was this not every girl's dream? Plus, she would become a personal assistant to the mega-rich, world-famous deity of music – none other than Reed Baratolli. Her life was about to change beyond recognition. So, for now she would help her mum with the washing up and tomorrow she would enjoy the Fourth of July party and then … she had the rest of eternity to figure out who and what she would become. Independence Day indeed.

CHAPTER 10

15th July 2013

Friends had once described a brown circle at the bottom of a test tube. Her friends had described blue stripes or a pink dot with a matching pink stripe. She had heard many stories over the years of how various females had encountered this life-changing moment. In her case, the truth was simple, blunt and unmistakable. The words 'pregnant' simply appeared at the end of a white plastic strip, as yet still dripping with warm urine. HCG – human chorionic gonadotropin; she was cooking a fertilised egg and according to the white plastic, she was three to four weeks along. Oh, the cruel preciseness of modern technology.

Saskia sat alone in a hotel room close to Heathrow Airport and cried. Not big tears, just slow and inaudible sobs. By instinct, she should have felt motherly, perhaps nurturing and fiercely protective of the small clump of cells growing inside her. Instead she felt fearful and isolated. She had not wanted this outcome.

Outside the triple-glazed hotel window with its shabby grey net curtains, the drab English weather seemed to agree with her. The pit pat of constant raindrops and the dullness of the bleak afternoon matched both her tears and sudden depression.

She hadn't taken a holiday in well over a year. Just for a magical minute, she slipped back in time and remembered the fun she had enjoyed on the slopes of Tignes with Florence, Becky and the lads. For one solitary moment in her life she had let go and allowed herself to feel free and irresponsible. The French Pyrenees now seemed far away and very long ago. Gallons of dirty water had rushed under the bridge since then and now, she simply felt trapped and ridden with a bone-crushing guilt. She recognised that for some women this white plastic strip would signify the most wondrous discovery in their lives. Maybe for her, one day this would also be a beautiful, magical moment. But for now, the HCG in her bloodstream was simply a badly timed hormonal irritation. Pregnancy – want it, love it, hate it, couldn't care less one way or the other ... she considered how many differing emotions those words on a plastic stick encapsulated. At this specific moment in time, parasitic was the word that came to her mind. Her uterus had been invaded by a blood sucking freeloader.

She looked at her watch. Twelve noon; the enigmatic Mr Smith would be with her soon. This was the first time she would meet her employer in person. She had wondered why, of all times, he had chosen to meet with her now. It was all very last minute, but his instructions had been clear yet ambiguous. She was to pack a suitcase for a week and bring her passport. He wouldn't tell her if the location was warm or cold, just simply to pack at least one outfit in an outlandishly bright colour and to call him and simply declare the colour. She did as was instructed, stating 'lime green', and then hanging up as per his directive. No emails could be exchanged and nothing was to be discussed over the phone. It was all very clandestine.

Meeting in the airport terminal was out of the question due to security cameras. She was sure her boss was sending her on a covert mission somewhere and naturally hers was not to question. She wondered what Mr Smith would think of her newly discovered pregnancy. She concluded she would be sacked on the spot. Her job was to remain reclusive and avoid intimacy in all aspects of her life. Being pregnant would surely betray her as disloyal. She kept reminding herself that she only had a few more mortgage repayments to make and then she would own her own little idyll Cotswold retreat. As soon as each inch of wattle and daub belonged to her, she vowed that nobody would dominate her life ever again. Not her mother, nor her father's many children, or the Ouroborous. Nobody would tell her how high to jump. The more she thought about it, the angrier she became. Mr Smith and his weird group of investors could go screw themselves once she no longer required their handsome monthly salary. However, just for now she had to keep a lid on her feelings. Motherhood did have a certain appeal, but the timing was incredibly bad. She threw the plastic device in the bin and sat watching the rain outside the hotel window. She awaited his knock. She cast her pregnancy from her mind. She would deal with this unwelcome situation later.

The expected knock came on the door, precisely at the moment the big hand and little hand of the clock co-ordinated on the number 12. She drew a deep breath and held her body rigid, as though she was a soldier on parade. For some reason, she felt incredibly nervous.

She slowly opened the door and stood to one side. She hadn't expected the company of two people. The first to enter was a man whom she presumed to be Mr Smith. He was younger than she had imagined and was dressed most business-like, wearing a city-broker-type pinstripe suit. Following demurely behind him was a pale, thin young woman, with fair hair and a timid expression. She had engrained dark circles beneath her eyes, and Saskia couldn't help but deduce that she looked quite frail and possibly poorly. Mr Smith held out his hand. 'Pleased to meet you in person at long last, Miss Usov. As I am sure you have already guessed, I am George Smith and today I am accompanied by Isolda.' Saskia tried her best to look pleased to meet them both and shook their hands as per formal tradition. In truth, her thoughts were a million light years away.

Mr Smith had little time for pleasantries and seating himself at a small circular table, he beckoned both females to join him. 'Do you have your passport and have you packed a suitcase, Saskia?' Saskia moved her eyes towards her Louis Vuitton case and nodded her head. 'Fantastic,' he responded. 'We are sending you off on an overseas mission for a week, but please just consider it to be a well-deserved vacation. Isolda is part of my team and she is here by way of a witness. Expensive items will change hands, so I hope you don't take offence to her presence. She also has all the paraphernalia you will require for your journey, so I will now hand you over to Isolda who will explain everything to you. You must listen very carefully, Saskia, as you cannot write down any notes. It is imperative that you use that extremely smart brain of yours to remember all you are about to be told.'

Saskia had butterflies in her tummy. This was something that she had not experienced since being a small girl waiting for her mother to collect her from boarding school. On this occasion, the expectation was more one of foreboding than excitement. The mysterious Mr Smith had brought a witness with him. This was bound to indicate something of immense importance.

Isolda pulled a folder from out of her handbag, and Saskia couldn't help but gasp at her tiny, bone-like fingers. Placing a printed sheet of A4 paper in front of her, Isolda explained, 'At 16.40 you will catch a flight from Heathrow terminal 5 to Côte d'Azur Airport in Nice. We have booked you into business class. You will arrive in terminal one where a chauffeur will be waiting for you. He will be looking out for someone wearing a lime green outfit, so you will need to get changed into this attire prior to your flight. He will be holding out a card with the name "L. Green" and his tie will be matching the colour of your suit. If for any reason his tie does not match the colour lime green, you must not get into his car under any circumstances.'

Saskia's gut instinct that this mission was something more serious than just a casual trip to the South of France was beginning to feel worryingly accurate. Looking at Mr Smith directly in the eyes she asked, 'That sounds a bit menacing, sir. What if his tie is a different colour? What does that mean? What should I do if we don't … err … colour co-ordinate?'

Mr Smith replied, 'Dear Saskia, please do try to relax a little. Yes, indeed, your mission is vitally important to us, but we have put everything in place to ensure your safety. We are not asking you to do anything illegal. You are simply transporting a very precious diamond to its new owner in Nice, and we want to ensure that it arrives in the hands of the right person. We own the diamond, it hasn't been stolen or anything like that, but it is worth a lot of money. If you can just listen to Isolda, she will explain everything in detail.' Mr Smith had cut her short with a quickly executed closure. She now fully understood that what she was being asked to do was deadly important. As requested, she shut up and listened.

Isolda continued, 'We have rented out this hotel room in London for three weeks … just to give you some flexibility with your itinerary. Once you get back to the UK, you can check out anytime you like. There is a safe in the wardrobe and you will need to leave both your personal mobile phone and work phone behind in the safe. Phones can be tracked and we don't want anyone monitoring your movements. In the folder, you will find a new temporary phone for you to use whilst in the South of France. It is just a cheap "pay as you go" but it has been fully topped up and should be adequate for your time overseas. I have input a number in the phone which will call Mr Smith directly. This is his high-priority line and should only be used in emergencies. Only four people will know the colour of the suit you will wear for this flight, and that would be you, Mr Smith, myself and the chauffeur. In the unlikely instance that the chauffeur is wearing a different-coloured tie, it would indicate that he has been replaced by an impostor. This will not happen. We can assure you of that, Saskia. However, by way of making contingency plans, should this happen – make your way to a public place, call Mr Smith and await your instructions.'

Saskia went pale. She wondered if she had an option to refuse what was beginning to sound more like a scene from a *Mission Impossible* film. She then reminded herself of her cottage and the mortgage that was outstanding. Plus, a vacation in Nice in July whilst the weather in England was wet and drab did have a certain appeal. 'Okay,' she responded. 'I understand what you have told me so far. Please carry on, Isolda.'

The young woman with the ashen face then pulled yet more paperwork from the folder. She continued, 'We have booked you into the Palais de la Méditerranée, now known as the Hyatt Regency Hotel. We want to reward you, Saskia, and we thought you deserved some pampering whilst you were away. On completion of your delivery, you will also be rewarded financially and a £250,000 bonus payment will be made into your account.'

This number had caught Saskia's attention and her body language mimicked her feelings as she now sat upright and paid more attention. After all, she wasn't being asked to do anything illegal. She was a mere diamond courier. The numbers floated in front of her eyes. £250,000; she could pay off her mortgage and quit her job. Maybe she could be a stay-at-home mum, bake bread and make home-made jam from the plums growing in her orchard. Had she just described herself as a mum? She was shocked. Maybe the pregnancy hormones were altering her outlook on life after all. Oh, the power of mother nature. Weird given that less than an hour ago, she had been considering a termination. She pulled herself together and mentally re-entered the room. She responded, 'That's very kind of you, Isolda, I mean Mr Smith, I mean George. Please go on.'

George Smith now stood up and paced up and down the room. He had been unsure if Saskia had what it took to accept this challenge, but he had been equally sure that he could buy her compliance, and his gamble had been proven correct. His face wore a serious expression. He continued where Isolda had left off. 'The chauffeur will drive you to the Hyatt Hotel; however, before you arrive he will take a diversion down a lonely, dark lane. Do not be afraid, Saskia, as this is all part of the plan. The exchange will take place in the car and we don't want any prying eyes.'

Isolda removed yet another folder from her considerable handbag. She continued, 'This is a magazine detailing the agenda for a software trade fair at the Georgia world congress centre in Atlanta and an entrance ticket has also been attached. You need to hand these to your driver. We understand that you speak fluent Russian, Saskia, as indeed does your driver. You need to communicate with him in Russian at all times. You should explain that this trade fair should be given as the official reason for his visit to the US.'

Saskia's resolve to comply started to waver. She had been mentally joking with herself when she compared this odd situation to that of a script from a spy film, but this incredible scenario unfolding before her was now exactly how it felt.

Isolda then placed a sealed envelope in front of Saskia. It had been secured in such a way that it was not intended for Saskia's eyes. Isolda stated in a matter of fact way, 'These are for your chauffeur. They are plane tickets from Nice to Atlanta and then onwards to Miami after the trade fair; the driver can make his own way home from Miami. The plane to Atlanta leaves less than three hours after he drops you off at the hotel, Saskia, so do not delay. Make these exchanges as quickly as you can so your driver can get himself back to the airport. He will not have much time and it is imperative that he makes the flight.'

Saskia sat in silence. She knew to only ask questions that were relevant and to avoid any probing altercations. 'Curiosity could kill the cat' had always been her motto as far as her Ouroboros employers were concerned. Isolda continued to pull yet more stationery from her handbag. She handed Saskia a copy of Tolstoy's book *War and Peace*, written in the author's native Russian. She explained, 'This book is also to be given to your driver. You are to tell him that there are details in here of the two addresses he needs to locate. They will be coded in the usual way and he will find the details on the pages numbered as his house address and his mother's birthday. He will understand this instruction. He is a professional.'

George Smith was standing at the window watching planes take off in the distant vista. He had allowed Isolda to play centre stage so far, but it was now his job to close this meeting. He moved over to the table where both women were seated and he removed a small pouch from his jacket pocket. Opening the silk pouch, he carefully laid a single cufflink onto the table. Saskia gasped at the crimson sparkle bling which met her eyes and which continued to beam a spectrum of rainbow light around the dismal room.

Mr Smith explained, 'Saskia – this is but one half of a Jacob & Co.'s emerald-cut, red-diamond octagon cufflink. Isn't it a thing of divine beauty? I am told that this is an Asscher-cut red cape diamond. How many carats would this be Isolda?'

His female assistant didn't have to hesitate before she promptly replied, 'Actually only six carats in the centre, but it is their rarity which gives red diamonds their value.'

Mr Smith continued, 'Saskia, we don't want to create too much attention to this piece, so have attached an 18-carat white gold necklace onto the flip-back latch so that you can wear this around your neck. As stunning as this piece may be, we don't want to show it off, so may I suggest you wear it under your shirt. You only need to give the driver the actual cufflink, so you can keep the necklace we have attached it to. Call it a present from us to you.'

Isolda interjected, 'You should inform your driver that the other half of the cufflink will be awaiting him in Miami once he has accomplished his mission in Atlanta. Just so you are aware, Saskia, the cufflinks as a set are worth over $4 million, which is why we have gone to so much trouble to ensure they are given to the correct chauffeur with the right coloured tie. The red cape diamond is a rare and much-desired gem. Maybe now you understand why we needed to be so precise with our instructions?'

Saskia looked concerned. She asked, 'What about airport security?' Mr Smith responded, 'They shouldn't be too concerned about mere jewellery, Saskia, and anyway – from a distance, the gem looks too big to be real. Unless they have a magnifying glass on hand and are expert jewellers, they will assume your necklace to be crystal or glass.'

Saskia was lost for words as it seemed that too many big numbers had been floated inside her head in such a short, condensed period of time. George Smith noticed the look of shock on her face. He genially touched her hand. 'You can refuse to do this if you want, Saskia. We are in a hurry and it would be very last minute, but we could always try to find somebody else if this was all too much for you.'

Saskia thought about the money and carefully considered what such a large bonus payment would mean to her life. It was a game changer. It denoted far more than George Smith could have ever guessed. It was indeed life or death money. With no mortgage and money in the bank, she could afford to have her baby. Without it and as a single parent … well … she didn't want to become a replica of her own mother. Indeed, this was a life or death mission. 'I will do it,' came her immediate response.

'Good, very good,' added Mr Smith. 'Now quickly – repeat what you need to do.'

Saskia was smart. She had good memory recall. She promptly replied, 'Change into lime green suit, put both my mobiles into hotel safe, go to terminal 5, 16.40 flight to Nice, look out for driver with matching tie and holding up the name L. Green. If wrong guy with wrong tie, speed dial Mr Smith in public place. If the right driver, go to hotel, pull up in dark lane first, speak only Russian, hand over *War and Peace* and tell him to look for page numbers that match his address number and mother's birthday, then hand over entrance ticket and agenda to trade fair. Remove cufflinks from necklace and give to driver, inform him how to locate the other cufflink in Miami when the project is completed. Give him flight tickets to Atlanta and Miami and tell him to get a move on – drop me off so he can get his backside back to the airport fast, go directly to jail, do not pass Go, collect £250K.' Phew – she paused for breath. George Smith smiled; he found her reference the game of Monopoly quite amusing.

He was pleased. 'Glad you like to play games Saskia. If you like the throw of a dice, you should check out the casinos of Monte Carlo whilst you are over there.' Mr Smith was in a hurry to leave. He grabbed his coat and gestured to Isolda that it was time to go. She held out her thin, cold hand to bid Saskia farewell. She added, 'Don't get overly worried about all of this, Saskia. Trust me; it will all go to plan. You will be fine.' After those odd and possibly misplaced words of reassurance, the most unusual of couples then vacated the room.

Saskia pulled the hotel kettle out of the drawer and flicked on the switch. As she waited for it to boil she retrieved the white plastic stick she had disposed of earlier in the day. She placed it with its words stating 'pregnant' next to the multi-million-dollar red diamond. For a while she sat, looking at both items side by side. In her heart, she knew that the man she was about to meet – the driver with the matching lime green tie – was being paid to do something illegal. This burgundy piece of rock denoted half of his imbursement. Delivery of this rock to the Russian driver would most likely be a 50% payment upfront…but for what? Looking back at the positive pregnancy test, she knew that one thing could pay for something else. It was a difficult decision to make, but she felt she had no choice.

Looking at the time and hurriedly gulping her tea, she pulled her lime green suit from out of her suitcase. She frowned. It was closer to luminous neon green than lime green. What an awful item of clothing. Still, she wouldn't be missed in a crowd and she assumed that this was the intention. As she searched for her equally horrendous matching shoes, a small blue talisman fell from her case. She suddenly realised that she hadn't used this suitcase since she had been skiing in Tignes. Now here she was, off to France again, but for a very different reason. She lightly rubbed the sides of the blue altar stone and thought of Soul. She wondered if Soul ever thought about her whilst she held her half of their twin amulets. She looked back to the table and the bit of plastic. The words 'pregnant' continued to shout at her as though it needed to be heard louder than any piece of rock. She threw the stone back into her suitcase. Time to dress up in her coded suit and do whatever it took to get whatever it was, that may pay for something that she may or may not want. Whatever the end result, the money would mean that she was in control, rather than be a victim of circumstance. She would do Mr Smith asked.

CHAPTER 11

Friday 19th July 2013

11 a.m.; Saskia forcefully slammed down the lid of her laptop. She hadn't meant to be so disrespectful to her computer, but the rush of adrenaline when she saw that a quarter of a million GB pounds had been deposited into her bank account in their glorious sterling numerical vastness, sort of hijacked the moment.

She took a minute to compose herself, and then wandered over to the balcony of her sea view suite. For a short while she was absorbed in watching the people below pass by – going about their normal business and casually strolling along the Promenade des Anglais. The little people on the promenade seemed to have a cavalier disregard for time. She observed them as they ambled along the seafront in no particular hurry. Saskia envied what she presumed to be their normality and considered that boredom and a lack of schedule, was a perfectly fine ambition. The opposite of boredom was perhaps being driven down an isolated dirt track in the middle of a foreign country and handing some Russian stranger a rare diamond.

Saskia wasn't stupid. Of course, she recognised that this was down payment for some sort of dastardly deed. She hadn't failed to notice the Kalashnikov Bullpup Rifle that was indiscreetly propped up in the car well of the passenger seat. It was within arm's reach of the driver, and at the time she wondered if it had been placed there as a warning to her, or for protection in case of an ambush. Whatever the reason, it caused her to shake with uncontrollable fear.

She had composed herself as best she could whilst she delivered various items and instructions to her chauffeur, but the moment he dropped her off at the Hyatt Hotel, she crumbled. Pregnant or not, the first thing she did when she reached her hotel room was to down a glass of neat brandy in one urgent gulp. It would turn out to be an oft-regretted quick fix, but at the time it was all she knew to do to treat shock. Only now had she managed to finally stop trembling. It had been the worst and most terrifying experience of her life. She concluded that her £250K had been more than justified, and in retrospect even considered that she had been underpaid for the psychological trauma she had just endured. She vowed, 'Never again.'

Still exhausted after four sleepless nights followed by hormone-induced morning sickness, Saskia lay back on a sun lounger and allowed the morning rays to ignite her skin with a gentle tan. As she tried to doze off, she couldn't rid the thought from her mind that some terrible task had been completed. Money was now sat in her bank account and that fact concluded that the mission had been successful. The Russian driver would either be in Miami or on his way there by now. She wondered who would be waiting at the other end with the matching diamond. Enough! She mentally scolded herself for pondering over such thoughts.

Recovering from her recent experience in the middle of a remote French field, she had made the decision that she was going to use her time in Nice as a well-earned break. She would recharge her batteries and then contemplate her future. She would not watch TV. She would not read the news. She did not want to hear about some bank vault being blasted apart and rare red diamond cufflinks being stolen. She did not want to hear about any crimes involving a Russian with a Kalashnikov.

She absolutely had no intention of ever finding out what she had just been involved with. The rest of her time here would involve good food, good books, good sleep and that would be it. With that thought imprinted in her mind, her eyes grew heavy and soon she was in the deepest of slumbers.

***

1 p.m.; Don Morris had made a call into the Oxford office of MeDeVe Ltd to ask the office secretary Kerry about his itinerary for the following week. Don enjoyed his new job and loved working with his former university professor Roland De Vede. Somehow it offered him a pleasant midway point between being office bound and being out on the road. He had been in Ireland of late and had enjoyed his time with the professor and his friend Frank. The research into some long-lost prophecy and the connection with Irish hieroglyphics had been enthralling. Aside from that, he had managed to get in a few rounds of golf and several pints of Guinness. Indeed, Don was now in a happier place – until that is, he made the call with Kerry.

Kerry was animated, but not in a good way. 'Have you heard the news, Don?' He had no idea what she was talking about. 'I have been away working, Kerry, and I haven't had much in the way of down time. Catching up with the global economy has been the least of my concerns. What are you talking about, lass?' Kerry could hardly get her words out fast enough. 'Oh, bloody hell, Don. I don't know what to do. I have just been in the kitchen and I asked Simon if he knew who Katya Beselovaya is. Mercy had some emails from her and I needed to find out what to do with them. Anyway, Simon rushed out to get yesterday's newspaper from his desk and it was on the front page, "Russian Heiress found dead in boyfriend's Atlanta apartment".'

Don was lost for words for a few moments. He asked, 'What else does the article say, Kerry?' Kerry's voice was trembling as she replied, 'It says here that Katya Beselovaya was found dead on Tuesday night. When I checked Mercy's inbox, it seemed that Katya emailed her the day before she died. Do you think I should inform the police, Don? Maybe the email could be important?'

'Where is Mercy at the moment?' asked Don.

'She is in North Wales,' came the reply. Kerry's tone was one of panic. 'One of her clients is in hospital there. I know she was intending to get back soon. She has the MacDonald case to close after the weekend, so she needed to get back.'

Don composed himself and tried to calm Kerry down. 'Look, Kerry, it isn't your job to call the police. The email belongs to Mercy and not to you. You need to try and get hold of her as soon as you can and give her the heads up. If the death looks like it could be suspicious, the chances are that the police will have already been through Katya's emails and will be more than aware of what she wrote to Mercy. I will let her father know in case she gets in touch with him. In the meantime, please stop panicking. Katya's death may have been just an unfortunate accident. Until we know more details, let's stop jumping to conclusions.' With that, he hung up.

The colour drained from Don's face. He tried to call his friend and former boss, but both Saskia's work and personal phones kept ringing out unanswered. He was concerned and wondered if there was any way that Zac – with his technical wizardry – could put a trace on the phone's

location. Forever the workaholic, it wasn't like Saskia to ignore
incoming calls.

Over the last couple of years, they had remained friends and met up
at least once a month for a pub lunch. It had only been in the last couple
of weeks that Saskia had confided in him that the infamous socialite
Katya Beselovaya was in fact her half-sister. Saskia was by nature self-
sufficient, independent and maybe a tad reclusive. From what Don could
deduce, Saskia had only one family member that she had any feelings for
and that was Katya. Poor Saskia; she must be devastated. Where was
she? He needed to find her. Why wasn't she picking up?

***

2 p.m.; Saskia had overslept. It had been a much-needed afternoon
nap; however, in the absence of any sunscreen it had left her with a
slightly red face. She decided to amble out to the town centre and go in
search of some face cream to calm down the fiery blaze on her cheeks.
Walking past the plasma screens in reception, a headline caught her
attention.

She froze. It was one of those moments when time stands completely
still. The people on the TV – they surely couldn't be talking about her
sister Katya, and yet … they were. The name was the same. The face on
the photograph was the same. But … they couldn't be talking about
Katya, could they? Yes, they could. They mentioned Atlanta and that is
where her sister lived. But … they couldn't be talking about Katya, could
they? As much as she didn't want to believe it, the news programme was
indeed referring to Katya. Her sister was dead.

Shock can affect different people in different ways. For Saskia, it was
a blur of nothingness – maybe confusion, certainly denial. She walked

out of the hotel and headed for the beach. Sitting cross-legged in the sand, she looked out to sea and found solace in the serene far horizon. It was a beautiful day. Children made sand castles and filled their moats with sea water. Seagulls dive bombed unsuspecting passers-by to relieve them of their ice-creams. Saskia remained watchful and compassed. Quietly and calmly, she tried to compute the reality of the news headline. Katya was dead! Katya was dead! It was assumed to be a heroin overdose. She was found in her boyfriend's apartment in Atlanta on Tuesday night. She still had a tourniquet around her right arm. As denial became belief, the hard, cold facts started to hit home. Katya was a party girl. She smoked pot, she drank too much and she sniffed the occasional white powder, but to inject heroin – never. Katya was terrified of needles. Then other facts started to hit home. Atlanta; Katya was in Atlanta. She was found on a Tuesday night – Saskia had met with the scary Russian man on Monday night. He would have been in Atlanta at the same time as Katya met her demise. The place, the day, the mode of death! Saskia gasped. Could she have been the person who paid an assassin? Without definite answers, this thought would surely eat away at her brain and then destroy her mentally. Katya had some dodgy associations; this was true – but who would have a reason to kill her? Surely not the Ouroboros? They were just a bunch of eccentric property developers, were they not? Maybe they were a cover for something else, something more sinister? Saskia began to kick herself for being so unquestioning and blindly obedient.

Saskia decided that she only had one course of action, and as reluctant as she was, she would have to visit her father. She knew he would be completely demolished by Katya's death. Although he had two daughters, only one had been legitimate and so he often introduced Katya as his only daughter. To begin with this hurt, but over time Saskia accepted that she hardly existed in his eyes. With the passing of time, the hurt didn't hurt as much. Her father Sergei was a ridiculously rich Soviet oligarch. Extremely well-connected, very determined and ultimately powerful, she was sure he would leave no stone unturned until he knew exactly how his favourite child had died. As much as it pained her, she had to know the truth.

How could she find out his address? She knew he was a tax-exile living in Monaco, but knew little more than this. She tried to visualise a map of France and was sure that Monaco wasn't too far away. Down at the bottom and somewhere to the left. Maybe driving distance … or maybe she could hire a helicopter. She decided to go to the British embassy with her passport. They would surely understand her situation and help her locate him.

She considered the oddity of life. Just this time last week, her life had been fairly normal. She was a creature of habit and liked to stay in at night and drink green tea. Just one week later, she was in the South of France, had been enlisted as a diamond courier, had experienced a close encounter with a possible assassin, had a dead sister and was now about to come face to face with her long absent father. Oh, and she was pregnant. Locked inside the calamity of recent events, she had quite forgotten the white plastic stick in the London hotel room. Surely nothing more could happen to turn her world upside down?

CHAPTER 12

20th July 2013

The taxi dropped Saskia off barely a minute past midnight. Exhausted and tense, she stood for a while, just staring up at the remote-controlled, CCTV-monitored, electrified gates of her father's mansion in Monaco. Part of her wanted to run away, but like it or not she knew she had to face him. She needed answers, so it was time to step foot inside his shady world.

As far as she was aware, her father had only purchased the place a few years back, so thankfully this was somewhere she had never visited before. She presumed that some new wife, mistress or maybe his financial advisor had bullied him into it. She could imagine some crusty-faced accountant saying, 'Become a tax exile, Sergei.' Saskia concluded that this seemed the more likely scenario. The father she remembered would have never allowed a wife to control him. Money was a far more appealing mistress.

Pressing the intercom was hardly a home from home welcome. She soon found herself being scrutinised by security guards and made to submit her passport, which was then duly scanned. Being fingerprinted simply to visit her estranged family was neither a welcoming nor pleasant experience.

The taxi driver had been refused entrance and so she had been made to take the walk up the long driveway alone and unescorted. Late at night, unaccompanied yet being watched; this felt like a slow, miserable walk. Men in black with menacing blacker Dobermans patrolled the gardens and surveyed her suspiciously. As she looked up, she could even catch the glint of cameras hidden within the foliage of the trees. As she moved along the pathway, she noticed that the cameras moved in synchrony – surveying her every move.

As illustrious as the fanciful Roman columns may have appeared, and as artistic as the exterior mood lighting adorned the façade, this house was not a home. It screeched out the word 'paranoia'. For a split second this gave Saskia some hope. Maybe if Katya had been murdered, it could have been a gangland killing to avenge her father Sergei? Surely only someone with something or someone to fear could be incarcerated in a house like this?

A male butler answered the ram-proof, bullet-proof door. He was expecting her. 'Good evening, Miss Usov. Your father has asked me to show you to your room so you can freshen up.' He took her overnight case from out of her hand and replaced it with some sort of communication device. 'Press button number 4 when you need me to come and collect you, and I will take you into the lounge where you will find the rest of your family are awaiting you. The red button is a security panic button in case you need help urgently.' Saskia didn't like the sound of that possibility, yet was impressed that she had been expected. She assumed that the British Consulate had called her father in advance, possibly to check she was who she claimed to be. Ascending the palatial white marble staircase, she demurely followed the butler down a very long corridor to her awaiting room. The butler was very courteous and polite, and yet somehow quite aloof. She reminded herself that he was a paid employee and not some favourite uncle.

She collapsed on the queen-sized four-poster bed, and as sumptuous as it was, she had rarely felt as uncomfortable in her life. It would have been too easy to close her eyes and fall asleep, but she was here for a definite and serious reason. She needed to know what had happened to her half-sister, and if anyone was in possession of such detail, then that person would be her estranged father.

The butler's button number 4 worked a treat and before long she was being shown into an enormous cream-coloured lounge area. Looking down, all she could see was the bear skins scattered randomly over the milky marble floor. It wasn't to her taste and if anything – made her stomach feel quite queasy. The thought of slaughtered animals as floor decoration didn't sit easily with her. She clasped her tummy as a stabbing pain hit her below her naval. It lasted but a few seconds and then went away. Composing herself, she raised her eyes to scan the crowded room.

The expensive décor was wasted on Saskia, as all she could see was a long line of men with serious faces, most of them dressed quite formally. She vaguely recognised the faces of her half-brothers – two for each of her father's former wives. Their familiarity was only by way of photographs that Katya had shown her several years back. She hadn't met at least half of her siblings and others were but distant childhood memories. Her father parted the wave of suits as he rushed to greet her. The suits watched on unimpressed and with a tinge of jealousy. Saskia was now the only daughter left in the family and she could detect that her brothers were concerned that she would now pick up the mantle of favourite child.

After an unexpected, crushing hug, Sergei pulled away to take a good long look at Saskia's features. He announced, 'Ty tak pokhozha na svoyu mat'; Saskia understood that he was telling her that she was identical to her mother, and from the scowls of disapproval from her many half-brothers, this was a statement that was not well received. After all, her mistress mother had lasted longer than any of Sergei's marriages to any of their mothers. She glared back at them. She knew that they considered her mother as little other than a highly-paid prostitute. Saskia had long since tinkered on her calculator and deduced that their mummies, along with their handsome divorce settlements, had actually commanded a far higher price tag for services rendered. This thought made her feel smug and psychologically untouchable. Had she still been a little child she would have pulled her tongue out at them by now, but alas she was a grown woman and, anyway, she had no need to feel inferior. She was now Sergei Beselovaya's only remaining daughter. Her status in the world had just received a promotion.

The whole strange scenario began to feel like a game of chess. Her brothers could no longer move their father out of her reach, nor could they take her out of the equation since her position was under his protection – checkmate!

Eventually she responded to Sergei's comments. 'Papa, my Russian is not too good. Could we please speak in English?' Yet more silent tuts and frowns followed this request. Saskia really didn't care. She had been schooled in an exclusive English establishment because her father had banished her mother to far distant shores, and if they wanted to communicate with her, then it had to be in her adopted tongue. Her terms or nothing! Sergei soon began to realise that his younger daughter was not only a stunning replica of her mother, but also had more Eastern European backbone than any of his spineless sons put together. She reminded him of Katya, and with that thought, his eyes began to well up with tears.

He went to sit down and, uninvited, Saskia sat down beside him. 'What happened to my sister? Please do not spare any details. I need to know everything.' Sergei was too distressed. He could not speak. He knocked down a neat vodka as though he was trying to anaesthetise his heart. He placed both hands in front of his eyes. He could no longer face the world and hoped his fingers would filter out reality. Katya's only full brother Dima came to rescue the situation. He understood the nature of the relationship between the two sisters and was sympathetic to Saskia's distress. He also understood the dynamics of the family and how historically Saskia had been belittled due to her illegitimacy and the perception of her mother's profession.

Sitting down beside her, Dima began to explain. 'Katya was found by her boyfriend last Tuesday evening in the apartment they shared. He called the ambulance but she was pronounced dead on arrival by the time they reached the ED. The police were called because the death was sudden and unexpected. They found a syringe, needle, tourniquet and traces of heroin on her bedside cabinet.' Saskia started to shake and a few tears made their escape. 'She would never have touched heroin, Dima. Katya has done many crazy things, many times with many people, but not if it involved making a hole in her vein. No way – never! She was terrified of needles. It was a real phobia of hers.' Dima put a comforting arm around her shoulder. 'Yes, we know that, Saskia. The toxicology reports are not back yet, but the police suspect her death was made to look as though she had taken an overdose. They found things that simply do not add up.' Saskia sat bolt upright. She clasped her tummy as yet another piercing stab took her breath away. The nausea started to rise up through her throat. She didn't feel at all well. 'What things?' she asked. Dima looked to his father, and Sergei nodded his head to gesture he should continue.

Dima continued, 'Her boyfriend stated that there was a chemical smell in the room and he thought it could be ether. A damp muslin patch was found under the bed. The police have sent it over to forensics, but they suspect it could have been used to make Katya unconscious before injecting her. Nothing has been proven as yet, so it's just a hunch at this stage.' 'What else?' asked Saskia. 'You said that things did not add up, so there was more … things … wasn't there? What aren't you telling me?'

Dima kept looking to his father for approval before answering Saskia's questions. He replied, 'The last person our sister ever spoke to was a man called Reed Baratolli. She called him the day before she died. He is a fairly famous guy. Have you heard of him?' Saskia nodded affirmatively. 'I don't follow the world of celebrities, Dima; however, I do know this man's name. Isn't he some sort of musician, songwriter, music producer and rock god?' Dima replied, 'Yes, that's the same man, mostly just referred to as Reed B. Anyway, Katya rang him to blackmail him. She had something on him. It transpires that he tried to sexually assault Katya at some party and after that incident she was all out for revenge.' Saskia was confused. 'That makes no sense, Dima. To begin with, how do the police know the details of this alleged phone conversation, and secondly, why would the woman with more money than sense want to blackmail anyone? What would she possibly have to gain? Also, I know Katya well enough … or at least I think I knew her well enough, to understand that she doesn't … or didn't … do the whole revenge thing. She always tended to let things go.'

Once again Dima looked to his father for support and on this occasion Sergei stood to his feet and answered on Dima's behalf. 'Saskia, I think that I should answer your questions from now on. My son is becoming overly stressed by all of this. I know that you loved Katya very much, but this is a difficult time for all the family and it is hurtful to talk about. What I am about to tell you is classified information and under no circumstances must you disclose this to anyone. The police have only shared this information with me because of who I am – do you understand?' Saskia nodded compliantly, 'With crystal clarity, Papa.'

Sergei took a sip from a crystal glass that had recently been refreshed with chilled vodka. He looked troubled, as though he was struggling to find the correct words in English. He began, 'It appears that Katya was good friends with an English lady called Mercy De Vede. She ran some sort of investigation agency in England and she had done some detective work for Katya in the past. I believe that they were old friends and that their relationship went back many years. Anyway, it seems that Mercy needed a favour from Katya. It transpires that Reed Baratolli's wife was one of Mercy's clients and was over in the UK at the time on personal family business. The police believe that Mercy's company were acting in some sort of protection and security capacity. I am not sure of the exact details, but Reed's wife was due to fly home to Miami for a party Reed had planned for her. I know that sounds trivial, but actually it was a big family reunion and I believe it was an important event. This all sounds very bizarre, but your sister had been asked to blackmail Reed; however, not for money as most people would assume. As you just stated earlier, your sister had no need for money. Instead she required his co-operation. It appears that his wife would not be attending this party back in the US, and it was Reed's task to come up with a cover story to explain his wife's absence. I know this must seem petty to your ears, but for some reason this was a big deal. I am sure there must be things behind this that we simply don't know, but from what I can tell, this was the reason for the call.'

Saskia looked confused. She felt sick and tired. She longed to be curled up within the giant four-poster bed that awaited her, but she was troubled. None of what her father had told her made any sense. She responded, 'That's a heck of a lot of detail. I don't get it. How do the police know about this and why would that lead them to believe this was connected to Katya's death?'

Sergei took another swig of vodka and inhaled deeply on his chocolate-coloured Cohiba Behike cigar. The smoke caught the back of her throat and made her cough, but Sergei didn't even seem to notice. He often failed to notice people. He answered his daughter as best as he could with his self-taught command of the English language. 'Katya made a tape of the conversation and emailed the link to her friend Mercy. The police found the recording on her hard drive and played me the tape. Let us just say that the conversation was chuvstvitel'nogo kharaktera, or as you would say ... I don't know what you would say ... secrets were disclosed.' 'Such as what?' asked Saskia. Sergei replied, 'When Mr Baratolli picked up the phone, he assumed it was his accountant. He accidentally let it slip that he had been scheming to divorce his wife and was planning to hide his assets away in some off-shore account. As if that wasn't bad enough, Katya then accused him of feeding his wife a cocktail of tranquillisers and benzodiazepine to keep her under control and locked away in his Miami mansion. You must remember that Katya has a degree in pharmacology so she would understand the terminology. Complete waste of time and money since she has never worked a day in her life, but nonetheless she had enough knowledge of drugs to accuse him of keeping his wife in a drugged state. These were very serious accusations, Saskia. Even as I listened to the recording, I was shocked by what my own daughter was saying. I did not know that my child could be capable of such venom.'

Saskia was speechless. She was equally as shocked as her father. She had always seen Katya as a fun party person and couldn't relate to this other person with an acidic tongue.

Sergei continued, 'Oh it gets worse. She accuses him of being a womaniser and of using his career to have time away from home for opportunities to bed women. She then accuses him of attempted rape. Oh, and then she told him that she knew his wife Eenayah had gone missing in England, but that his only concern was not for her welfare, but more a fear that this could delay divorce proceedings. Then she told him he was a bigamist as he had just got engaged to Amanda Primetta. I mean – shit – do you know who the Primetta family are? As if the conversation wasn't bad enough, mentioning Amanda brought the Mafia and American politics into the equation. This conversation was pure dynamite, Saskia, and 24 hours later your sister is dead. I am only telling you what I remember, but in itself this phone call could be enough to have someone killed. I listened to it all, word for word, and that is my opinion.'

Phew. Saskia gave a big sigh as the colour drained from her face. 'Are you saying that this could be a professional contract killing, Papa?' Sergei shrugged his shoulders and mirrored Saskia's sigh. 'The police believe that this is a real possibility. There are plenty of people who hate me enough to cause problems with my family. Katya herself hung around with some dubious people in the criminal underworld, and as for Reed Baratolli; after that phone call, he must be the number one suspect. In all of this mix, let us not disregard the Primetta family and their associations. It doesn't look good.'

Saskia was in shock. This was everything she had hoped she wouldn't hear, and yet at the same time multiple motives seem to steer blame away from the Ouroboros. The name of two cities kept floating through her mind; Katya lived in Atlanta and Reed lived in Miami. The Russian driver who had met her in Nice Airport had plane tickets for both cities and she had given him one half of very expensive cufflinks in payment for something. She had placed the diamond in the driver's palm like 30 pieces of silver. She dare not contemplate the thought that she may have been involved in her own sister's assassination.

She asked, 'But her apartment would have had security, surely? The police would have had access to CCTV footage. Did they not see anyone enter the building before she died?'

Dimo now re-joined the conversation, sensing that his father was finding the discussion too trying. The general mood in the house was heavy and austere. Sergei was trying to be strong on behalf of all his children, but his heart was broken and his sorrow was something he could not disguise, nor indeed was anything he wanted to disguise.

Dimo answered his sister's query. 'Yes, one man entered her apartment in the late afternoon and stayed for less than an hour. Reception put him on the intercom to Katya. She seemed to know who he was and invited him up. He was wearing a baseball cap which threw a shadow on his face. There wasn't a clear enough image on CCTV to identify who he was. He came and went on foot, so likewise there wasn't any car registration plates to identify him. It is early days, Saskia, but we are assured that the police are doing all they can to get to the bottom of all of this. Some things remain confidential, so they could be keeping some details back. I am sorry we cannot tell you more. We are as frustrated about this as you are, but we have to respect that this is a criminal investigation and they can't tell us everything.'

Saskia did not entirely believe Dimo's statement but neither did she feel too well. She knew the name Mercy De Vede. Who had mentioned this person to her before? As though her half-brother could read her mind, he then added, 'oh and just to complicate things – the lady who asked Katya to make the phone call – Mercy De Vede...she crashed her car yesterday and is presently in hospital. The police are not sure if the car had been tampered with in some way.' Saskia fell silent. Who had mentioned the name Mercy De Vede to her before? It was drilling a hole in her head. Eventually, exhaustion got the better of her so she wasn't able to stay around much longer. She stood up and gave both Dimo and her father a hug. It wasn't so much an emotional embrace – more a thankful gesture. She blanked the other miserable suits who had watched silently in the background. Having pressed the number 4 button, the butler duly arrived to escort her to her bedroom. Her father's house was a maze of rooms and corridors, and so she was grateful for his assistance and the convenient communication device. However, it had not escaped her attention that this device also meant that she was not allowed to wander around the house at will. Indeed, the place was a virtual electronic prison.

She dared not let her imagination run loose. She needed to sleep and tomorrow she would leave for home. The womb-like comfort of her own cosy cottage was tugging on the umbilical cord and beckoning her back. She no longer wanted to stay in her father's high security world. The whole situation was surreal and now she needed the panacea of Cotswold normality.

***

Saskia was tucked up inside a heavy tapestry duvet and in the deepest of slumbers. Suddenly she was awakened by a sinister bestial voice. The menacing tones stirred her from the pleasant dream she had been submerged in. Loud and clear it simply said the words 'turn over'. Startled, her eyes popped wide open. Nothing was in the room. She was quite alone. She decided that her mind had been traumatised by recent events and her imagination had possibly just been given a kick from hell. She ignored the voice and went back to sleep.

She was lying on her side, when without thinking about it she turned over and lay on her back. The most horrific stabbing pain then hit her instantly. It was as though a knife was being thrust into her pelvis. She awoke with a scream. The pain seared through her abdomen. The unexpected sudden agony was enough to make her vomit. She rushed to the toilet to throw up a frothy mixture of water and bile. After heaving on an empty stomach for at least five minutes, she then pulled down her PJs to expose the skin of her stomach. Her skin was intact; no marks, no slashes, nothing to indicate that she had been cut. She concluded that it must have been some sort of nightmare. Walking back to her bed, she felt a warm trickle meander down her leg.

'Oh no,' was the instant thought that came into her mind. She knew immediately that she was bleeding. Rushing back to the bathroom, the bright red stains on the toilet tissue became an immediate confirmation. Shouting at her as loud as the white plastic stick had stated 'pregnant', the red blood clots now clarified 'no longer pregnant'. She didn't know if she should be happy or sad. In the last few days she hadn't even had the time to think about her circumstances. She pressed the number 4 on the buzzer and awaited the butler. He would surely find the requirement for sanitary pads a most unusual request.

As she awaited his arrival, she contemplated her situation. Had she gone through with this pregnancy, the baby would never have known a father. Although she would have managed financially, there would have been no caring hands wiping her brow as she went through the pains of labour. Neither would she have had the support of another parent able to relieve her of night feeds and twilight nappy changes when too exhausted to function. Then when her child was older and naughty, there would be no threat of a father to go and tell. No back-up, no relief, no other person to share any traumas or joys with. She had been raised herself by a single mother. She knew it would have been a difficult journey for both of them.

Yet, looking down at the blood dripping on the white sides of the toilet pan, she also had other laments. Little more than the size of a fingernail, the sadness was not about the loss of a tiny embryo as it had been but an hour ago, but about the loss of the person it could have become. The first smiles she would never see, the first day at school she would never experience, the first bicycle he or she would never ride. She would not witness her child get married, and indeed right now, there was a little boy or girl somewhere, who would never grow up to meet and fall in love with her child. There were also grandchildren she would never hold. Indeed, the 'never events' were the greater sorrow. The grief of losing a human that would now not be born and losing a life that they would never have and one she would never share.

She had to shut these emotions away now. They were too raw. She had grieved for the loss of her child. And now she had to move on. Her thoughts moved away from her recent pregnancy and onto her memories of her sister.

Dearest Katya, a larger than life, fun-loving person who entered a room like a tornado of pure light and energy. Saskia hoped beyond hope that her involvement with the Russian driver was little more than coincidence. She had already convinced herself that this was the case. Emotion made way for logic as she asked herself why a group of elderly property investors with an interest in ancient relics, would possibly want Katya dead. It made no sense. There was nothing to link them. She now understood that both Katya and her oligarch father had more than enough enemies between them, with the means and justification to fund a contract killing.

Saskia did dismissal very well. Dumped at a boarding school by her evil mother as she was, and ignored by her father as she had been, Saskia had a ruthless cold streak. She could allow herself a moment of sentimentality and then kill the moment as though it hadn't even existed.

The butler tapped at the door. She would send him off to bring what she needed to mop up her life, and then she would leave. She wouldn't be coming back for any funerals or requiem laments. As far as she was concerned, her baby was gone, the man who made the baby was gone, her sister was gone and now it was time for her to be gone. She would be gone far away from the suits who hated her and a father who now only showed her a glimmer of affection because she had been pulled off the reserve bench. She would leave in the morning.

CHAPTER 13

22nd August 2013

Don Morris had a soft spot for Ireland, and so it felt most odd heading back to Dublin without his mentor, boss and general sidekick – Professor Roland De Vede. Don had the greatest respect and admiration for his former lecturer and now of late – his employer. He revered the professor as a teacher, author, historian, genealogist, but above all else as a friend.

He had taken the ferry over from Holyhead, with the full intention of slowing the journey down. Ireland was a special place, and like a trickle of the blackest Guinness at the back of the throat, it was a flavour not to be rushed. Sure, he could have jumped on a plane, but he felt this mode of travel was most fitting and therefore vindicated.

Don wandered up to the upper deck. He wanted to feel the wind in his hair, and taste the salty spray from the Irish Sea on his face. He was grateful for any remaining cobwebs to be blown from his mind. This ferry crossing would give him precious thinking time before meeting up with Frank O'Byrne again. He had so many questions swirling around in his head, but he needed to shine a light in a few dark corners before he could untangle the tethers. So much had happened in rapid succession. As of late, life had become like a house of cards – falling in dramatic succession, yet being unable to remember which suit crumbled first or who gave the first card the push.

He thought about Patsy. He always thought about Patsy. She was never very far away. She had continuously begged that they visit Ireland, as some of her cousins lived near Cork. Alas he had always been so busy in his job as a BBC researcher. Too busy to ever find the time. Then he did find the time, but all too late. Patsy's time had run out. He presumed this to be all too sad and common a tale. Maybe it was something about being at sea, but he remembered his dear wife being obsessed by the film *Titanic*. She played the soundtrack so many times, that he often felt he was drowning in uilleann pipes and Irish tin whistles. Memories – so many memories. That blasted theme tune drove him crazy. Walking over to the stern, he had to smile as he could almost hear Patsy quoting lines from the film, *'It's been 84 years, and I can still smell the fresh paint. The china had never been used. The sheets had never been slept in. Titanic was called the Ship of Dreams, and it was. It really was.'* His lovely wife, she almost knew the script off by heart. Now it was he who could quote the lines to perfection.

He then cast his mind back to two years ago. It had been a beautiful sunny English afternoon when he first encountered a most unusual young woman in a lavender field near St Helens. It was a strange meeting, in a place that one would not normally associate with the industrial north. Yet it existed in all its shades of unexpected lilac glory, like a pocket of heaven just off the busy Manchester to Liverpool dual carriageway.

At the time, it seemed to Don that Saskia was an angel, flown to Earth to rescue him from the murky depths of despair and depression. Back in the workplace, and having found a meaning and purpose to life, he embraced the bizarre project he had been given. Living and working within a radius of the local village, he discovered many new friends. Saskia also became his friend, and they often enjoyed a Friday afternoon pub lunch together in the Cotswold retreat where she lived. Don always worried about Saskia. He looked upon her as a daughter and his was a sincere fatherly concern. He needn't have worried so much, as he was soon to discover that his angelic-looking employer had guts made of steel and fists of concrete. She certainly didn't require any sort of paternal protection. Nonetheless he remained concerned. The loss of her only sister must have been a stomach-wrenching blow, even for one who acted as though she was invincible and indestructible. Her dry indigo eyes didn't fool him for a second.

His memories then fell upon his time when he was working with the professor and his fiery daughter Mercy De Vede. Saskia reminded him of Mercy. They had the same single-minded sense of purpose and determination. When his work with Saskia and the Crank caverns had been completed, it was MeDeVe Ltd that had offered him a new job. Oxford felt like a new life – new town, new apartment and maybe a new beginning. He simply could not believe that Mercy had been killed. How could one who had so much life, now lie so still? Don's mind was crammed full of so many unanswered questions. What exactly had happened to Mercy? Was it just a fluke coincidence that her friend Katya just happened to be Saskia's sister? Was there such a thing as coincidence, in lives driven by a greater purpose? The day before she died, Saskia's sister had a conversation with his boss. No matter how many times he thought about it, it still seemed like an unexpected twist of fate. Recalling the cairns at County Meath and the strange hieroglyphics, Don couldn't help but wonder if the ancient biblical prophesies uncovered by the professor and Frank O'Byrne could have had any bearing on the events of the last few months. He was dying to meet Frank again. He didn't want to put him through an interrogation, but he needed some sort of closure. Don was a researcher by profession, and so a closure to some, may count as an opening to him.

The cranes of Dublin harbour came into view. He would soon have his moment with Frank, and he was determined to walk away knowing more. He hated the fact that the *Titanic* theme tune kept playing in his head as the ferry approached the dockside. Perhaps this was Patsy's punishment, for him never finding the time to bring her here. Don mentally concluded, 'Regrets – not the best place to dock ones' boat. Best not to harbour them if at all possible. However, sometimes when one has a busy, full life, they are a natural consequence of not being omnipotent.' It felt like an excuse, but it was the best exoneration he could award himself. Guilt and regret were not calming bedfellows in the midst of a sleepless night.

***

In the smart streets of middle-class Dublin, Don stood outside Frank O'Byrne's trendy Georgian-style abode and noted the for-sale board at the front gate. He hadn't visited Frank's home before. His genealogist boss had kept him too busy fighting nettles in overgrown cemeteries to include him in their best-buddy encounters. Frank answered the door wearing a solemn face. He was a kindly looking, portly man with vivid carrot-red hair and matching beard.

On inviting him in, there was a mere token exchange of greeting between the two men, possibly out of politeness. Frank's home seemed to be very white and exuded a minimalistic, clutter-free mood. Don felt quite uncomfortable. Frank had excluded him from some of the final conversations he had exchanged with the professor about Eenayah Baratolli, and Don couldn't help but feel a sense of rejection or maybe mistrust – or perhaps both. Frank showed Don into his office as opposed to any of the less formal rooms in his house. This action did not go unnoticed by Don.

'So, Don, what can I do for you?' was Frank's opening gambit. Don was not in a mood to dance around any handbags. He responded, 'Thanks for seeing me at short notice, Frank. I do appreciate you making time for me, but I do have some questions for you. A week ago, I was invited to a company conference call, chaired by young Simon. You may recall that Simon is the professor's grandchild.' Frank simply nodded his head to confer that he knew who Don was referring to. Don continued, 'The call came as a big shock to everybody. It appears that MeDeVe Ltd has shut shop, although there were some hints that perhaps Simon may open up his own detective and investigation company at some point in the future. However, for now I have joined the ranks of the unemployed. Look, I know my situation is of no concern to you, Frank, but I sure could do with some answers and I know you know something. What happened? That's all I am here to ask of you, Frank. What the hell happened?'

Once upon a time, Frank O'Byrne would have been addressed as Father Francis. As a Catholic priest, he was deemed to be a savour of souls and a source of solace and succour for the poor and needy. Yet his present dispassionate demeanour seemed to bare no traces of his former profession of pastoral care.

Don sensed a brick wall. He stood up and, leaning forward on the table, looked Frank directly in the eyes. He was aware that as body language gestures go, he was now being forceful and maybe even intimidating; however, Frank wasn't playing ball and Don wasn't leaving the playground until someone threw his ball back over the fence.

He addressed Frank once again. 'Do you recall the day we visited the cairns? Our young tour guide Brigid dropped us off at the pub after we had been to see Mary Ryan's headstone in St Mary's cemetery. You will recall the hieroglyphics on Mary's tomb were identical to those inscriptions engraved within cairn T. It seemed like an astounding discovery and at the time I recall we were all quite excited about what this could possibly mean. Anyway, Frank, we were in the pub and I went off to the toilet. As providence would have it, I had forgotten my phone on the table and I was expecting an important call, so I came back to get it. You didn't know that I was just behind you, and I heard you say to the professor, *"I am sorry, my friend, but I don't even know if Don can be trusted. He is a paid employee of your daughter's and he can be bought and sold."'*

Don stood bolt upright, shook his head in dismay and shot Frank an angry look. He walked over to the window and for a moment he was quite lost in himself. Don had always considered himself to be a moral person – a good employee and a good husband. In his entire lifetime, he had never heard himself described as someone who could be 'bought and sold'. He was perplexed, dismayed and deeply saddened. He was far from home, and at this very moment he so wished Patsy was by his side. He needed her. He gulped as he fought back a tear. He held out his hand for an imaginary hand to fill his, but his palms remained empty.

He then felt plump, freckled fingers pat his shoulder as an arm came around his back. Frank tugged at the lost man staring into nothingness. 'Come along, Don,' beckoned the former priest with a rueful tone, 'let me make you a hot toddy. I am sorry if I insulted you and I apologise for my lack of hospitality. I do not have any excuses to offer you, but I do have my reasons. Let us move into the snug where it is more comfortable and I will tell you what I can.'

***

Don wasn't sure which smell met with his nostrils first. As the door opened, a steaming tray entered the room and the aroma of lemons, cloves and sweetened whisky perfused the air. Frank carefully placed the warm glasses on the table, along with some star-shaped Oaten biscuits. 'I made these myself,' Frank proudly proclaimed. 'As an eternal bachelor, I had to learn how to feed this growing stomach of mine from a young age. Take a sip of your toddy, Don. It will put hairs on your chest.' Don did as he was told, inhaling the cloves and lemon long before the comforting liquid graced the sides of his mouth. He started to relax. The brick wall was starting to come down. Perhaps Frank was beginning to realise that Don was not the enemy.

Frank's tone was gentle and repentant. Hostility was not his normal choice of hat and he felt acutely embarrassed by the cool reception he had given his visitor so far.

He began, 'Don, I just want to say that I am sorry. I did not mean to affront you, but in certain situations information can become quite dangerous, and it could be better to know less rather than more. In part, the professor wanted to protect you. At the time, it seemed that people who knew too much may be at risk. However, there was also a requirement to protect his daughter's client, Eenayah Baratolli. Her life seemed to be tumbling into mortal danger, and even now she is lost to the world. Nobody knows if she is dead or alive. Was this an overreaction on our part? Could it be that we were two silly old men with overcharged imaginations? You can make that charge if you like, Don, but just look at the facts. Eenayah Baratolli went missing. She fell off a mountain, we know not how or why. Mercy tried to protect her by changing her identity whilst she lay unconscious in a hospital bed. However, her identity was unmasked and the next thing that happens is that the ambulance transferring Eenayah to some sort of brain injury recovery unit takes a detour. For now, Eenayah Baratolli is somewhere and nobody knows where. We don't even know if she still breathes. For all intents and purposes, she has vanished into thin air. Then, of course, there is Mercy De Vede; the professor's ex-CID daughter and the woman hired to protect Eenayah. She also had an accident and ended up in the same hospital as her client. She was in the process of being transferred over to Oxford, but was given what was presumed to be a deliberate morphine overdose prior to the journey. The nurse who gave the medication cannot be traced, and I understand the police are treating this as a criminal investigation. In all of this, let us not forget Mercy's friend, Katya Beselovaya, daughter of a Russian oligarch. I do not know all the full details, Don, but I do know that Mercy involved Katya in some plot that involved Eenayah's husband – the famous Mr Reed B. The next thing we all read in the Sunday papers is that Katya has been found dead in her boyfriend's Atlanta apartment.'

Frank's eyes looked vacant and bewildered as he took a long, deep slug of the much-needed hot toddy. He continued, 'Whilst reading the same Sunday papers, one cannot help but notice the catalogue of tragedies that has since dogged Reed B. I cannot say I really like the man, but I do feel sorry for him. His entire life has gone into freefall since his wife vanished. His record company is on the verge of collapse and it seems some dodgy accountant woman has hidden most of his savings in a fictional offshore account. The last I heard, Reed Baratolli was in ruination. Do you not understand, Don? More or less anyone who has had anything to do with this case appears to have been blighted with some curse. People have gone missing, relationships have ended, careers have collapsed, some have died; there are forces at work much greater than we can even imagine. I know you are a researcher and so by nature you are a curious chap, but I beg of you to walk away from all of this and do not dig any deeper. Both you and the curious little kitten may be killed.'

Don also took a large, forceful glug at what remained of his hot toddy. He was not to be so easily deterred. He responded to the final comment by adding, 'Which is exactly why both me and my feline friends have nine lives held in reserve. I can read the newspapers and find out all the information you have just shared with me, Frank. So … tell me something I don't know. What are the lines of Tamar?'

This was a question Frank did not want to answer. In all their recent explorations of genealogy, tomb stones and ancient Irish hieroglyphics, this had been the one missing jigsaw piece they had hoped to keep to themselves. Frank stood up and left the room, leaving Don sat alone and confused. He didn't quite know what to do. He went back over to the window and pondered on the for-sale sign. It seemed that even Frank O'Byrne was making an escape. He wondered about the professor and where he had run away to. Rumour had it that he was under some sort of police protection. There was even gossip to suggest that his daughter Mercy had not died from the morphine overdose, and maybe had joined her father in some safe retreat. After all, she was ex-Metropolitan Police and didn't these guys all look after their own? He paced up and down the room. Where had Frank disappeared to? Why had he just walked out? It was a most odd situation.

He did not have to wonder long, as within ten minutes Frank returned to the snug. He apologised. 'I am sorry for just walking out on you like that, Don. I had to consider my next actions carefully.' He handed Don an A4-sized brown envelope. Don was mystified. 'What is this?' Frank's face was etched with worry lines and his eyes bore a solemn glint of resignation. He sighed as he responded, 'I have just made you a photocopy of an essay a student of mine wrote many years ago. This goes back to the days when I taught theology at the university. The paper is about the Ledanite prophecies. The essay will tell you all you need to know about the mysterious lines of Tamar, but in brief this was a story removed from the Old Testament, possibly as one of many missing scrolls. It tells of a woman who was convinced that she was the carrier of a mystical seed. These days we may refer to this as a DNA mutation. Anyway; so convinced was she of this, that she would do anything she could to become pregnant so she could pass her biological heritage on to future generations of kings. Tamar succeeded, by way of the royal and sacred lines of King Solomon and David, and via her eldest twin son Pharez. It is told that her youngest son Zarah, and his descendants, set sail to a new kingdom in the North, and of course dear, sweet Brigid told us all about this story when describing the hieroglyphics. The Ledanite cult also believed that Tamar had twin daughters – Leda and Sheol. Leda was an exact genetical copy of her mother Tamar. I guess these days we would call her a clone. According to the Ledanite prophecy, an unbroken line of clones would continue to be born as twins until Tamar herself could be reincarnated into one of them. The essay talks about a deeply secretive society which protects this holy line. It is described as ultimately powerful because of its diversity. How can one beat something which is multi-cultural, multi-religious and operates on a global scale? We kept this information away from you to protect you, Don, as it seems the Ledanites will stop at nothing to guard the keepers of this extraordinary DNA. During our investigations into Eenayah's genealogy, it soon become apparent that she was part of this inheritance and that many of the clones prior to that were the ones you found – the ones whose tombs had been marked with the same ancient transcriptions. It seems like this was some sort of symbolic messaging system within the Ledanite following.'

Don was silent. What could he say? For so long he had only known part of the story and in a way, it was a relief to now fill in some of the missing gaps. However, as was always the case with such mysteries, it opened up more questions than it answered. He stared at the A4 envelope in hushed contemplation. He eventually asked, 'What of the other female twin – Sheol?' Frank shrugged his shoulders nonchalantly. He replied, 'It was told that Sheol was given supernatural powers, but only so she could protect her twin sister. Sheol herself was not a clone, even though she was Leda's twin. It was believed that these magical abilities would be transferred down the descendancy of Sheol's line, in order to protect many generations of clones. History tells of many magical humans who are direct descendants of Sheol. However, according to the essay, Sheol's descendants, who could be both male and female, were not always so good and virtuous. There are those who could misuse their powers for evil purposes – so much so, that they sometimes captured the souls of the dead for their own malevolent reasons. Over the years, the Jewish even used the word Sheol as meaning, "the place of the dead". It took on board a wicked connotation.'

Don was still confused. He asked, 'How does any of this connect with Mercy and Katya?' Frank drew a deep breath. He knew he had given Don far too much information, but he also knew that without it Don would persist and persist to the point of nuisance. He was a man with nothing more to lose and time on his side – the most dangerous sort of a man.

With reluctance, he replied, 'Eenayah was a clone of Tamar. All of the investigations the professor did into her genealogy revealed centuries of patterns that confirmed this. However, my understanding is that the Ledanites saw our investigations as meddling. The writer of this essay was my student and a former Ledanite himself. He is now a Buddhist priest hidden away in a forest cabin in County Wicklow, and he warned us that no good would come of Mercy's intent to protect Eenayah. This was not seen to be Mercy's job and she would be removed from that assumed position. It was made crystal clear with the cold clarity of glacial water that this group of believers would stop at nothing.'

Don gulped as though his windpipe was in temporary paralysis. He muttered some four-letter expletive under his breath. He hadn't disclosed his relationship with Saskia and couldn't help but wonder about her and her sister Katya. Was this just a coincidence and, if not, what was their connection to all of this?

Frank could see that Don was deeply engaged in his own thoughts and was struggling to come to terms with all he had been told. Still in shock, he asked for his hat and coat, making some feeble excuse to now leave.

Frank walked him to the door. Standing outside, Don pointed to the for-sale sign. 'Where are you off to?' he asked Frank. Frank looked up at the sign. The stark sunlight caught his leathery skin and he looked older than when Don last remembered. He considered that time had taken its toll on the ex-priest. 'Over the hills and far away,' came the response. 'And what of you, Don?' asked Frank. It seemed almost like a terminal conversation between two people who may never meet again.

'I don't know,' responded Don. 'I can't think that far in advance. I guess it depends on young Simon, and if he can find some space for me in his new company.' Don held up the A4 envelope. 'Oh, and thanks for this.'

Frank shook his hand firmly and added, 'Look after yourself, Don, and look after that envelope. If I was you, I would read it, burn it and flush the ashes of it down a toilet. Just in case I haven't drummed the point into you as well as I intended, I want to emphasise how dangerous this cult can be. Keep away from them, my friend. You have the closure you came here for, now forget all you have been told and move on.'

Don tipped his hat in a gesture reminiscent of a former time and made his way down the path. By the time he turned to close the gate, Frank was safely back inside and that was the end of that. Would he ever see him again or was this yet another last time? He was unsure.

CHAPTER 14

3rd June 2016

Another place, another time, long ago and far away. Counting the years …

Like sand in an egg-timer, the lives of many people had by now drifted into a different space. Almost three years had passed since Eenayah Baratolli had been kidnapped and held captive by the Ledanites. Three years since Frank and Don last met in Dublin for a slightly awkward conversation. Three years since Katya Beselovaya had been found dead in her boyfriend's Atlanta apartment. Three years since Mercy De Vede had allegedly been killed by a morphine overdose. Three years since her company MeDeVe Ltd had been dissolved, and three years since her nephew Simon took over the business, creating SiDeVe Ltd. It was also three years since Mercy's father – Professor Roland De Vede – had disappeared off the planet. Three years since Reed Baratolli was put under the microscope of suspicion. Two-and-a-half years since Eenayah's twin sons were born in a cave and illegally adopted. Two and a half years since Darcy Kyfinn deserted her Welsh home and the Ledanites for a new life in New York. Two years since Reed Baratolli changed his identity to Anthony Mort and set up the VOTS charity for the homeless. Over five years had passed since Soul touched the rocks of Crank and became aware of a strange unearthly presence. 651 years since three pilgrims came across the cave and recognised those locked within it as 'unbeknown'. 223 years since three young children were killed within the Crank caverns.

Indeed, lives had changed and much water had flown beneath the bridge of epoch. Meanwhile, back in Wales and in the heart of Snowdonia, other plans were afoot. New lives, new dreams, new times.

***

Darwydden Castle Manor had been immersed into a hive of frenzied activity, as preparations were being made for the biggest celebrity social event in Wales, not that the rest of Wales could boast much in the way of competition. Garlands were being shipped in by the truck load, as every part of the hotel was to be dressed in abundant, delicate shades of pastel flora. Crews of roadies lifted enormous amplifiers and screens from articulated trucks, as the stage was set for tomorrow's elite performers. Several helicopter landing spots and even a grassed runway had already been marked out in anticipation of the rich and famous arriving by air, whilst awaiting limousines were at the ready for those travelling by ground transportation.

The hotel staff were in a highly-elevated state as some of the younger members hung around on the battlements with binoculars – desperate for a star-studded view of the incoming wedding guests. Slightly outside the hotel parameters, members of the paparazzi were camping out, having had much of the same intention. Predictably a matching army of security guards had been enlisted to keep prying eyes and long-range camera lenses at bay. Keeping such a high-profile event under control had been like a military operation; however, wrapped within the secluded Snowdonia mountain range, Darwydden Castle Manor seemed perfectly suited to the luminary requirement for privacy.

Entire refrigeration units had been assembled at the back of the kitchen, simply to cater for the pernickety needs of numerous exacting guests. As Nico presumed ownership of the entire cooking ensemble, he couldn't help but tensely patrol the catering arrangements. Ruby had to remind him, 'You are the groom, Nico. For crying out loud, relax and let someone else take the strain. You are off duty for the weekend.' Nico could do many things in life, but as one of the most illustrious chefs in the Northern Hemisphere, relax was a term that didn't often hit his vocabulary.

His bride to be – Tia – and her guests wouldn't be arriving until tomorrow afternoon, and this seemed like a good arrangement all round. The bridal party wouldn't catch a glimpse of the marital venue until everything was at its glorious best, but more so it gave Nico time for a Friday night mini-stag celebration with his own guests. Indeed, tonight was party time for the groom and his many friends, family and associates. Even with that thought buzzing around his head, Nico was in a state of excitable agitation. Tomorrow was going to be a big day, but no venue could live up to the high stakes better than the splendid Welsh bastion he resided within.

***

Florence and Saskia giggled like adolescent school girls as the limo drove up the driveway towards the drawbridge of the hotel. Overhanging yellow laburnum trees created a buttery archway above the car as it drove, immersing the car roof in a strange lemon glaze. Nothing could ever be considered drab or normal about Darwydden, and as though it had a life of its own, it seemed to shimmer with pride. As they finally caught sight of the hotel, Saskia gasped at its serene, medieval beauty. Even though Florence had visited her sister Becky here many times in the past, she also found a 'wow' blasting its way past her lips as the house bedazzled them with its fiery welcome.

As the bright blue of daylight sunk into the dulcet navy of dusk, iron-framed oil lamps had been lit along the drawbridge. The scene was a fitting welcome for the two guests and would not have been out of place in a *Harry Potter* movie. As Florence absorbed the lavishly fantastical scene, she couldn't help but murmur, 'Jammy beggar; can you believe Nico landing an Oscar-winning actress? I mean, Tia Lembugo. How the hell did that happen?' Having suddenly realised what she had said, she turned to her friend, 'Oh, I am sorry, Saskia. I quite forgot that you and Nico had a thing going for a while. Are you okay with all of this?' Saskia was dismissive and shrugged it off, responding, 'Don't go tiptoeing on egg shells for my sake, Florence. It was a long time ago. When was it we all went to Tignes together?' Saskia went quiet as she made mental calculations and counted on her fingers. Eventually she piped up, '2012. That was four years ago, Flo. Water under the bridge and all that.'

Eternally indiscreet, Florence continued to probe, 'But it was hardly just an alpine holiday romance was it, Saskia? I mean, weren't you guys dating for over a year?' Saskia remained flippant as she replied, 'Just under a year and a half is the mathematically correct answer, Florence. He dumped me because he didn't want to get involved in anything serious, or at least that is what he told me – but I suspect that the truth was that he had already met Tia by then, so … what can I say? Men lie! Best not to dwell on these things. I have been dying to see this strange hotel for a long time and what better excuse than watching my best friend perform as a bridesmaid.' Florence smiled like a Cheshire cat at the mere reminder that, indeed, she was to be a bridesmaid at a celebrity wedding. Her few seconds of fame were awaiting.

Saskia sunk into the back of the seat and let out a deep sigh. 'Nico never did invite me here as his girlfriend. Can you believe that? Anyway, I am here now, so let's just enjoy the moment. Nico means nothing to me anymore. I have no emotional baggage, Florence, so let's just focus on having fun, eh?' Saskia was being honest. She never hauled her dirty laundry around in her luggage. She had inherited this brittle survival trait from her mother.

Nevertheless, Saskia had been less than honest about her other undercover interest in visiting Darwydden. With her own subterranean project, finally being given the green light by the planning department, she was 'professionally curious' to see how the owners of Darwydden had created their own very special buried grotto. Maybe she could steal a few ideas.

The chauffeur opened the rear doors, and a strange mixture of sweet honeysuckle and smouldering oil infused their senses. As the young women walked into the reception area, a harpist played Pachelbel's Canon in D major. At that moment, Saskia knew that Nico's wedding would be quite perfect. She rubbed her empty belly and a sad thought gate crashed from somewhere in her past. It was not a thought she wished to contemplate. She would check in, bathe, drink, party, sleep – in roughly that order. The past would be dismissed in the expert way that only Saskia, and those few of a similar aptitude, would ever be capable of executing like a sniper.

Stilettos picked their way across the cobbled courtyard to the converted stables. Both young women were in an exuberant, animated mood. Their laughter was only ever so slightly drowned out by the overhead helicopters. They each looked up at the various flying machines making their approach – quite asphyxiated by curiosity as to their contents. Florence could hardly believe she was about to become a bridesmaid to none other than the fantastically glamorous Tia Lembugo. This deserved a celebration, and with champagne and nibbles already being prepared by room service, the girls intended to make an early start.

***

Soul looked down at the passing miniscule buildings sheltered within the glens of the Welsh countryside, and quietly smiled to himself in snug contentment. He was arriving at a gig in a helicopter and, at long last, he was beginning to feel as though he really had arrived. Feeling relaxed and confident about tomorrow's performance, he sipped on his iced water with all the self-assurance of a successful performer. The young magician had gone through many years of despair and reinvention following several stage catastrophes. Indeed, he was almost at the point of giving up when his sister Eve persuaded him to reinvent his act and embrace the more traditional conjuring world of showmanship. Soul still employed some of his natural clairsentience, but he also understood that a modern audience demanded bigger, better, louder and more fantastical visual illusions; and so he adapted his act. Finally gaining entrance into the coveted inner sanctum of the 'Magic Circle' was a real step up in the world and made him one of an elite few. Yet for Soul, signing a contract with the Magnus Management Agency was the real game changer. Magnus had a global network of contacts, commanded a reverent level of respect and worked with an enviable list of 'A-Listers'. Indeed – Soul's professional career had gone supernova from the moment Magnus signed him onto his books.

Sitting quietly besides Soul was another of the Magnus school of prodigies. Soul glanced over at the young American boy and couldn't help but notice the discreetly inked tattoos on his wrist. Soul was about as observant as any human could ever claim to be. This was a man who could see magnetic forces and count the invisible particles from solar flares, so the scars of self-abuse hidden beneath the wings of a butterfly were more than glaringly obvious. He had attempted to make conversation several times since they had taken off from London's Canary Wharf, but the boy had plugged in his earpieces, turned his music up high and drifted off into a deep sleep. Like many of his age group, he was adept at being anti-social.

Soul had little other source of amusement but to glance out of the window and gaze down at the passing terrain. The ground was silent and calm, until Soul saw something strange – something so extraordinary that it caused him to jump out of his seat and in so doing knock his chilled water over the other sleeping passenger.

Micah woke up with a sudden jerk. 'What the shit?' he exclaimed. He had been in a trance-like slumber, and being roused by ice cubes down his shirt was not an ideal awakening. He was confused. 'What the hell are you doing, mate?' Soul then turned to look at the boy sitting next to him and noticing his damp shirt was full of apologies. Offering him a napkin, he could only utter, 'I am so sorry, pal. I saw something out of the window and it made me jump. I have a spare T-shirt in my hand luggage. You seem about the same size as me. Do you want me to get it for you?' Micah could immediately see that something had shaken up the man sitting next to him. Small beads of perspiration had formed on Soul's brow, and as repentant as he claimed to be, his eyes were transfixed on something outside of the helicopter window. Not waiting for a response, Soul had taken the shirt from his bag and handed it to Micah, yet all the time looking outside.

Micah was baffled. He replaced his wet shirt with Soul's clean, dry replacement, and yet throughout this change of dress, Soul did not look upon him once. Micah was concerned. What was it that was capturing the other passenger's attention with such interest?

Nudging Soul's ribs with a forceful dig to get his attention, Micah held out his hand and with a low-pitched American east coast accent stated, 'Sorry to sleep throughout the flight, mate, but I had a heavy night last night. My name is Micah and I am the singer-guitarist dude playing at tomorrow's gig. I believe you are with Magnus as well, but sorry and all that; I can't remember your name. I do recognise your face, though.' Soul was still distracted, but found enough good manners to respond to the boy. 'Oh yes, Micah; I have heard some of your music. You are good – very good. Love your new single. I am Soul; the stage magician. Look … I am really sorry about soaking you and all that. I just saw something that I have never seen before and it sort of shocked me. Are you okay now?'

Micah instantly recognised the name. He had heard all about Soul and felt slightly star-struck wearing the T-shirt of someone so famous. He knew him to be renowned in the world of illusion. An Icelandic guy who lived in Britain, and who even had his own TV series shown weekly in the States. He replied, 'Err yeah … I'm okay, pal. Taken the shirt off your back, hope that's okay. Nice to meet you anyway. Can't wait to see you perform. You are the top act tomorrow, or so Magnus tells me.' Soul shrugged his shoulders and said nothing. Something outside of the helicopter was capturing his attention far more than the young, apologetic musician sat beside him.

Micah's patience grew thin. He stood up and went to look out of the window himself. He couldn't see anything. 'What the hell are you looking at? It's just sky out there … oh and trees and mountains and … wow … take a look at that castle. Is that for real? Awesome! Is that the gig? Is that where we are landing? Surreal mate, bloody surreal! I have heard so much about this place. Can't wait to check it out, and can't wait to check out Tia as well. What a looker! The geezer marrying her is a bloody lucky bugger!'

Soul looked anxious. He gripped the arm of his chair and closed his eyes tight. His breathing was fast and loud. Micah looked on totally bemused. He was beginning to think that perhaps Soul had a phobia of flying, but then again, he had seen his stage act where he climbed on the wings of a plane and then just disappeared after take-off, literally vanishing in mid-air. With this image imprinted in his mind, he couldn't possibly believe that Soul had flight fear issues.

Eventually Soul opened his eyes and, looking out of the window, heaved a mighty sigh of relief. Micah instinctively patted his shoulders as a comforting gesture. 'What got you, mate? Something had you worried. Are you okay now? Was it a UFO fly-by?' Soul still looked nervous and uneasy. He looked up to the sky, down to the ground, forwards and backwards from where they had flown. He replied, 'Yes, everything is okay, Micah – we are through it now. Sorry if I freaked you out.' Micah asked Soul if he needed a shot of Brandy to calm his nerves.

Brandy was the ultimate solution that Micah's Canadian Gran used to solve these sorts of situations. Soul politely refused. 'Thanks for offering, Micah, but no thanks – I don't drink a whole lot when at work. Let's not forget I am a control freak. No big deal; the danger has passed.'

Micah couldn't let it go with such a simplistic explanation. Whatever it was that Soul had seen out of the window had been enough to make a seasoned stage magician; one who conjured up all sorts of daring death-defying tricks – to break out in a cold sweat. He was determined to find out what had alarmed his fellow passenger. He tried the direct approach. 'Exactly what was no big deal and what danger has passed? What the hell did you see out there, Soul? You just gotta tell me.'

Soul could see by the look on the young musician's face that he wasn't going to give up on this line of enquiry, so he decided to be bluntly honest. 'It was a blue dome.' 'Blue what?' responded Micah as he choked on his drink. Soul continued, 'I have never seen one of them before, but then again you can only see them from above, so you need to be in the air. I wasn't sure we could get through it, but then I sort of figured out that there are lots of copters already parked on the ground, so if they made it through, it must be harmless. It had me shitting bricks for a minute or two, though. Hey Micah, you do know I am weird, don't you? You didn't really expect a normal answer from a freak like me?'

Micah wasn't expecting that reply. He didn't know what he was expecting, but it sure wasn't a blue dome. He responded, 'Blue dome – that is weird. Do you mean … like those force fields that you see on some UFO movies?'

Soul finally relaxed enough to let out a small laugh. 'I have never thought about it like that before, but actually a force field isn't such a bad comparison. Seems you are obsessed by UFOs though.'

'A-ha,' announced Micah feeling semi-triumphant, 'so you thought we were going to hit it and ping off into the atmosphere or crash or something?'

'I guess that thought crossed my mind,' responded Soul. 'So then, what caused it?' enquired the young musician.

Soul was becoming tired of the incessant questioning. He thought to himself, 'Gee … this is like sitting next to an inquisitive 5-year-old that won't shut the hell up.'

Like it or not, this conversation wasn't likely to end anytime soon.

'Have you ever heard of ley lines or ghost lines, Micah?'

'Yeah sure … I mean maybe … I mean no – we don't have them in Connecticut.'

'You sure do have them in Connecticut. They are everywhere.'

'So, what are they then? Nobody back in my old town of Hartford ever talked about these lines.'

Soul looked at his watch. They had five minutes to kill before landing so he considered that he may as well educate his young fellow traveller in all things New Age.

'Ley lines are simply lines of energy around the Earth. Some people believe they are fictional, but I know they are for real because I can see them and feel them. Mostly they are connected to geographical features. Look, the best way I can ask you to imagine them, is to think about standing on a bridge looking over at a fast-flowing wide river. A river is a moving, living thing, with many undercurrents. In some places the water is deeper, darker and slower. In some places, it is narrower, shallower and the water flows faster. In other places, it may be still and stagnant. It has many channels of differing energy both at the surface and on the river bed. The Earth is just the same, but unlike a river, most people can't see the Earth's energy flows. Just because you can't see something, doesn't mean it doesn't exist, Micah. You can't see or smell or touch radiation, can you? But … we believe it exists.'

Micah understood and nodded accordingly. 'Fair point, mate – I get it. So, what about these ghost or ley lines, then? What are they?'

Soul continued, 'Our ancestors were more in touch with nature than modern people are now. They knew all about ley lines and they believed that the spirit world walked along these lines of energy – call them spiritual super highways, if you will. They often protected their villages by burying their dead in tumuli around the outskirts and along the path of a ley line. They believed that their ancestors would walk the ley lines and protect the villages – hence the term ghost lines.'

Micah placed some fresh gum in his mouth and pondered on Soul's response. 'But, isn't this a pile of mumbo jumbo? Has any of this ever been proven?'

Soul pointed out of the window to a line of church spires. 'Look at the horizon, Micah. See how the spires follow a line? Those burial mounds I mentioned before – well, as time passed, people often built their churches on top of these mounds and so what we can end up with is a line of churches that inadvertently follow a ley line.'

Micah stood up to look out of the window and appeared fairly impressed. He shrugged and nodded. 'Fair dues, man. They do line up, but what is any of this to do with a blue dome thingy?'

Soul could hardly wait for the helicopter to be on terra firma and quite wished he hadn't awoken Micah until after they had landed. But there was no way he could duck and dive from Micah's questioning. He had dug himself a hole & would need to keep filling it until they landed.

He replied, 'If you think about a ley line being about a mile high or so, some of it over ground and some of it under ground, then a ghost line could be considered good protection against a spear or a warrior on horseback, would you not agree?' Micah initially struggled to use his imagination, but eventually agreed that a horse wouldn't make it over a half-mile-high wall of protective super-charged energy. As a young guy who had just celebrated his 21st birthday, he spent most of his spare time playing in a world of virtual reality on his PC, so imagining such things came fairly easy to a gamer.

Soul continued, 'But what if you wanted to protect someone or something from invaders from above as opposed to a threat at ground level? A low-lying ghost line wouldn't keep out fearsome foes capable of flight, would it now?'

Micah loved the whole UFO conspiracy scenario and was now fully engaged with this peculiar conversation. 'Go on, this is fascinating stuff, Soul.'

'I have never encountered this before, Micah, but I have heard that if the four points of a double set of parallel ley lines were to be activated, that they could be made to curve so that they met in the middle, thus forming a dome. I have been told that the dome reflects the sky, so tends to be a silvery blue colour to those sensitive enough to see such things.'

'Someone like you, Soul?'

'It's what I do, Micah. I cannot read your fortune or tell you the winning lottery numbers, but I do have a connection with nature that most modern humans seem to have lost. It hasn't done me a whole lot of favours in life. I am an anomaly and I scare women away, but it is as it is.'

Micah's veneration of his travelling companion shot up several notches as he began to understand that Soul's stage performance wasn't just an illusion. He asked, 'So you said that this dome creation had to be activated. Does that mean that blue domes aren't a natural phenomenon, as you say ley lines are?' Soul was impressed that the young 'up and coming' rock star had picked up on this finite level of detail.

'Well spotted, Micah. The ley lines are natural, but having them curve inwards to make a dome shape is the work of some very powerful entities. Not only that, but in time they would weaken so just keeping them activated would be an ongoing task. That dome isn't here by accident, that's for sure.'

'Still, we didn't crash into it, did we? It didn't exactly keep us out,' stated Micah.

'I don't think it was meant for us, Micah. It is there to keep something out, I just don't know what or why and by whom. We are not the problem.'

Micah was mystified and quite taken by the whole conversation. 'This is like something that's just climbed out of an Xbox. Fascinating! So do tell me, Soul, what do you think the dome is protecting?'

Soul pointed outside the window towards Darwydden Castle Manor. He replied, 'That, Micah. The dome is encapsulating the building we are about to walk into. Interesting! If they have an empty bedroom going begging, I am sorely tempted to stay an extra day to try and figure out where the ley line hot spots are. You have no idea how rare these domes are. Something very important must reside inside this building and I am curious to know what it is. Anyway, it would be good to stay over an extra night. I guess I should play the part of the good son and catch up with my mother.'

Micah nearly choked on the water he was gulping. 'Hey man, you are a dark horse. You never mentioned that your mom was here to see your gig. Has she seen you on stage before?' It wasn't a conversation Soul really wanted to get into, but he knew his young companion well enough to recognise that Micah was like a dog with a bone. 'She isn't here for my gig, Micah; she works in Darwydden. She doesn't agree with what I do for a living, so we are not exactly what you would call close. She has watched me perform before, but she hasn't seen my new show. It will be interesting to see if she even turns up. She has quite strict morals and doesn't agree with me using magic for money. She says it is unethical and I say I am hungry. How about your parents?' Micah looked uncomfortable with the question. 'Similar answer to yours, mate; my mom doesn't watch me,' responded Micah. 'Sure, she stood there and watched as my stepdad kicked me so hard that he broke five of my ribs, dislocated my shoulder and shattered my left collar bone, but as for watching me play – she had no interest. I came to New York to curl up and die on the sidewalk. If it wasn't for Tony Mort, BK and Magnus, I would be pushing up daisies right now. I get on with my real dad just fine and he does come to the occasional concert, but not my mom – no, my security wouldn't allow her and her shitty husband anywhere near me. What about your father?'

Soul looked down as the turrets of the castle hotel loomed closer. He preferred not to talk about his father, but trapped next to Micah in mid-air, he couldn't exactly walk away from the lad's cross-examination. Soul answered with tired reluctance, 'My father died when I was a young boy. After that my mother got jobs all over the world – mostly looking after the super rich and their offspring. Hey, I am not complaining. Eve and I grew up in some amazing places. My mother has done well for herself, but as I mentioned before – we don't see eye to eye. She goes her way and I go mine. End!'

With the finality of that three-letter word, the helicopter touched down on the ground with a bump. As Micah prepared to disembark, he tried to yell over the sound of the still-spinning helicopter blades. 'Count me in if you are going on a paranormal adventure. I am really into this stuff and would love to join you. Don't forget me, will you, mate.' Soul beamed back in Micah's direction. He had a feeling that like it or not, he had just found a new little puppy dog who was going to follow him around wherever he went.

As the two men walked away from the landing zone, distant screams of adolescent female voices could be heard. Soul guessed that the reception committee wasn't exactly meant for him. Looking over to the handsome young musician walking alongside him, guitar thrown casually over his shoulder, he guessed that his companion was the likely source of adoration. He smiled to himself. It was a smile that hid a deeper concern – a strange puzzle. Exactly what was Darwydden concealing behind its stone fortress guise, and more so – who was shielding what, and for what reason?

CHAPTER 15

Morning of 4th June 2016

Ruby Kyfinn was very much the lady of the manor, but she was the queen bee who preferred to merge into the background of the hive. Hard work and perspiration had built up her home from a crumbling ruin, adjoining an even more crumbling Welsh castle, to the swish upmarket hotel which had since become one of the top wedding venues in Europe. Toiling over a thankless job in London, and missing the earlier years of her son Harry's life, had been an immeasurable sacrifice. Only now could she finally breathe a sigh of relief and relax whilst others scurried around doing her bidding. She now employed a small army of such workers, to make sure every task was completed.

She sat down at the large oak kitchen table, cupping a mug of coffee as though her life depended upon it. On occasion, she drifted into her own private world. People knew to leave her well alone when the 'little girl lost – faraway look' glazed over her eyes. Her twin sister Eenayah had officially joined the ranks of 'missing people' during the summer of 2013 and, to date, she had ever been found. It was a mystery that remained unsolved and one that continued to baffle the police.

Ruby tried not to dwell on the past, but sometimes the past would not lie down and die. How could she exile her memories? She sighed. No matter what success or material wealth she had since accumulated, Ruby had the deepest sadness that stuck in her throat like a fish bone. It was an ache that never went away. The last place she saw an image of her twin was when she was sitting at this very kitchen table. Was it her sister's spirit or some chemical synapse in her brain that created a cruel deception? She guessed she would never know the truth, but liked to believe it was a true manifestation. It was but one of many silent prayers: 'I wish I could see you again, Eenayah. I wish there was some sign you could send me to let me know you are at peace.' It was always the same prayer and it was always followed by silence. Such deafening silence, was a bitter sweet lull in her otherwise busy life.

The moment of stillness was not to last long. In the background, she could hear shrieks of hilarity as the younger staff members engaged in some frivolity along the hallway. The atmosphere in Darwydden was pure electricity today, and she knew that she needed to play the part and be the perfect hostess to her VIP guests, but – just for now – she wanted to hide in the kitchen.

A soft, warm hand made its way to the cusp of her neck, gently stroking it as one would a baby. Ruby turned around sharply. 'Roserie, what are you doing here?' Roserie smiled and responded, 'More to the point, what are you doing here? Don't you think you should be doing something productive to help everyone prepare for today's big event? It's mayhem out there in the hallway and now Darcy has made an appearance, I doubt any work will get done.' Ruby smiled. She knew exactly what Roserie meant by that last comment. Darcy was Owyn's larger than life, flamboyant sister. Ruby hadn't seen her since she left for New York a few years back. Darcy always had a fascinating story to tell and Ruby couldn't wait to play catch-up. However, Darcy was also a big distraction and if she stopped to listen to her sister-in-law's adventures now, she may as well give up on doing any work for the rest of the day. She decided upon a cunning plan, and would take the original servants 'back stairs' so to avoid her.

Ruby looked at her watch. 'It's only 10 a.m., Roserie. I have plenty of time yet. Have the entertainment arrived?' Roserie replied, 'They all came in last night. Did you not hear them? They were having quite a party outside at the BBQ. There has been a fair amount of cleaning up required this morning; the result of a few high jinks I would rather not mention. Still; Nico had a good time and that is all that matters. Did you not hear them? Where have you been, my dear girl?'

'Bed,' came the stark, monosyllabic reply.

Roserie was concerned. Without her make-up, the dark circles under Ruby's eyes were clearly visible. For one who slept so much, she looked visibly drained. 'Shame,' responded Roserie. 'I would have liked to introduce you to Soul and Micah. Later, maybe.'

As if by order, the morose mood within the scullery was soon broken by boyish laughter. Seven-year-old Harry leapt into the kitchen and dived under the table, as the 2-year-old twins followed in hot pursuit by way of an overly zealous version of hide and seek. With a hot pan bubbling away on the stove, Roserie was far from amused. She scolded the children in her loudest Spanish tones, 'Harry, you have plenty of places to play hide and seek in within this vast house, so must you hide in the kitchen where there are lots of dangerous things?! Take Angelo and Alessandro out to the garden and go play on the swings, and stay out of mischief, boys. We have many important guests staying with us today.' No child would ever dare disobey Roserie; as lovely and matriarchal as she may be. The children vacated the kitchen in as much of a whirlwind of vivacity as they had entered it.

Ruby couldn't help but snigger to herself. She so loved the troublesome boys. If anyone could lift her mood, it was the children of

Darwydden. 'Okay, well I guess that's my signal to finish my coffee and start work,' announced Ruby. 'Would you happen to know where Owyn is hiding?' Roserie simply pointed in a downwards direction. 'Where do you think your husband is? Where does he always hide?' Ruby wasn't totally sure why she had even bothered to ask.

The vast underground cavern beneath Darwydden had been converted into a hi-tech grotto by the brilliance and IT wizardry of her fanatical husband. He had created a holographic extravaganza which had even been reported upon in both technical and bridal publications … two totally separate magazines with diverse readerships and not normally ones to run the same story. Darwydden may not have been the largest wedding venue in the world, but it did have one of the most unusual settings, and with Owyn's ability to create a virtual world of make-believe, it was certainly one of the most visually and audibly astounding. Owyn tinkered with his precious lasers and computerised light shows, as a mechanic would tinker with a car engine. It was fair to conclude that Owyn was obsessed.

Ruby made her way down the medieval-crafted stone steps into the voluminous subterranean cavern that nature had conveniently placed beneath her home. The steps were illuminated in yellow and green coloured strobes. The hotel accommodated wedding parties most weekends and Ruby seldom had any involvement with the various bespoke themes. As such it had almost become a game for Ruby to best-guess the outlandish themes of each bride and groom. The flashing lime and lemon stairwell was proving a challenge. She had no idea what to expect after the last step.

Upon entering the cavern, all became obvious as Ruby spotted that the glass-covered lake had been converted into a tropical, sun-drenched beach, whilst gentle white and turquoise waves lashed upon an imaginary shore. As she walked onto the dance floor, she could even see tropical fish swimming beneath her feet. To her delight, a shoal of blue and yellow angel fish, seemed to follow her as she walked along the glass lake. Looking upwards, holographic Amazon parrots flew overhead, and 3D palm trees surrounded the stage area, appearing to sway gently to a cybernetic breeze. Each of the guest tables had been set up with thatch umbrellas to add to the authenticity, and floral displays of Poinciana and Hibiscus decorated the aisles. On the ceiling, the wispiest puffs of cloud actually drifted across an azure sky and a seemingly real sun truly exuded heat from its position overhead. Owyn had set the movement of the sun to mirror the actual time, so that tonight there would be the most stunning apricot sunset. This would be followed by deeply divine seductive dusk. Owyn had then encoded that the flickering stars of the Milky Way would adorn the ceiling. He had even allowed for a few holographic shooting stars to fly unnervingly close to the bridal table. The cavern's own natural waterfall had been garnished with jungle ferns, whilst a strategically placed fog machine transformed the far right of the cavern into a humid rainforest.

Ruby found her husband industriously working away on the mood-aroma … as yet quite undecided between a gentle sea spray or a cocktail mix of coconut, mango and pineapple. Ruby did a 360-degree turn to take in her surroundings. 'I do believe I am in Paradise. Is that the theme, Owyn? Have I guessed it correctly?' 'Nearly right, Ruby, but I need more specifics. I will give you a clue. What nationality is our celebrity bride to be?' Ruby smiled, fully understanding that Tia was Jamaican and that the national flags embellishing the room, along with Nico's Italian flags, made this multi-cultural union more than visually obvious.

Owyn smiled back at his wife. Something he rarely did these days. Ever since her twin had mysteriously vanished, Ruby had withdrawn from her marriage, preferring the isolation of her own thoughts to a conversation. Owyn hadn't put up a fight. He was happy spending most of his time down in the caves and entertaining himself with various gadgets. Over the years, they had slowly and steadily floated apart – like driftwood caught up in different undercurrents. It wasn't a problem. They both accepted things the way they were. Their domestic stability was tolerable.

Owyn typed something into the computer program and looked smugly satisfied. He declared to his indifferent wife, 'Done it. I will vary the aroma with the time of day, so when it's dusk I am going to effuse the room with some sandalwood and Brunfelsia Jamaicensis or "Jamaican Lady of the Night" as we would know it. Perfect!' Ruby stifled a yawn. Owyn could clearly see that she had little interest in something of which he felt immense pride. He was the ultimate wizard of ambience and he enjoyed the title, but to his wife it seemed that what he had achieved was much of a nothingness. Her reaction was a disappointment, but Owyn had grown used to Ruby's apathy.

'Oh Rubes, I almost forgot to mention. Tonight's magician has been wandering around the cavern. He wants a word with you. Maybe he wants to set up some wires for a levitation stunt?' Ruby was less than impressed by the sarcastic gibe. She had read all about Soul's rise from oblivion to fame and she was aware that not all of his tricks were cleverly disguised acts of deception. She felt there was something strangely real about the young performer. Owyn asked, 'Anyway, why has Nico booked a magician? Bit of a strange act for a wedding, don't you think?' Ruby responded curtly, 'Have you forgotten that Soul's sister Eve is friends with Nico, and so there are forces of nepotism at work here, dear husband. Besides that, having a magician mingle with wedding guests at their tables, to dazzle and amaze, is far from being a new trend. Maybe you should just stick with what you know best and go smell some more … flowers.' She walked off in a huff.

Owyn shook his head and continued to press more buttons and twiddle more nobs. Communication with his wife seemed to be like falling helplessly into the abyss. He made a mental note that from now on, he should avoid ironic exchanges with his better half. She didn't understand his world, and neither did she want to.

***

Soul was crouched down like a stalking cat. He was attempting to view the unusual craggy arena from ground level … possibly working out angles and areas of dappled shade. His disappearing act worked best in the shadows. On seeing Ruby approach, he stood to his feet with a warm and welcoming beam. He always researched important engagements prior to the gig, and so he had recognised Ruby's face from the hotel website. He wished he had the psychic skills of his sister Eve so he could work out the complexity of the human persona … especially of the female sex. However, his ability was constrained to all things minus a heartbeat and he accepted his own limitations. Nonetheless, the approaching woman was giving off a vibe and unusually for Soul, it was one he could sense.

She was an attractive woman and he presumed her to be in her early forties or maybe late thirties. It was hard to tell her age as she had obviously taken good care of herself and was immaculately dressed for so early in the day. Judging from the pace of her movement, she was keen to meet him. It seemed he had one fan at least. Yet, a dark cloud hung around her like a cloak. Soul didn't typically have the capability to see auras, but the one Ruby was wearing was so intense that even he couldn't fail to notice it. The word that came to his mind was 'stagnant'. Ruby was stuck in a moment of time – a place from the past of which she couldn't escape. Something dark, something sinister even – was weighing heavily on her shoulders. Unusually for Soul, he had an inexplicable perception that he was here to help her. Combined with the rare blue dome which shrouded Darwydden in a protective psychic light, Soul was convinced that something unusual lay within the walls of this sprawling, gothic mansion. Unintentionally touching the stony floor beneath him, a slight tingle of electricity shot through his hand. The random thought occurred to him – 'Not just within the walls, something also below the ground.' He moved his hand away sharply. He hated these uninvited moments of clairsentience. In truth, he despised what he considered to be a useless gift. Little did he know then, that his rare ability was going to spin his world around on its axis.

Ruby lowered herself to shake his hand. 'Good morning, I take it you are Soul. I am the hotel's proprietor and I am also a big fan of yours. I am so delighted to meet you. My name is …'

Soul cut her short. 'Of course, I know who you are. I am delighted to meet you, Ruby.' With that Soul performed a commonly used magic trick of making something appear using a sleight of hand. He had picked a red rose from the garden that morning, in anticipation it would come in useful at some point of the day. As he said the name 'Ruby', he would instantly present her with a red rose, which apparently would appear from out of nowhere. Shockingly, the trick did not go to plan.

Ruby gasped, as Soul held out an exquisite claret-coloured gem. It was shaped like a heart and for all intents and purposes, the trinket looked like a real ruby. Soul looked bemused. He had planted a rose in his pocket, so how could this now be a ruby? His face was contorted by bewilderment. He wasn't aware that he had gained a new ability to add to his portfolio of magic tricks.

Ruby assumed that this was all part of the act. She exclaimed, 'Wow, you are really good, Soul. The way you even look like you have surprised yourself is the icing on the cake. You are quite the actor. I can't wait to see you perform this evening. If I didn't know better, I would even think that this bit of glass was the real thing.' Soul gestured that she should hand it back to him. His face wore a serious expression. If anyone could detect if a stone was a real gemstone or not, then it was Soul. Material objects were his domain. He closed his eyes and focused on the energy that came from the blood red rock. The energy was strong and visual. It was showing him pictures.

He spoke as the images and thoughts flashed into his mind. 'This isn't a trinket. This is a real Burmese ruby. I believe it was mined from the Magok valley. It is well over four carats in size, so this is far from some cheap gemstone. It has considerable value.'

He hesitated, whilst Ruby looked on feeling quite confused … not totally sure if this was an extension to his magic act or some kind of personal psychic reading. He continued, 'This stone was never intended to be an item of jewellery. It sat enclosed within something, but I can't see what. It feels like cardboard, but that makes no sense. I will come back to that later as maybe it will become apparent if I focus on the owner.' He took more deep breaths and his eyes flickered as multiple images pelted his visual cortex like an optical machine gun.

'The person who purchased this stone was a woman, a very wealthy woman. She purchased it to give to a man as a birthday present. I think the man could have been her husband. It is hard to tell as she was quite detached from him. I have a feeling that she was trying to mend their relationship. I sense distance … great distance. I then see it being stolen. The thief has dirty fingernails and he is removing it from its surroundings with a rusty old knife. Give me a moment to think, Ruby. If I focus I may be able to see what the stone was set inside.'

Ruby was mesmerised. Her gut instinct told her that this was no stage act. Soul really was reading the red stone as though it was communicating to him. She was enthralled. After a few minutes, Soul continued. 'My God, it was in a book. That was the cardboard I saw earlier. The stone was placed in the front cover of a book and given as a gift … only … the woman never got to give the gift.'

As he said the words, he saw the hands that touched the book as it was handed to the person it had been intended for. His optic nerves were bombarded by the brightest, whitest, purest light – an intense luminosity that he had never before witnessed. At that moment, he knew. The book had been touched by an angel. The angel was familiar. He knew her. He hesitated to say the words. He recollected the stage show where he told the potential recipient of an engagement ring that someone in the past had died wearing it. From that former mortifying experience, Soul had learned the lesson that the truth was sometimes best undisclosed. There was no way he could share this with Ruby. Even he found this revelation too hard to believe. How could an angel be a courier? Far stranger than this, how could she be who he believed her to be? He knew it was best that he keep this information to himself.

He opened his eyes and handed the heart-shaped stone back to its new owner, cupping it tightly in her hand. He pronounced, 'I was supposed to hand you a rose that I already had tucked away in my pocket. I have no idea how this became a ruby. This is a degree of alchemy that even I am not capable of … I wish it was, but sadly I am not that talented. Darn it, I would be rich if I really could do this all the time. However, I do know that this ruby was intended for you as a gift and also as some sort of sign. It did not belong to the thief who stole it, and somehow … I know not how, it made its way into my pocket and from there into your hands. You may not believe me, Ruby, but take it to a jeweller and have it checked out. I think you will find that it is genuine. I am so sorry, but clairsentience exhausts me and I need to be fresh for tonight. Please don't think me rude, but I need to go and lie down now. Sleep recharges my batteries. Take care of your Ruby.'

Soul felt faint and the colour had drained from his face. As he went to walk away, one last thought came to mind. He turned back to face Ruby, who was stood motionless looking at the precious gemstone in her hand. He shouted back, 'One last thing. The man and the woman I spoke about; I believe that this was your sister and her husband. Maybe if you ask around you can find out if your sister gave her fella a book with a ruby set in its cover. Any which way – it belongs to you now. Some sort of peace offering or something to do with peace. See you later this afternoon. Sorry I must go.'

Ruby couldn't move. She didn't look up to watch the weary magician walk out of the cavern and neither did she notice her husband go skidding on the glass-covered lake. She simply stood and thought. Then she remembered; Eenayah was going to give Reed a book for his 50th birthday, but her twin went missing before she could execute her intentions. Did the book have a gemstone inserted into the cover? She wasn't sure, she couldn't remember. How did the book get to Reed if Eenayah wasn't there to give it to him? So many questions and no answers – there were never any answers.

CHAPTER 16

Afternoon of 4th June 2016

The wedding guests congregated in the main reception, sipping 'Darwydden Ghost' – an aromatic champagne cocktail made with pomegranate liqueur and amaretto, blended with coconut cream and topped off with a liberal splash of grenadine and a cheeky lime twist. Ruby seemed to be partaking more than most. Eve made the mistake of commenting on her rapid intake, noticeably looking at her watch (which stated 2 p.m.) and adding, 'Go for it, Ruby, after all it's 5 o'clock somewhere in the world.' This was met with a shocked response and a fiercely contemptuous look. Ouch – Eve deduced she had hit a raw nerve. She ruminated that either Ruby was an alcoholic in denial, or there was something in her comment that hit Ruby in the pit of her stomach. She deduced that her latter assumption was probably the more accurate. The elegant proprietor of Darwydden was holding onto some inner grief, and it had not escaped Eve's attention that there was a distance between Ruby and Owyn, both a physical distance and an emotional disconnection.

Eve had a tendency to notice people. Some would describe it as a sixth sense, but she would often shrug it off as simply being common sense. Her brother Soul was intensely jealous of his sister's talent, comparing his ability to chat to bricks as being a futile gift by comparison. He had a habit of belittling his own unusual ability.

Eve loved to people-watch, and the renovated castle gate reception, with its knights in armour and wall-mounted stag's head, was now playing host to some diverse human specimens.

The celebrities gathered together in close groups, totally snubbing anyone outside their glamorous inner circle. Eve noted that should an outsider attempt to join any of these elite groups, the stranger would be met by saccharin smiles and then the back of well-groomed heads.

Tia's Caribbean family were the loudest, happiest and most genial, totally unaffected by the snobbery of other notable guests.

However, it was the executive employees of Darwydden which confused Eve the most. They shared a secret. She couldn't detect what it was, but covert glances and concealed gestures signalled a common bond. She mentally whispered to herself, 'Interesting … wonder what you are all hiding.'

Ruby's best friend and the hotel's assistant manager Becky, broke the flow of her thoughts by striking a dinner gong which sent ringing vibrations through her bones. Not dissimilar to flocking sheep together, Becky then herded everyone into the great hall. This was a wooden-clad, rectangular room, embellished with antique oak beams. The petal-strewn aisle led to an altar area, above which overhanging Orange Blossoms dangled beguilingly from the minstrel's gallery. Decorated in gilt and illuminated by large white church candles, the gothic scene was worthy of the most noble of nobles … let alone a starlet of Tia's notability.

To the left, Tia's Jamaican family and other VIP friends filled each of the pews, by far outnumbering the handful of Nico's Italian kinfolk and former chef colleagues. Becky hovered around the rear of the hall, looking visibly edgy and tense. She had been allocated the task of wedding organiser – a job of which she was perfectly experienced. Still clutching onto a clipboard as though her life depended on it, she hushed each of their guests into their places … or rather sheep pens. Despite the fact that everything was so far going to plan, she had an uneasy frown etched upon her overly stressed face.

Becky was secretly unhappy about her brother-in-law's pairing. She considered Tia to be an exceptionally talented classical actress and a lovely lady, but the fact remained that she wasn't one of them. She wasn't a Ledanite. Nico's engagement had proven to be controversial, and his marriage would be life-changing. Becky felt sad about the whole situation. Nico would be moving away from his job and his home at Darwydden, as well as moving away from their clandestine little society. She didn't consider this to be any cause for celebration, but nonetheless she would play along with what she considered to be a charade. Becky was old-school. She didn't believe in marrying outside their beliefs, and noticing the obvious void in Owyn's marriage to Ruby, she felt justified in making this assumption. In her eyes, marriage should be based on trust, and how could trust exist when one person was hiding something from the other? However, along with all the others, she reluctantly accepted that her brother-in-law had a mind of his own. It was his decision and they would all need to adjust accordingly.

Tia glided down the aisle with unassuming elegance and style. Wearing a simple hand-embroidered medieval wedding gown, the cream linen complimented the brown tones of her flawless skin. Simple had never looked so exquisite, as the belted waist and long, floating sleeves accentuated the bride's slim outline. Eve couldn't help but smile as the bride wafted past to the tones of Elizabethan lute music. Wearing a braided twine of cream rosebuds in her hair, and holding a small bunch of flushed orchids, it was completely obvious to Eve that this was a bride confident in her own skin. For one so classically dazzling, a diamond-encrusted tiara and outlandish bejewelled gown would have distracted from her unpretentious beauty. Modest yet totally perfect, Tia was indeed a bride to behold. Her pure simplicity needed no embellishments.

Eve scanned the room to check on facial expressions. It was more than obvious that not everybody in Nico's circle had been delighted with this union. It was then that she spotted a strange haze around Ruby. Eve did not like to describe herself as a spiritual medium, as it was a profession she had personally rejected. Rightly or wrongly, she had associated her gift with Victorian séances and parlour tricks. However, occasionally her psychic senses gate-crashed the party uninvited. This was such an occasion. It seemed that Ruby was being haunted in more ways than one. The haze was that of a trapped soul. Eve sensed that although it wasn't evil, neither was its presence entirely good. It certainly wasn't good for Ruby, and seemed to be dragging her down to a deep, dark place.

Eve then looked around for her brother Soul. He was nowhere to be seen. Eve hadn't seen her brother's new act, but presumed him to be backstage preparing for his magical extravaganza. She couldn't wait to see what fresh tricks he had up his sleeve. She made a mental note to pull him to one side for a different sort of conversation later. Something very strange was manifest at Darwydden Castle Manor, and she longed to compare notes with him. She wondered if her sibling had also noticed something unusual about this place? She wouldn't need to wonder much longer.

∗∗∗

As the guests were ushered out of the Grand Hall and into the caverns below the house, Soul stood to attention at the top of the stone staircase. He was disguised as a waiter, and handed out refreshment to the passing masses. This was all part of his act, and the guests were unknowingly already participants in his game. Soul stood aside and gave them time to take in the extraordinary sight of a Caribbean island submerged next to the dungeons of an ancient Welsh castle. The cave resonated with an echo of multiple reactions, from gasps to shrieks and then rumbles of laughter. People were transfixed – looking around with gaping mouths and wide open eyes. Owyn stood in the background, getting some sort of fix from the reaction of the guests. This was his reward. It was why he did what he did. To him, this was art and he fed from those who became part of his moving, breathing canvas.

Although now a stage performer, Soul began his career as a table magician – casually wandering around his audience as they sat eating and drinking. He enjoyed the connection with the unwitting quarry, and still in his waiter's outfit (complete with moustache and curly dark wig), Soul the magician was about to perform. The unsuspecting diners would soon be victims of his enchantment and wizardry. It would be unexpected, and that was part of the fun – caught off guard and for a moment confused – until he revealed his true self in a spectacular light show conjured up by Owyn's pure genius.

The ten bridesmaids were all congregated together one below the top table. The waiter approached them, offering to fill up their glasses. He spoke in a dodgy Spanish accent, not unlike the fictional character of Manuel from the TV series *Fawlty Towers*. Florence grimaced as she saw the waiter move along the table with a large jug of water. Once the other bridesmaids realised that alcohol was absent from the serving tray, they appeared equally as disappointed. Begrudgingly they each took a sip of their H2O. Losing patience, Florence shouted out, 'Can we not have something a tad stronger, sir?' The waiter smiled mischievously. 'Take another look,' he responded. Each of the young women gasped as their eyes were diverted downwards to note that each of their glasses (now champagne flutes) were filled with bubbling 'Armand de Brignac-Ace of Spades', with the exception of Molly – who only drunk red wine – and indeed she had red wine, and not only that but in a burgundy glass perfectly crafted for the 1985 Chateau Poujeaux now awaiting her glossed lips. 'How the hell did he do that?' exclaimed Molly. 'These glasses weren't even on the table before!' The girls were puzzled. Tia's younger sister Meenah piped up, 'Have I just imagined something, or did that guy just turn water into wine?' The bridesmaids laughed nervously.

Leaving the young women still in awe, Soul then moved over to the arctic domain of the celebrity table. He approached the great thespian, Sir Bernard Benedictine. Handing him a pen and notepad, he asked, 'Excuse me for being so bold, sir, but would you do me the honour of autographing this for my niece Sophia?' 'Yes, of course,' responded Sir Bernard, ever so slightly ruffled by the waiter's cheeky, opportunistic request. The actor handed the signed notepad back to whom he assumed to be the waiter. Soul looked bemused. 'Thank you, but I am confused, Sir Bernard. You have written this in my handwriting and also used my signature. The actor grabbed the paper back off him and stared at it in disbelief. He made several more attempts to sign his own name and on each occasion neither the handwriting nor signature was his own.

By now, the entire table had become involved in this strange mystery. Each of the celebrities passed the notebook and pen amongst themselves, but nobody could make the pen write in their own handwriting. The TV presenter Maddox Burnham scrutinised the waiter with deep, analytical eyes. The magician was about to be rumbled. Finally, Maddox announced, 'I know that face. You are Soul, are you not?' Soul winked back in his direction. 'Guilty as charged, Maddox, but please don't tell the next table as I am about to make some of their jewellery disappear and reappear inside a melon and that guy's underwear.'

The celebrity bods all gestured a silent applause and sniggered like naughty school children. Maddox's girlfriend covered her mouth with her index finger as though she was now part of some special secret society. 'How did you do that?' she asked. Soul replied honestly, 'Some things I do are out of my kitbag of illusions, and some things I do are from my ability to interact with energy. Changing the energy of a pen so it only reflects my own handwriting is something I have been able to do since being a child. I will now take away my influence on the pen to make it neutral again. You can all try to write with it now – it should be fine.' With that he walked away, leaving the celebs to pass the pen around to test out his explanation. Their bemusement amused him. To Soul this was a simple trick, yet for some reason it always seemed to impress.

He continued to move around the tables with his card tricks and sorcery, until it became apparent that his identity had been exposed. The word was out and it was spreading. Moving as fast as a Mexican wave from table to table, the guests were whispering that the pretend waiter was in fact the renowned magician 'Soul'. With his cover blown, now was the time for Soul to make his grand entrance and then – his grander exit. He would perform at midnight at the outside arena, once Micah had finished his set. However, for the moment Soul and Owyn had conjured up an interesting light show deep beneath the bowels of the manor.

As Soul, still dressed as a waiter moved to centre stage, three other holographic images of him (also in waiter's attire) appeared from out of nowhere. One emerged from the cascading rainforest waterfall, another ascended from beneath the lake, like King Arthur rising up out of Lake Avalon, and the other simply pixelated in behind Soul's shadow. Closing his eyes tightly and dropping his head, Soul dramatically thrust his arms in the air whilst a light show of lasers played rhythmically upon his body. Colours and images danced to the sound of 'Isle of the Dead' by Sergei Rachmaninoff. Bolts of lightning appeared to escape from his fingertips, and his head was surrounded by a halo of fire. Without any apparent movement of his hands, his waiter's disguise seemed to evaporate. The three holographic images mirrored this action. Soul now wore a more recognisable outfit – his trademark long, dark coat, which emphasised the fairness of his long, flaxen ponytail. The costume change did not take place behind some dinky little sheet, but in full view of his mesmerised audience. Like some Teutonic warrior, he commanded the full attention of everyone in the cavern. All eyes were transfixed on this Viking-like god.

Then seeming to have the ability to part gravity as though it was the Red Sea, Soul appeared to push something aside and walk up invisible steps. Hovering in the air, a tunnel of fire soared from the stage. The guests gasped as they felt the scorching heat from the blaze warm their faces. The white rose that had just appeared in his hand was instantly burned to a cinder, yet Soul floated inside the middle of the fire unharmed. Slowly his image faded, the flame died down and nothing was left. Aside from the three holographic images linking arms down on the stage, Soul was gone. The audience were in shock. The silence in the room was deathly. Nobody knew what to do or say.

One by one the holographic images came forward – bowed to the wedding guests and then vanished. Then the final image came forward and to everybody's surprise, it turned out to be flesh and blood. Soul took a bow and then announced, 'Thank you for participating in my little games. I trust that you have all located your jewellery and all handwriting has now returned to normal. The music show starts outside at 6 p.m. with DJ Izy Starker who has just flown in from Ibiza, so for those of you who want to dance the night away – enjoy. Micah and his band will be on stage at 8 p.m., and I am going to be doing something dangerously insane from the top of the castle battlements at midnight. In the meantime, I would like to welcome the comedian Eddie Bayn to the stage, who will entertain you for the next 40 minutes. Of course, I cannot leave without a toast, so can we all raise a glass to the beautiful bride and her fortunate groom – "Tia and Nico". Actually, why waste valuable energy. Everybody please stand, leave your drinks on the table and simply hold out your drinking hand.' With that, all the glasses in the room miraculously lifted from their various tables and made their way into the guests' hands. Pure, fantastical magic which defied all explanation and several laws of physics.

Cloud of smoke – massive blast – waiter's uniform left crumpled on the floor. As exits go – it was impressive.

After the comedian had completed his session, many of the guests made their way to the outside arena. Saskia was part of the tipsy throng trying to bag a good position near the stage. However, before doing so, she managed to catch up with Eve. Still slightly out of breath, she tugged on her arm. 'Eve, just wanted to say wow. Your bro stole the show tonight. I believe a lot of influential showbiz types were very impressed. I don't think Soul will be short of bookings anytime soon. How the heck did he do all of that? Was some of it natural magic? People can't stop talking about it.' Eve shrugged. 'It puzzles me as well, Saskia. That was the first time I have seen his new act. I do know that Owyn made a huge contribution. If Soul has his head screwed on properly, he should consider hiring Owyn. They would make a fantastic partnership. The visuals really made it.'

Eve was anxious to locate her husband Gérard amongst the crowd, so started to walk away. Many new guests had arrived for the evening celebration and a throng of bodies were beginning to collect around the outside beer tents and rostrum. Saskia wasn't giving up on the chase. She pulled Eve back, tugging at her arm. 'Eve, I need to hire Soul again. Now he is some famous hotshot he may not want to do some local clairsentience jobbie, but we really need him. Nobody else can do what he can do. He will be well rewarded. Can you have a word with him, please? It is very important.'

Eve wasn't overly impressed with the way Saskia had treated her brother back in Tignes, and neither did she care for the way Saskia had grabbed her arm so brusquely. 'Ask him yourself, Saskia. For some strange reason, he has a soft spot for you, so he will probably oblige. A pretty face and he turns to blancmange – typical man. You don't need me to do the asking for you. Anyway, I thought you had already approached him about your little project, back in Tignes. That was a while back now. What happened? Did he not want to work with you again?'

Saskia sensed the acidic sarcasm in Eve's tone. 'Please don't judge me harshly, Eve. My little project, as you call it – was delayed. I am aware that he could have done with the money back then, but hey I am not the magician here. I couldn't just wave a wand and put the timelines back on track. Complications and all that. As for the personal stuff, I am sorry, Eve. I know you tried to hook us up, but the timing was all wrong. My job means a lot to me. Keeping business and pleasure separate is mandatory in my world. I wish I could tell you more, but I can't. Please believe me when I say that I had no choice. Soul is a good-looking guy and a nice person. I mean, what is not to like? But … back in France there was someone else on the scene anyway.'

Saskia glanced in the direction of the bride and groom as they took to the floor. Eve noted a momentary look of sadness in her eyes, before she composed herself and turned away. Suddenly the truth hit Eve. She shook her head and gasped, 'I can't believe it. Sometimes I am so busy trying to see what is hard to see, that I miss the easy stuff when it's right in front of my eyes. You and Nico … of course. Oh dear oh dear, and wasn't he also seeing Tia at the same time? Didn't he start dating her either just before or just after we went skiing in France? Well, Saskia, you excel in complicated, that's for sure. So, let me get this right – a guy liked you, but you liked someone else, who liked someone else. I am sorry – this one flew over my head. I was distracted; I had problems of my own at the time. I am so sorry sweetie – I was wrong to judge.'

Saskia lowered her head and tried hard to hold back the tears she had so far been unable to release. The DJ played the song by the group Passenger, '*Let Her Go*'. Several cosy couples became overly smoochy and intimate. Something in the lyrics made the moment intense. They seemed to mean something to Saskia, and looking over to Ruby, who stood watching quietly on the side-lines, Eve could see that the words were hitting her in the heart as well. It was all too much.

Eve looked down at Saskia's stomach and instantly understood. 'Oh … you poor girl, I am so sorry. There was a baby, wasn't there?' Saskia simply nodded – she couldn't speak. Eve asked, 'Do you need my brother to go back to that weird Crank place? He hated it there. This is a big ask.' 'Yes please, Eve, we need him.' Eve gave Saskia a motherly cuddle. It felt like maternal hot chocolate and was a level of nurturing and comfort unfamiliar to Saskia. Eve held her shoulders so that Saskia faced her full on and looked her directly into her eyes. 'Leave it to me. I am sure my brother will help you. In the meantime, wipe away that sad face. This is a party. Go find Florence and let your hair down … and when is this music going to start rocking? It's all too sombre and twee. I need to have a chat with the DJ.' Saskia nodded in agreement, uncomfortable with this rare show of vulnerability.

As if on cue, Micah and his band stormed on stage playing the Fall Out Boy track '*Centuries*'. With the tempo raised, the volume on high and the mood lifted, Eve patted Saskia's shoulders and hushed her away. 'Go find Florence and the other girls. Forget about Nico – his marriage won't last anyway. Oh dear, I wasn't supposed to say that, but let's just say that Nico and fidelity are not on the same page. He isn't worth your tears, girl.'

Eve watched as Saskia ambled away in no particular hurry. She was aware that Saskia had inherited some Eastern European grit and was a true survivor. She would recover. Still, she was sorry that Saskia had not got it together with Soul. She believed they would make a cute-looking couple. In the meantime, she noted that Owyn's sister Darcy was literally intertwined around her brother's torso, and Soul didn't seem to be raising too many objections. 'Ah well,' considered Eve. 'Not my job to interfere. The night will take people where they want to go, but daylight will wake them up and shine a torch into the faces of those who would rather forget.'

CHAPTER 17

Morning of 5th June 2016

The day after the night before, and whilst most guests were sleeping off hangovers, there were those sober few up with the larks. Dr Gérard Bouvier was a fitness freak and was not about to miss an opportunity to jog through some exquisite scenery on a bright summer morning. With the amazing mountainous backdrop of the Snowdonia National Park, Gérard was in his own personal zone. Forever wondering what lay beyond the next corner, Gérard expected to have the heather-coated hills to himself. It was therefore quite a shock to find a young woman sat on a rock in the middle of nowhere. As he looked into her dark eyes, his blood ran cold. He turned on his heels as fast as he could and darted back to the relative safety of the hotel. His heart pounded and the sweat poured from his brow. He kept running – not slowing down and not looking back.

By-passing his usual requirement to shower, he headed directly for the breakfast room and an emergency caffeine fix. He knocked back two coffees and struggled to regain his breath; his mystified wife noted the odd behaviour. Eve was concerned. 'Gérard – what on earth is the matter? Have the paparazzi been chasing you? You look like you have seen a ghost.' Gulping back a glass of water, Gérard finally responded, 'I think I have.' Initially Eve thought he was joking, but then noting his pale complexion and the seriousness of his expression, she realised he was being completely sincere. 'That girl, that girl,' was about as much as he could stutter. 'What girl, Gérard? What are you talking about?' He finally caught his breath. Although super fit, he had sprinted back to the hotel at a speed which his body wasn't used to. Eventually his breathing returned to normal and he felt able to talk. 'That dead girl. The one who was shot. The one that lost me my job. That girl – I have just seen her.' Eve finally understood. 'But Gérard – that was over four years ago, and on another continent. How could you remember what she looked like?' Gérard was adamant. 'She hasn't changed much, Eve. I would recognise her anywhere. I opened her chest up. I pumped her heart with my own hand. You don't forget things like that. It was her, Eve – the same girl. I swear.' Eve knew her husband well enough to know he was telling the truth. He was in genuine shock. Other diners were beginning to stare. Eve took her husband by the arm. 'You need to lie down, honey. Let's go back upstairs. This is a very strange place. We need to get away from here soon. I also feel uneasy. I have been seeing things as well.'

As she helped her husband to her feet, Ruby walked in to refresh the coffee pot. She looked over to Eve. It was a long, helpless stare. She wanted to talk. Eve understood the signal. It was a call for help, but right now Gérard was her priority. That incident four years ago, almost gave Gérard a nervous breakdown. They had swapped continents after the various investigations and legal processes had been concluded. It severely affected all the staff who had been involved in the case. How could a dead woman simply come back to life? More so, why would that same woman now be sat alone on a Welsh hill thousands of miles away? It made no sense, but Eve knew her husband was telling the truth. As lovely as it was, Darwydden Castle Manor was a peculiar place. They needed to pack!

***

Micah was keen to join Soul on his paranormal detective mission – so much so that he had set his alarm clock for 8 a.m. and was knocking on Soul's door before the young magician had yet dressed. Entering the room and catching some female feet exposed at the bottom of the duvet, he winked at Soul and gave him a laddish nudge in the ribs. 'Hey mate, you have company. Are you sure you want to do this now? I mean … if it was me.' Soul looked back at the scarlet-painted toenails emerging from his bed. 'If I am worth it, she will wait. If not, she won't. Life is quite simple … that's before we screw it up with complications. Anyway – we need to do this before folks start to wake. Once the energy from lots of "warm bloods" blends with the ley lines, it blurs everything. I can talk to the countryside better when it is quiet enough to listen. Anyway, don't tell me you left an empty bed behind? Young, good-looking rock star like you – surely not?' Micah shrugged and didn't reply. Indeed, he had left an empty bed, but wasn't prepared to admit as much. It was a male ego thing. His persona was that of the rock and roll lifestyle, but in private – Magnus kept him in check and had warned him about the drugs, booze and groupies. Micah had started out in life on the wrong tracks, but he sure as hell didn't want to end it that way. He was a reformed man, not that he would ever share this info with Soul. To the rest of the world, he lived the persona. But in private …

It was a divine June morning. The dew was still sticking to the blades of grass and a blanket of early morning mist draped the valley in a white miasma. 'Where are we going to?' asked Micah, as they walked briskly towards the church. Soul cast him a glance as though to say 'stupid question'. 'I told you about it on the way over, Micah. Churches are often found on ley lines, so this is the best place to start. Now all I need to do is locate the other three hot spots.'

Standing outside the chapel, Soul pointed directly ahead. 'Well, the second marker is easy enough to locate. See that hill over there with the folly on top – it's the tallest point within a mile and I reckon there is a direct line of energy between the steeple and that folly.' Micah stared as though if he tried hard enough, he would also be able to view the invisible energy line. He was slightly disappointed that nothing dramatic appeared to be happening.

Soul knelt down, touched the floor and closed his eyes. 'There are tunnels under the ground here. I think they were escape routes from centuries ago – probably used by frightened Catholic priests. One leads to Darwydden, one to the village and one to that hill. I honestly can't feel any more than three. Shit … people have been killed down there, and here's a surprise – these tunnels are still being used. That figures.' Micah was entranced. 'How the heck do you know all of this?' he asked. Soul responded, 'It's like looking at an X-ray film and seeing a ribcage. Man-made structures disrupt the natural energy of the Earth and look as different to me as bones and flesh do to a radiologist. Hey … I come in real handy when there's a blocked drain.' Soul laughed at his own joke.

'So how do you know the tunnels are still used?' Memories of Micah 'the ever-questioning child' back on the helicopter journey came flooding back to Soul. 'Do you not remember what I told you about the analogy of a river?' replied Soul. 'Stagnant water is still. It looks and acts nothing like the moving water being carried along in a fast current. When something moves, it moves the energy around it. And that, my dear American friend, is how I know these tunnels are still being used. It makes sense and it is sort of what I expected. Somebody must be activating this dome, and I don't mean just one person. Many people at all the different markers need to focus at the same time to keep this energy bending the way it does. I am guessing some of them must walk inside these tunnels. Generating a dome of this magnitude can be no easy task, but I believe I have weakened it, so I must be a threat.' Micah was intrigued. His new best friend literally had him spellbound. 'You are a threat … really? How have you weakened it? I don't understand.'

Soul rose to his feet, his knees creaking as he stood. 'I know when I use the word "power" it makes me sound like bloody Merlin; however, I can't find a better word to use. My power has increased tenfold since I have been here. Honestly, mate – I have never done that glass-raising thing before. I didn't even know it was possible and I can promise you – there were no wires. That was pure, supernatural anti-gravity. I have felt strangely energised since I have been here, so I suspect that I may have been draining the dome … unintentionally, of course.' 'Is that a problem?' enquired Micah. 'Well yes, it's a problem to the folks that have gone to a lot of trouble to create it. There is something in Darwydden that many people want to safeguard, and they won't be too happy about me plugging into their power socket.'

'Where next?' asked Micah. 'The village,' replied Soul. 'One of the tunnels leads up there and I suspect the third marker comes from a house in the village. It would be interesting to know who lives there. We need to look for a house with lightning rods. Before you ask – lightning often tries to earth itself along a ley lie. 'What about the fourth one?' asked Micah. Soul looked around the vista, turning full circle. 'No idea,' replied Soul. 'Maybe somewhere underground along a subterrarium river.' 'Don't tell me,' responded Micah, 'rivers run along ley lines.'

Soul joked, 'You learn fast, little glass-hopper. Indeed, all natural features can attract energy lines. Well done.'

As they were about to head for the village, a small, black Scottish Terrier dog came running around the corner, almost crashing into Soul's ankles. Micah loved dogs and crouched down to catch him. 'Hey little man, where are your parents? What are you doing running around off your leash?' He stroked him tenderly and the small dog responded by licking his chin zealously. In the near distance, he could hear a female voice shouting, 'Dantalion, Dantalion – come back. Where are you? You naughty little dog.'

A young woman with striking strawberry hair came running from the direction of the cemetery. Spotting her dog, a look of complete relief washed over her face. 'Oh Dant, you bad boy,' she exclaimed. Micah handed the Terrier back to his owner. 'This little boy is yours, I take it?' The young woman smiled beguilingly. 'Indeed, he is. Thank you for catching him. I need to get him some puppy training.' Soul sensed the beginnings of flirtation emerging between Micah and the young woman. He wasn't normally attuned to human emotions and he blamed the dome's energy for gifting him with an unusual degree of perception. Seeing as they both grinned at each other like cats who had just found the cream, it wasn't a difficult signal to miss. The young woman held out a tiny porcelain-like hand, and had the appearance of a delicate china doll. 'Well, thank you anyway. My name is Océane.' 'What a beautiful name' commented the hormone-infused young man. 'Lovely to meet you, Océane. I am Micah.'

Soul inwardly groaned. He sensed that their ley line detective mission may be nearing an abrupt end. Leaving the young couple to make small chat, he carried on with the job in hand. He drew lines on the local map which he had brought with him from the hotel and played around with the compass app on his phone. As Soul moved further towards the church vestibule, he threw a stick for the mischievous young puppy. Dantalion went to retrieve it, but then stopped short at the chalk line Soul had marked on the floor earlier. Océane seemed to be so engaged with exchanging phone numbers with Micah, that she hadn't noted the odd behaviour of her dog. Soul was intrigued. He threw the stick several times in several places and on each occasion the pup chased after it – unless it meant crossing the chalk line. Soul crouched down to stroke the dog, who then growled at him with a sinister glint in its orange eyes. A cold shiver went up the back of his spine.

Another woman then came running through the main gates of the church. She looked fairly angry and was shouting Océane's name. On seeing Micah and Soul, she shot them a disapproving look. By this time, Soul was on the phone to his sister Eve, who was telling him about Gérard's earlier experience whilst out running. Soul moved out of earshot, but carefully observed the interaction between his young friend and the two women. He spoke in hushed tones.

'What happened exactly?'

'Can he be sure it was the same woman?'

'What did she look like?'

'Can he remember what she was wearing?'

'What was her name? I mean, if he had to write the death certificate he must be able to remember her name.'

'Okay – so are you guys about to leave now?'

'Fine, I will try to catch up with you next week if I can.'

'Oh, before you go, can you get reception to order me a ride home to London? I am good to go just after lunch? Say about 2 p.m.'

'Great. Thanks for that. Best get Gérard back home and I will talk to you later. Bye – see ya.'

Soul moved back over to the group, smiling casually as he approached them. He said, 'Morning ladies. We were just about to walk over to the village and grab a coffee. Would you care to join us?' He gestured towards a small gate at the end of the path as being the general direction to the village. Both women seemed keen, but then the older one hesitated and pulled her younger companion back. The dark-haired woman mumbled, in a southern American drawl, 'Err, thanks for the offer but we have to get back now. Enjoy your coffee. See you later maybe.' Soul went to shake her hand and replied, 'Yes that would be nice, Arabella. Micah has your numbers so who knows, maybe we will.'

The older woman had a stunned look upon her face. Micah chased after Soul as he walked hastily away and towards the smaller exit at the edge of the cemetery. 'Soul, slow down. How the heck did you know that woman's name? Gee, your powers really are on fire right now. Why are you walking so bloody fast? Slow down man, I am recovering from a heavy night.'

Soul eventually stopped dead in his tracks and looked back to check that the women had left. He replied, 'Sorry, mate, just wanted to put some distance between myself and those bloody demons. They knew we were here. They must be good – darn good.' Micah was stunned. 'Bit severe, pal. They both looked a bit on the cute side to me.' Soul put a fatherly arm around Micah's shoulder as an older brother would to a younger sibling. He pointed back towards the entrance to the church vestibule. 'See those chalk lines, my friend? They are where the ley line, and therefore the dome, starts and ends. I was a tad suspicious when the little dog couldn't cross the line to retrieve the stick – especially as it was named after a demon. I tested out my theory by inviting them for a coffee; however, coffee in the village would mean them walking over the ley line. I wasn't surprised that they declined the offer.' The look on Micah's face was one of pure astonishment. 'But what about knowing Arabella's name?' he asked. Soul didn't want to go into too much detail, but Micah deserved some sort of an answer. 'My brother-in-law used to be a trauma surgeon in the States. He once got pulled up in front of a medical tribunal because he wrote a death certificate for a woman who was later found to be alive. He has had a bit of a shock this morning, as he swears blind that he bumped into the former corpse when he was out for a run. The dark-haired woman matched his description, so let's say that I just made an educated guess.'

'Shit – If that's the case, what are they doing here?' shrieked Micah. Soul shrugged his shoulders. 'I have no idea, but I think the dome has probably been created to keep them and their kind out of Darwydden. He pointed up to the gargoyles mounted high upon the church walls. 'The lovely ladies you have just met may appear gorgeous on the outside, but on the inside, they could look like one of these mythical monstrosities, so don't let your eyes fool you, young man. I am checking out of here soon, so let's go grab some coffee in the village and get the hell away from this place. It's freaking me out, and trust me – I don't scare easily.'

With that, they walked away, leaving the chalk marks and their recent encounters far behind them … certainly for the time being.

CHAPTER 18

13th December 2016

Don Morris and Frank O'Byrne sat in one of the many cafés of Strasbourg's side streets, sipping café noisette with Pineau des Charentes. Having presumed they would never meet again, the death of a mutual friend had delivered them both in the Alsace-Lorraine region of France, alongside tourists frequenting the Christmas markets. Don glimpsed at his watch with a heavy heart and said, 'Time to go, Frank.' When they last met, they had almost expected it to be a final encounter, but fate had a different plan.

The taxi drove them through the old town, where a giant and splendidly decorated Christmas tree, from the Vosges Mountains, shimmered in the town square. Curiosity diverted their eyes outside the taxi windows, to the tall, half-timbered medieval houses. Glistening with snow, Strasbourg was the perfect caricature of a Christmas card. However, Don and Frank were visiting the region for a far more sombre reason. Stress levels rocketed as a car accident outside the train station, on the Boulevard de Metz, created an unwelcome diversion. They were now running late. To run late for one's own funeral was a notion that randomly came to mind, aside from the fact that this was the interment of a long-lost friend. More heavy sighs followed that sombre trail of thought.

The taxi dropped them off outside a partially open 8ft-high metal gate. They found themselves in a cemetery that would not be out of place in a horror movie filmset. The headstones were mostly concealed under a blanket of snow, and the cemetery was shrouded in sinister, low-hanging fog. The pathway had been cleared of snow and an austere-looking undertaker, with a leather-clothed hand, waited at the gates to lead the funeral party towards the church. With no words exchanged, a simple gloved point in the right direction was adequate communication. In this instance, the latecomers were directed towards the site of the grave itself.

Crunching through other people's footsteps, the gents grumbled amongst themselves. 'Bloody embarrassing,' muttered Frank. 'Shut up, at least we're here,' responded Don. 'We should have set off sooner,' retorted Frank. This was met with a sneer and an impromptu snowball from Don. 'That wasn't a fitting action … childish idiot,' protested Frank – who as a former priest had more respectful veneration for their immediate setting.

Fine sleet was falling from the heavy grey clouds, and so the gents were faced with a sea of black umbrellas. They discreetly moved alongside the other attendees, hoping that their late arrival would go unnoticed. The priest was giving his final blessing. 'Anima ejus, et ánimæ ómnium fidélium defunctórum, per misericórdiam Dei requiéscant in pace.' Those closest to the open grave threw soil upon the casket and some of the women threw flowers.

Don leant down to place a small white Gypsophila wreath with white Calla Lilies next to the mound of heaped earth. A simple card stated, 'Bless you, Professor Roland De Vede, a great friend and teacher. Forever missed, respectfully from Dr Frank O'Byrne and Mr Don Morris. RIP dearest Roland.' They stood motionless for a moment, perhaps lost in their own personal memories of former days. The last funeral that Don had attended was that of his wife Patsy, and as old emotions came crowding back, he was anxious to leave as soon as was appropriate.

As they turned to go, one of the drivers gestured that they should get into his car. Prior to that, they spotted a woman pointing them out before embarking into her own limo. They couldn't quite see who she was, as her face was covered with a black lace mantilla mourning veil. However, they did notice the 6-inch Jimmy Choo stilettos as her legs swung into the back of her limousine. They only knew of one woman who would persist in wearing killer high heels in the midst of an icy winter surface, "Mercy De Vede" – the professor's daughter. Don muttered, 'That surely can't be Mercy. She is dead, isn't she?' Frank responded, 'Well there were rumours to the contrary. Who would blame her if she did invent her own disappearance. Events at the time were quite disturbing. I mean, someone did try to kill her. I may be tempted to fake my own death if someone was after my guts for garters.'

Frank and Don walked nervously towards the awaiting car, silently pleased that they didn't have to hang around for a taxi. It was 4 p.m. in the afternoon and the light was fading as the sun prepared to greet the southern hemisphere. The arrival of dusk lowered the temperature by several degrees. As the light in the cemetery dimmed, the low-lying fog nipped ominously around their ankles. Meanwhile, some of the older crypts looked ready to fall apart and spill out their contents. The gents were happy to swiftly vacate the scene and join the funeral cortege.

The journey in the unexpected, yet much welcome, limo took place in respectful silence until they reached the Kammerzell House restaurant. On arrival, they were ushered downstairs towards the vaulted cellar, known as the 'Léo Schnug Roome'. Frank was familiar with the venue, having done some research on the city prior to their journey. He poked Don's ribs. 'Hey Don, get this place. I do believe that this room was named in honour of an Alsatian artist – Léo Schnug – who painted the allegorical frescoes around 1904.' Don pretended to be impressed at his friend's cultural awareness but made no comment. Maison Kammerzell, with its distinctive décor, was probably the most charming of Strasbourg's winstubs and the perfect location for Roland De Vede's funeral reception.

A small crowd gathered in the cellar room, sipping Muscat á Petits Grains and nibbling on hors d'oeuvres such as amuse-bouche, garlic snail appetisers, intermezzo and a varied selection of sausage-based entrees. Neither Don nor Frank knew any of the other mourners, and as the others communicated in French or German, the two gents linguistically kept themselves to themselves.

Within 15 minutes or so, a waiter approached them. He seemed to be well-versed in their mother tongue and addressed them in fluent English, 'Monsieur O'Byrne and Monsieur Morris, could you please accompany me upstairs to the vaulted alcove. Professor De Vede's daughter would like a private audience with you.' Don and Frank followed the waiter, at the same time signalling to each other in a sort of impromptu sign language. They each understood that the professor only had one daughter and that was Mercy. There had been some rumours that she was still alive, yet until now this had been little more than speculation. Mercy was a durable character and many had considered her immortal, and so her alleged death had shocked many at the time.

As they entered the intimate frescoed room, a woman stood with her back turned towards them. Her flame-coloured hair was piled up into a severe bun and she wore a black mesh-splicing A-line dress. From behind, she looked ever so slightly "Dior retro" and yet she was immaculate. Her long-heeled shoes bore the trademark of the person they suspected she must be. She turned around and her bright red lipstick smile looked genuinely pleased to see them. 'Mercy De Vede – oh my, so it is true – you are alive,' – the words just fell from Frank's mouth. Don was speechless!

Mercy looked at the gents with genuine fondness and, in an uncommon gesture, went to hug them both. 'Thank you for coming to my father's funeral,' she uttered. 'When I didn't see you in the church, I feared that you hadn't been able to make it. I take it that the invitations took you by surprise?' Don remained speechless, so Frank spoke on his behalf. 'Mercy, I can't believe it is you standing here. We were so shocked when we heard about your death, and I believe that I speak for Don when I say we are both delighted you are alive and well. We are confused, but very pleased. We are also dreadfully sorry about your father. We would have come to visit him, but when you allegedly died, he seemed to vanish off the face of the Earth. What happened?'

Mercy gestured towards the seating area in the alcove. 'Don … Frank; please sit down. I have been standing in a freezing cemetery for what seems like an eternity and I am in need of this Cognac.' Mercy downed her shot in one. Her face looked deeply sad and she had puffy dark circles under her eyes. As Don studied her face by the light of a candle, he could see that the woman, who was once alight with raw energy, now looked tired and drained. Only dying embers lingered from a once blazing fire.

She began, 'Gentlemen, my father had the greatest respect for both of you. You just being here means so much to me. I guess you would like some sort of explanation?' Both nodded back in unison, so Mercy continued. 'You know how much my father adored me, so when someone attempted to kill me with a morphine overdose, it more or less destroyed him. For several days, I was in intensive care and it was touch and go. My life was literally hanging by a thread and it could have gone either way. It put my father under a lot of stress, and during that time he had a stroke. I recovered and he recovered, but he was never quite the same again. The police felt it was for the best that I remove myself from the Baratolli case, both for my safety and my father's well-being. You know, I am a tough old bird – ex-police detective and all that. If it was just about me I would have stayed. I am not one to run away from anything. However, my father couldn't cope. So, I brought him back to his birthplace – Strasbourg. Many of his family still live here and I needed their support. After the stroke, he lost the use of his right arm and he struggled to eat. It affected his memory, he could hardly walk and obviously, he became depressed. He was such an extremely intelligent man, so to be locked within a body and a mind that couldn't function, was so frustrating for him. Little wonder that he lost the will to live.' A sob made its way from her painted lips. She continued, 'It has been a long and difficult journey.' Mercy held her head down low. Her pain was obvious.

Don finally managed to speak. 'We are so sorry, Mercy. You did the right thing in coming here, but we just wish we could have met him again before he passed away … just for one last time.' Frank gave Don a subtle kick, deeming it inappropriate to make the professor's bereaved daughter feel guilt-ridden.

Mercy stood up and wiped her eyes with a lace handkerchief. Mercy would never lower her elevated standards to use disposable tissues. She took a deep breath. 'Anyway, he had a pulmonary embolism – a blood clot in his lungs. He passed quickly. He was mostly bed-bound at the end, so it was for the best. He wouldn't have wanted you to remember him as an invalid. Nothing can hurt him anymore. He loved you both as friends. I am sorry you didn't have the chance to say farewell.'

Don and Frank could only repeat the message that they were both so sorry. Mercy composed herself. 'Now is not the place and time for a serious conversation. I need to get back downstairs to join the other mourners. I have quite a few relatives I need to socialise with. Without their help over the last few years, life would have been intolerable. I do need to speak with you both at some point, however. I am still in daily contact with Simon and I have been keeping tabs on you – not in a snoopy way … more out of concern. You both have associations that worry me and we need to have an earnest conversation about them. I don't want either of you to put your lives in danger and there are forces out there – human and otherwise, which may bring you harm. Trust me, the last few years have opened my eyes.'

With that final, enigmatic sentence, Mercy left the room, leaving Don and Frank equally puzzled and curiously gobsmacked. By way of an afterthought, she popped her head around the corner of the door. 'I will meet you at your hotel tomorrow – breakfast at 9 a.m. – order me a pot of tea with brown toast and orange marmalade. No worries, I know where you are staying.' Mercy seemed to be back in control …

***

At precisely 8.58 a.m., Mercy De Vede marched into the reception of the Au Cerf d'Or hotel. She was wearing a tight, navy-blue pencil skirt, matching pillow-box hat, a figure-hugging white jacket and of course Mercy would not be Mercy without 6-inch stilettos in white, gleaming polish … without a scuff mark to be seen. As per command, her steaming hot tea and brown toast awaited.

Struggling to sit in her unyielding attire, Don and Frank couldn't help but notice that any trace of yesterday's puffy eyes and dark circles had been eradicated by clever use of make-up. If Mercy was grief-stricken, then for the moment she was hiding it. Business-like and without the need for small talk, she leant forward and launched into the conversation.

'Gentlemen, thank you for seeing me and also thank you for coming to my father's funeral. I wanted to talk with you in private and away from last night's gathering. As I mentioned yesterday, I fear you may have become ensnared in something most peculiar.' Frank responded, 'Peculiar – that's a strange word to use, Mercy. What do you mean?'

'When I was in intensive care and drifting in and out of consciousness, I had a most unnerving experience. A woman approached me. She looked to be in her mid to late thirties and had long, platinum blonde hair. She was unusual looking, quite stunning – but there was something strange about her. She made me feel uneasy. She was wearing a long, red dress with a matching cloak. It was totally inappropriate attire for a clinical setting. She just stood next to my bed, looking down at me with a fixed stare. Maybe she was smiling, but to me it seemed more like a sneer. I looked around to see if anybody else had noticed her, but I honestly think that they couldn't even see her. She stroked my forehead, but it wasn't a comforting caress. It was as though she was demonstrating that I was weak and she was in control. It was as though she owned me and it sent a cold shiver down my spine.

Then she spoke. She told me that on this occasion she had allowed me to live, but that I was to take what had happened to me as a warning. She said that I had meddled too much and become involved in something that was none of my concern. She then said that I was to leave England and should walk away from everything and everyone I had ever known. To ensure that I would obey her, she told me that she would give my father a stroke. She said he would recover from this; however, if I didn't do as she said, he would die within a matter of weeks. Then, in front of my eyes, she faded away. I thought it was some sort of hallucination, possibly brought on by the morphine overdose. However, shortly after this, I got the news that my father had indeed suffered a stroke. This was almost three and a half years ago, my dear friends. I nearly died. My father almost died. I do believe that the woman I saw was some sort of evil spirit. She certainly wasn't on the side of the good guys, not that I knew who the good guys were. It was a crazy, mixed up time in my life.'

Mercy's composed façade started to melt for a moment, as suppressed emotions began to surface. She continued, 'I only wanted to protect my client. Eenayah Baratolli was a lovely lady, but sad, lost and mixed up inside her head and her heart. However, she was also part of some weird ancient prophecy and it seemed as though two opposing armies were out to get her. One was some strange religious group who called themselves the Ledanite. I am aware that you knew about them. However, the other … well … I think the other side were demonic –

similar to the woman in red. Apologies Frank, as I know you are an ex-priest, but I have lived my life as an atheist and of course have never believed in the paranormal … until that day in the hospital. I can't even believe I am saying this now, but I suspect there was a malevolent force involved in Eenayah Baratolli's disappearance. So, dear friends … possibly for the first time in my life, I did exactly as I was told and here I am, in my father's home town of Strasbourg, many miles from the spires of Oxford.'

Mercy stopped to take a sip of tea and measure the reaction of her audience. Frank looked down and moved breadcrumbs around on his plate, seeming to be deep in thought. He finally responded, 'I am so sorry, Mercy. I didn't know the full story. We were all told you had died and then MeDeVe Ltd shut shop and then Roland disappeared off the face of the Earth. We all presumed he was grief-stricken. You were his world, so nobody questioned his disappearance. I do believe you. I think there has been a war between angels, demons and some sort of secret society. I do believe Eenayah was caught up in the middle of all this. Yes, I did just say that out loud and yes – it sounds ridiculous and no sane person would believe it – but I have reason to deem that there is an unearthly tale beneath the story.'

Mercy looked at Dr Frank O'Byrne with deeply critical eyes. She could read body language as well as some may read a newspaper, and she knew he was holding something back. 'Frank, when you feel able, please share with me what else you know. Perhaps what I have told you has scared you into silence, but I need closure on the Baratolli case and I hope one day you can tell me what really happened to my client.'

Don sat in stunned silence. This had to be the politest confrontation
he had ever witnessed and it was being played out in front of him. Mercy
continued, 'Frank, I understand that you are involved in some charity
work for the homeless?' 'Yes, VOTS – View of the Stars. It's a global
charity franchise. Is there something wrong with charity work?' 'No,
nothing at all, Frank. It is a very credible and successful charity. I think
it's admirable the way the charity doesn't just put a roof over someone's
head, but awards them medical attention, psychological support, helps
them recover from various additions and puts them back into
employment. I have read all about VOTS and it seems like a clever
concept. Neat idea getting sponsors to provide many products and
services free of charge as a tax exemption, plus great free publicity for
them to boot. Whoever thought up this concept is certainly vert smart.'

'Kirk Anderson and Tony Mort are the brains behind it, and yes, they
are smart guys. Where is this leading?' asked Frank. 'Dearest Frank, I
used to believe in coincidences until I became involved with the Baratolli
and MacDonald cases. Okay, so I admit that there is such a situation as
luck, both bad and good. If I was to hand you a hat full of numbers and
you were to pull out the lottery numbers, I would think this was a one-off
chance of good fortune – a happy coincidence. However, if you were to
pull out the winning numbers again and again, every week – I would
suspect you of being a cheat. A sequence of apparent coincidences makes
me nervous, Frank. Some things are simply not logical or natural.'

Frank was confused and grew inpatient. 'I don't understand what you
are trying to say, Mercy.' Mercy delicately chewed away on her toast to
give herself thinking time. How could she phrase this appropriately?

'Tony Mort, hmm, nice guy. His full name is Anthony Reed Baratolli Mort, just in case you didn't know. Reed Mort was Eenayah's bad-boy husband. It is odd that you spent time with my father investigating pre-history connected to the woman who was your boss's wife.' Both Don and Frank looked visibly shocked. Frank spoke first. 'I didn't know Tony's full identity, Mercy, but even if I did, I would still have worked with him. He may have been a bad boy once, but he is a reformed character now. Anyway, I am an ex-priest working for a homeless charity. Where is the shock in that? It is no big deal – it is just a co—' Frank stopped himself from completing the word. Don jumped into the conversation. 'Mercy, I know your feelings as regards Reed. Don't forget that I was around when all of this crap was going on, but like Frank, I am confused as to why you think any of this connects with us.' Mercy had more cards hidden up her sleeve.

She replied, 'I have been keeping a close eye on things, gentlemen. I happen to know that Darcy Kyfinn also works for VOTS in a business development role. She has done well for herself. Started out in the soup kitchens and worked her way up. Not bad for a Welsh girl with zero qualifications. I wonder who helped her up the ladder. Did you know that she is the sister of Owyn Kyfinn, who is married to Ruby, the lady who was Eenayah's twin sister? Darcy is part of that crazy Ledanite cult that targeted me and my father. Sounds like a bit of a family business to me.' Frank became tetchy. 'I didn't know that Reed and Darcy were related by some former marriage connection. It is a bit of a … oh I am going to say the word anyway – coincidence – but I don't really think it matters that much.'

Mercy continued, 'I almost forgot to mention Reed's little musical prodigy – Micah Laski. He has done very well in the music charts of late. I believe he was even playing at a wedding in Darwydden over the summer. All very cosy and nepotistic.'

Frank responded tersely. 'You are reading too much into this, Mercy. Micah was a homeless person himself once … an abused kid from Connecticut who ran away from home to die on a frozen New York pavement. He was rescued by Kirk and Tony … or Reed if you want to call him that. He is a talented young man and Reed gave him a chance. He would have probably got the booking at Darwydden anyway as he is a popular artist, but even if Darcy did get him the wedding gig – does any of that matter? It was his luck.' Mercy simply shrugged and replied, 'Too many numbers being pulled out of the hat, Frank. All I am saying is please be careful. I know you are a good guy and my father loved you, but you are still closely linked with a family who are connected to something strange and mysterious. Nothing is a coincidence and they may want to keep you close to use you at a future date. Just be vigilant, that is all I am saying.' Don had mostly listened in stony silence, but knew that it was soon to be his turn. He couldn't think how he would even be vaguely connected with the Baratolli saga, post his employment at the former MeDeVe Ltd. He was just an ex-BBC researcher. What crime could he possibly be accused of? Mercy arrogantly clicked her fingers to order more tea, and then proceeded with the second half of her deliberation.

She began, 'When I quit my job as a detective in the Met to set up my own investigation bureau, everybody thought I was taking a huge risk with my career. Thankfully, my father supported my decision, so I did it anyway. It was a struggle to begin with, as I didn't actually have any clients and yet had salaries to pay. The agency was on its knees and I almost quit. Then … by coincidence, this young woman answered one of my ads in the classified section of a local London paper. She thought her boyfriend was being unfaithful and asked us to investigate him. We did, and he was. She then thought her next boyfriend was stealing money from her and she asked us to keep an eye on him. We did, and he was. Then along came the next boyfriend, who she suspected had a hidden wife and family in Australia. She wanted us to keep tabs on him. Guess what?' Don answered the question. 'Yes, we get the drift – you did and he was. However, what has any of this to do with me, Mercy?'

Mercy continued, 'Be patient, Don, as all will become clear. The lady I am referring to became a good friend of mine. Because of this lady and her endorsement of MeDeVe to her many wealthy friends, my company grew and thrived. I am referring to Katya Beselovaya. You will know this name, Don.'

Don shook his head with incredulity at his own forgetfulness. 'Yes, of course, Mercy; Katya was your friend. 19th July 2013, I even remember the exact date. I was in the office when I heard Kerry and Simon talking about the headline in the newspaper – "Katya Beselovaya found dead in boyfriend's Atlanta apartment" or something along those lines. If I remember correctly, you asked Katya to do you a favour and make a call to Reed Baratolli. The tabloids interpreted this call to be one of blackmail. Reed was the last person Katya spoke with before she was found dead, and one of the last conversations she had with Reed was to threaten him. The police knew this because you had asked her to record her conversation with him. I recall Reed being arrested on suspicion of murder and his record label hitting the floor soon afterwards. I even recall you being suspected of master-minding the whole plot. However, 19th July also stands out in my mind because that was the same day you drove your car into a ditch and broke your collarbone. Just two days later, you were given an overdose of morphine by an unidentified nurse. I believe you were on your way back to Oxford and the injection was supposed to ease your journey home, but of course you were unconscious before you could get there. The police were waiting to interview you, and the press assumed that somebody didn't want you to talk. The next thing we heard was that you had died, presumably murdered by the mysterious nurse. Yes, Mercy, I remember it well. It was a messy time. But it was also confusing because then everything suddenly went quiet. MeDeVe Ltd was dissolved, we were all made redundant, the offices were closed down, your father vanished and you also evaporated without so much as a funeral. The press speculated for a while and it was headline news for a few days, then everybody sort of forgot. I never forgot, Mercy. It was an awful moment in time. I lost my job. I lost my boss. I lost a dear old friend. Not long before that I had lost my wife. How could I forget?'

Frank noticed than Don was visibly shaking and he felt sorry for his companion. Amongst all the hive of activity and accusations that were flying around during the summer of 2013, it was easy not to notice lesser victims – but they were victims nonetheless. Don downed some Espresso, and then shook even more. He continued, 'I know what you are going to say next, Mercy. I was employed by Saskia Usov, who I later found out was Katya's half-sister. I would say that this was a mere coincidence, but you will tell me there is no such thing. She needed a researcher and I am a researcher. Saskia even acted as a reference so I could get a job with MeDeVe and you would have checked her details for sure. So you knew who she was, Mercy. Indeed, I also had links with your friend Katya, even though I never met her in person. So what? We live in a small world.'

Mercy had sat patiently and listened to Don, but now needed to throw in some dynamic punches. She began, 'When I heard that my dear friend Katya had died, it almost destroyed me. This woman not only rescued my company, she was also my friend. I asked her to make that call to Reed by way of a personal favour, but I should never have involved her and I deeply regret the day I picked up the phone to her. Hindsight, people say it is a wonderful thing. I think it's more like salt being rubbed in an open wound. Somebody wanted her dead, and it is possible that her association with the Baratolli case could have been the reason. Once I had recovered from my own dance with death and was here in Strasbourg, I kept in touch with the police and followed the investigations with great interest. I wanted to know who killed my friend – and it was murder. Katya didn't take Heroin and everyone who knew her well, would be aware that she had a phobia of needles. There was no way that she would inject herself with that drug, especially using her right hand when she was left handed. I guess the killer hadn't done his research.'

Frank interjected, 'You just said the killer was a male. Do the police know who did it?' Mercy replied, 'The CCTV picked out a tall man entering her apartment about 20 minutes before the estimated time of death. His face was covered by the shadow of a baseball hat; however, Katya buzzed him in and – according to the guy on the security desk – he exchanged words with her on the intercom, speaking in Russian. The police believe she must have known him, but then again Katya knew a lot of dodgy people. I loved Katya, but she did live life on the edge.'

Frank repeated the question, 'So, do the police know who murdered Katya?'

Mercy considered her answer carefully and answered evasively. 'It soon became clear that this was a contract killing. There are only so many people in the world who are known contract killers; it is a small, elite group. All the police really needed to do was find a Russian man who was in Atlanta at the same time as Katya's death, and of course border controls in the United States are fairly diligent.'

'Well,' asked Frank, bursting with curiosity.

'Well,' responded Mercy. 'They did locate a guy who entered the States on the premise that he was attending a software trade fair at the Georgia World Congress Center. The guy never turned up – he didn't even register. The man involved – who I cannot name for obvious reasons, was actually an ex-soldier from the KJB era. He worked for the federal security services back in the '80s. He was registered as unemployed back in his home city of Moscow, and so there would be no reason for him to attend a software trade show. It raised a red flag. When the FBI tracked his movements, the finger seemed to point in his direction. His flight to Atlanta was booked in England, yet he flew in from Nice. He was hardly in Atlanta any time at all, before he caught a flight over to Miami. As this is where Reed Baratolli lives, of course this tied in with Reed being the main suspect. Maybe he hired the killer? It was a reasonable suspicion.'

Yet again Frank pushed for more details. 'All this was over three years ago, Mercy, so there must be some end conclusion to this story.

Reed is a free man now, be it that he is mostly known as Tony Mort. So I presume that there was no evidence to tie Reed in with Katya's murder?'

'Correct,' responded Mercy. 'It was even felt that this man's trip to Miami could have been a pre-calculated attempt to frame Reed. Nobody knows for sure. However, the guy did make a mistake. He hung around in the States for a while, hopping over to Los Angeles, San Francisco and even taking a bit of a vacation in Hawaii. That was an error on his part. If he had done the deed and got the hell out of the USA as soon as, he may have averted arrest. However, by the time he was checking out to go home, he was already on the FBI's radar. He was detained at Honolulu International Airport wearing what was probably the most expensive cufflinks in the world. The guy was unemployed back in Moscow and the immediate suspicion was that the cufflinks were either stolen or payment for the killing.'

'What then?' asked Frank. 'Then, dear Frank, it became very complicated. The diamonds on the cufflinks were very rare red diamonds. Natural red diamonds are so exceptional that few jewellers will have ever seen them throughout their careers. Fitting them into cufflinks was a very clever guise. To the untrained eye, they could have easily been mistaken as lesser-valued rubies and easily sneaked through customs.' 'So how was Reed's name cleared?' asked Don. 'There was nothing whatsoever to tie Reed to Katya's death other than a recording of an unpleasant little phone conversation, plus financially Reed was in ruins. His accountant had stolen his money and, given his new economic demise, it made no sense for him to give away something so valuable. But what is even stranger, is that the diamonds were never registered. For something so rare to be unregistered is unthinkable. Not only that, they were never for sale, never purchased and therefore never stolen. They almost didn't exist, at least not officially. There could be only one conclusion, and that was that the diamonds had come straight from out of the mine and given to the man in question.'

'What of the man in question?' asked Frank. Mercy replied, 'He was arrested for other crimes, but they could not connect him to Katya's death and so sadly nobody has ever been convicted of that particular crime. What is even more appalling is that because the diamonds have no official owner, once our Russian friend gets out of prison he can claim them back. He is sat behind bars on a fortune and nobody can do a thing about it.'

Don heaved a mighty sigh. 'That is a hell of a story, Mercy, but how does any of this relate to me? You mentioned yesterday that I had associations which may bring me harm.' 'Indeed I did, Mr Morris … indeed I did. Tell me, have you ever heard of a group known as the Ouroboros?' Don went pale and perceptibly gulped. 'Yes, I have, but then you probably already know that, Mercy. Saskia is employed as a solicitor for such a group, and for a while I was also an employee.'

Mercy allowed herself a partial smile. 'Yes, I am aware that you know that I know. The Ouroboros are a secretive little association. I have a friend who is a city investment banker in London and I believe that they are widely known as "the moles". They have a bizarre business methodology, in that they seem obsessed with anything under the surface. They buy castles with dungeons, old houses with underground tunnels, coastal areas with caves and, oh … they own mines. Lots of mines. I am told they are the biggest global investors in emerald, gold and diamond mines. Not only that, they own a mine in South Africa which can source rare red diamonds. In fact, it is now known that the diamonds in the cufflinks came from the Ouroboros mine.' Don was confused. 'What are you suggesting, Mercy?' 'I am giving you a "heads up", Don. Your friend Saskia has been under police observation. You see, it turns out that she was in Nice on the exact same date and time the Russian man was there. He flew out just after she flew in. Plus, she works for the organisation who owns the mine these diamonds were quarried from.' Don was shocked. 'Saskia loved her sister. Katya was the only person in her disjointed family that she did love. She would never have taken part in her own sister's murder.'

Mercy was sympathetic to Don's plea as she could clearly see he was fond of his young friend. 'I am not saying she was knowingly involved, Don, but I am saying she could have been an unwitting mule in the payment to the contract killer. If the Ouroboros had a reason to want Katya dead, it could be that they are also involved in this odd mystery that I refer to as the Baratolli case. Not only that, but I understand that Saskia attended the same wedding in Darwydden Castle Manor, the wedding that Micah and Darcy attended … the very place owned by Eenayah's sister Ruby.'

At that point, Mercy looked down at her Cartier watch and stood up to leave. She felt mentally exhausted and traumatised by recent events. She added, 'At the beginning of this conversation I mentioned that I may well smell a rat if too many lottery-winning numbers were drawn out of the same hat again and again. I now smell that rat. There are far too many coincidences that bring you both into the same small circle of improbability. You need to be careful. You know what happened to me and to my father – not to mention Eenayah and Katya. There are killers out there and I don't think they are like you and me – as in mortal.'

Both gents got up to bid her farewell. 'Where will you go from here?' asked Frank. 'My father's estate was worth a fair amount of money and I am the biggest beneficiary. I have no need to work again, but Strasbourg holds too many painful memories for me. I will not stay here. I don't know where I will go next, but I doubt it will be England … or Wales for that matter. One car accident too many, you could say.' A sad look was etched on Don's face as he asked, 'How can we get hold of you if we need you?' Mercy handed both the gents her business card with the instruction, 'Put my number in your phone under the name of an alias and then destroy these cards. I do not wish to be found by anyone other than you two and my immediate family. Keep an eye on the time. You need to be at the airport in an hour and the roads are busy. Take care – it has been sad yet lovely to be reunited with dear old friends of my father.'

Mercy gave both men a hurried hug as she turned to leave. 'Remember what I said – too many winning numbers from the same hat cannot be a coincidence.' She left …

Frank turned to Don and said, 'Wow – information overload – what do you make of that?' 'I am not sure,' responded Don. 'I don't intend to tell Saskia about her possibly being a mule. I don't think she would tolerate that painful thought. It would kill her. We should do as Mercy says and just be vigilant. Do you think we will ever see her again?' 'I doubt it,' responded Frank. 'Somehow I think that was a final goodbye. Then again – it is Mercy, so never say never.'

CHAPTER 19

14th December 2016

Her fingers felt numb and cold to the touch. The ravages of Vincristine had left its vicious mark on her peripheral nerves, and the constant flow of chemicals had traumatised delicate veins. She curled herself up in a foetal ball as cramp gnawed at her stomach and terrible images shot through her mind. Eve shivered as hot beads of perspiration chilled her skin and a fever toyed with her temperature. However hard she tried, she could not avert the visions that played out in front of her eyes. Images, nightmares, hallucinations – it mattered not. It was like watching a film. It all seemed so real and close enough to touch.

Soiled ancient hands grabbed at delicate, clean ankles. She could see a woman, either unconscious or in a deep sleep. She had been hauled out of her bed covers and was still in her nightdress, being dragged along a creaking wooden floor. Eve could clearly hear the pulling noise, as the sleeping body rubbed against the oak surface. She could both hear and smell the heavy breathing of the accoster. Looking up, she could see the spectral face of the owner of the grubby hands. A woman was dressed in an ankle-length linen skirt. It was deep red, the colour of old blood. She wore a dark shawl, wrapped tightly around an old-fashioned tunic. A cream kerchief covered her head, and a long, dark plat cascaded from beneath the headdress. She wore a neckless of amber. The woman was dressed in the clothing of someone who had stepped out from another era – a time long gone, by maybe a thousand years or more.

In the background was the faintest vision of yet another woman. She was dressed completely in white and stood motionless – yet like an eerie mist. This other vision appeared to float a few inches from the floor. Her eyes looked sad, lost and pathetically tragic. She watched impassively as the ancient woman continued to drag the sleeping woman across the bedroom floor. It was a surreal glimpse into something paranormal. Three women – one in spirit form, one sleeping and another hauling a body along a floor. It was a disturbing sight. What could it mean?

Eve was restless. She tossed and turned as her mind tried to vanquish the nightmare scenario. Suddenly, in her mind's eye, the sleeping woman opened her eyes and screamed. It was an ear-piercing cry from the soul. The noise echoed around Eve's head with a menacing reverberation. Eve's eyes danced between each of the three women. They were one and the same. The same exotic Eastern look – the same chocolate-brown eyes – the same mocha-tinted hair … and yet they were different. Eve recognised the woman on the floor. She now knew exactly who this was. She shot bolt upright from her damp, sweat-drenched bed, heart pounding like a bass drum.

In the distance, she could hear the passing rumbling of a train in the night. To Eve this was normally a comforting noise. It assured her that there was a world outside the window, busy and industrious as she lay in her bed. But now, alone in her room and drenched in perspiration, she felt anything but comforted.

Where was her brother? This had not been a nightmare. This was a vision. What she had seen had just happened and it was real. She needed to contact Soul – now!

***

Soul was still in a state of delayed jetlag following Monday's flight from New York; yet despite his exhaustion, something in his sister's voice made him jump in his car and head up north. He was shocked to see the frail shadow of a woman who greeted him at the door. Not normally a demonstrative type, he rushed to embrace her. 'Eve, what is the matter? You look awful. Where is Gérard?' Eve's voice was faint and weary as she replied, 'Oh, Soul – thank God you are here. I gave Gérard some time off. Poor guy was at the end of his tether, so he has gone skiing with his parents in Tignes. He has been through so much with me and my stupid illness, and I just felt he deserved some time out. He will be back on Christmas Eve. Hope he brings me something nice back from France.' She tried to smile, but what appeared on her face was more of a strained melancholic grimace. Soul hugged his sister once again. He was more than aware that with the chemotherapy and radiotherapy, both her mind and body had suffered multiple blows. He squeezed her tightly.

Eve had always been so fit and healthy. Soul considered his sibling to be nothing less than a complete health freak. Perhaps losing their father so young had jolted them both into a life of organic eating, exercise and a desire for all things herbal and pure. So, when Eve also discovered a lump in her left breast … the diagnosis felt cruel and unfair.

As Soul walked through the mosaic-tiled hallway of Eve's Victorian home, he noticed a small suitcase waiting by the door. 'Are you going somewhere, Eve?' 'We both are,' came the reply. 'I had a vision last night, Soul, and please don't tell me it was the painkillers playing with my mind. I am a psychic – I know the difference between hallucination and reality.' Soul was stunned. He hadn't known what to expect as he put down the phone and headed for Eve's marital abode. He assumed that her health had taken a turn for the worse, and so the revelation of a random, clairvoyant experience came as a huge surprise.

He sat, or rather tumbled – into an antique rocking chair positioned beneath a stained-glass picture window. 'What kind of vision? What did you see?' Eve sat on her suitcase and held her face in her hands. Her expression was deadly serious. 'It was Ruby Kyfinn. Some entity … a woman in old clothing, had pulled her out of her bed and was dragging her along the floor. While this was happening, they were being watched. I recognised the spirit watching her. Her features were similar to Ruby's. I believe it was the manifestation of her twin sister Eenayah Baratolli. I then saw the face of the woman holding on to Ruby's ankles. She had the same face as Ruby and her twin, only dirtier and older. I don't know who she is, Soul. She was the same as the twins, yet different – maybe from another century. It made no sense. I do know I was being sent a message. Someone, something, is trying to get Ruby's attention, as well as getting my attention. I can only presume that Ruby is in some sort of danger. We need to go to Darwydden and we need to go now – and I mean NOW.'

Soul wasn't sure how to respond. His neurons were turning cartwheels. Eve had an innate spiritual ability. It was something she had been born with and something which frightened her. Throughout her life, she had wrapped herself in protective bubble-wrap and closed her mind from psychic events. However, every now and then, the clairvoyance would sneak in unsolicited and make its presence known. Last night was obviously such an occasion, and knowing his sister as he knew her, he had no doubt that her supposition was correct. 'Have you spoken with mother about all of this?' 'She has enough on her plate,' replied Eve, 'it would be nice to see her again, but I don't want her to know anything about these visions. You know how she frets. Let's just keep her out of this, please.'

Soul had previously decided never to visit Darwydden again, despite his connections with the place. He knew that something within its walls abhorred him, because without intent, he drained the power from its protective force field. It had been a mutual detachment – he from it and it from him. Now he was being forced back over its medieval drawbridge. 'Are you sure, Eve? You don't look well. I am concerned about you.' Eve pulled herself up from her suitcase and then pointed down at it. 'Can you be a love and pick this up for me? I have already called the hotel and made arrangements for us to stay. They were fairly full with it being Christmas, but they managed to find two rooms in the private family quarters. I informed them we were friends of Ruby's, and that did the trick. I didn't want to involve our mother. It may compromise things if the hotel staff know we are related. Anyway, best make a start before it starts to snow.' Eve opened her front door and cast her eyes upwards. 'Those clouds look awfully heavy to me.' Soul looked down at the suitcase, and – resigned to his fate – lifted it from the hallway. He had little choice in the matter. 'Fine – if you are sure. Let's point the car in the direction of North Wales then.'

***

The narrow country lane meandered its way through a dark pine forest. It was covered in a sheet of white and the roadside was lined by heavily snow-laden trees. As the wheels spun uncontrollably on the freezing surface, Soul was relieved to be driving a 4x4. Hidden potholes threw them around the car and at one point Eve had to get out to empty her stomach contents. As Soul heard his poor sister retch, he considered the wisdom of travelling out to such a remote place in such inclement weather. Her body wasn't well enough to take this punishment, yet she had insisted.

As the sun fell behind the mountain range, the light suddenly dimmed and the temperature plummeted. Soul tried not to show it, but he was concerned. The lane was tapering and the loose, gritty surface barely kissed the sides of the valley walls. The drop along the sides of the road appeared to be steep and unforgiving. Soul tried not to look down and focused his attention on the road ahead. Manoeuvring the vehicle over the slippery surface of an ancient bridge – only held in place by a stone buttress – Soul silently prayed they were close to their journey's end.

The turrets of Darwydden were soon visible above the treeline, and it was with a huge sigh of relief that they neared their destination. The snow had started to fall again and, whipped up by a wind that blew down from the mountains, the scene was akin to a blizzard. The geography of the valley agitated the snowflakes into a milky tornado, which served only to terrorise them further.

The long driveway leading up to the moat and drawbridge had been adorned with glimmering Christmas lights, giving a welcoming glow which was much appreciated by the weary travellers. Fighting the snowstorm with an inadequate umbrella, Soul guided his fragile sister into the hotel reception area. The comforting smell of charcoal and the warmth of a blazing fire embraced them with a congenial greeting. The cheerful receptionist offered them a choice of Brandy or Sherry. In need of a quick pick-me-up, Eve availed herself of one of each. The siblings sat in silence by the fire whilst their luggage was taken to their rooms, and Ruby made her way over to greet them.

Within minutes, their hostess had arrived. She looked delighted to see them both, although visibly shocked by Eve's appearance. It did not escape Soul's attention that Ruby wore a substantial bruise on the side of her temple. He began to consider the possibility that his sister's vision may have actually been a glimpse into something which had actually happened. Could Ruby have really been dragged out of her own bed by some latter-day doppelgänger? No doubt they would find out soon.

Ruby guided them down a long, marble hallway, walking by an oversized mirror that would not let anyone escape the often cruel reflection enforced upon the passer-by. For a moment, Soul stopped to touch the mirror. In his mind's eye, he could see Ruby's twin looking at her figure with a critical gaze. He felt a shiver run down his spine, as he was left with the unnerving feeling that it was the last time Eenayah may have ever gazed upon her own reflection. He was overcome by a sensation of uncertainty – the never knowing of 'the last times'.

Entering the private family quarters in the east wing, Ruby directed them towards the large farmhouse-style kitchen. She seemed pleased to have the company of her impromptu guest. 'I have baked a Nut Roast and Shepherd's Pie. I presumed you would be hungry after your journey, but I didn't know if either of you were vegetarian, so you have a choice. How were the roads?' Eve pulled out a large, rustic chair and positioned herself at the shabby chic table, attentively laid out for three people. A steaming hot pot of tea, a loaf of 'just basked' crusty bread and two cast-iron casserole dishes were awaiting the visitors. Roserie had known they were coming and, concerned about Eve's condition, had made sure the cook had prepared something. The array of home cooking was indeed much-welcomed sustenance.

Outside, the snowstorm had ceased and, as Eve was facing the window, she could see the white caps of the aptly named Snowdonia Mountains in the distance. A full moon had broken free from its cloudy cover and blessed the mountain peaks with its lunar shimmer. The valley sparkled as though carpeted with a billion diamonds. For a moment, Eve was completely entranced by the beauty of her surroundings. Then, suddenly remembering Ruby's question, she responded, 'Oh … erm … sorry, Ruby. The journey here, yes, that was okay … until we hit North Wales and were met with a torrent of this white, fluffy stuff. The Horseshoe Pass was a bit gruesome. We thought they were going to close the road – in fact, I think we were one of the last cars they let through before they sealed it off.' Ruby joined them at the table and, pouring the tea, added, 'I heard on the radio that the police have just shut the A543 over the Denbigh Moors, so indeed you are lucky to make it through. I am so glad you are here, though. Confused and somewhat puzzled by your visit, but nonetheless glad. I had wanted to talk with you both since Nico's wedding. Anyway … why are you here, exactly? Have you come to visit your mother?'

Soul had so far remained silent as he found small talk somewhat irritating. As such, he was pleased that Ruby had cut to the chase and asked a direct question. He responded on Eve's behalf. 'Nothing to do with family business on this occasion. Mystic Meg here had some weird dream about you last night. She believes it was not so much of a dream than a vision. She saw you being dragged along the floor by the ankles and she swears it wasn't just a nightmare. Tell me, Ruby, exactly how did you get that bruise on your face?' Ruby looked startled at the unexpected inquisition. She responded, 'I fell out of bed. I do that sometimes when I get restless. It was a stupid thing to do. Woke up in the middle of the night on the floor. Must have given my head a right old crack. I fall out of bed quite a lot these days and these old beds are quite high off the ground. On some occasions I have been in such a deep sleep that I have even spent the night on the floor. Not a great experience, I can tell you. I don't usually end up with all these bruises, however. Thank you both for your concern, but I really am fine.' Eve joined in with the conversation, gently probing, 'So where was Owyn? Why doesn't your husband pick you up when you have these err … falls?'

Ruby looked embarrassed and gave a cutting reply. 'If you must know, we don't sleep in the same room, Eve. He snores and we have a big house with lots of rooms. I don't have to put up with snoring when I have options.' Eve wasn't convinced by the reply. She had noticed the void between the couple at Nico's wedding. She suspected that Ruby's relationship had hit upon difficult times. However, she took the hint that Ruby's marital situation was none of her business.

Soul stood up and walked over to the kitchen window. He needed to give himself thinking time. Ruby was obviously on the defensive and yet he sensed she needed their help, but was maybe too afraid to ask. As he looked over to the hillside, something caught his attention. 'What is that glow up yonder?' Ruby walked over to the window to look for herself. She replied, 'You are in the heart of Druid country here, Soul. The cycles of the moon have a ritualistic significance for folk around these parts. They light fires on the hills on a full moon, and you can hear them chanting on a new moon. It freaked me out when I first came to live here, but you get used to it after a while. Welcome to weirdsville.'

Eve was overcome by curiosity, so walked over to the window to see for herself. Indeed, the whiteness of the hillside reflected an orange aurora.

Ruby continued, 'You may have noticed a large Malachite statue of a woman in the hotel's reception area. She is standing behind a solid-silver wheel with two little boys playing at her feet.' Of course they had noticed it. The figurine was facing them as they sat down by the fire, and they had both commented on its rare beauty. Ruby continued, 'She is Arianrhod – the lunar Welsh goddess. I am not an expert on ancient religions, but Owyn once told me that she was associated with the Milky Way and was mother to twin boys – Dylan and Lugh. Her name means silver wheel or disc. I have often joked that if she did exist at all, she was probably an alien from some far constellation. I have since learned not to joke about her. The villagers all have statues of Arianrhod in their homes for protection and they take all of this mythology quite seriously. Some refer to her as the goddess of reincarnation, because it is said that the dead are carried on her oar wheel to Emania – which either means the moon or land of the dead, or maybe it means both. Who the hell knows? I am not a native pagan. Anyway, she is the deity of reincarnation and karma and that's about as much as I can tell you. Owyn is the real expert as regards Celtic history, as indeed is his sister Darcy. You should ask them about the local mythology. Either of them could wax lyrically about the subject for hours on end. I guess that being a twin myself, I always found the whole opposing twin theory quite interesting. Dylan represented the dark and Lugh the light, all very yin and yang. Anyway, as weird as it sounds, I suspect they are lighting those fires for Arianrhod. You should have been here on 2nd December – it was like

4th July up in the mountains. Fireworks and all that jazz. I know that all of this must sound very colloquial and pagan, but the old way is still the way of life around here. Darwydden is caught in a time capsule. I guess it's been like this for centuries and may be for centuries more.'

'Where is Owyn?' asked Eve. Ruby didn't reply but looked out of the window towards the direction of the fires. Her eyes gave the answer. Eve and Soul were beginning to understand that Ruby had been excluded from whatever secret society existed within the local area. 'I am not part of what happens around here,' was as much as she would say.

Ruby quickly changed the subject to distract her guests away from the fiery sorcery outside her kitchen window. 'Please, come and sit back down. Eat before the food gets cold. We have plenty of time to catch up on the peculiar sagas of this area when you have a full stomach. So, Soul, have you seen much of Darcy on your travels? You guys seemed to be getting along very well at Nico's wedding.' As she said it, Ruby looked over at Eve and winked suggestively.

Soul became slightly embarrassed at the mention of Ruby's sister-in-law – a young woman with whom he was presently enjoying a closeted amorous encounter. Eve noticed a slight blush in his cheeks and instantly understood the significance. He responded, 'Well … yes – she lives in New York and so do I, so it's convenient. She is doing fine. Still working for that homeless charity and enjoying herself by all accounts.' 'That's good,' responded Ruby. 'I hear through the grapevine that you guys hooked up at the wedding. Hey, your love life is really none of my business, Soul, but just watch out for Darcy; she is a feisty one and a hell of a flirt. Wear a suit of armour.'

An awkward silence followed. It was broken by an unexpected announcement from Ruby. 'Apologies, but I need to leave you for a moment whilst I swap these stupid shoes for some trainers.' She looked down at Eve's footwear. 'Yep, you are dressed just fine. By the way, I really am so happy that you are both here. I have been eager to see you since the wedding. I hope you can help me. Anyway ... I have something to show you later, but for now, please finish your food and I will be back in about 20 or 30 minutes.'

With that, Ruby vacated the kitchen – leaving her guests quite speechless.

As she left the room, the siblings spoke in hushed tones.

'Remind me, Eve, why are we here exactly? This was a bloody crazy, fucked-up idea.' 'Because I had this weird vision, Bro.' Soul felt uncomfortable. He added, 'Dearest sister, this place is creepy on steroids. The last time I was here, two demons and their devil dog were patrolling the perimeter. Oh, did I mention that this particular perimeter was constructed of bowed ley lines – which I suspect defies the laws of physics as we know it. In fact, I can deduce that the fortnightly trance party over in the hills, could well be our enchanted forest friends reinforcing the dome.' Eve whispered back, 'You think that your bowing ley lines are freaky. My doctor husband was out for a gentle jog outside the village and bumped into a woman he once wrote a death certificate for. Not to forget that he nearly lost his job when she suddenly decided to have a heartbeat again.' 'Yes, I know Eve – I met her if you care to remember. She was one of the she-devils Micah and I met in the cemetery. Hey, but this is your call, Sis – you are the psychic. You dragged us out here in a snow storm even though you feel like shit and I am knackered from a transatlantic flight.'

'Don't make me sound like a freak, Soul, you were the one who jumped from the battlements and survived.'

'Just wires and illusion, my dear sister! Inner knowledge from the Magic Circle and nothing that science couldn't explain.'

'Levitating the glasses at a wedding toast did not involve wires and illusion, Bro. Admit it, this place is weird and … to a degree, so are you.'

'What? I am weird? Really … and this comes from one who can listen to dead people.'

'Oh, so listening to stones is one step nearer sanity, I take it?'

'Look, Eve, let's stop this argument. Neither of us are as pathetic as a woman who is totally at ease with her husband lighting fires on a full moon in worship of some star-trekking pagan deity.'

'I agree, dearest brother. So okay – let's think this through. Ruby will be back soon wearing trainers and I think that means we are going to be taken to a stiletto-adverse environment. We are both in agreement that Darwydden is like a refuelling service station on a ghost super-highway. Before Ruby makes her reappearance, can we guess what all of this is about?'

Soul replied, 'This is your call. You made us come here. You throw the dice first, sister.' Eve closed her eyes and attempted to call upon a seldom-used sixth sense. She sat in silence for around a minute. 'I think this is about her twin, Eenayah. She has never recovered from losing her. She wants to know the truth and because of our … unusual abilities, she believes we can help her. That's as much as I can pick up right now … so your turn.'

Soul knelt down and touched the cold stone of the kitchen floor. His eyes were shut tightly as every sense in his body tried to listen to what the stones were telling him. He appeared to be deep in concentration for about three minutes before announcing, 'There is a lingering odour of an unusual perfume. I don't know what it is but the stones are telling me it is "The Sacred Tears of Thebes". Eenayah's spirit came to this place. Cardamom, basil, myrtle, sandalwood, musk; these aromas are her trademark. She came here to say goodbye to Ruby.' Soul hesitated for a moment. 'Oh my God – Eenayah Baratolli was never found, and that's because her body is buried somewhere deep beneath these floors. She is far underground, very far underground. Bloody hell – she was thrown to the bottom of a deep ravine. She was put there purposely so she would never be discovered. Eenayah was killed twice. I don't understand what that means, Eve. She was sacrificed. It wasn't just a killing in the normal sense, if there is such a thing as a normal killing. It had a greater meaning and had a religious association. It was a group collaborative. I cannot tell how she died, only that it was connected to some sort of ritual … and childbirth. That doesn't make sense. I wouldn't often put birth and death in the same sentence, but on this occasion, they were linked.'

Soul's eyes opened and he sprung to his feet. He looked upon the pale, drained face of his sister and his heart fell. His concern suddenly focused on the living with little concern for the dead. 'I wish we hadn't come back to this place, Eve. You are not in a fit state. Here is my proposal – we play along with whatever Ruby is planning for tonight, and then tomorrow we get the hell out of here and we never come back here again. I mean never! I am also concerned about our mother's welfare, so I will be talking to her about this as well. I'm not happy with her working in this place. Do you understand me when I say the word never?' Eve silently nodded and agreed. She had come to much the same conclusion.

***

As promised, Ruby collected her guests exactly 25 minutes later and led them back down the long corridor and into the library. It was an imposing rectangular room, handsomely decorated with enriched panelled ceilings. Along the main wall was a grand mantelpiece of oak, cedar and walnut, delicately inlaid with other ornate woods. It was a striking room, and for a moment her guests took some time to look around and drink in its impressive ornamentation. Ruby was rightfully proud as she informed them, 'I renovated this library single-handedly. Every single book was acquired by me personally. God knows how many car boot sales I walked around in the pouring rain. Owyn had no involvement in any of this at all. Whilst he was secretly converting the caverns beneath the house into a disco hall, I had my head firmly above ground. He has zero interest in this place and the mysteries that are hidden behind these walls.' Eve and Soul were confused and said nothing. Ruby continued, 'Please turn away and close your eyes. I will let you know when you can turn around.' It felt like a childish game of hide and seek, but nonetheless they complied.

After a minute or so, her guests turned to see an open door where once had been only bookshelves. It led into a dark, cobwebbed aisle. Ruby handed them both a torch. 'We are in the 21st century now, guys – AA batteries work a treat. I don't do candles and flaming torches anymore. Mind the step and follow me.'

They proceeded up a steep wooden staircase, until they reached a narrow upper corridor. The air was old and musty, and even Ruby breathed heavily as her body called for oxygen. Eve tried hard to keep her claustrophobia at bay, as she rubbed shoulders with the panelled walls. Soul was a man with a broad, Viking-like body frame, and so he struggled to manoeuvre through the inner corridor. Proceeding sideways, he cursed under his breath. 'Where are you taking us, Ruby? Whatever this place is, it has clearly been designed for little people.'

Ruby seemed to be taking them on a most unexpected history tour. 'This is the corridor of the lower rooms or at least this is what I call it. It winds its way around the whole of the medieval part of the house. When walking around these inner corridors, the little people … as you call them, would have been about ear level with the upper part of the ground-floor rooms. Some sort of inexplicable acoustics pushes the sound upwards and makes it really easy to listen in on private conversations. There are even little spyholes in parts of the timber. Follow me – there is more to show you.'

Yet again they ascended a second steep wooden staircase, which led up to the top of the house. By way of the same architecture, the narrow corridor wound its way around the medieval section of Darwydden; however, on this occasion one's ear level was at the same height as the external eaves. Ruby was obviously far more elated by this 'ye olde snooping technology' than her guests, going into great detail about the meaning of the term 'eavesdropping'. Yet again, spyholes had been cleverly disguised into the eyes of monstrous gargoyles and gave the snooper a clear outlook to the driveway and gardens.

Ruby pointed to the end of the corridor, where the medieval building adjoined the old castle, as though one had been bolted onto the other by way of an afterthought. She continued, 'There is a spiral staircase at the end which leads down into the caves and the tunnels. I suspect this was once an escape route. We think that the castle we see now was built around 1285 by King Edward I during his invasion of Wales. However, local folklore states that there was a castle here long before the 13th century. Some even say this was the site of Caer Sidi, the abode of their moon queen – Arianrhod. To many, this is a sacred place.'

As fascinated as Soul was by this mythological history lesson, he had to intervene. 'Ruby, my sister is sick. We would love to hear all about Darwydden, but we don't have the time and Eve hasn't got the energy. I am still not totally sure what we are doing here. I don't mean to be rude but ...'

Ruby got the hint. She produced a large, crudely-cut key, which dangled on an equal-sized rusty ring, and led them towards a concealed room. Steering them in, she lit several battery-operated lamps that sat upon a well-worn table. Soul picked up the vibrations from the room in an instant. 'This is a prayer room,' he declared. 'I can almost hear the incantations of Catholic chants. I can feel the energy of devotion, piety ... but alas also fear. There is a priest hole underneath the floorboards. If you haven't found it yet, Ruby, come up here with a crowbar next time as it's in here, I swear. There was no altar – that would have been a giveaway, I guess. The Protestant Reformation was a cruel time. I can smell their distress. Their faith and determination to worship as they please, is almost tangible.'

Ruby gestured for her guests to sit and then poured them some wine. They seemed surprised. She responded accordingly. 'I have lots of hidden supplies – don't worry. I come in here when I want to get away from life. In here … deep within the walls of Darwydden, there is no Wi-Fi signal, no phone connections and zero disruptions from the outside world. I had no idea what this room was used for until you told me, Soul, but it doesn't surprise me to learn it was a place of contemplation and prayer. I often meditate in here – along with a glass of claret. Before you ask, I have brought you here for a reason. In fact, you both brought yourself here for a reason. This isn't just a quaint history tour of an old house. I am not gifted with the unusual senses you both have, but I can tell what you are both thinking.'

'And the reason is?' asked Soul. Ruby took several hasty gulps of her wine before replying. 'I want to know where Eenayah is and I know that only you guys can tell me. Not the police, not anyone … just you.' Ruby's statement was met with stunned silence. She continued, 'Look, before I came to live here, I had a brain. I was the European Sales and Marketing Director for a well-known pharmaceutical company. I didn't do priest holes and pagan fires. I did spreadsheets, financial targets, nice hotels and London wine bars. In fact, Becky was once my single London friend who went with me to all those bars and introduced me to numerous ridiculous-sounding cocktails. I was a young woman in my thirties and I was normal. Look at me now. Everyone thinks of me as a strange crazy woman who hides inside the walls of a medieval house – and they are right. 100 per cent bloody spot on.' A tear fell to her eye and yet more hurried slugs from her glass followed. Soul and Eve remained quiet and simply listened … not knowing how else to react.

Ruby banged her glass down on the table and continued. 'Then I got married and I thought it was fate and love and all that crap. Then we adopted a little boy – "Harry" – because nature screwed up my internals … and I wanted to do the whole mother thing because I had wanted a baby for so long. However, Owyn wanted us to put all our energy and money into … this! Just look at it, look at me. I am living in a mausoleum.'

Ruby raised her arms in the air to signal that she referred to her surroundings. 'I was pushed into paying a mortgage for a crumbling abomination, and working longer and harder hours just to fix a hole in the bloody roof.' She started to cry and then got up to pour yet more wine … which predictably didn't last too long in the glass. She wiped her tears and faced her shocked audience. 'My twin sister gave me a lot of money … and I mean a lot of money. She made an electronic transfer into my bank account the day before she went missing. For a while it made me a suspect in her disappearance. Dearest Eenayah; her timing was never great, but nonetheless it was a generous gift. Her gift released me from my toil. I can never repay her for that. I didn't even have the chance to say thank you.'

Eve was curious. When Eenayah Baratolli went missing, it made headline news in all the tabloids. After all, she was married to a famous multi-millionaire music mogul. Eve recollected that her disappearance was strange, sudden and unusual. There were those who had their motives and those who were suspects, but with no body and no concrete evidence, no charges were ever made. The investigation remained open, but somehow drifted into a cul-de-sac.

Eve found herself drawn into the conversation. 'What happened to Eenayah? I mean, how much do you know?' Ruby drank yet more wine and replied, 'Nothing – I know nothing. When someone you love dies, it always hurts. When that person dies young, it hurts more because it wasn't yet their time and it seems unfair. When that person was taken by an accident rather than an illness, that seems cruel, and when by illness – at least you can say they are no longer suffering. But when you can't even bury the body of the one you love because you don't know where they are … that my friends … that is the cruellest piece of shit ever. I don't know what happened to her. I don't know why. I don't know where she is. Eenayah was my twin sister for God's sake.' She wiped a tear away from her eyes. Ruby tried not to be angry, yet containing her bitterness was eating away at her sanity. Both Soul and his sister could clearly see that this was a lady in need of closure, and no matter how painful the truth may be, the 'not knowing' was the far greater pain.

Ruby continued, 'When you have a twin, there is a connection which pre-dates birth. There can be no greater human bond. When Eenayah went missing – so did I.' Ruby entwined her fingers into Soul's hands and looked directly into his Icelandic blue eyes. 'I know that you know where my sister is, Soul. She is dead and her body is down in the caves somewhere. I need you to take me there. I just have to see for myself.'

Soul was somewhat taken aback by the sudden confrontation. He asked, 'What makes you think I know where she is?'

Ruby gave him an uncharacteristically icy stare. 'This house has eyes and ears. Have you not learned that by now? Darwydden is a Frankenstein of a building that has travelled through time. It is a Victorian gentleman's residence, connected to an Edwardian abode, attached to a medieval manor house, bolted onto a Norman castle. Beneath its very foundations are the dungeons of that castle, and the castle that existed before that. The old castle vaults link into a myriad of caves and tunnels – some natural and some manmade. This was an ancient place of worship long before any of these structures were crafted. Everything here is connected to everything else, like veins and arteries. I have brought you into one of many secret areas, to show you the inner corridors which allow one to move around Darwydden covertly and undercover. So, dearest Soul – please do not deny the conversation you had in the kitchen with your sister, because the walls heard every word and, by default, so did I. Why do you think I left you alone?'

Soul's cheeks reddened with embarrassment. 'I am sorry, Ruby. I didn't mean to deceive you. I just didn't want to bring you yet more grief.' Ruby tenderly stroked his blushing cheeks. 'I know, Soul. I can tell that you are a man with a good heart. Try to understand that my life is in pieces and if I am to survive, I need to move on. I heard you talk about Eve's vision and perhaps that is why something keeps pulling me out of my bed. Something brought you here for a reason, and that something is real. I have the finger-marks on my ankles to prove it. Look … I am not an idiot. I have a vague idea about what has been going on here behind my back. The management team – and that includes Owyn, Becky and her husband Amedeo – are all part of some little secret society. They whisper in huddled corners and give each other knowing little looks. However, right now they are up in the hills and the caverns are empty. Whilst we have the chance, please … take me to Eenayah. Soul, you are the only person I know who can listen to the rocks. They know where she is. They will tell you.'

Soul looked dumbfounded. He looked over to Eve, who was equally speechless. He put a brotherly arm around his sister's shoulders. 'You stay here, Eve. You are not well enough to go underground. You do know that I have to do this, don't you?' With that, Ruby took him by the hand and led him out of the prayer room towards the cavern steps. Her facial muscles relaxed and a smile almost formed on her mouth. At long last and well overdue – a chapter in her life was about to close.

***

Eve stayed behind as instructed, and relished in the environment of being somewhere dark, silent and peaceful. Alone with her thoughts, she connected with the divine ambience of the former prayer room. As her brainwaves soared up into the exosphere and her breathing slowed – she entered a pre-meditative state. Connecting with a greater universe, she felt a presence enter the room. She understood it to be the woman in the vision, a spirit entity that could only communicate with images. Eve opened her eyes to see the dark, shadowy mist in the corner. As the woman's features began to take form, she recognised a similarity to Ruby. 'Who are you?' she asked. There was no response, so again she asked the question.

'She cannot understand you,' came a voice from over her shoulder. 'Nor can she reply in a language you would understand. Her tongue is that of ancient Hebrew.'

Eve swivelled around in shock, almost falling off the bench as she turned. 'Mother, what are you doing here? Ruby presumed the hidden room to be a secret.'

Her mother replied in hushed tones. 'Ruby only knows of me as the children's nanny. She doesn't talk much these days. I have been worried about her for a long time. As for this being a secret, those who live here know that these inner chambers exist.' Eve's eyes remained firmly fixed upon her mother's eyes, and now that her clairvoyant senses had been heightened, she also began to see a soft glow around her mother's outline. She had not seen it before. Eve gasped, 'Oh my ... I have never noticed it before, but you are not exactly human. What are you?' Roserie smiled and touched Eve with a delicate angelic touch – she had no need to answer her verbally. Eve instantly understood that she was in the presence of something amazing and other-worldly. A mother she knew, yet had never known. She didn't know what to do. Should she curtsy, kneel ... bow? 'What is going on?' was about as much as Eve could utter.

Roserie gestured towards the shadow. 'This is the spirit of Tamar. She is Ruby's great grandmother many times removed. She lived thousands of years ago and, in fact, you can read all about her antics in the book of Genesis. Between us, we worked hard to bring you and your brother back to Darwydden. We needed you to come back so you could rescue Ruby and get her away from this place and the people who wish to control her. They are Ledanite. They don't mean Ruby any harm but sometimes people unintentionally confuse right and wrong.'

Even for one who was a clairvoyant medium and had the ability to communicate with the spirit world, Eve was clearly shaken. She repeated her earlier question, 'So, Mother, who or what are you really?' Roserie smiled. It was the soft, delicate smile of rose petals floating on the wind in the shape of drifting lips. She replied, 'There is an action, and at the beginning of that action is a cause. Some would call that destiny. After that action is an effect. Some would call that the consequence. I am there at the beginning and I am there at the end, and in between the cause and effect. You humans get up to lots of things to keep me on my toes. I am known by both names – call me the angel of destiny or the angel of consequence, as you see fit. It all depends where along the line we met.' Eve understood perfectly and responded, 'Can I just stick with calling you Mother? It's easier to say. I have no idea where on the line I am standing right now, but I suspect we are into consequence territory and I may be here to pick up the pieces.'

'You are a clever woman and a precious daughter, Eve. That is exactly where on the line you stand. Very soon, Ruby will return to this room. She will walk back in with an insight into her sister's death, which will push her to the edge of insanity. She will know for certain that her beloved twin died many years ago. Soul will reveal to her that she was pushed from a cliff by the demon Tobiah. The demon tried to kill her because she was pregnant with very special twin boys who were part of a hidden biblical prophecy. Yet Ruby's sister had not been unfaithful to her husband. Eenayah had been raped, deliberately and strategically. The Ledanite organised this incident. Ruby will discover that Eenayah was the clone of Tamar. It is the spirit of Tamar that you see in the corner, the lady who can only speak in ancient Hebrew. She has been trying to protect Ruby and that is why she will not leave her side. It was Tamar who appeared in your dream and Tamar who has been trying to bring you and your brother back to Darwydden. Ruby and Eenayah were not identical twins. Only Eenayah carried the mutant gene which had been passed down from clone to clone for over 4,000 years. Only a clone such as Eenayah could give birth to the twin boys. These were twins who would be the reincarnation of Tamar's own twin boys, as told in the book of Genesis.'

'Wow,' Eve sighed as she struggled to take in the information she had just been given. She walked over to the dark, misty figure in the corner. The spirit's facial features were hazy and its essence was weak, but nonetheless she could clearly see a resemblance to the twin sisters.

Tamar held out both hands with palms facing upwards. She looked at Eve and whispered the words, 'Toda rabah.' The spirit began to fade and within minutes had totally vanished. Tamar was gone.

Roserie walked over to the corner to join Eve. She put her arm around her waist to comfort the sickly child. 'Tamar has just said thank you. She can leave this place now as her work is done. Darwydden has been haunted for long enough. Tamar also wanted me to tell you that she feels a terrible sadness about what happened to Eenayah. She carries the tortured ache of regret like a weight on her back, and yet she had always known that the boys should be reborn. The world needs whatever it is they were prophesised to bring to this planet of yours. Know that Eenayah's spirit is free and happy. It is Ruby's welfare that is now of concern. Soul has been given full insight into events from the past and the truth will come as a massive shock to Ruby. She will need help to get through all of this.'

Eve enquired, 'I feel almost too scared to ask, but what else will Ruby discover? I feel there is more.' Roserie shrugged with heavy shoulders of sadness and replied, 'She will have final confirmation that her husband and best friend are part of a cult, the secret society known as the Ledanite. Their one mission in life was to ensure that eventually one of the clones would give birth to the twin boys. She will realise that her relationship with both Owyn and Becky was planned and contrived. They were only close to her to stay close to Eenayah. Basically, she will find out she was used and both her marriage and friendship was little more than a sham. She will discover that Becky's twin boys do not belong to Becky biologically and that in fact they are her nephews. The boys were born in the caves. They were cut from her sister's womb as she lay dying. Their birth was never registered. They have no identity. They were being kept at Darwydden to protect them from the demons outside. Yet by keeping them in this prison, they stood no chance of growing into the powerful young men they were destined to become. Ruby will also know it was the Ledanite who kidnapped her sister, removing her from her hospital bed and hiding her inside the caverns until the twins were ready to be born. Soul will not hide anything from her and the truth will be brutal. Ruby will know all that has gone before and even come to understand that her own husband was one of many who threw Eenayah's body into the ravine. I am sorry, Eve, but her knowing all of this will have a dramatic consequence and will spark off a chain of events which even I cannot control.'

Eve was flabbergasted. She didn't know what to say. 'The consequence, the cursed consequence. What can I do to help her?' was about as much as she could ask. Roserie replied, 'I must go soon, Eve. They are making their way back from the caverns now and I do not want them to see me. You cannot tell them I was here. I will answer you quickly. There was a woman who tried to help Eenayah when she was alive. She goes by the name of Mercy De Vede. She was also threatened with death for her involvement in all of this, and so she feigned her own demise so she could go into hiding. Your brother Soul knows a young woman called Saskia. She knows someone – a man who knows where Mercy is. The man's name is Don Morris – you must locate him. Ruby will make a run for it. She will take her son Harry and the twin boys and she will leave Darwydden. Her life will be in immense danger and she will be in a serious emotional state. She needs someone smart and strong to help protect her and Mercy is the person who can do that. When Ruby escapes, as she will – you and your brother need to find her and then find Mercy De Vede. I am sorry, Eve – I must go now. One last thing – do not tell your brother Soul who or what I am. I will tell him in my own time, when the time is right.' Roserie then ran off into the dark inner corridors of the manor house.

The door slowly opened and Eve caught her breath. She waited in anticipation, not quite knowing what to expect. Soul entered the room alone. His face was pale and he looked exhausted. He had the glimmer of a tear in his eye – something quite unusual for an impassive Viking type. 'Oh, Eve – that was not easy. That was awful. Why was I made to see and hear all of that history? Why was I compelled to tell her the truth? I hate my ability sometimes.' Soul looked up to his sister and noted that she was equally pale and forlorn. 'Let's get out of here,' he added.

'Where is Ruby?' asked Eve. 'Probably packing her cases and planning on doing the same thing, I suspect. At least now I know what the blue dome was all about and what it was trying to protect. I hate this place, Eve. It's creepy and weird. We are not staying here tonight. We will find some local pub to camp out at, and once the roads are open again, we are getting as far away from here as we can. I am also going to have a word with Mum. I know she loves working here, but I doubt she will have any children to look after by next week.' With that, Soul took his sister's clammy hand and led her away from the medieval prayer room. He took one last look inside before he shut the door. 'Someone else has just been in here. I can sense it. You don't have to tell me about it now, Eve. It can wait for later. Let's go.'

CHAPTER 20

28th February 2017

It was 6 p.m. on a dank, murky Venetian night. The backdrop was
that of a dark gothic metropolis, seductively illuminated with minimal
lighting. An eerie mist ascended from the various waterways, as two of
the masked guests made their way through a labyrinth of narrow
alleyways. This seemed to be a place where shadows lingered and
footsteps echoed, rebounding from the walls of jaded baroque buildings.

The two strangers felt out of place amongst the historical vapour of
courtesans, casinos, brothels and the infamous Casanova. Their thoughts
invoked bizarre imaginings of mysterious footprints and headless bodies,
with dismembered body parts of Jesuit traitors floating down the Grand
Canal. Adrenaline levels soured and hearts raced. Looking at a tattered
piece of paper, they followed their instructions with immense
concentration, until they found themselves in the assassin's alleyway.
They had been instructed to wait at the bridge for a gondola to transport
them to some clandestine location. They waited in silence, the
anticipation almost terrorising their spirits. Breathing in the atmosphere,
they could almost smell the musky sweat of the spice merchants and
sickly perfume of the Doge's harlots.

The invitation had been strange and mysterious. It was as unnerving
as it was enigmatic. Yet neither of them felt willing to resist the chance
of a free vacation in Venice, along with the opportunity to attend a
masquerade ball. Neither of them knew who sent the invitation or who
paid for their flights and hotel. This unknowing seemed to add to the

mystery of the event and added yet more layers of ambiguity to the illusive setting.

The gondola moved with slow deliberation through the tiny watery alleyways. Aside from the comforting swish of the oar against the water, there was a strange, uncomfortable quietness. A calm, almost meditative aura pervaded the moment. Peering down a passing canal, they could see a distant courtyard which was alive with colour and debauch panache. The entire population of Venice seemed to be promenading their flamboyant costumes in public, like strutting peacocks. The distant, ostentatious laughter drifted up the canal and met with their ears. It offered some small comfort, breaking an otherwise menacing silence.

Finally, they arrived at what they presumed to be their secret destination. The gondola pulled up alongside a large, ornate doorway. The 12ft wooden door looked as though it had not been opened in centuries, the hinges creaking as it was forced open. The steps leading inside were covered with a slippery green slime and looked equally untrodden upon. A butler, dressed as a Venetian noble, appeared from behind the door and threw down a Turkish rug to cover the weedy steps. He offered a white-gloved hand to steady the guests as they made their way out of the swaying vessel. The gondola left as silently and swiftly as it had arrived, vaporising into the silvery mist.

Inside the landing hallway, Murano glass chandeliers were illuminated by numerous candles. A sickly scent of olibanum wafted towards the guests, as the heavy doors were firmly slammed shut behind them. A sudden dread pounded in both their hearts as they suddenly realised they were alone in a strange place and at the mercy of an anonymous host. Isolated, solitary and far from home.

They were led down a corridor filled with mosaics and Byzantine wall art. The religious imagery almost seemed to be at odds with the debauch flavour of the evening's festivities. As they each cast their eyes upon the exotic yet pious artwork, the two guests silently and individually pondered on the schizophrenic confusion between holiness and debased sexuality.

A huge brass sculpture of the goddess Reitia stood proudly alongside an equal-sized winged lion. Reitia was holding a saucer of hamil al musk charcoal and Frankincense. It created an aromatic cloud, which crept along the ceiling of the darkened corridor like a meandering serpent.

Finally, the butler spoke to them as he led them through yet another large door, this time opulently carved and misted with gild. 'This way Gentili ospiti.' He pointed to their seats, which formed part of a semi-circle. He continued, 'At 8.30 p.m. precisely a water taxi will collect you and take you to the Venetian Palace Ca' Zeno close to the Basilica dei Frari. Your entrance tickets are waiting for you on your chairs. The hostess will be joining you soon, but in the meantime please help yourself to the frittolle and galani. Enjoy your evening.'

The two guests looked around – they were not alone. Surrounded by other masked strangers in lavish lace and finery, and in similar disguise to themselves, they wondered why they had been brought here and by whom. A waiter approached them with a silver tray and offered them a pale orange drink in a tall thin glass. He explained, 'This is Campari, Grapefruit and Prosecco.' They each took a sip and enquired as to its name. 'Death in Venice,' came the austere reply.

Although their facial expressions were hidden by papier-mâché, the duo turned to face each other and noted subdued trepidation in each other's eyes. They sat quietly, curiously observing the other party guests. They had little choice but to wait for whatever was going to happen next. This was turning out to be a most unusual evening.

Eventually the presumed hostess drifted into the room, followed by an assemblage of around six or so followers. She was wearing a black lace ball gown, tiered with golden thread and decorated with Swarovski crystals. Her matching mask totally covered her face. Several Medusa-type extensions projected from around the mask, covering some of her hair. Her jester's façade dangled with tiny chime balls which rang as she moved. The end result was the presentation of a mysterious, unidentified female. Her followers clustered around her as though she was their queen, and indeed she conducted herself with all the self-assurance of royalty. Stepping onto a podium, she covered her face with a black lace scarf whilst moving her mask to one side and taking hold of a microphone. She commanded an effortless control of the crowd, who by now had gathered around to hear whatever it was she was going to say. A hushed silence fell upon the ballroom.

She began, 'Ladies and gentlemen, welcome to Venice. I trust that you all had a pleasant journey and located your respective hotels with relative ease. It is easy to get lost in this beautiful city, but then again, easy enough to be rescued. Anyway, I suspect that you are all wondering what you are doing here, so I had better begin before curiosity gets the better of you. Many of you will know me, others will know of me and to some I am a complete stranger. However, you are all connected to each other in one way or another, and so I considered that a masquerade ball was the most appropriate way for you to meet. Without the benefit of reading facial expressions, we all need to put more effort into verbal communication.'

Pausing slightly, she beckoned for her guests to sit and then continued. 'Let me introduce myself. Many years ago, I began my career in the Metropolitan police force. I climbed the ladder to become a detective inspector and then many years back, I left to set up my own investigation bureau.' She turned to point out the small group who had followed her into the room. 'These extremely talented people once worked for me. Between them, they can scale any wall, crack any code, trip any security system, hack into any computer server, jailbreak any phone and video your every movement without you even knowing you are being watched. Beware – any one of these guys can move stealthily amongst you, listening, observing and peeling off your layers like an onion skin. Your skeleton will be exposed and you won't even know it. My dear friends, back in the day my team could collectively outwit the finest investigative brain on planet Earth. However, sadly these wonderful people are no longer part of my team, and that pisses me off big time.'

The hostess did her usual pause in order to read the reaction of her guests, but with stunned silence and concealed faces, there was little for her to read. She continued, 'My company – MeDeVe – was like my child. I raised it from conception, and losing it was like a bereavement. Worse still, I lost my father, my dearest friend and regrettably a client I was hired to protect. Even my own life was put in jeopardy. So, dear guests, I had little choice but to lie down and play dead. My home and all my belongings were sold and my company dissolved. I even had to leave the country. All of this pain, loss and heartbreak occurred because I became connected to one person, a lovely but tragic woman called Eenayah Baratolli. All of you in this room will know that name. None of this was Eenayah's fault. Her memory carries no blame. In truth, she was the ultimate victim and now lies dead without the dignity of a funeral.'

Her voice trembled as her throat narrowed. With a dry mouth and quivering vocals, she kicked aside her emotions and continued. 'Dear guests ... I was an atheist. I didn't believe in anything aside from the law and justice. I didn't believe in heaven or hell, myth or magic. However, because of my involvement with Eenayah, I discovered that there is another world hidden behind the world we see with our partially closed everyday eyes. It is a strange, invisible world, but it has intelligence and deliberation. There are species and entities within this other worldly realm. They are not human, but they live alongside us and try to control us in subtle, cunning ways. Some of you listening to me right now must think I am as mad as a box of frogs. Well yes, I am mad. I am fucking fuming. I may have retired from my job as CEO of MeDeVe Limited, but I am not retired from finding out the truth. So, dear guests, consider tonight to be my coming out ball. Tell the world – Mercy De Vede is back. I am alive and well – perhaps slightly mentally unstable, but still worshipping my religion of law and justice. The truth will be exposed and wrongs will be made right. In the meantime, I hope you all have a dazzling evening here in Venice, and I will enjoy mingling with you before you depart for tonight's ball.'

With that, Mercy's nephew Simon stepped forward and raised his glass of orange Prosecco. 'To my courageous Aunt – the formidable Mercy De Vede. Welcome back to life.' The room followed suit, each raising their glasses in stunned shock and muted silence.

Carmen stepped forward in an attempt to lighten the mood. She was obviously a silicone-enhanced woman, whose bosom size contrasted with her tiny wisp of a waist. She commenced, 'Dear guests, by way of entertainment, can you please draw a picture of what or who you are on a "post-it note" and stick it on your chest. Although you are in disguise, many of you will know each other, so we hope you will find some amusement in guessing each other's identity. At 8.30 p.m. we will be setting off for the Casanova ball. Don't be too worried about the title. If you want to stand to one side and watch the cabaret, you may do so. Likewise, if you want to be part of the cabaret, you may do so. That's just the way life is. Venice caters for both saints and sinners, the watchers and the watched.' With that, Carmen raised her gilded-crystal glass high into the air and most inexplicably, tilted it so the contents spilled down upon the marble floor. 'Here is to a night of mystery and excitement – enjoy.' She then rustled her scarlet ball gown with childlike delight, and headed back towards the rest of Mercy's entourage. Decadence suited Carmen – indeed, fitting her hand like a glove.

Saskia turned towards her companion Don, who was in the process of drawing a caricature of Donald Duck on his 'post-it note'. 'Oh bugger, why is she walking in our direction?' came her dazed enquiry as she observed the hostess scanning the room with missile precision. Don smiled from behind his mask. 'Because, dear Saskia, Mercy is my former employer. I should have guessed that she was behind tonight's escapade. Mercy never did do things by half. This is a lady who doesn't know how to dilute life. You had better be on the lookout, as I am guessing you will be one of the first on her calling list.' With that, they noted Mercy moving towards them with deliberation. 'Told you so,' chirped up Don.

'But how does she know who we all are?' asked Saskia. 'She ordered the costumes,' he responded. 'I can bet she has studied every single outfit in detail and knows the identity of everybody wearing whatever it was she selected for us. She leaves nothing to chance. Mercy De Vede is quite a remarkable woman.' The admiration in Don's voice was audibly obvious.

As predicted, Mercy made her way towards Saskia and Don, but maybe less predictably selected Don to speak with first. Gently pulling him to one side, she asked, 'How well do you know Miss Usov?' The question was direct and quite brusque. Don shrugged and answered accordingly. 'I have known Saskia for five years or so, Mercy. She employed me before you did. Remember, she acted as a reference for me when I applied to you for a job. You know all of this already, so why do you ask?' Mercy replied abruptly, 'You know why I am asking, Don, so why do you respond with a silly question. Her sister Katya was my friend. You can't have forgotten that fact, surely? Tell me – I am curious. What do you know of the Ouroboros group – the organisation she allegedly works for?'

There isn't much to tell you that you don't already know, Mercy. We touched upon this in Strasbourg. They seem to be an odd group of investors – incredibly secretive and extremely wealthy. They funded Saskia's conversion programme after she left university and they pay her a salary far greater than many young solicitors would earn. Reading between the lines, I am guessing that she doesn't probe too much because she doesn't want to lose a well-paid job.' 'Hmm,' retorted Mercy. 'So this is a lady who can be bought for 30 pieces of silver – just like her mother could. I take it that she confided in you that her mother's sexual services were procured by her oligarch father – until that is, his courtesan became pregnant with Saskia. I believe he dumped her the minute the baby started to kick. It is quite a sad little story really. Pregnant prostitute offloaded by her wealthy client. Quite sad …'

'No, I didn't know that, but it hardly surprises me. She holds a lot of bitterness around her childhood and seems to hate both her parents in equal measures. I guess that would explain a lot,' Mercy sighed, feeling unexpected sympathy for Don's young friend. 'I guess you are right,' she replied. 'Katia told me a lot about her half-sister. I don't think the relationship between the sisters was as rosy as the picture Saskia would like to paint. I am guessing that this is a lady with such a rigid poker face that she needn't even wear a mask tonight. I look forward to meeting her, but not quite yet. I intend to save the best to last.'

Don liked his young friend Saskia and felt Mercy was judging her too harshly, but neither did he want to enter into some fractious debate with his formidable former boss. As Mercy turned to leave, Don followed her and judiciously pulled at her arm. 'I almost forgot to mention – the Ouroboros, I did some research for them a few years back and I still have copies of the files I created for them. They are on a memory stick in my office back home. I have no idea if this information is of any help, but I can send them to you if you are in need of some heavy bedtime reading.' Mercy pondered upon the idea. She had almost overlooked the fact that Don was also once an employee of this peculiar organisation. 'You have my attention, Don. What are they about?' she asked.

'Centuries ago, some kids got lost in some tunnels in North West England. It was in an extensive warren of caverns and old mine shafts in a place called Rainford. One of them escaped and told a far-fetched story about strange beings that lived underground and captured the children. The story spread and became something of a local legend. The Ouroboros paid me good money to spend five months drinking in the local pubs with the villagers and investigating the myths surrounding the story. I have no idea what happened after that. You need to talk with Saskia. I believe she was involved in the legal process of them purchasing the caves and mines. I do know she was involved in years of disputes with the local planning department at St Helens, but I can't give you any specifics. Whenever I met up with her, she would always be grumbling about the council and how they made life difficult for her. The Ouroboros obviously had an interest in the area, but for what and why … well, your guess is as good as mine. They are a strange bunch.'

Something struck a chord with Mercy. Had it not been for her mask, Don would have noted her renowned 'I'm onto something' look. 'One other thing,' he added, 'the only person in the Ouroboros I know by name is the guy who speaks with Saskia. He seems to be her main contact – in fact, I think he is her only method of interaction with her employers. He is called George Smith. I am going out on a limb a bit here as I know this must be a common name, but there is a tomb in the nearby cemetery. The headstone bears the mark of the Ouroboros – the winged skull and the snake in a circle devouring its own tail. It is the grave of a man called George Smith. However, what is most odd is that the burial records for the year he was buried cannot be located. Every other year is documented in the parish records but for this one year. In my head, I can't make any logical assumptions, but it just seems a fluke – that's all I am saying.' She squeezed his hand by way of a thank you, then scanned the room for her next target. Don had given her much to think about, but she had other people to meet. Mercy wasn't a lady known to waste time.

***

Eve had just completed drawing a sketch of a naked woman with a fig leaf over her groin, whilst her brother's 'post-it note' was adorned by a magician with a wand. Huddled in a corner, they both giggled like schoolchildren whilst creating their badly sketched identity pictures.

Soul had been concerned about the health of his sister, but then noted her depressive state and decided that a trip to Venice may do her some good. He persuaded Gérard to let her go, arguing that the mind needed to heal every bit as much as the body. However, cruising along dimly lit canals through a creepy, ghostlike smog, he had begun to doubt the wisdom of the decision. Now, safely in the glitzy confines of garish glamour, they were both quite enjoying Mercy's extravagant 'coming out' party. The atmosphere in the room had lightened, whilst alcohol had helped to elevate the geniality of the gathering. Even though the harpsichord player's rendition of 'Fugue on a theme of Albinoni' added a slightly baleful edge to the night, the general laughter rose above the musician's dark, majestic notes.

Eve nudged her brother towards their hostess. 'We need to introduce ourselves, Soul. I have heard so much about the great Mercy De Vede, and after all, she did come to Ruby's rescue. Eve did not volunteer the additional information that it was in fact Roserie, an angelic entity whom Soul only knew as his mother, who had shared some of this information with her, back in the hidden chambers of Darwydden. The evening was turning out to be unusual in its own right, and did not require the embellishment of former strange events to make it even stranger.

The siblings held out their hands in greetings and each were met with a soft, gloved hand with an uncommon and most unexpected firm grip. Mercy looked at their 'post-it notes' and commented, 'Well – you are either the goddess Venus hanging out with Rasputin, or I am in the company of the amazingly talented Soul and his equally gifted sister Eve.' Eve giggled nervously, 'Indeed you are correct, Mercy. Well guessed, and it is wonderful to meet you at last.' Soul interrupted his sister, 'Oh … but we are related to Rasputin. If the rumours are correct, our great-great-grandmother Isolda was one of his many mistresses.'

'In that case,' added Mercy, 'maybe that's where you two get your unusual abilities from. Any which way, it's great to meet you both and I also want to thank you for pointing Ruby and the boys in my direction. They are all safe and under the team's protection.' Hesitating slightly, she added, 'This is not easy for me to admit, because even though I was born a Catholic, I don't usually do the whole regret and repentance thing. However, I have had many sleepless nights about the loss of poor Eenayah Baratolli. I was hired to protect her and I failed. As such, I will do everything in my power to make sure that the same thing doesn't happen to her twin sister, her son and her nephews. History will not repeat itself – this I promise.'

The siblings were both taken aback by her humility and penitence. It was not what they expected from a woman of Mercy's reputation. Soul then asked, 'How are the boys? Has Owyn, Becky and the rest of the cult members not made an attempt to find them? Surely they will have called in the police?'

Mercy laughed contemptibly as she replied, 'Think about what you have just said, Soul. This bad-arse secret group or whatever it is they call themselves – I think it says Ledanite on the tin; these folks kidnapped a woman. Eenayah was being transferred by ambulance for medical treatment at a specialist brain recovery unit. The ambulance was hijacked or stolen, maybe both … and Eenayah's life placed in jeopardy because of that action. Prior to all of this, I believe she was ritualistically raped by her father-in-law. Let me keep a score. Yep – that's all of four crimes chalked up already. Then they held her prisoner underground whilst the pregnancy progressed, which could also be classified as a crime, I guess. Then by all accounts they cut the boys from out of her stomach without her permission – I think that's technically referred to as assault. Plus, let us not forget that these babies were born in a cave. Their births were never registered. They never left the confines of Darwydden, nor attended school or nursery. According to society, these twin boys do not even exist. No birth certificate, no NHS number and they were not even registered on a recent census report. Trust me – I have searched. So tell me, Soul – how do you report missing people who technically have no identity? As such, Eenayah's children do not exist. I understand that after they were born, their mother died. Not only did these Ledanite screwballs not register her death, but they also disposed of her body illegally. Ruby informed me that you sensed she had been thrown into a gully. Is that correct, Soul … because I am into a counting crimes mode? Oh, I think I have run out of fingers.'

For a moment, there was dazed silence before Soul responded, 'Yes, I saw all of this. There was no mistaking what happened. The energy beneath Darwydden is ancient and very strong.' 'Then,' responded

Mercy, 'wearing my former CID hat, I would say that people guilty of kidnapping, hijacking, theft, imprisonment, manslaughter, rape, spoliation of evidence, not registering a birth, illegally performing a caesarean section, assault and finally preventing the lawful and decent burial of a dead body – are hardly going to call in the police – are they? Crime after crime – I rest my case.'

Once again Mercy had stunned her compact audience into silence. She added, 'Look, don't worry about Ruby. She has been hiding behind a mask for a long time. At least you can take yours off before bed. She has had a lot to come to terms with. She is just beginning to realise that she has spent her entire life being manipulated and that's a hard pill to swallow. We are not just talking about human crime here, but about supernatural crime – and boy is that a term I thought I would never utter. I assumed that dealing with common criminals on the streets of London was a challenge – but demonic felons take my job into an entirely new universal dimension. Anyway, sorry about my rant. It was a privilege to meet you both, but I have to go and mingle now. Before I go, I want to reassure you that Ruby and her boys will be safe with me. They already have new identities and the team are starting to build new lives for them. The Ledanites will be pissed off major league, and I am sure we have not seen the end of them – but this time around I am prepared. Got to go – have fun and stay safe. Venice is a schizophrenic place of charm. It reminds me of a Christmas tree – bright sparkling lights perched on prickly dark branches. All wrapped up in glitter, but with sharp needles to pierce your naked feet. Take care in such a place. It cannot decide what it is. Arrivederci.'

With that terminal remark, Mercy walked away and hovered around … searching for her next confrontation. Soul and Eve remained motionless and slightly overwhelmed by the forthright candour of their awesome hostess. They simply stood and watched as she went on the hunt.

Mercy had already homed in on her next target. The yellow spiral curls flopping down from behind the woman's lilac mask gave her away. Moving closer and peering through vintage opera glasses, Mercy spotted her 'post-it note' broadcasting the scales of justice alongside the Soviet flag. Mercy only knew of one legal person with Russian connections – Saskia Usov. More than anyone in the room, she savoured her meeting with Ms Usov the most.

She boldly parked herself alongside Saskia, then turning to face her full on, said, 'You are Saskia, are you not? Hello, I am Mercy.' Saskia had been anticipating this moment all evening and fully understood that the delay was Mercy's way of teasing her and extending her uneasiness. She knew all about women like Mercy. After all, her own mother had similar cold and calculating traits.

Saskia tried to appear casual and nonchalant. 'I am pleased to meet you, Miss De Vede.'

'Are you now?' responded Mercy curtly. 'You could have fooled me,' she added. Saskia bit her tongue. Although she had mentally prepared for this meeting, the acidic tone in Mercy's voice still came as a jolt. The young woman fought back, 'In fact, YES, I am pleased to meet you, Mercy. Why would I not be? After all, you were one of the best friends of my beloved sister Katya. I mean … Katya could have been alive right now if you had not involved her with the Baratolli case – but hey … a friend is a friend and any friend of my sister's … and all that shit.'

Mercy was impressed. Saskia had a bite. She retaliated by softening her tone. 'Look, Saskia; I am sorry for involving Katya in the case I was working on and if I could turn back the hands of time, I would. However, we both have her blood on our hands. I will admit as much and now it's time that you came clean. You are a smart woman – I know that for sure. When somebody hands you half of a cufflink set, which contains one of the rarest diamonds in the world, and asks you to deliver them to someone you suspect to be a criminal, there must be a teeny-weeny part of your privately educated brain that considers it could be payment for something illegal. You can wrap this up with all the fluffy cotton-candy excuses in the world, but I know that you know that the man you met happened to be in Atlanta on the day Katya was killed.'

Saskia went into defence lawyer mode. She wasn't sure if Mercy had any of this on tape. After all, MeDeVe investigation bureau had once boasted of an impressive reputation of being able to solve insolvable crimes. Mercy had every reason to hate her. She should say nothing. Her mind was gyrating in circles as she tried to work out how Mercy could possibly know of her meeting in Nice. Mercy's reputation was formidable. Was there anything this woman didn't know? My God – what if she was right? Had she taken part in her sister's own death? Saskia dare not contemplate such a horrible thought. Yes, she had floated that possibility past her conscience, but then relegated it to the back of her mind in the same way Saskia – the little girl – had dismissed her own mother's parental cruelty. The minutes ticked past, and still she had said nothing.

'Your silence is interesting,' whispered Mercy into Saskia's bejewelled ear. She continued, 'Look, dear, I can see that you are not going to enter into a conversation with me, so there is little point in knocking on a shut door. Just understand that I know far more than you think. I am more than aware that as much as you publicly professed to love your half-sister, you were also insanely jealous of her. She was your father's only legitimate daughter, and I suspect that you felt secretly delighted when her death now meant that you were Sergei's only remaining girl in a sea of boys. However, I do know that you didn't kill Katya. The Ouroboros paid for an assassin to kill her and I want to know who they are and why they did it. Katya was my friend and like a dog with a bone – I will not let go. I will not rest until I unmask the Ouroboros. When you are ready to talk, you will know where to find me.'

Mercy waited and still, no reply. She was faced with the silence and the expressionless, deadpan face of a Venetian mask. 'Okay,' added Mercy, 'we will play this your way. I am not judging you, Saskia. My team have been investigating you and I can see that your life has been difficult. You had a wealthy father who didn't care about you and disposed of your mother like she was a piece of trash. You were then left with a mother who resented you and then also abandoned you. You have since worked long, hard hours to bring some stability into your life and I can see how the attraction of easy money overruled your morals on this occasion. Don Morris is a very dear friend of mine and was formally a confidante of my father's. He holds you in the highest regard and he is a good judge of character. I don't think you are a bad person, Saskia. I may be a mean bitch from time to time, but I would never kick a person when they are down. Even wearing your beautiful Venetian mask, I can still see deep sadness reflected in your eyes.' Mercy knew what to say and when to say it.

Saskia unintentionally rubbed her lower stomach. She had wanted to tell Mercy that she was pregnant and that she needed the money to raise her unborn child, but then again that would have been an admission of guilt and so her lips remained sealed. Mercy noticed everything and so did not fail to observe the discreet tummy rub. She gently touched the young woman's arm. 'You will be fine, Saskia – your secret is safe with me. All I ask is for a meeting with George Smith. Get me that meeting, and what I have discovered about your involvement with Katya's death will go untold. I suspect we understand each other. You do know I could destroy you in a second don't you? Do as I ask.'

Mercy rudely placed her business card down the top of Saskia's corseted bosom and then walked swiftly away in the direction of Frank O'Byrne. Ms De Vede had delivered her message with unmistakable clarity. Inside her mask, Saskia seethed with rage. She had just become a victim of blackmail and placed into an impossible position. Her king was in check and there was no way to remove the threat, other than comply. How was she ever going to extract herself from this situation? She felt in turmoil. That darn woman had beaten her at her own game. She had shown but one second of vulnerability … just one bloody stupid second.

Saskia then spotted a man and a woman laughing near the bar. She had clocked his 'post-it note' earlier in the evening and knew it to be Soul. Don, forever delighting in celebrity gossip, had already told her that Soul was dating Darcy and that they had just bought an apartment together in New York. His choice of woman had surprised her … and if she could be truthful to herself (something of a rarity), this revelation had also hurt her. She had known that once upon a time, Soul had been attracted to her and the feeling had been mutual. However, she had rejected him as some poor Icelandic wannabe magician and as a hired help that she could not become involved with. In her mind, work and pleasure were kept in separate compartments. The man she now observed was still as handsome as he had ever been … in a tall, statuesque Viking way, but now he was also rich, successful and, if Don was to be believed – very happy. She tried not to sulk, but somehow the emotion enveloped her. Right here and right now, she so hated happy contented people.

Saskia approached Soul and his sister with some reluctance and introduced herself. They were both surprised to see her at Mercy's party and gave her a warm, affectionate welcome and a polite hug. She hated herself for resenting their frivolity and laughter. How could they enjoy such an evening when the whole thing had been staged by Mercy De Vede like some weird 'who dunnit' theatre. She continued to curse Mercy silently, thinking, 'For fuck's sake, why can't these idiots see through this pathetic masquerade? Was it Miss Scarlet in the kitchen with the rope or bloody Mr Green in the library with the candlestick? They are all being played and are too stupid to even see it.' She resolved to get the hell out and catch the next plane home. Just one more item of business to secure and she would be gone.

Saskia interrupted the socially pleasant conversation with Soul and his sister Eve, as best she could. 'Soul, I am not feeling too well so I am going to leave early, but will you give me a call, please? You may recall the Crank caves I asked you to investigate a few years back?' Soul shuddered as he recalled the abnormal energy of the place. Saskia continued, 'Well … we, as in the Ouroboros, own them now and have converted a farmhouse into a spa. You would be impressed if you saw it. It covers one of the entrances into the tunnel system. To get as far as we have has taken us years and multiple arguments with planning committees. Anyway; I won't go into that now as it's a long story. The Ouroboros need you to perform one last task. I have been trying to find your contact details, so just stumbling across you in Venice of all places, was a stroke of luck.' Soul was one of the few guests wearing a half mask and so his wide white smile was clearly visible as he replied, 'I am sorry, Saskia. I only work as a stage magician these days. My former clairsentience days of doing personal energy readings are well and truly over. I am sorry. I don't do touching rocks anymore. By the way, do you still have your half of our twin talismans – you know, the altar stone? Just curious.'

Saskia had expected this response and his attempt to move the conversation away from her request failed to impress. 'I understand what you are saying, Soul, but I am asking you to do this as a personal favour. The Ouroboros investment group are disbanding and my job will shortly be redundant. If you can do this one last thing, I will get a big bonus payment which will leave me secure during my days of unemployment, and as for you – you can write your own cheque.' Saskia turned her attention to Eve. 'I am sorry, Eve. I heard about your cancer diagnosis. Your psychic abilities are underused, yet also recognised as being immense. You would be of great assistance to the Ouroboros, alongside that of your brother. Your presence seems to amplify his abilities. I am aware that you and your husband have struggled to cope on just one wage since your illness. If you could please come along with Soul, for just this one last time – my boss "Mr Smith" will pay for the best treatment money can buy, anywhere in the world. You will also be paid handsomely in cash. I am sure you could do with the money right now. Oh, and Soul, no I don't have my altar stone thingy anymore. Turned out that it wasn't that special anyway.'

Saskia had played the ace up her sleeve. She was more than aware that Soul didn't really care much about money and that he had detested his experience at Crank. However, she also knew that Soul loved his sister Eve more than anyone else in the world. His own minor phobias would be trivial by comparison. The lure of money to help heal Eve was irresistible bait.

So, she had thrown him a proposal which was difficult to refuse. He knew Eve was in need of financial as well as medical help. 'Let me call you tomorrow, Saskia. I need to discuss this with Eve first. Oh and by the way, Saskia. Bad idea throwing your altar stone into the sea – seven years' bad luck and all that. Not to worry; it found its way back into my pocket.' With that, Soul opened up his hand. The two matching stones sat comfortably in his palm – one of them still wet and smelling of brine.

'Neat trick,' remarked Saskia, feeling both impressed and confused. She had indeed thrown her copy of the stone into the Adriatic. With Don's gossip about Soul and Darcy still ringing in her ears, she had thought about the magician with anger as she thrust the talisman towards the water. However, maybe the anger was more aimed towards her own stupidity at letting Soul escape. Nonetheless – here was the stone, back in his hand and bearing the faint, salty aroma of the sea. She concluded that Soul indeed had abilities that went above and beyond that of just an entertainer with a rabbit and a hat.

All in all, Saskia was happy with Soul's response, which she considered to be at least a consideration to work with the Ouroboros. After all, it wasn't an out-and-out rejection. She clicked her fingers at the waiter and ordered a water taxi, turning to take one last look at the tall magician with the long, blonde ponytail. She sighed – it was a sigh from the heart. She was attracted to him, she always had been. Life had just got in the way. It was not to be, but she was her mother's daughter and could flick a switch. Such frail emotions would not linger for long.

***

The foggy night was infused with drunken laughter as Saskia sat alone on the Piazza San Marco – directly facing St Mark's Basilica. She sat and watched the gondolas bob up and down in the moonlit water and contemplated how easily the blackmailed had become the blackmailer. She had hated this life. She would be glad to get the Ouroboros out of her skin.

A shadow approached her, seemingly out of nowhere. Wearing a long, red velvet cloak, its face was partially hidden by a cowl. The female figure removed her hood to reveal long, platinum tresses that fell to her waist. Saskia looked at her watch. 'Mother, you are late.' 'I am never late, darling daughter,' came the reply. 'I was simply waiting in the shadows and observing you fill your lungs up with smoke. You should take more care of yourself. That stuff will kill you. After all, you are only human. So, do tell – what happened?'

Saskia sucked on her cigarette. She so hated this habit, but her cells called for nicotine. 'Well, to begin with – I actually quite like Eve, although I think giving her cancer was a nasty thing to do. Did you have to go to such extremes, mother dearest?' The woman in red grinned as she looked down upon her human offspring. 'Had I not given her a tumour, which made her so sick that she lost her job, neither she nor Soul would have agreed to do what we ask – and believe me, they WILL agree. Do not forget, Saskia, we have a binding contract with the Ouroboros and this is the one last tick in the box before we are all set free. After we do as they ask, they will be gone forever and this planet will be ours to rule again. In my opinion, a few rogue cancer cells were a small price to pay. Anyway – she isn't exactly going to die from any of this. Just a bit of hair loss and a financial reality check. Nothing that money and a wig can't put right. You are way too soft, Saskia.'

Soft! The word spun around Saskia's head a few times. She had never been accused of being soft before. She rose to her feet. 'They will call me tomorrow; I am sure of it. Soul will not risk his sister's life. We have them in the bag, mother. It was a neat trick you played on them – intensely cruel and typically evil, but affective.' With that she turned to leave and Emmanuelle walked back into the water from whence she came.

Neither one of them knew that from within the deep, dark recesses of the church, they were being watched with great interest. The layers of the onions skin were being unpeeled.

CHAPTER 21

19th March 2017

The wind howled like an angry animal, whilst partially frozen raindrops spattered down on the car rooftop with noisy deliberation. Although still late afternoon, bruised storm clouds had turned the day into night. Heading away from the main dual carriageway, the streets became lanes and then the lane degenerated into a muddy farm track. As the Range Rover bounced through potholes, Saskia apologised to Eve, who was anxiously clinging onto the sides of her rear seat. 'I am sorry. I am trying to pick the ruts out with my headlights, but I can't miss them all. We should get all of this tarmacked soon, but it was last on the list of many priorities. This bloody project has tested me to my limits.' With that, they hit another pothole!

'Why now, why today?' asked Soul. 'This date may not mean much to you,' responded Saskia, 'however, to religious folks, scientists and pagans alike, after midnight tonight it will be the March Equinox. At 10.29 a.m. local time tomorrow, the sun will shine directly on the Equator and so for one day of the year, there will be nearly equal amounts of day and night throughout the world. Many people see the equal distribution of light and dark as being symbolic. To others, it is simply the beginning of spring and to Australians the beginning of autumn. To the Ouroboros it means nothing more than favourable astrological conditions. I don't want to steal Mr Smith's thunder. He will explain more when we arrive.'

Soul hadn't taken to the area when he had first visited it in 2011, and now – six years later, he was still on edge as they bypassed the farm track leading to the Crank caverns. The energy around the area was oppressive, and sparks of unseen electricity caused the hair on his arms to stand on end. Although she had never visited the area before, Eve was equally as tense as her brother. Gazing out of the rear passenger window, she sensed despair, desolation and – strangely enough – imprisonment. She went to touch Soul's shoulder to get his attention, and a zap of static electricity cracked on her fingertips as they made contact. They both screeched 'Ouch!' at the same time, as the tiny energy zap caused momentary pain. Yet again, Eve tried to get her brother's attention. 'Soul, what is this place? People have been lost here, trapped even. I perceive a strong desire to escape. I can almost hear the landscape screaming out. I swear, I have never been to anywhere like this before. I thought Darwydden was off the scale in terms of having a weird factor, but this place ... I can't put it into words.'

Saskia turned right onto a long gravel driveway and up a hill. The vista of the surrounding area was magnificent. Even on a dreary day, the hills of Wales and the Peak District could be seen on the horizon. Even steamed-up windows, and sprays of water from the wheels, could not occlude their faraway majesty. Ahead of them, the car headlights captured the sight of 12ft-tall electronic gates. The overhanging trees had low-dangling branches, which moved in the wind as though they were trying to grab the car before it escaped through the now-open gate. Soul almost thought he heard them sigh in disappointment, as the car moved out of their twiggy reach. Everything about this area seemed to be alive with noise. The brook babbled, the granite driveway mumbled, the walls gossiped and the trees complained as their barked tentacles creaked in the wind.

Saskia explained, 'We purchased an old farm building a few years back and it's taken forever to get it to this stage. Of course, we couldn't do much with the listed part, but the barns and outbuildings were ripe for conversion.' 'Why buy a small holding?' asked Eve. 'Good question,' responded Saskia. 'A lot of the surrounding land is greenbelt, so it's untouchable; however, the farm was ideal. This was one of the places we found which had direct access to the tunnel system below, so just think of it as one big entrance porch. The portals to the tunnel system took a lot of finding. We created lifts down into the lake and built an awesome spa area around it. What I don't know about spa water now isn't worth talking about, and don't get me onto the subject of the "Town and Planning Act, section 54A". I have spent years working with the Mineral Planning Authorities and circumnavigating the "Planning and Compensation Act 1991". If you think getting planning permission for the development of an old farm was tricky, just try getting it for an underground construction. That's why all of this has taken so long. Years and years of playing tiptoe with the planning inspectorate and holding hands with the countryside and environment agency.'

Eve was intrigued. She was captivated by anything that promised eternal life and beauty. The big 'C' word had a tendency to focus the mind on all things health related. 'What's so special about the underground lake?' she asked. Saskia was happy to wax lyrically about the sodium-rich 'soda water' which was naturally effervescent due to rising carbon dioxide bubbles. She then described the formation of the Halite crystals around the perimeters of the lake, at which point she handed her mobile to Eve so she could flick through her photos. Eve let slip a 'wow', as she viewed the aquamarine cubes which brought a surreal, bejewelled splendour to the underground cavern. Saskia continued to explain, 'The colour range of Halite is mainly caused by impurities. I am told that the deep blue and violet colours are actually caused by defects within the crystal lattice. Hey, whatever or however, they add magnificence and colour. Don't you agree?' Eve simply nodded as she scrolled through pictures of sugar lump quartz and giant rock crystals. Like mini-glass prisms, they reflected every colour in the spectrum when illuminated. Eve handed the phone back to Saskia, commenting, 'Who would think, looking at the drab flatness outside the window, that under those muddy fields lies a wonderland of natural beauty. What a find. I can understand why your colleagues were so keen to develop this Saskia.'

Eve was so taken by the conversation that she quite forgot they were visiting Crank for far more serious reasons. She continued to probe about the health and beauty benefits of the spa water. Saskia was more than happy to lighten the mood, and so went on to explain how the high silica content of the water could strengthen the spongy cells in-between the collagen and elastin fibres, therefore augmenting the skin and slowing the formation of wrinkles. If Eve could have found a swimming costume and jumped in there and then, she would have done so. She was sold and ready to sign on the dotted line for a lifelong membership.

Soul stifled a yawn. He was bored with the subject matter, but impressed with the way Saskia seemed so enthused about the spa project. He mentally reckoned that years of having to convince various planning boards about the benefits of a local health farm had indirectly caused her to convince herself. However, despite the superficial chatter, his skin prickled as though he was being hit by a deviant voltage. He felt deeply uneasy. He knew that he hadn't been asked to Crank to cut the ribbon on some grand opening of a beauty spa.

Driving closer to a sprawling, darkened building, Soul caught sight of an almighty tower. It was a colossal construction, pointing skywards like an arrow. Saskia parked the car and they all disembarked. Still transfixed with the tower and looking upwards, Soul asked, 'What have you made here?' The tower was mirrored and reflected the nearby scenery, almost making it invisible until in close proximity. The mirrors created a perfect camouflage for a structure, attempting to fit in with what was essentially a farming community. Saskia explained that this was a condition of planning consent and that the tower was a lift shaft. Soul didn't quite buy her line. He sensed an unusual energy surrounding the tower and was sure he could see a second structure hidden within it – a pyramid shape, maybe? A hidden pyramid – why would anyone go to so much trouble to make such a construction. He baffled him.

Saskia locked the car and guided her visitors towards the main entrance. Soul struggled to walk. His neck was still cranked backwards as he observed the unusual construction which had transfixed him. 'This reminds me of a control tower at an airport, except that it is something more than that, isn't it, Saskia?'

Saskia made no comment as she led them both into the huge reception area. It had all the guises of a spa – with soft aromatherapy fragrances floating through the air, and meditation music playing sympathetically in the background. The reception was but an empty desk, and the sumptuous leather chairs in the waiting area had yet to be sat upon. The ornate vase, decorated with gilded, cast-copper alloy, awaited the arrival of flowers that had yet to be delivered. Soul was by nature a tactile person and couldn't resist touching the Cloisonné enamel. 'You have been on one heck of a spending spree, Saskia – Ming dynasty, early 16th century, I believe. Mr Smith must have a big open cheque book.' Saskia ignored the comment. Indeed, money meant nothing to George Smith, but this was information she wasn't prepared to divulge. 'Wait here, please. Do help yourself to coffee or tea. I will tell Mr Smith that you have arrived.'

Soul moved over to the 'Fracino Cybercino' coffee machine, picking up a bag of Kopi Luwak. He turned to his sister, 'I won't tell you what they put in this to make it, Sis, but this stuff is the most expensive coffee in the world. We should try it. Or perhaps, we should avoid trying to work the complex coffee machine and just go for some simple Da Hong Pao tea instead. I understand that these leaves cost more than gold, but hey … no expense spared in this place, it seems. Now … where did they hide the kettle?'

'What is this place?' asked Eve, spiralling around to take in the unreserved opulence of the lobby? 'Well,' responded Soul, 'we know that it's pretending to be an upmarket health resort. However, I suspect it is trying just a bit too hard. Oddly enough, it reminds me of Venice and Mercy's surprise masquerade ball. I would guess that this entire development is little more than a mask to conceal its true self. Perhaps that's how Saskia managed to wangle the planning consent … by driving this forward as a business to bring employment to the local area. She is a smart woman and she would know the legal loopholes.'

'You saw something didn't you, Soul? When we got out of the car and you were looking up at the tower, and you were mesmerised. You didn't say anything, but I can read you like a book. What did you see?'

Soul finally located the kettle, but then went in search of water. 'Can you believe that after spending all this money on posh coffee and tea, they don't even have bloody water? I told you that this was all one big pretence. I feel we are on a film set, Eve. I was really looking forward to some Da Hong Pao. Darn it!'

Eve lost patience and asked her question for a second time. Soul gave up on his tea-making exploits and came to sit by her side. 'Okay, so what did I see? Well … the tower hides an inner pyramid. I could see the shape inside the outer structure. There are folks who believe that the numerology and dimensions of the pyramids have some deeper magical or mathematical meaning. I don't know if that is true or mumbo jumbo. You are talking to a guy who failed both maths and physics at school, but all I can say is that, be it steep and narrow, there is most certainly a hidden pyramid in that tower and that's for sure. I am not saying that it isn't a lift shaft – it probably is – but a lift to where, exactly?'

'You saw something more than just that, Soul. I am your sister so you can't fool me. Your eyes were not focused on the tower, but above it. What is in the sky above it, Soul?' Her brother became unusually coy and reticent. In recent years, he had tried to focus his efforts on becoming a stage performer and had underplayed his ability to see, feel and hear a side of nature mostly impalpable to those normal folks around him. His peculiar abilities were an embarrassment to him … yet that is why he had been brought to this place, surely. He decided he should share what he saw with his sister. If she laughed, she laughed. What the heck. He had become used to being the victim of cruel taunts.

'There is a hole in the sky – a hole above the point of the pyramid shape.' Eve fell silent for a moment – she hadn't quite expected that reply. 'What do you mean, a hole in the sky?' He continued, 'Above the apex of the pyramid, there is a hole in gravity. Gravity pulls us down towards the Earth. It gives us weight and basically stops us falling off the planet, as stupid as that may sound. I can see gravity every bit as much as I can see magnetic fields, and I am telling you, Eve, there is a hole in the sky above the tower right at this moment. It's a sort of channel, a place where gravity simply doesn't exist.'

Eve looked confused. 'So why are we not being sucked into it and thrown out into space, then?' Soul played with his fingers and appeared to be troubled. 'I told you, I failed physics at school – how the hell should I know. The darn hole is very small and in a very precise position, so maybe we are too big or just sat in the wrong place … with no water to even make a blinking cup of tea. Why do you always presume that I know everything? I don't have all the answers. My IQ isn't that great.' He sighed with exasperation.

At that moment, a woman they had never met before entered the room. She looked familiar, but neither sibling could make the neural connection. With a Southern American drawl, she pronounced 'We are so sorry to keep you waiting and I must apologise as I can see you have no drink. Let me make you some tea. My name is Arabella, by the way, and I am Mr Smith's PA. I will take you through to meet him in a moment. Don't worry, I will bring your tea in as soon as its brewed. I can tell that you are both quite thirsty after your journey. Isn't the weather awful outside. I hate all of this English drizzle. Tiny little raindrops seem to make one so much wetter than the big stuff we have back home.'

They watched Arabella with great interest. 'She just poured hot water from an empty kettle,' whispered Soul into his sister's ear. 'So what, you turned water into wine. Could you not have just made some water for us like she just did?' 'It doesn't work that way, Eve, and anyway – that was just a party trick.' 'Stop underestimating your abilities, Soul.' Arabella spun around and listened to the feuding siblings with a degree of amusement. She gestured that they should follow her.

Soul and Eve entered a dimly lit room. It was decorated with pitch-black walls, which contrasted sharply with the soft amber-diffused lighting. Arabella directed them towards a sumptuous leather settee. Eve considered that it was designed to disarm them. 'Little chance of attack or defence when at a lower level and sinking into a sea of cowhide,' she thought. A large mahogany office table with matching captain's chair faced them and of course was at a higher level. With no books displayed upon empty shelves, nor family pictures exhibited on the desk, the room appeared unlived in. The filing trays remained empty aside from one blank piece of paper, possibly added for effect. On the blackened walls, one single picture hung in isolation. It showed a man performing magical tricks for a small, appreciative audience. Soul wandered over to the wall and touched the frame. He turned to his sister Eve and proclaimed, 'This is by the French artist Alexandre-Évariste Fragonard. It's called "The Magician". Do you think this is aimed at me in any way? It is an original, of course.' 'Yes, of course it is,' uttered Eve – by now accepting the fact that what few random objects did reside in this strange building, they would be nothing other than the genuine articles.

Soul wandered around touching the walls, trying to conjure up an image as to their history. 'Interesting; all energy has been blocked from the building. In simple terms, this is akin to being in a sound-proofed recording studio. I have no idea how they have managed to do this. All physical matter carries an energy vibration, even if only slight. I can only think of one material which acts in this manner, and that is Preseli Bluestone. Someone has gone to a lot of trouble with the construction of this … erm health farm. I don't know what this place is, Eve, but it sure the hell isn't some swanky spa.'

Eve's thoughts meandered back down a lonely lane and to Mr Smith's PA. 'How do I know that woman and why does her name ring an alarm bell in my head?' Arabella had been heavily made-up, her eyes blackened by Kohl and further accentuated by ultra-thick lashes. She was wearing a mauve cowl-neck hoodie dress, which partially concealed her face. Wearing knee-high corset boots with platforms, her height and stature had been overly stretched. By all intents and purposes, she was in disguise.

With her thoughts still focusing on footwear, the office doors swung open and the highest, glossiest set of emerald stilettoes, boldly entered the room. Arabella beckoned the owner of the shoes to take a seat. The shoe woman disobeyed and perched herself on the edge of the table, waving Mr Smith's PA away with a dismissive wrist action. As her eyes adjusted to the light, she became aware of the others. 'Eve … Soul … what a surprise. I didn't know you had also been invited to this gathering, but of course I am delighted to see you both again. I am especially delighted not to be in this trendy mausoleum on my own. What is this place?' Eve laughed. 'Pleased to meet you again, Mercy, and indeed – we were just thinking the same thing.'

Mercy moved closer and sat on the arm of the cowhide settee. Eve silently admired her flawless presentation. Mercy's reputation had proceeded her into the room, and her ability to always dress as though she was attending a wedding, a christening or Royal Ascot was well known. Mercy spoke in soft tones as though the room had been bugged. A lifetime of working as a detective had made her quite rightly overly cautious.

Mercy whispered, 'The woman who led me in here, I know her.' 'She introduced herself as Mr Smith's PA,' responded Eve in equally hushed tones. 'Yes, she did,' replied Mercy, 'but I am sure that once upon a time she was Reed Baratolli's PA. I recall seeing her photographed with him in some magazine article about his record company. I never forget a face and with her goth, rock-chick image, she doesn't exactly dress to blend in.' 'She said her name was Arabella,' added Eve. 'Yes, Arabella – indeed, that was the name of Reed's PA. They are one and the same person … how odd! I am curious; I wonder how Reed's former PA found herself a job with the Ouroboros?' reflected Mercy with a quizzical look on her face. 'Coincidence,' responded Soul, eventually joining in with the conversation and appearing to look bored. 'I long since stopped believing in that,' added Mercy, moving over to a chair in the corner. 'Well,' added Soul, 'maybe it's because she is a demon, then. These walls have ears, but when we have time alone my sister should tell you what happened to her doctor husband when he worked in the US.' Eve shook with the sudden realisation that Arabella was in fact the corpse that mysteriously came back to life. Mercy looked slightly shaken by Soul's remarks, commenting, 'So Reed's PA was a demon then? Why should that surprise me? I wonder what demons are doing working with the Ouroboros?'

Soul looked worried. Thinking out loud, he asked, 'Why are we here?' 'Well, I think we may be going to find out soon. I can feel someone hovering outside the door and about to enter the room,' responded Eve, as her psychic senses tingled. About two seconds later, the door handle moved and Mr Smith walked in.

George Smith was also a man who dressed to impress. Wearing an Oxford blue Brioni pinstripe suit and a starkly contrasting crisp white shirt, he looked like a chief executive ready for a meeting in the boardroom. Soul had already noted the pricey Breitling hanging from his wrist, prior to looking down at his own ripped jeans and muddy Nike sneakers. Eve also did a selfie clothes check, quickly realising that both her and her brother had come sloppily underdressed for the occasion, whatever the occasion may be.

Mr Smith took a seat and studied his audience with great interest. Talking with an English upper-class accent and with a mere trace of suave, Scottish charm, he addressed his guests. 'Soul, Eve, Mercy – your names have come to my attention many times over the last few years, so I am delighted to meet you all at last. You may well be wondering why you are all sat in here together. Mercy, you demanded some answers and I can understand the reasoning behind that. You have had a difficult few years and so I suspect that to get some sort of closure, the truth may be an aid to recovery. However, I do not approve of the method you used in securing this meeting with me. Blackmailing an employee of mine is not a method I would sanction. I will tell you what you need to know and you may ask your questions, but after today you should leave Saskia well alone. Saskia is a mere employee and nothing more. Do I make myself clear?'

Soul and Eve looked at one another, and in a rare moment of sibling telepathy, considered that George Smith had no right to give a moral lecture about blackmail, considering that Saskia used the same coercion technique on them in Venice.

Mercy De Vede was not normally a woman who could be easily silenced; however, in her world it was a rarity to come across a person as forceful ... and as well dressed, as she was. Mercy found herself walking through the unknown terrain of admiration. She hardly dared admit it to herself, but she was quite taken with Mr George Smith. Unusually speechless, she simply nodded in compliance.

Mr Smith then addressed his other two guests. 'Soul, Eve – thank you both for coming here. You are both very unusual beings with rare talents. Soul, I know you do not like it here at Crank. I understand that your senses must be on fire, because indeed this is an unusual place and I am sure you can perceive that. However, I need to ask a massive favour from you. I cannot promise that what I will ask you to do will be safe; however, I can promise you that we will do whatever it takes to cure Eve's condition and from today her life will be made safe and without financial pressure. I am not asking you to do anything which is illegal. You will be helping me and my kind. I have friends who have been trapped on this planet for centuries and you can help return them to where they should be. Today will be a long day. Please follow me; we need to go elsewhere.'

As requested, the bewildered trio followed George Smith into a large, oval-shaped room. The entire length and breadth of the curved wall appeared to be made out of glass. They sat politely around a large, matching boardroom-type table. They were soon joined by several other mysterious strangers, whom George Smith simply introduced as other members of the Ouroboros, aside from one woman who he named as Isolda and one other female who he referred to as Arian.

Soul appeared to be confused. Isolda looked pale and thin, and although she had a face he didn't recognise, she looked familiar. She walked over to him to shake his hand and the vision that flashed into his mind from the touch of her skin nearly threw him off his seat. There was no need for any other words. George Smith would explain everything clearly to the others, but in that instant, Soul knew everything. He knew who Isolda was, and – more importantly – he knew what she was.

Mr Smith moved to the head of the table, and without so much as flicking a switch or pressing any buttons, the room's lights started to dim and the glass walls became one large plasma-type screen. Before long, an orbiting view of Earth – as would be seen from outer space, was visible from each wall.

Mr Smith stood for a while – smiling in awe at the planet, as though admiring an old friend. He began, 'My friends, I have much to tell you and very little time to say what I need to say. So, apologies if I cut corners, but we need to get through this in haste. Time is not on our side.' He moved closer to one of the screens and pointed to the rotating Earth. He began, 'Let us start with the beginning. This remarkable planet of yours was formed about 4.54 billion years ago, give or take 50 million on either side. Its birth was noticed from far away, observed from the outer edges of what you call 'Space'. Humanity is not the only intelligent life form in this universe, and there are ancient civilisations who have long since been able to view the distant corners of the cosmos. The development of this new planet has been watched with interest and fascination by many. To begin with, its colour was most unusual. With your primitive eyes, you can only see the Earth as blue and white, and that is because your retina and brain can only register three primary colours and then millions of secondary blends. In truth, there are six primary colours and many millions more secondary colours. To those with advanced sight, your Earth is a rare shade. Against the blackness of nothingness, it stood out like a glistening beacon. Of course, there is nothing in your language which describes this colour and neither can I illustrate it to you. How does one portray colour by using words? I can only assure you that from far away the Earth gleams with a rare, serene and beckoning hue. Any questions so far?'

His question was met with total silence. Nobody dare speak. Eyes were open wide and mouths gaped in stunned surprise, yet no noise emerged. 'Good, then I will continue,' added Mr Smith. 'For a very long time your planet lay dead and was far too hostile an environment to cradle life. Then about 245 million years ago, plants started to grow, seas became fertile and large creatures dominated the Earth. Your palaeontologist and geoscientist refer to this as the Mesozoic Era.'

With that statement, the planet on the screens were magnified to such a degree that the audience could see actual dinosaurs moving around. Mercy raised her hand. 'Excuse me for asking, Mr Smith, but I presume that what we are seeing now is a computer-generated mock-up?' Mr Smith smiled at the naivety of the question. 'No, not at all, Mercy. This is an actual aerial view that I dug out from our archives. You are the only humans to ever see your planet as it was when dinosaurs controlled the world. I hope you appreciate how privileged you are to receive such an insight.'

By now, of course, the trio had all realised that Mr Smith was not human. As that thought sunk in, a look of trepidation collectively visited their faces. 'What actually happened to the dinosaurs?' asked Eve nervously. Mr Smith paced up and down the room, mentally debating his answer. 'I should be honest with you,' he began. 'Those huge creatures ravished the Earth for around 180 million years, and what I mean by that is, they virtually ate it. Devouring it piece by piece, not unlike modern humans. The vast majority of them were herbivores or plant eaters. It was quickly getting to the stage that the plants could not replace themselves in time before being consumed. Their existence threatened the planet and put the development of other lifeforms in jeopardy. They had to be removed. This part of your history could be referred to as the "K/T extinction event". The dinosaurs were killed alongside 50 per cent of other life forms on the planet. It was a necessary clearing and a collective verdict. One does not exterminate a multitude of species without great deliberation.'

The room remained ghostly silent until Eve raised her hand. She could not help herself as she asked, 'Do you mean that you – or your kind – zapped them into oblivion?' Mr Smith was amused and laughed discreetly at her question. He replied, 'Not me or my species, Eve. We are well down the food chain and we simply don't possess that sort of planet-zapping capability. Sadly, we also are a primitive species compared to others. The universe has a power and intelligence all of its own and it can create or destroy at will. You may wish to call this God, or perhaps you have other names you can use. However, this power is not owned by any single culture or species. Thankfully, the universe is a power that asks and listens. It simply asked permission and as a celestial community, consent was given. From then onwards, a series of meteorites and other global calamities did their work. All life has a cycle, Eve, and these wonderful monsters had reached the end of their evolution. They had to go in order to make way for an intelligent life form – humans.'

Mr Smith paused for more questions, but as none came forth from the tightly pursed lips of his dazed guests, he continued. 'The dinosaurs last walked on this Earth about 85 million years ago and, following their extinction, there was a long and necessary period of rest and recovery. Then – fairly recently in the history of your world – Neanderthals evolved. We are only talking circa 200,000 years ago – quite recent by universal time standards.' He paused. 'I do not want to spend precious time giving you a lecture on palaeoanthropology, but it was important to set the scene for what we are going to share with you next. This planet recently lost a wonderful, iconic musician who created lyrics about my kind, *"There's a starman waiting in the sky/He'd like to come and meet us/But he thinks he'd blow our minds"*. Well, hello – we are here and we have been here for a very long time. Not always, but mostly we walk amongst you disguised as humans and there are many genuine reasons for this, but using Bowie's lyrics, the whole blowing your minds issue was a genuine concern.'

Over on the walled screens, planet Earth's tectonic plates could be seen cooling and shifting, along with the overlying continents. His guests were transfixed on the images, so Mr Smith sat down and gave them time to watch and ingest all he had shared with them. Gulping some of his own spa water, he then gestured for Isolda to take over.

Her slim frame stood tall and warriorlike. With all the composure of a Saxon princess, her crown was circled in gold twine and her shoulders draped with fox fur. Her eyes were fearless and bore the mark of one who had seen too much, yet her delicate face appeared taut and tense. She began, 'Good morning, dear friends – George has given me the "blowing your minds" part of this presentation. Thank you for this privilege, sire. I am not sure where to begin or how to say this delicately, so I will plough right in. Be prepared to be shocked.'

Eve looked at her brother Soul, who had so far sat in reserved silence. The moment he touched the hand of his ancestor Isolda, he knew instantly that she was an old soul in a deceptively young body. He had already seen the truth long before it was spoken.

Isolda began, 'There were once many different variants of humans on this planet, and yet today only Homo sapiens survive. When mankind started to evolve from apes, the race began. You may call it a competition if you like. It is the missing link question that has puzzled you for millennium. How did mankind emerge from apes? The answer to that conundrum is that – as a collective – other intelligent species, who possessed a similar cell construction of DNA to the apes, came to Earth to genetically engineer your species using their own chromosomes. You may refer to them as aliens. We see that as a derogatory blanket term; however, if it helps us to communicate with you better, we shall use your language. There were about eight different extra-terrestrial visitors in total, of which my kind were not included because we do not possess compatible DNA. The body I wear right now is but a suit of armour to protect me from your environment. If you could really see me for what I am, you would understand that the Ouroboros are distinct from many other forms of life. We were here merely as judicators – our part in all of this was to be unbiased judges.'

'Blimey, you were right when you said that this would be mind-blowing Isolda, and I am struggling to believe you, but intensely curious. What happened next?' asked Eve.

'Eight different types of Homos species emerged. The experiment was mostly deemed a failure, as for the greater part, seven of these were not well adapted to Earth's conditions and failed to evolve beyond a few thousand years. Homo sapiens persisted and the competition was won by a species not unlike yourself in both physical form and attitude, yet from a distant constellation. The successful species derived from Corona Borealis, which is a constellation of stars moving around the North Star. Their sun is called Alphecca, which has a twin star. For your general interest, this is known as a binary system – each star revolving one around the other. Their planet is Emania – the planet with two suns. My friend Arian here is Emanian, although she does have a holiday home on the dark side of the moon. It's just a convenience thing. You may think of her as the mother of all Homo sapiens, and in some cultures, she is deemed and worshipped as such, as well as being known as the moon goddess, for obvious reasons. Apologies, but she does not speak your language and cannot understand you. I can translate if you have any questions.'

Again, the room fell silent, so Isolda continued. 'There were some humans who retained knowledge of all this, and so passed these stories down over many centuries, mostly by way of bedtime fairy tales to their children. The goddess Arianrhod, who ruled Emania, to this day is still worshipped in some pagan religions. Primitive humans often worshipped what they didn't understand, yet in truth they understood far more about nature, the cosmos and their origins than modern-day man. 21st century Earth beings have gained technology, but lost contact with the worlds outside their own. We find that sad. You are all part of a greater universal family, yet have isolated yourselves within your own geography and kill each other with your futile territorial wars. It is an unfortunate trait you inherited from your Emanian forefathers.'

At the same time, both Eve and Soul looked at each other and uttered the word 'Darwydden'. Ruby spoke of the Druids in the mountains, who still connected with the Emanians and worshipped Arianrhod. Things were slowly beginning to fit into place. Soul finally opted to speak, asking Isolda's opinion of the more successful biological invaders.

Isolda did not hold back the punches. She responded, 'Yes, it was a surprise and maybe a disappointment that the Emanians won the genetic battle on Earth. If Arian could understand me, she would probably agree that there were far more gifted and less violent species, aliens who could have added different flavours to humanity. Not meaning to be disrespectful to Arian and her kind, sometimes science shakes the ingredients from the bottom of a bottle. To borrow a human phrase, "Shit happens!" The good news, however, is that some humans bred with the differing Homos before they became extinct, and so managed to retain DNA from several of the other seven species. They are few in number, but mutant strings of chromosomes still exist in humankind. We have observed such deviants with great interest. Through the passage of time and breeding, these unlikely shreds of DNA naturally become diluted and dissipated, but in a few select humans they remained dominant rather than recessive. It has been an interesting experiment, Soul. I hope I answered your question truthfully.'

Mercy finally chipped in. 'So how does any of this relate to Tamar and the biblical prophesies. As fascinated and overwhelmed as I am by all you have told me so far, I am here for a specific purpose, Isolda. I need answers. Who are the Ledanite cult and how do they link in to all of this?'

Isolda sat back down and pointed to a woman who had so far remained silent and whose face was partially hidden by a hood. 'Let me introduce you to someone who has had more involvement with the Ledanite than myself and is better equipped to answer your questions – my dear friend Carmen.' Mercy nearly fell off her chair as her former 'honey trap' employee removed her cape to reveal her identity. 'My God,' she gasped, 'can I not trust anyone on this Earth anymore? Carmen the alien. Well – such a phrase I thought I would never utter. I am stunned, and do apologise if the "A" word is an insult in the galaxy community, but I don't know what else to say.'

Carmen spoke in soft, reassuring tones – in total contrast to the usual giddy blonde Mercy had come to assume she had known and loved. 'The "A" word is fine by me, Mercy. I am the one who should apologise. I hadn't meant to be deceitful, but our kind cannot advertise our existence. To move amongst you, we have had to become one of you. I am sorry.' What else could Mercy say but, 'Apology accepted, but now, young lady – or whatever you are – tell me about the Ledanite. It seems you are an authority on the subject.'

Carmen responded as per command. 'Tamar was a remarkable woman, and one we respect and admire for her fortitude. Over 4,000 years ago, and in the era she lived in, she was unique as a female. I knew her quite well and as a person she was exceptional. She was rare, in that she had inherited the traits of all eight species, but only the finer traits. She understood that she was special, but not in a conceited way. She simply wanted to pass on some of her rare abilities and genetic coding for future generations. She told me that it was for a time when mankind was facing some of its greatest challenges. However, you must understand that Tamar was a woman living in Palestine thousands of years ago. This was an era and culture which viewed women as inferior beings. A woman as superior as Tamar had to tread carefully. She could only survive by marrying into a powerful royal dynasty and by her ensuring her descendants were protected through the turbulence of history by their stately birthright. The lineage of King David and King Solomon – along with Joseph and Mary – owes its roots to the lines of Tamar and her son Pharez. Nevertheless, the question you asked, Mercy, was about the Ledanites, so let me move on before Mr Smith looks at his wristwatch again. Tamar had twin girls later in life. She made one of the twins her exact clone and the child's name was Leda. Remember that Tamar had powers not bestowed to mere mortals, so she possessed this unusual reproductive cloning ability. Leda was the first in a long line of clones, leading right up to your client Eenayah Baratolli. The Ledanite followers were actually descendants of Leda's unidentical twin, Sheol. Her mother gave Sheol supernatural powers, so she and her descendants could protect Leda and her descendants, using whatever magic was required. The Ledanite followers – as descended from the lines of Sheol – believed in Tamar's prophecy above and beyond all else. They guarded the clones quietly and covertly. Through the passage of time, some clones produced more than one clone, maybe by way of a back-up. Fast forward into the future, and there was quite a collective of women genetically identical to Tamar. Not big numbers, but let's say enough of them to keep Tamar's unusual DNA protected for future generations. Their only mission was to protect them, in the hope that one day Tamar would be reincarnated into one of the clones. This was so that Pharez and Zarah could be reborn as sons who would become great leaders. This prophecy did exist and maybe even made its way into the pages of the Qumran Caves Scrolls. However, if it was ever incorporated into the Old Testament, then it was torn out. The prophecy was a secret, only meant to be shared from Ledanite to Ledanite.'

Mercy felt overwhelmed with the depth and bizarre nature of this information, but was also slightly cross that Carmen appeared to be defending a group whom she saw as meddlesome and dangerous. Not one to mince her words, she said as much. Carmen bit back, 'I am not justifying their actions, Mercy. Some carriers of Sheol's alien powers did misuse their abilities for their own gains. History is littered with such tyrants. I am sure that Isolda, as his former mistress, could tell us all about Rasputin's escapades. Just know that any earthling with such abilities can only be a descendent from Sheol, and that includes you two.' Carmen looked over at both Soul and Eve, who were now looking quite ashen following the disclosure that their own biology was part of this strange alien lineage of DNA. 'However,' continued Carmen, 'the Ledanites were only trying to do the right things for the right reasons, and yes ... sometimes they made mistakes. To err is human, is it not?' She sat down with an aggressive crossing of her arms. She hadn't meant to let her temper get the better of her, but Mercy seemed to be missing the point.

George Smith stood back up and took control of the situation. The conversation seemed to have become overly heated. 'We don't have all day to construct a post-mortem, Mercy. We are all aware that Eenayah Baratolli was an innocent victim in all of this, and that you also became caught up in a peculiar, tangled net. However, what has happened has happened. You now have Eenayah's sister and her twin boys under your protection, and for the foreseeable future, that is your job. It is a worthy job – you are blessed and privileged to have this responsibility. Just understand that many people throughout history have made huge sacrifices for these boys to be born, so take good care of them, please. If anyone on this wonderful planet of yours has that capability, it is you, Mercy De Vede, and the universe is eternally grateful.'

Eternal, universal gratitude – Mercy liked the sound of that. It matched her ego. She fell silent within her own self-righteous glow.

Soul interrupted the bonding ceremony which seemed to be blossoming between George Smith and Mercy De Vede to ask his own questions. 'So – aside from the whole Tamar prophecy and the fact that my sister and I have just discovered that we have a snippet of alien DNA from the line of Sheol – can you now tell me about your species, Mr Smith, and why you need me? What is this place you have created here at Crank, and please don't try to convince me it is simply a beauty spa. It has taken too much time, research, money, dynamite and resources for this to even secure a return on investment. The truth, Mr Smith.'

George Smith had always intended to tell the truth, but he recognised that Mercy had her dragons to chase first and it made sense to satisfy his audience's interest in order of priority. He commenced, 'My species come from the constellation Aquila and our planet revolves around its brightest star – Altair. Humans have not yet discovered some of the galaxies in my backyard, and neither will you for a long time to come. Despite our appearance, we bare little relation to your physical composition. However, like you, we have an inner energy and an outer shell. As judicators of the human experiment, we came to Earth to observe the process of human evolution. For us, this was a disaster. If you were to see us stripped bare, our inner souls burn like a raging fire, yet we live on a dark, cold planet. We breathe air, but the mixture we prefer is higher in carbon dioxide, lower in oxygen and we really love the sweet aroma of methane gas. Oxygen weakens us, we burn too bright and fade too fast. Our outer shells are much like your own. We are very small in comparison to Earth people and our skin is white and fragile like tissue paper. We communicate by the colour of our skin, so our skin is translucent and fluorescent in nature. We emit light by a substance in our tissue that has absorbed electromagnetic radiation. It is how we talk to each other.'

'So how can you talk to us now, George?' asked Mercy. 'How do you have a voice?'

'I am merely borrowing the vocal cords of the body I inhabit. I will tell you more about this soon, Mercy, but for now let me share with you what happened when we first visited your planet 200,000 years ago. Our friable skin became sore under the glare of your ultraviolet light. Earth's winters are just about bearable, but because we don't have sweat glands, the heat of even your coolest summer was too much for my kind. Many of us perished, and those of us who survived only did so because we learned to adapt to these conditions. We went to live underground, in deep places where the darkness and temperature suited us better. Some humans did know of us and referred to us as the Mithras. Others worshipped us as deities of the underworld. You will find a rich source of mythologies which talk of our kind. Older cultures knew of us, whereas modern man dismissed our existence as fantasy – the fairies at the bottom of the garden, so to speak.'

'So, you clearly look like a convincing human now,' observed Soul. 'What happened? What changed?'

'Some of us adapted and evolved. That tends to happen with all species after a while. Those of us who did adapt, discovered that we could discard our fragile bodies and inhabit a dead human body. We found that our intense inner energy could rejuvenate the cells, prevent the carcass from aging and even make it immortal. The shell I am wearing is the body of a real man. George Smith was born in the year AD 1680. The spirit of the human – George Smith, is long dead. He no longer needed his corpse, and so I can live in this shell for as long as I wish. I have inherited his looks, his vocal cords and his estate in Scotland. However, at some point humans will realise that George Smith is not aging. So, we need to keep moving around, avoiding friendships and relationships so to avoid suspicion. Either that, or we find a new shell to leap inside. We have done nothing wrong. The body we take, would only rot if left in the ground.'

Whilst consumed in heavy conversation, George Smith had not noticed that Saskia had crept into the back of the room and had been listening attentively. She spoke loudly, trying not to mask her anger. This was anger born through years of servitude and discreet diplomacy. She shouted, 'When exactly were you going to tell me all of this, Mr Smith? When Don Morris researched this area, he found a grave in the local church yard. We did wonder about it at the time, because the headstone was decorated with the sign of the Ouroboros. The person interned within was allegedly a Mr George Smith who died in 1720, and yet Don could find no burials for 1720. The parish records for that year and that year alone were missing. Are you now saying that everybody in the Ouroboros organisation knew – noticeably not me I may add, that you took the body of some George Smith chap? Are you linked to the St Aidan's grave, which I now presume to be empty aside from Kitty that is?'

Mr Smith put his head in his hands. He had not intended for Saskia to discover his true identity in this way. After a moment's pause, he addressed her. 'Perhaps if we are playing the truth game, Saskia, it is now time that you told the audience who and what your mother is.' Saskia's face went red as the fury built up inside her. She walked to the head of the table and faced the bemused onlookers. 'Fine – let's get all the cards out on the table. My father is a despicable Russian billionaire who uses and abuses everyone around him, but if you cut him he bleeds. My mother simply played him at his own game. I am not justifying what she did, but I believe her intention was to secure my future.'

Mr Smith responded, 'Your mother, tell us who your mother is, Saskia.' Saskia held her head low, possibly with a mixture of sadness and shame. She hardly dare look Soul in the face – she couldn't imagine what he must be thinking. 'My mother goes by the name of Emmanuelle. She is a demoness, that is … a very high-ranking female demon. So, whilst on the subject of mixing DNA, you now all know that I myself am only half-human. You have chosen to come to quite an unusual party, Soul.' Soul simply shook his head with both disbelief and disappointment. He had always held a soft spot for Saskia, though she had constantly spurned his advances. Nonetheless, he felt saddened by this new revelation.

Mercy now joined in the conversation. 'Bloody hell – Emmanuelle! She was the bitch who killed my father, or at least she gave him the stroke which killed him later.' Saskia was acutely embarrassed, 'I am not going to defend my mother, Mercy. She is a demon and by definition she does evil shit. However, she has always told me that she can only kill people who are dying anyway. She simply gives fate a nudge.' Soul interrupted, 'By definition, doesn't that mean all of us, Saskia? We are all dying, surely.' Saskia noted the look of contempt in Soul's cold Icelandic eyes and her heart felt heavy. More than anything, he was the one person she hadn't wanted to disappoint and having Emmanuelle as a mother, was hardly good news.

George Smith stepped back into control before the room ignited with an ill-timed argument. 'Now is not the time and place for such debates. Let me set the story right. In this human body of mine, I have all the abilities of a human. I have no superhero powers aside from the ability to keep this carcass alive and to prevent it from aging. That is it – no magic puffs of smoke, no alien probes, no wizardry or impressive paranormal stuff. I am simply Ouroboros energy in a human body. The same applies to many of us around this table. Occasionally, we need favours doing. Those of our people who could not adapt to jump into other skins became trapped within this Earth, many of them in caves, tunnels and old mine shafts. They naturally gravitate to these environments and can survive indefinitely in a state of hibernation, but that isn't the point. We need to rescue them and send them home. This human body of mine cannot walk through walls to find my lost friends, but demon spirits can. Rightfully or wrongfully – we traded with the likes of Emmanuelle. They located each and every one of our kind, moving spiritually throughout the unseen underground of your planet. In return, they ask us for favours. I am sorry, Mercy; Katya was your friend. I am sorry, Saskia; Katya was your half-sister. I apologise unreservedly to both of you, but Katya was deemed to be interfering with something that was none of her business. The demons didn't want to see the Ledanite prophecy come true, mainly for their own immoral reasons. Emmanuelle also wanted to punish Reed B, so she ordered Katya's death, and we had no choice but to comply. Indeed, we paid for it with the blood-red diamonds from our own mines. I am sorry, Saskia, but you were the one who made the transaction. At the time, I was not aware that Katya was your sister. You always told us you were an only child. It said as much on your CV. I don't have the ability to read minds. I don't know what else to say, but sorry. Your mother was correct in what she told you – the demons cannot kill someone unless they are already dying. They can help them make mistakes and trip them up so they break their necks – but direct murder, no, I have been assured that this is something they are not allowed to do. However, this human flesh that I wear, is capable of killing anything – dying or otherwise. The species that succeeded in creating your present human species – the Emanians, they are also killing machines, and that is why they won. They beat all the other competition by a process of extermination, and they didn't play fair.' George sent a fiery look in Arian's direction as he made the statement. As ethereally beautiful as she was, her slender frame was capable of immense carnage.

Eve stood up and stepped forward. 'I am a psychic medium and I can see the spirit world. So why did you not ask the angels to walk through your walls, Mr Smith? Why enlist the vile energy of demons?' Mr Smith looked puzzled by the question. After a short pause, he responded, 'In the world I come from, there is no good or evil. We do not make that definition. Your world confused us. We saw people you describe as good – politicians and religious leaders – create wars and urge mortals to kill one another. We didn't understand any of this as we assumed killing was a crime in your Earth laws. If we made a mistake, then that is unfortunate. To us, the demons were willing to help whilst the angels ignored our pleas. As strangers to your world, this made the demons the better spirits to deal with. How were we to know any different? Can you explain the difference between right and wrong to a baby?'

One could have heard a pin drop. The truth had been outed. Pandora's box had been opened. They all now knew that Saskia was half-demon and had unknowingly contributed to her own sister's death. They all now knew that her boss – Mr Smith – was wearing a body which died nearly 300 years ago, and he was in fact an alien in disguise. Eve and Soul now knew they descended from the lines of Sheol, and that their great-great-grandmother Isolda, was also borrowing the outer skin of a Saxon woman who lived in England many centuries ago. Mercy had her answers; this was the truth she was seeking but not the truth she expected. The atmosphere in the room was deflated. All went quiet, as each mulled over a new truth.

Eventually Soul broke the silence. 'So, okay – we all now know who everybody is. A slightly dramatic introduction even by my standards, but hey … the mask of illusion has fallen. My next question, Mr Smith, is …

what do you want with me and my sister? I presume this wasn't designed as some sort of alien meets demon counselling session?'

'I am glad you asked, Soul, as I was wanting to get around to this part sooner rather than later. We need to do what we need to do during the Equinox; 20th March at precisely 10.29 a.m., and not a minute later.' As he finished the sentence, an image appeared on the wrap around glass. It displayed the solar system with the light of the sun illuminating half the planet in light, whilst the other side of the Earth was shrouded in darkness. Automatically zooming into the latitude of 53.490665, longitude of -2.738947, GPS co-ordinates of 53° 29' 26.394'' N and 2° 44' 20.2092'' W, a shaft of thin, lilac light emerged in a straight line, piercing the Earth's atmosphere and entering deep space. Its source was from the apex of the hidden pyramid at Crank and its end destination infinite.

Mr Smith explained as his guests looked upon the image – each equally mesmerised. 'I will get to the point – the demons can walk through walls and see the energy of our kind, but they cannot physically pull them through the walls and return them to us. They cannot interact and engage with energy – not like you can, Soul. You earthlings big the demons up into something that they aren't. They prey on the insecurity and fragility of their victim, but are fairly useless beyond saying "boo". As for my species – the ones trapped beneath the soil of your Earth – many of our kind have already perished. The life force eventually drained out of them, sapped away by the brutality of time. Unless they had been able to find a discarded human skin to live inside, they would have died. Those of us who have survived, have evolved to conserve, repair and immortalise a human form. It protects our energy. Without that overcoat, we die, just as humans die. Living inside your empty and exhausted bodies has been our only way of survival. Dear friends, we have spent many years searching for any remaining survivors. We wish to depart this planet and return home, but not before we have located all members of the judicial team. We believe we have found three of them right here. When the boys who got lost in the Crank cavern perished, our kind managed to get into their shells. It is my understanding that the boy's death was an accident and my kind tried to rescue them, but they were children and they became frightened and lost. The myths and legends troubled the human population and they shut the tunnels down by blowing up the walls with dynamite. Our kind, still wearing the bodies of the dead boys, are deep inside the cave system. We have tried our best to rescue them and – yes – we had to construct a so-called spa to create a legitimate excuse to expose parts of the tunnels. How else could we explain the fields shaking and the sounds of explosion? However, our best has not been good enough. We have failed. If we cannot recover their bodies, we can only recover their spirits, and this means literally pulling them out in the form of pure energy.'

Mr Smith pointed to the screen and the lilac line of light. 'If we can get their energy inside this light at the exact moment of the Equinox, we have a chance to save them and send them home.'

Soul now understood. Eve now understood. Mercy understood. Saskia, eventually after many years of being the victim of silence and subterfuge, finally understood. Soul spoke. 'Mr Smith, I can see, feel, smell and sense energy – occasionally I can even change its vibrations to make it into something else – but I cannot become it. How can I just walk through walls of solid rock and recover your alien colleagues? I cannot walk through walls.'

'Yes, you can,' retorted Mr Smith. 'You are one of the few humans who descended from the gifted line of Sheol. You are a rare person – one bestowed with a magical fragment of DNA as a dominant gene, rather than the more common recessive version. You must believe in yourself, Soul. Self-doubt has always been your impediment. You are a direct descendant from the same genealogical line as Franz Anton Mesmer, Grigori Yefimovich Rasputin, Jean-Eugène Robert-Houdin and Count Alessandro Cagliostro. You should surely find confidence from your forefathers' ability. They were no more gifted than you are. Your grandfather Abaris, many hundreds of years ago, changed the energy from bones into a palladium – an inanimate object with an energy so great that it protected a city from attack. I can go on and on, Soul. How many more examples do you need? Should we subpoena Merlin?'

'You said it was dangerous. How?'

'I have given this much thought, Soul, and I can see only limited options. Either you free your spirit from your body to perform this rescue – in which case, your mortal body may perish if you are absent too long. Or … you convert your entire physical body into pure energy so that you can enter and exit the rock as one being. The latter option, though more difficult to achieve, should be your preference, I suspect. I must also warn you that my species possess a formidable inner energy. It is so potent that for you to simply touch it could possibly burn a hole in your aura. I cannot be sure, but contact with them may be fatal for you. I am asking you to do a selfless act, with no guarantee for your safety.'

'Is there not one other person on this Earth capable of helping you, George? Am I really the only hope for your lost friends?' Mr Smith looked troubled. What he was asking was almost too big of an ask. 'There is just one other. A young gypsy girl has developed an ability to move around mentally and spiritually, but we doubt she can interact with energy like you can, Soul. She is too much of a risk and this window of opportunity will not stay open for long. I am sorry to ask this of you.'

'What if I say no … just walk away?' Mr Smith touched his hand in an unusually intimate yet brotherly gesture. 'Soul – you are a kind man. In the past, men with great powers like yours have often been tyrants. You are unusual in that you are anything but. However, nature is the great equaliser. As with the Equinox, the universe enjoys balance and so for every oppressor, there is a liberator. For every right, there is a wrong, for every up there is a down. It was in the name of equilibrium that you should be born a gentle, empathetic man. However, I will not bind you to any agreement which will cost you your own life. You are free to walk away. I would only request that you do not disclose the secrets I have shared with you today. In case you are wondering, you will still be paid and we will still do all we can to help Eve. I am not holding you to ransom. This act of benevolence is of your own free will, or not at all.'

Soul felt overwhelmed and momentarily lost in his own thoughts. He respected the fact that George Smith was not aiming a gun at his head, and yet this hybrid alien had read him exactly right. It would always be Soul's instinct to help others, even at his own cost and maybe even at risk of his own life. 'Can I have time to think?' he asked.

Mr Smith smiled in a caring, fatherly fashion. 'Soul, you are mentally drained and not in a fit state to make any decisions right now –

let alone command a high voltage of pure energy. The Equinox is not until tomorrow and so we have at least 16 hours for you to chew the cud. Can I suggest that you and your sister be the first to swim in our underground lake. The health-giving properties of the spa are not some phony make-believe marketing ploy. Once we have completed our mission, this place will be put up for sale as a legitimate and very expensive health retreat. You should all go and enjoy the facilities whilst they are still free. It will do you all good to get some much-needed relaxation, especially for you, Soul. The term "recharging your batteries" was never a more fitting saying. Mercy, you are also welcome to stay. My staff will prepare rooms for you all and bring you costumes to wear. Have a good night's sleep, Soul. I will meet you for breakfast and you can give me your decision then. Would that be okay?'

Soul simply nodded whilst his sister had a grin the size of a cut melon. The thought of embracing the special properties of the underground soda water had lightened her spirit. Saskia held her hand up and coughed, 'Err, erm.' George Smith looked back at the wistful, wanton face of his employee. He yielded to her puppy dog eyes. 'Okay, Saskia – you have worked long, hard hours for many a year – you deserve some time out. Go and splash around with your friends, but 8 a.m. prompt – I want you all to be sat at the breakfast bar. I am making it your responsibility, Saskia, to have everyone there on time. Am I understood?'

The group were mentally exhausted. Their heads hurt – brain cells filled with bizarre information that they were all still struggling to compute. The lake seemed like a good idea. Time out to talk between themselves, get a grip of the enormous task Soul was being asked to consider. Time of quiet contemplation. Maybe a 'last time' situation!

Saskia nodded, smiled and then hurried her friends over to the lift shaft that would deliver them to an exotic, subterranean world. A world of crystals, colour, translucent waterfalls and restorative miracles. She had always wanted to bathe in the lake herself, but had never dared dream it would be possible. For now, it was – but for all the wrong reasons. Tomorrow was another day.

CHAPTER 22

20th March 2017

Saskia ambled coyly into the breakfast bar, looking the epitome of natural beauty in her simple Broderie Anglaise dress. Soul was munching his way through a bowl of organic granola when he looked up and caught sight of her heading in his direction. He felt an unlikely mixture of emotions – anger, sadness, regret – but mostly a warm fondness for the spiral-haired lady about to sit opposite him.

It was awkward! Neither of them really knew what to say next. Saskia wasn't usually one to blush, but the redness of her cheeks seemed to be amplified by the crisp whiteness of her dress. 'I'm sorry,' she uttered. 'Don't apologise,' responded Soul. 'After all, why would someone like you want to sleep with someone like me?' 'Do I need to remind you that you have a girlfriend,' snapped Saskia.

Soul didn't respond and swigged down his fresh orange juice in one gulp. He hadn't intended to be unfaithful to Darcy, but then again Darcy hadn't exactly been the loyal girlfriend waiting at home with granny slippers and a cup of hot chocolate. His flirty Welsh lady friend had never made any secret of the fact that she had wanted an 'open' relationship with Soul. He had understood from the beginning that Darcy was a sexually liberated Celtic live wire, and not one to be tied down. She had a take it or leave it attitude. He took it – but he didn't like the situation. Not that Saskia could possibly know any of this. She had always been the one he had desired, but years of rejection had worn him down. It was quite simple – Darcy was available and Saskia wasn't. He sighed a deep, remorseful sigh and felt angry for giving up on her so easily. The thought 'faint heart never won fair maiden' came to mind.

As Saskia got up to locate the serving counter, Soul caught her arm and pulled her back. He whispered, 'Look, thank you for last night. I was just a bit upset to wake up and find you gone. An empty pillow can be a tad insulting.' Saskia replied with gritted teeth, 'I work here, Soul. I have my own room here, furnished with all my own belongings. I am not a teenager anymore. I don't do the whole sneaking down the corridor at 7 a.m. thing. Do you really think I want my boss to see me leave your room with dishevelled hair and mascara smudges? I am beyond all of that. Let's just forget that last night ever happened. You have a big, important morning ahead of you and I have an empty stomach. Excuse me.' With that, Saskia wiped his hand from her arm as though an insect had landed on her. She shot him a fiery look and walked brusquely away. As rejections went, it was acidic.

He had desperately wanted to explain to her that although Darcy was his girlfriend, she was also a player and that he would be more than happy to end the façade of their coupling. He had wanted to tell Saskia that he loved her – that, in fact, he had always loved her. But, as always, his timing was lousy. The moment had gone.

Eve entered the room looking pasty-faced and with dark circles under her eyes. Soul could tell that she hadn't slept – probably because she was worried about him. Maybe more so than anyone else, Eve knew that her brother was about to attempt something very dangerous. As her skeletal frame sat down beside him, Soul was reminded as to the reason he had agreed to any of this. He tenderly touched his sister's cold, thin hand. 'Are you okay?' he asked. Eve looked him directly in the eyes. It was a deeply probing, brain-piercing scan. She then looked over to Saskia, who was availing herself of a full English breakfast. 'Oh no, Soul. Please tell me that you didn't?' He had never been able to hide anything from his sister. She could read every neural transmission that fired within his cerebral cortex. 'Please don't give me a lecture, Eve. I am a grown man.' Eve loved her brother. She hadn't intended to give him a matriarchal 'telling off' – but she was concerned. 'You needed all your energy for today, Soul – that's all I wanted to say. That alleged "early night" you had after the spa session was supposed to recharge your batteries. Your energy was not meant to be wasted pleasuring Shirley Temple over there. Have you any concept of what George Smith has asked you to do and do you have any plans, tactics or strategies as to how you are going to achieve any of this? Have you given his request any serious consideration at all?'

Soul focused on stirring his coffee cup. It was an unnecessary action, anything to avoid his sister's livid, ice-blue eyes. He gave her question some thought and eventually responded, 'Well, from what I understand, the Ouroboros – or whatever name they bloody well call themselves – have mislaid some of their cabin crew. I understand that they presently reside in the former bodies of three young boys who went missing in the Crank caverns hundreds of years ago. Mr Smith is going to take me to some wall in the caves and somehow, I know not how – I have to get myself through the wall and into the cavern where they are trapped. Then by some means, I need to pull their energy out of their borrowed human bodies and deliver their energy into this funky lilac light – which, at precisely 10.29 a.m., will suck them up through a hole, George Smith and his team have punctured in gravity. Oh, and just in case I forgot to mention it, I think they have also created a rift in the Earth's magnetic shield as well. Let's hope the birds don't start falling out of the sky. So, Sis, should this all go to plan, then happy days, as they get to go back to their own planet. As for me, I have to do all of this without killing myself and to an exact time schedule. Let us not forget that I have never dematerialised myself before and I am not sure I can even walk through a wall. Have I remembered everything, Eve, or is there some minor detail in my understanding of the gravitas which needs modification?'

Eve shrugged, 'Well, erm, yep … you seem to have a handle on it, Bro, and it's nice to hear you using big words. Gravitas – 6 letters, not bad for a school dropout. Just one thing you need to remember, though – your body is still very much alive. The cadavers George Smith and his mates wear died centuries ago. The second they quite literally jump out of their skins, the human remains will disintegrate. You have far more to lose. A body and its spirit are connected. If for whatever reason you fail to dematerialise and instead allow your spirit to step out of its body and run free – isn't there a danger that your body will just die?'

Once again, Soul avoided looking at his sister's face, by now more worried than angry. 'I once considered including teleportation as part of my stage act. I never quite got around to it, but I did do some research into out-of-body experiences and astral projection. My understanding is that I need to reach some fourth dimension. Oh shit … I wish I had done more research into this stuff. I just got freaked out by it, so took it no further.'

Unbeknown to Soul, George Smith was now standing behind him. 'No need to worry about any of this,' he exclaimed – placing a reassuring hand on Soul's broad shoulders. 'Mastering astral physics and time-space travel will be simple for someone as gifted as you. We will teach you all you need to know. Your sister Eve is here because as a person with occult perception, she can view the local etheric environment. She will guide you and, if need be, pull you back. Your only risk is in touching the raw energy of the three trapped ones. However, the fear will only be in your mind and we can teach you how to overcome this. You have always been fearful, Soul, and this has thwarted your progress as a truly gifted magician. Once you conquer your fear, you will gain an immense insight to a remarkable universe. The lessons you are about to receive will possibly make you the most powerful man on Earth. We are comfortable with this. We may be another species and unimaginably diverse from humanity, but we recognise your grace and kindness as a man. As such, we are happy to share this knowledge with you. We feel certain you will put this power to good use.' With that, Mr Smith handed Eve a dappled red apple. 'Take care of your brother, Eve, and we will take care of you. However, time is against us, so now we need to take you both into the caverns to meditate. You haven't eaten, Eve, and your glucose levels are low. You need more energy than what presently flows through your blood. Eat this apple – it will perk you up.'

At that moment, Mercy De Vede entered the breakfast room; her emerald stilettoes making a clickety-click noise, which could be heard long before she could be seen. Trying to read the body language of George Smith alongside Saskia, Eve and Soul, she asked, 'Have I missed anything?'

There was a slightly gauche reticence before Saskia piped up, 'No, nothing worth writing home about.' It was a statement delivered with a hint of sarcasm. It was meant to hurt and this did not go unnoticed by the ever vigilant Miss De Vede. 'Okay, I get it,' responded Mercy, 'we have secrets in the room. No worries, I will dig out the skeletons soon enough. As you were.' With that she saluted the team by way of a mock military gesture and made her way over to the yoghurt and fruit bar. It was 9 a.m., and time was moving on as time inevitably does …

The Equinox was nearly upon them … and a window of opportunity which would not stay open for long.

***

George Smith gestured that Soul and his sister should follow him. He called over to Saskia and Mercy, 'Isolda will bring you in later. We just need minimal disruption for the moment.'

He led them through an unusual octagon-shaped archway and down a long corridor painted in an opaque amethyst colour. The siblings presumed that they were heading for the lift down to the underground lake and spa complex. However, Mr Smith took an unexpected left turn towards a cleverly concealed exit. Opening a half-hidden door, they moved into yet another corridor made entirely out of mirrors. Both Soul and Eve felt disorientated, as the mirrors reflected mirrors within mirrors into an infinity of glass. Losing perception of their special awareness, Mr Smith noted the bewildered looks on their faces. He explained, 'We have had to make a lot of structural alterations to this farm building and the various tunnels that lie beneath. Without planning permission, the detonations would have sent off alarm bells. You can see what a quiet area this is. Just farms, fields, hills and a handful of houses. Such a disruptive process as building all of this would not have gone unnoticed.' Soul nodded as though he understood. 'So, you had to dress it up as a spa rather than an interstellar staging post.' 'Exactly,' responded Mr Smith with a smile on his face. He liked Soul's wit and dry sense of humour.

The trio then entered another elevator, which took them down into a different part of the subterranean system. Soul appeared calm and relaxed, but Eve fidgeted. It was clear that his sister was feeling apprehensive. As they exited the elevator, Mr Smith pointed in an upwards direction towards a slender tunnel which ran alongside the lift shaft. He explained, 'This channel leads up to the tower you probably noticed on the outside of the building. It leads directly to the apex of an inner pyramid. It may interest you to learn that the meaning of the word pyramid translates to "fire in the middle". The angles within its shape project radiation towards the central chamber and it is this that gives it the power of upwards acceleration towards Earth's atmosphere. The internal construction of the channel is made from piezoelectric rose granite, so the tunnel even generates its own magnetic field. Maybe now you understand why we chose you, Soul. Your ability to interact with matter and energy is unique. This is the channel you need to lead the entombed energies towards. You may need to push them inside, but do not enter yourself. Directly above the apex there is no gravity, and as you have also noticed, Earth's magnetic field has also been deactivated at this precise point. The combination of this and Earth's magnetopause, at the noon to midnight meridian during the Equinox, will have a dynamic effect. In astrophysical terms, it will be like firing a bullet into the galaxy. Our trapped astronauts will ride home on a solar wind ... winds usually rendered ineffective by your planet's magnetic field. The conditions will be perfect.'

Soul was overwhelmed. Physics had never been his best subject and most of what Mr Smith had just told him flew way over his head, but none of that mattered. He had lived his life believing that his unusual powers were a fruitless folly. Aside from helping him carve a career as a stage magician, he had deemed his abilities to be unusable. However, now he was being held in esteem as a unique individual. He now longed to touch the inside of the pyramid's inner channel and link with this force of immense magnitude – a power beyond his wildest imagination. Despite the temptation, he heeded George Smith's cautionary advice to keep well clear. Eve could hear what her brother was thinking, and gave him a warning glare.

Close by the channel, they found themselves faced with a substantial granite wall. Mr Smith touched it. 'This is solid rock. It lies directly below the main crossroads of the village. If we detonate this – and it would take a considerable amount of dynamite – it would demolish the village above. We would not cause such wanton destruction to save just three lives. This is the rock you need to move through, Soul.' Soul laid his hands on the granite and closed his eyes. He remarked, 'This is around 100 yards thick, George. This isn't a wall, it's a solid mass of impenetrable matter. I can feel the energy of those hiding behind it. Their energy is magnificent and sizzling like a fire – but they are afraid. My God, they are trembling with fear.' Soul was shocked by his own words. He hadn't considered that the alien life forms had emotions. For the first time since they had arrived, he felt compassion for these poor, trapped creatures. He could tell by their energy that they were ancient beings with a wise yet gentle essence. He touched the rock face again. 'You have drilled another substance into the granite. I always fell asleep in my chemistry classes, but I can sense a phyllosilicate mineral containing aluminium and potassium, with the chemical formula of KAl2(AlSi3O10)(F,OH)2. I have no idea what I have just said, George, but I do see twinned green crystals with flat, five-pointed stars. Why have you done this?' George Smith was impressed. 'We have inserted some Muscovite crystals to help your spirit move through the wall. Muscovite will encourage the devas of the Devic kingdom to assist you. You may not understand this as yet, but at some point in your future, you will learn to harness the power of prana. This is a lesson for another time. Just know that this has been done to help you.'

'What do I need to do, Mr Smith? How can I help them? They are in an elevated state of distress.' Mr Smith pointed down at his own body and explained, 'What I wear is a human shell. I need to keep it warm; allow it to sleep; hydrate and feed it. I can keep this body functioning forever, as long as I maintain its condition. My colleagues trapped behind those walls wear the shells of young boys who died in 1793. Their bodies have not been cared for and they are deteriorating. To be blunt, the human bodies are at the point of death. As with your species, we cannot live without an outer shell. It is now or never for them, Soul, they understand that.'

Mr Smith pointed to what looked like two massage tables. 'Unlike our demon collaborators, your body cannot walk through solid matter, but your spirit can. Conversely, unlike them, you can connect to my friends – pull them out of their prison and into the chamber of the pyramid. To do this you need to meditate, in order to change your brain function. You need to aim for an alpha/theta brain wave condition. Basically, you need to mimic a REM sleep state.'

Soul looked down on the ground as self-doubt invaded his ego. George Smith sensed his reticence. 'You can do this, Soul. You have conjured up far more impressive magic than merely astral projection.' Soul asked, 'Why is Eve here? What do you want with my sister?' George Smith responded, 'She is connected to you telepathically, Soul. She can watch you as you enter the cavern and communicate with you. If you get into any sort of trouble – and we don't anticipate any problems – she has the capability to astral project into the cavern herself and pull your spirit out. We know Eve is fragile and we do not envisage her needing to do this, but neither do we want you making a martyr of yourself. My friends have been trapped in here for a long time, but we do not want you harmed just so you can help them return home.' Soul didn't need to be asked twice. He recalled the fear and desperation of the strange aliens incarcerated within the caverns. 'Let's do this, George. It's worth a shot.'

***

Soul and his sister lay motionless on the black leather tables. George Smith watched silently, as other members of the Ouroboros crept quietly into the dark cavern. It was uncomfortably warm for them, but they understood that the heat would help Soul relax and reach the mental state required.

Whilst keeping one eye on the time, George Smith observed Soul carefully. The young magician's eyes were twitching erratically and the heart rate monitor indicated that his pulse was tachycardic. Isolda looked concerned. She commented, 'Eve looks so relaxed in comparison. Her respirations have slowed right down and her pulse rate has decreased to 50 bpm. She is where she needs to be. What is going on with Soul? He seems to be fighting it.' George had considered the same thing. Time was not on their side. 'I am going to try to talk to her,' he added. He touched her hand gently. 'Eve, Eve – can you hear me?' Eve responded positively. 'Where is your brother – can you see him?' 'Yes, I can see him,' she replied. 'He is out of his body, but just stood at the wall. I don't know what is wrong with him. He isn't so much afraid as distrusting his ability.' Isolda turned to George. 'I told you this might happen,' she scoffed. 'Brilliantly talented human – yes, indeed – but such low self-belief.'

At this stage, both Mercy and Saskia had been led into the room. The atmosphere was quietly tense. Eyes made contact with eyes and no words were spoken. Soul's heart rate continued to rise, whilst in contrast his sister was in a state of pure tranquillity. 'Should we give him some gentle sedation?' asked Isolda, eying up the IV cannula fixed into his veins. 'Perhaps it will help,' she added. George Smith wasn't so sure. He would have preferred Soul to be in a natural state of relaxation rather than a chemically induced REM. He mentally deliberated. Just as he was about to give Isolda permission to induce a deeper sleep state, Soul's arms suddenly slumped to his side, as though lifeless. His heart rate decreased dramatically to 30 bpm and his breathing was almost non-existent. Saskia was concerned. 'Can someone find out what is happening?' Eve heard her plea as though it was a prayer that came from the heart. The emotion in Saskia's voice surprised her. His sister spoke up, 'He is behind the wall. He is okay. I can see the entire cavern as though I am looking through his eyes. There are many spirits in there – human spirits. I can see the souls of the three children who perished. There are many others who died in here. It is an awful place – so much pain and dread.

The smell is rancid. Skeletons and decay everywhere. I see the alien life forms in the children's former bodies. Soul is trying to reason with them. They are too scared to come out of the boys' remains. They are terrified. Soul doesn't know what to do. There is also a woman in there. Long red cape and long, light blonde hair. She is not one of them. She seems to be finding all of this amusing.'

George Smith looked at Saskia accusingly. 'Emmanuelle, no doubt! Why should her presence surprise me? Why have you dragged your mother along for the ride?' He continued to glare at his young employee, who responded, 'I haven't dragged her anywhere. She has a wicked mind of her own, Mr Smith. You should know that by now. I hate her more than you do. To her, this will be a form of entertainment.' Isolda touched George's arm. 'He only has 15 minutes on the clock, George.' Eve heard the comment, 'I will tell him that he must hurry up. What should he do if they refuse?' George answered, 'He has the ability to command their energy. He should reach for their hands and pull them out one by one. Tell him not to touch them for too long, as they could scorch his spirit.' 'Okay, I will tell him,' replied Eve. Her vital signs had hardly altered the whole time she had been in an altered state, yet now, her pulse rate increased ever so slightly. It was as though her mouth obeyed, but her heart was unsettled.

In total contrast, Soul's vital signs remained erratic – yet were so abnormal that he barely registered as alive on the monitors. Eve then suddenly gasped with such an unpredictable jolt that the whole room jumped. 'Oh my God,' she screeched, 'he has just pulled one out. The being is on fire. The child's body it lived inside has just crumbled into dust. That isn't a vision I care to remember. He is racing with the spirit towards the wall. My God, it has semi-merged with his own spirit. His hand and his arm are on fire, as well.' She paused for a moment before continuing. 'He is through the wall.' Everyone turned to look towards the tunnel – the inner channel containing the pyramid and an inner chamber. There was nothing to be seen, nothing to be heard. Only Eve had the capability to visualise the spirits. Mr Smith smiled. 'The light has turned rose pink. One of them must be safely inside. What a relief.' He exhaled as though he had dared not breathe prior to that moment.

'Soul has gone back into the cavern,' announced Eve. 'I can sense his mood. He feels confident now. He is in some pain, though. I hadn't been aware that one's spirit could feel pain. That is a new revelation to me. He has been burned slightly. The heat from your species is like a furnace.'

Up until now, Mercy De Vede had remained quiet, but curiosity finally got the better of her. She turned to face George Smith. 'What exactly is your species, Mr Smith? I mean, who are you, what are you, what the hell is your real name?'

'My species do not possess vocal cords, Miss De Vede, so we have no spoken name. We communicate by light and sonic sound waves. We live in a cold, dark, watery place. We are so intensely hot on the inside that we constantly need to cool down.' 'Hmm,' responded Mercy, for once almost lost for words. Years of training in the Metropolitan police force had not prepared her for such a wildly surreal conversation.

At that moment, Eve started to talk again. 'He is struggling with the second life form. It is resisting. Poor things, they are just so frightened. He has almost had to jump into its flames to pull it out. He has managed – only just – but yes, he has it. He is running with it. He is on fire. Can he recover from this, Mr Smith?' George Smith didn't know the answer.

Soul's blood pressure was falling dramatically low. Isolda drew up some adrenaline in case an intracardiac injection was required. Soul's mortal life now became a concern. A whoosh of pure pink energy lit up the inner chamber of the pyramid with a bright display of surreal light. Isolda proclaimed, 'The second one must be in there. It's 10.20 a.m. We only have nine minutes until the Equinox. Do you want to call time, George? I am concerned that Soul could be about to have a cardiac arrest. He is hardly alive.'

George Smith looked at the pale, limp body of Soul – a brave man who had displayed a heroic lack of concern for his own safety. A man he respected. A gifted magician who had come to the rescue of creatures so remote from his own biology and understanding, that he couldn't even imagine how they looked – and yet he had understood their distress. Displaying immense selfless compassion, he had responded to the distress call of beings far removed from humankind. George spoke softly to Eve, 'Please thank your brother for all his help, but tell him to get the out of the caves now and back into his body. He has saved two of my friends. The remaining one can always wait for another opportunity.' Eve nodded – she understood the instruction.

Saskia now looked genuinely worried and full of remorse at the way she had treated Soul earlier in the day. She ran to George Smith's side and tugged at his arm. Struggling to control her tears, she asked, 'If he dies, can you bring him back to life? You can do immortality, healing and all that weird stuff, Mr Smith. You can repair bodies – can you repair his?' George put a comforting arm around his employee. 'You are correct in saying we can repair and immortalise the human body, Saskia – but only if we live inside it and take possession of it. If Soul was to die and I was to jump into his body, it would be me and not him. The person you know – and I suspect the man you love – would be dead.' 'Can you not do it for just a few seconds, Mr Smith – jump in and then jump out again?' George began to feel immense guilt for ever involving Saskia and Soul with his rescue mission. With a heavy heart, he replied, 'No, it doesn't work that way, Saskia. I borrowed the body of a man called George Smith, who died in 1720. What you see when you look at me is a 297-year-old corpse. The moment I vacate this shell, it would turn into a skeleton and I wouldn't be able to recover it. The same applies for all of us in this room. Isolda is in the body of a woman born in Saxony over 1,000 years ago. If she exited her human body, it would become dust. We can't go leaping around like frogs. I am sorry, Saskia.'

Once again, Mercy's inquisitiveness had been stimulated. 'Who is, or should I say who was, George Smith?' Mr Smith shrugged – more than happy to diffuse the tenseness of the situation. 'All I know from the team who found a body for me, is that he was a wealthy Scottish land and mine owner. He came to Crank with a view to buy the mine. As he was exploring the entrance area, I believe the cave roof gave way and crushed him and a few others who were with him. His wife Kitty was also injured in the mine, and died shortly afterwards. For us it was a tragic, but convenient, accident. My associates pretended to bury them both and marked the coffin with our sign – the Ouroboros, the sign of immortality. We do this in case we ever need to return the body to its grave. You may see us as a ruthless bunch of body-snatchers, but we try to be respectful of the cultures and traditions of the species we work with. George Smith's body was a useful possession, in so much as he had no family and we could assume his wealth. I hope that answers your question, Miss

De Vede.' Mercy shivered. The thought of her talking to a walking corpse possessed by an extra-terrestrial life form was giving her the creeps. She concluded that she had been in some odd situations during her career as a detective, but nothing could remotely compare to this situation.

Eve had become deathly quiet and, still in a meditative state, had not spoken once during this entire debate. A single tear made its way down her cheek. Saskia noticed the tear. 'What's the matter, Eve? Are you sad? What's happening in there?' Eve let out a sigh that came from the pit of her stomach. 'I have tried to reason with him. He won't see sense. He wants to recover the last one.' George Smith looked at the clock on the wall, as it ominously ticked away second after second after second. 'He only has five minutes,' he responded, 'he has run out of time – get him out.' 'Do you want me to astral project?' asked Eve. 'Yes, yes, yes,' replied Mr Smith.

Eve became silent and her heart rate dropped as she moved over onto the astral plane. It seemed to be the longest five minutes ever. Time itself appeared to hang in the air and stagnate. The entire room was motionless, aside from Isolda, who hovered around the resuscitation equipment. For a Saxon princess, she was adept in modern medicine, but then again, a thousand years of learning had not been wasted.

A cracking sound came from the direction of the pyramids and the illuminous inner channel. It was similar to the sound of pure electricity wrapped within a thunder cloud. This was soon followed by a loud noise which was akin to a crack of lightning. The sound splintered the plaster on the walls as it vibrated around the room. The channel shone with the most beautiful pink-purple glow. 'I can't believe he has done it. He has rescued the last one,' applauded Mr Smith. He pressed a switch and a TV plasma screen revealed the outside of the building. Everyone watched in amazement as a pulsating light, unlike any type of light ever seen upon Earth – shot out of the apex. At first it emerged slowly and then it blasted out towards the sky at supersonic speed. Then it was gone. Some clapped in celebration. Some laughed with glee and others cried with relief. Their friends had been saved. The moment was such a dynamic visual experience, that for a few seconds no eyes were upon Soul. When at last they turned to face his lifeless body, he had no colour in his cheeks and his lips were tinged with a deathly shade of blue. The silent alarms had not alerted them to the flat, green line being pushed across the screen. Isolda moved into action and tried her best to resuscitate him. Mercy attended to Eve, shaking her and trying to wake her. Eve suddenly sat bolt upright. She was quavering and appeared to be in shock. She didn't know what to do. She was married to a doctor and had once been a nurse herself. She should rush to Isolda's assistance. She knew what to do and she should do it quickly – yet she remained resolutely calm. Instead, she slowly walked over to her brother's table and pulled Isolda away from her CPR efforts. 'It's too late,' she uttered, 'you can stop now.' Isolda looked back upon her, a twisted, confused look upon her face. Eve was totally composed as she continued, 'Soul has been sucked up into the channel with the three aliens. Wherever your planet is – he is there right now. There was nothing I could do to stop him.' The reality of the situation then suddenly sunk in and Eve collapsed on the floor. Her tired, cancer-ridden body was shaking with exhaustion. Her eyes wide open, staring into nothingness. Pupils dilated, eyelids motionless with disbelief.

Once again, time froze. In one sense, there was a relief. Gentle creatures that had been sent to Earth as judicators – to ensure that the development of the human species had been concluded correctly and justly – had been released from their earthly prison. Unbeknowingly, mankind owed their existence to the strange aliens. Extra-terrestrials who, in their various forms, had inhabited our Earth and lived amongst us for millennia … some hidden deep underground and some in a human veneer. However, at the same time, a valiant young man had finally conquered his greatest fear – his own self-belief – only to die in doing so. George Smith broke the silence. 'Soul isn't dead. Maybe his body has died, but Soul the soul is somewhere on a new world right now. Perhaps one day, we can rescue him and bring him home again. We will make effort to recover him, I can promise you all of this.'

Mercy asked, 'Why did you not go with them, George?' He replied, 'On your planet, the captain stays with his sinking ship. Plus, I have yet more to rescue and I cannot leave until I recover each and every one of my friends. So, the Ouroboros will continue to be moles, constantly searching all underground hideaways until we find the rest of our kind.'

Nobody noticed Saskia. In all the mayhem of the last few minutes, nobody saw her sink into a corner. Nobody heard her cries. Nobody saw her tears. She finally stood up and walked over to Soul's lifeless body. Maybe for the first time ever, she really looked at him and saw him for the gentle giant he had always been. 'Too late to appreciate through new eyes,' was the thought that crept into her mind as she held his limp hand. Fingers as yet still warm. Fingers that would soon be as cold as the mortuary slab where his body would rest. She noticed that his left hand was tightly clutching something. She opened his fingers to see his blue stone – their blue stone – the talisman they shared. She would take it for safe-keeping. She held the stone to her heart – a heavy heart, weighed down with remorse.

George went to pick Eve up from the floor. She had just collapsed, so carrying her out he said, 'We will take care of her now.' Mercy shot him a look of pure indignation and contempt. In a state of disbelieving outrage, she marched out of the room – slamming the doors and bringing seven years of bad luck into the mirrored hallway as she left.

***

George Smith found her in the car park, sucking on a vapour cigarette as though her sanity depended on it. He approached her cautiously. Three hundred years on Earth had taught him to avoid the angry female of the human species. Mercy saw him approach and stomped directly over to him. 'I can report you,' she said. 'I can blow the bloody lid off your entire escapade. Just wait until the authorities know what you and your ET types are doing on our Earth. How dare you come here and kill my friend as part of some deal and give me all that "not knowing right from wrong" baloney. How dare you kill Soul, allegedly our one and only superior human, and for what … to save a few shrivelled-up mates.'

Mr Smith responded, 'Do you honestly believe that anyone would take you seriously, Mercy? Sometimes small children do not listen to their parents, and then sometimes it is the parents who choose not to listen. There are some mysteries that remain forever unbeknown to those who choose not to hear. A long time ago, three men were making a pilgrimage to a holy well, when they stumbled across this area. They saw my friends, and not knowing what they were, they called them "the unbeknown". The name stuck and people grew to fear them. They were harmless, but because they looked different, they were bullied. Then centuries later, when the young boys became lost in the tunnels, the locals blamed my friends for their deaths. They put explosives throughout the cave system and sealed many of the tunnels. They knew our type lived in there, yet deliberately they imprisoned them. It was an act of supreme violence and ignorance. My friends tried to live in peace with the locals, but a frightened cat can scratch. Not all humans are the same and some do try to help us; however, sadly that is not the case most times. You may try to tell your story, Mercy, but few will believe that the unbeknown actually exist. I am sorry about Soul. He was a good man.'

Sorry seemed too weak a word, but Mr Smith didn't know what else to say. He could do little but defend his position. Mercy De Vede was furious and her rage was palpable, visible and audible. She went to walk away, but then turned around to confront him again. She pointed a finger directly at his face. 'Now, I am going to be the one telling you what to do and you will obey me as you owe me and my shitty humankind big time.' George Smith stepped back in astonishment. He hadn't encountered such a forceful woman as this before. She continued, 'You are going to get back in there and you are going to get your tiny alien ass out of George Smith and into my friend Soul. You will heal, conserve and immortalise his body until you find where the hell his spirit has shot off to. Then you will return his body back to its rightful owner. Mr George Smith's remains shall go back to the coffin from whence he came. I don't care how you get his bones back in there – but back in there they must go. Am I making myself clear?'

Mr Smith nodded humbly in stunned compliance. 'Good,' she shouted, 'I am glad we understand one another. One last thing – I am to become part of the Ouroboros inner upper circle, but by way of a judicator to ensure that your body-snatching team behave yourself. Prior to today, I have never been a religious person, Mr Smith, but now I am going to throw some biblical teachings in your direction so you had better catch what is coming.' Mr Smith remained silent, not knowing what to expect next. Mercy continued, 'If my Sunday-school teachings serve me correctly, I believe it is written, "Judge not, that ye be not judged. For with what judgment ye judge, ye too shall be judged: and with what measure ye mete, it shall be measured to you again – and why beholdest thou the mote that is in thy brother's eye, but considerest not the beam that is in thine own eye."' The words could not have been delivered any sterner, by an over-zealous preacher pointing fingers from a lectern. Miss De Vede meant business.

Mr Smith looked confused. Mercy was angry and was not going to remain quiet for long. She continued, 'Let me interpret some ancient Hebrew for you, Mr Smith. Your Saxon princess described the DNA of my species as science shaking up some shit sediments from the bottom of a bottle. Well the next time you come across all virtuous, just take a long, deep look at yourself in some of the shattered mirrors in your hallway. When you get to reflect upon your own actions, you may realise that you aren't so bloody perfect yourself. Now follow me and let's do this swap before a young magician turns to mush.'

Mr Smith interrupted her angry dialogue to implore, 'But Miss De Vede, supposing we did find Soul's soul – and supposing we could return him to his body – he would not be the same person. He would have seen and experienced things no other human has ever encountered. We do not know what kind of a human he would become after all of this.' Mercy shrugged her shoulders. 'You said yourself that he was a kind man, so what … maybe he will come back as a more galactically enriched kind man. His empowerment is a risk we will have to take.' With that, Mercy marched back inside, and the alien being that assumed the name of George Smith had no choice but to obey. Killer stilettoes were well prepared to stomp onto his borrowed ancient feet … should he even consider refusal.

***

For the moment, this is where the story ended. The body of Soul was revived, but minus his own soul. George Smith's bones were returned to his tomb, and allowed to rest with those of his beloved wife Kitty. The unusual grave still lies serenely in St Aidan's churchyard, as though untouched by the passing centuries. As agreed, Mercy monitored non-human activity on Earth, and continued to show no mercy. The judge indeed became the judged. The unbeknown, under their pseudo-identity of the Ouroboros, continued to walk amongst us – mostly assuming the identity of those long gone. Not aging and not dying, they kept moving – from place to place and person to person. The search for their missing peers, deep beneath the surface of the Earth, continued under many guises. One of these guises, the health retreat, was sold and commercially it flourished. The skin of many a wealthy Cheshire wife, had never looked so good after partaking in the therapeutic waters of the spa. Many sought out the healing waters of the underground lake, in complete ignorance of its chequered past. The term 'unbeknown' was gradually forgotten over time. There were those who knew, but – for the greater part – humanity had no concept of what had just happened whilst its eyes were closed.

As for the caverns of Crank – It was not an easy place to find and those not local to the area would not know of its existence. It was just an ordinary sort of a wood; a small scattering of trees that made up little more than an overgrown coppice. Yet the nettles, the dandelions and the freshly sprouting saplings hid a colossal secret. Tucked away in a corner of North West England was a place of universal importance. Not that anyone would ever know, and that was the way it remained. Its secrets slept silently in peace, veiled beneath the guise of mundane normality.

CHAPTER 23

19th March 2034

Harry Kyfinn may have just turned 24 years old, but he still did as he was told. The instructions had been quite precise, yet much appreciated. He was a stranger to New York and so, clutching his map of Central Park, he set about following the young woman's explicit directions. Talking out loud as he read, he mumbled, 'Enter the park by West 100th Street, keep left and head towards the boundaries of the ravine. Look out for Glen Span arch and a steep cascade falling over a rocky incline. You can't miss it. Close to this spot you will see a statue of a man playing a guitar with doves feeding at his feet. I will meet you guys there at 4 p.m. Love Candy xxx.' From what little he knew of her, young Candace seemed to turn everything into a magical mystery tour.

As he walked past the hollowed grottoes in the underpass, he noted two guys walking ahead of him. Even though he could only see their silhouettes in the distance, he recognised the confident swaggers of his cousins. After all, they had all grown up together under the watchful eye of Aunt Mercy and their ever-faithful nanny Roserie. Now both studying in the opposing establishments of Oxford and Cambridge, he hadn't seen either of the twins in over a year. The invitation to a world tour closing party in Manhattan, plus a chance for a catch-up with some old, familiar faces, had been too good an opportunity to refuse.

Intensifying his walking pace, he tried to catch up with Jeremiel and Sariel – the new identities which had been given to the twins by Miss De Vede. As much as Harry hurried, by the time he had turned the corner, the boys had vanished. The twins had been tricksters almost as soon as they could walk, and so he presumed that this was one of their enduring practical jokes. Harry was completely certain that the guys he spotted earlier must be them. He recognised the back of their heads and their dark, tumbling curls. He stood for a while as he checked his bearings. The air was still refreshingly cold, yet the delightful contrast of pink cherry blossom against a deep-blue March sky and a New York skyline, was quite breath-taking. He continued to walk in the general direction of the water – framed majestically by a line of Norwegian and Sycamore Maples. Passing by a large, white Oak, he was suddenly jumped on by two 6ft, giddy Englishmen, who then wrestled him to the ground. He cursed as he fought them off, 'Jez, Sars – get the fuck off me, you stupid morons.' One of the twins emptied a water bottle over his head, and then the lads quickly got to their feet to make haste. Harry shook his shoulder-length locks as a drenched dog would, and then gave chase.

He eventually caught up with them at the statue as specified by Candace. 'You bloody idiots,' Harry uttered, as he then went to give them both the biggest man hug ever. 'I have missed you and your constant attempts to kill me,' he continued. They laughed at their own immature high jinks. Testosterone-loaded male bonding was quite evident. Jez spoke first. 'So, Cuz, who is this Candace chick and how come low-life goons like us we get an invite to such a glitzy shindig? Hey – not complaining – brill excuse to be in NY city.'

Harry looked upon them nonchalantly. 'Long story, guys, but all you need to know is that Candy is connected via some past thing. Her parents knew our parents and so on. You will like her. Candace is a cool girl, but she is only 17 and a bit dizzy – so cut her some slack, lads … and paws off; remember that she is only 17. Anyway, where are you both staying?'

Jez answered first, 'We have checked into Aunt Darcy's condominium on 5th Avenue. Wow – what an amazing place. She has invited us over loads of times, but we always felt a bit awkward. You know the deal – it's never straightforward when there's been some big family feud. Whatever you do or don't do, you always end up offending someone … and so more fool us, we found an excuse not to visit.' 'First time in New York then?' asked Harry. 'Yep, there's a first time for everything, I guess,' responded Sari with a cheeky smirk followed by a nudge in his brother's ribs.

Harry continued to quiz his cousins. 'Have you met Micah yet?' he asked. Sari tried not to grin from cheek to cheek. Aside from politics, music was his passion and in his world Micah was one of the greatest musicians who had ever lived. He finally responded, 'My God; we finally get to meet Micah! Can you believe we are related to him? Well done to my cougar aunt for bagging herself a superstar toy boy. To answer your question Haz, no, not met him yet … we only flew in late last night and he was away when we got to Aunt Darcy's place. I am told that he will be back later today, so we get to meet him before Saturday's party. Finally, can't wait.' Seri rubbed his hands together in gleeful anticipation. Harry smiled to himself, recognising that although his cousins were just a mere four years younger than himself, four years made quite a difference on the maturity score index post-puberty. Barely out of their teens, the twins exuded boyish energy, the vivacity of youth and likeable stupidity.

They were being watched. They didn't know it, but many eyes were upon them. Harry's hair was being flicked, Jeremiel's shoelaces had been tied together and Sariel's remaining water was being miraculously emptied over his own head. Harry knew exactly what was happening. He put his Q-watch into video mode as he did a 360-degree turn. 'Come on out and show yourself, Candace. Like father, like daughter – stop with the trickery.' Now vaguely visible via heat recognition digital imaging, Harry walked over to the statue where Candace stood. She slowly pixelated into vision, giggling as her pink, dimpled cheeks became evident. Jez and Sari stared in disbelief. Of course, they were aware that Candace was the daughter of the great magician 'Soul', but they hadn't expected such a startling and dramatic introduction. Sari approached her first. 'Great to meet you, Candace. Do I shake your hand or pull a white rabbit from my hat? How the hell did you do that trick by the way? Neat!' The meeting was casual and light-hearted. Just four young people in Central Park enjoying the moment on a pleasant spring day.

***

On a small mound by the water, and completely invisible, sat a gaggle of four curious demons. They watched the youth of the moment as they teased each other in innocent jest. Emmanuelle had watched many past youths from many past centuries and this was nothing new to her – except that now something was different. There had been a change. She was observing her own granddaughter emerge from her camouflage of invisibility. The dynamics of the world and the future had altered slightly.

Tobiah asked, 'Do they know which statue they play beneath?' Emmanuelle responded, 'Time erases so much, Tobiah. The twin boys are the sons of Eenayah and the statue is dedicated to the man she was married to. The name Anthony Mort has been carved upon that stone. After his death, he was praised for his services to the homeless.

However, he holds a guitar and that is the only reference to his former life as Reed Baratolli. I guess they haven't noticed. Young mortals are often in such a hurry to grow up, that they fail to pay attention.' Océane commented, 'Given the close connection, you would think that they would at least recognise his name.' Emmanuelle gave Océane a sideward glance and, with a hint of sadness in her voice, she responded, 'So many humans tumble through life looking left and right before they cross the road, yet not really seeing what is on the road, or scanning the way ahead. Time wipes so much history away, which is why humanity keeps making the same mistakes. Let us not condemn this behaviour as it keeps us in employment.' Tobiah looked upon the statue with intensity. 'How did he die?' 'Suicide,' responded Emmanuelle, 'and before you go pointing any fingers, Reed's death was nothing to do with me. Perhaps he was consumed with his own guilt … I cannot be blamed for everything.'

Arabella finally piped up, 'Hey, but what are the politics here? One of them mentioned a family feud.' Emmanuelle replied, 'Which world war are you referring to? Aunt Darcy was none too happy when her boyfriend fathered a child with Saskia, and neither was Owyn too pleased when Ruby ran off with Harry and the twins, later filing for divorce and threatening police action. I mean, all human families have their issues and complexities, but these guys have knots pulled so tight, that even the passing of time cannot loosen them. The more they pull away, the tighter the knot. Arabella poked Tobiah in the ribs. 'They are on the move now. Let's follow. There may be other seedy gossip on the horizon. I enjoy this paranormal spying malarkey.'

***

The youngsters started to make their way out of the park and back towards West 110th Street. Harry looked puzzled, so asked, 'Is your father relieved about his world tour coming to an end, Candy?' She shook her blonde, pre-Raphaelite locks and nodded to indicate an appreciative 'yes'. 'Thank God it has ended – or nearly ended, anyway. He is exhausted. Touring drains so much energy out of him. His last show is tomorrow and he aims to go out with a big bang. As far as my father and magic is concerned, do not expect anything remotely average or normal.' Jez was intrigued. 'What kind of big bang is he planning?' Candace glanced at the young man with a look of thinly disguised disgust. 'You surely must know that tomorrow is a rare total eclipse, more so because it coincides with the Vernal Equinox?' Jez responded sarcastically, 'Oh yeah – sure. I knew that. Silly me for forgetting the Vernal Equinox.' 'So, what exactly is your dad planning?' asked Harry. 'He won't tell me. He won't share his special secrets with anyone,' replied Candace, 'but I do know that the timing coincides with totality, so there has to be a connection. Plus, right at this moment he is sat on a posh boat on the River Nile. I do know that he has invited a small, select audience, so it has to be something fairly extraordinary.'

'Sounds neat,' exclaimed Sari as he almost lost his footing on the pathway. He regained his composure and then continued, 'So, is this amazing last performance in Egypt then?' Candace laughed. 'Hell no, nowhere as predictable as that. Try northern Sudan. My mother has just flown out to join him. I believe the desert will be his stage. The small town of Abri is the epicentre on the path of absolute solar totality. My mother told me that it isn't easy to get to, but then again my father will see that as part of the fun. I have read the exclusive "A-list" invites and let's just say that manicured nails will be chipped. Sounds like a hell of a challenge. The guests have to get their pampered arses over to the tiny east-coast village of Wawa, then find themselves a boatman to ferry them over the Nile whilst trying not to look too appealing to the crocodiles. Once on the west bank, they have to walk, and yes I said walk … through the palm groves and there, on the brink of nothingness and desolation they will find my father's stage … as well as an ancient temple. The entire area will fall along the line of the full eclipse. Just 60 or maybe 70 people will have front-row seats to witness his alchemy whilst the world falls dark. None of this is a coincidence; it has all been carefully planned. Whatever it is, knowing my dad … it will be dramatic.'

Candace could have picked all their jaws up from the floor. Each of the lads were visibly stunned and enthralled by her description of events. 'Why the hell are you not at the show? It all sounds pretty awesome.' Candace smiled back at Jez. He was cute. She liked him. He had the deepest pool of brown eyes. Eyes she felt she could jump into and swim around in. Deep and beckoning. She composed herself, held her hormones in check and continued with the conversation. 'I don't really do basic survival, Jez. I think some of the guests will be staying in B&Bs in Abri and the greater majority will be camping next to the Nile on Sai Island. It may sound like an adventure to you, but to me it sounds like heat, dust, scorpions, dysentery and lots of other things that could kill me. No air con – no bubble bath – no Candace.' Jez sniggered at her reply and pushed her away in mock antipathy. 'You shallow little spoiled brat,' he responded, before giving her a quick kiss on her reddening cheeks. His twin detected chemistry and gave his brother a knowing look.

The unseen demonic spirits listened with much interest … and a splattering of devilish amusement. Arabella had a question burning inside her head. 'Are these twin boys really the reason that the Ledanite prophecy has existed for thousands of years, Emmanuelle? Are these guys … it? I mean, they seem so … normal. Shit – they are just average 20-year-old kids larking about in a park. What is the big deal?'

Emmanuelle replied, 'If you had ever bothered to turn up at school and partake in biology lessons, dearest Bella, you would have learned that genes can be either dominant or recessive. The twins have inherited the mutant gene from Tamar and her long line of clones, but I have to agree that it seems recessive in both boys. Neither one of them appears to have developed any powers of note, and I am guessing that this was why the Ledanite let them go so easily. Nonetheless – they will still become highly successful and prominent people – but just not in the way mortals refer to as supernaturally powerful.'

'Do tell us more,' quizzed Arabella, 'and don't start picking holes in my education. At least I found meaningful employment with you.' 'Only because the devil makes work for idle hands,' retorted Emmanuelle with a sneer. Océane grew impatient. 'The boys – Jeremiel and Sariel – Arabella asked you about them … what they are to become?'

Emmanuelle stopped to face her younger contemporaries. They were naturally curious and she owed them an explanation. After all – they had accompanied her on the Ledanite prophecy ride. She began, 'Okay, this is what I know so far, but do understand that destiny can be changed by free will. Angelo was the second born. Mercy De Vede renamed him

Sariel in order to give him a new identity. Let us not forget that these unanointed royal babes were born in a cave and were unregistered. Sariel will become Secretary-General of the United Nations. Unless we can get into his head and weave some corruptive thoughts, it is likely that he will strive to correct world poverty and bring pandemics under control. He will bring water where there is drought and food where there is famine. Climate change and the preservation of the Earth and all its species will be high on his "to do" list. He will be a great healer of mankind – not great by my standards, of course, but certainly in historical terms.'

'What of Jeremiel?' asked Tobiah. Obviously, he was Alessandro – the first born.' 'Jez, as he will be known, will become the Supreme Allied Commander of NATO,' replied Emmanuelle. 'He will rule over the air, land and sea. For such a man of war, he will probably become a global advocate of peace.' 'You say probably – what does that mean?' asked Arabella. 'It means that nothing is certain. He will probably marry my granddaughter Candace, and because she is one-quarter demon, anything could happen. The universe likes balance. If mankind falls too much in one direction, the opposite will occur in order to keep the equilibrium. Therefore, if civilisation becomes wicked, Jeremiel will address the balance – but he could just as easily come over to our side. I doubt it, but we can haunt in hope. It all depends on the temperature of the water at the time – do we heat it up or cool it down?'

Tobias looked to be deep in thought. '7th October 2009 – wow, that is 8,929 days ago, or should I say 24 years, five months, 12 days. How time has flown? We have so little concept of time in our realm, don't we?' Arabella looked puzzled. 'So, what happened 8,929 days ago, dearest Jack the Ripper?'

Tobiah shot her a gentlemanly acidic look before responding. 'I went to this criminology convention in London and listened to a certain Professor Roland De Vede making a keynote speech. He said much the same thing as you just did. He harped on about averages and outliers, but all in all, you said it in a much simpler way, boss. It's all about balance. Strange how things just pop back into one's mind sometimes. By the way – please don't refer to me as Jack the Ripper again. That was just a weird Illuminati phase, and I am so over it now. Oh and talking about the professor – didn't you kill him, Emmanuelle?'

The senior demoness seemed to take offence. 'He died on 7th December 2016 of natural causes, dear Tobiah. Maybe he didn't recover too well from the stroke I inflicted upon him, but I certainly didn't pull the last breath from his tobacco-laden lungs. He had a nice burial in Strasbourg, however. Quite brought a tear to my eye. Tuesday the 13th – unlucky for some, I guess.'

As both Tobiah and Emmanuelle drifted off mentally into their own personal memories, Arabella had become bored. She attempted to drag everyone back 8,929 days into the present moment. She asked, 'What do you think Soul is planning, Emmanuelle? According to what we just overheard, it is also the Equinox tomorrow, and we know what happened the last time Soul became involved in one of those. Maybe AKA Mr Smith has built another alien launchpad in the Sudan. He will be next door to the home of the pyramids, so it could work. The Ouroboros have never given up looking for their classmates, and isn't this the time of year when they phone home?' Emmanuelle scolded her newest initiate. 'I know you find all of this amusing, Arabella, but we have had a professional relationship with the Ouroboros for a long time. We scratch their back with our talons and they reciprocate with witch hazel and cotton wool accordingly. But you do have a point – if this is their final bailout, we should be around for the light show.'

***

As the demons gathered their thoughts and lay their plans, Harry, the twins and Candace had long disappeared from sight. Oblivious to their invisible spectators, they had set off for 5th Avenue and Aunt Darcy's apartment. Their conversation was full of mirth and the excitement of meeting the illustrious Micah. None could quite believe that he was once a homeless tramp on the streets of New York. They wondered how he had been rescued. None of them knew the full story. History had wiped the slate clean and the statue in the park was nothing more than just a piece of granite, covered in bird droppings.

CHAPTER 24

20th March 2034

It was dawn in Northern Sudan and an extraordinary day was about to unfold. Soul crouched down, and let the grains of sand filter through his fingers as though he was counting each grain like the sands of time. The Nubian Desert met with the water of the Nile, just as the night met with the day. He stood and watched as the most exceptional orange sunlight triumphed over the pale white light of the full moon. His tall, Icelandic frame cast a tall shadow against the shore. He knew that all too soon, at 10.44 Universal time. astral dominance would be reversed as the moon blocked out the sun from mother Earth. Later in the afternoon, the Earth would spin in partial dark and light. Just for one moment in one day, the balance would set the scales at equal levels. The astrological significance was acknowledged by many, yet only understood by few.

Soul felt at peace with himself – alone and yet not alone. He had grown accustomed to sharing his skin with the entity he knew only as George. The being from the Ouroboros had saved him, because he had saved them. They both had an equal will to survive, and the balance of that desire had placed both species inside the one body. It had been a strange, almost schizophrenic journey. However, Soul had not complained. He had witnessed the most remarkable sights from the far reaches of the galaxy; he had been truly blessed. George had found another human, one who had been able to travel spiritually to the constellation of Aquila, to rescue him and return him to Earth. At the command of Mercy De Vede, Soul's body had been conserved until his return.

'I have grown accustomed to living with you, George. I will be sad to see you go.' In his head, he heard a calm, refined voice. It spoke to him with the slightest hint of a Scottish brogue. It was the only voice George knew. 'I will miss you equally, Soul, but I am excited to leave. Do you know what to do?' 'Yes, everything is in place.' Soul found it slightly amusing that the life form from a far constellation had retained the voice and the name of a 17th-century Scottish mine owner. Nonetheless, he understood that for a species with no vocal cords, they had little choice but to improvise. In their own deep, dark, cold world, they changed colour like a chameleon to say 'hello'. With an alien identity, no human could possibly understand or imagine, a name borrowed from a tomb in St Aidan's churchyard back in the northwest corner of England, suited the purpose.

Soul admired this strange race. They had demonstrated their endurance again and again. With physical bodies, unable to withstand conditions on Earth, they had evolved to detach their inner energy and leap into the discarded remains of human dead. As distasteful as Soul initially found this concept, he also understood that a decaying carcass had no further use for its former occupant. It was the nature of nature to use whatever was available to ensure continuity of existence. Nature supported survival and the end justified the means. The Ouroboros had evolved to repair and retain the cells of the body they borrowed. Hence, the scorched and charred body of Soul the man, now stood tall and healthy. George had promised him that when he vacated their shared frame, that Soul would henceforth continue to age slowly. After all, George would not be leaving behind an empty shell. Soul could do little else but hope this was the case. He trusted George. He trusted the

Ouroboros. He had visited their homeland. He knew their type. He had seen worlds beyond worlds and corners of the universe no human had ever seen, or would ever see. He saw colours the human eye could not perceive. Laws of physics twisted and distorted into other realms of reality. Soul felt privileged and he would help this ancient species in whatever way he could.

He stood on the far northern shore of Sai Island and looked around at the recently constructed amphitheatre. The magician's audience were starting to arrive in their masses. The excitement was intense and the nearby chatter elevated. Some arrived carrying unbecoming welders' goggles, but most were holding on to their exclusively designed eclipse glasses with bejewelled tight grips. His team had set up areas of aluminised mylar sheeting with solar filters, just in case some guests forgot to come prepared. Soul knew there were bound to be a few. The quiet solitude of dawn was quickly becoming transformed into a circus. This was all part of the plan. The show was one big performance to mask the real activity taking place somewhere else.

The Ouroboros had been secretly funding years of archaeological excavations at the pyramids of Meroë. It had been a closely guarded secret that the labyrinths of Egypt had extended underground into the once Egyptian territory of Sudan. The Ouroboros also owned many of the gold and iron mines in the area and had access to the tunnel systems. An entire underground city, protected from the fierce heat of the sun, covertly existed out of harm's way and prying eyes. Those Ouroboros who had not evolved to leap into humans had sheltered their fragile skins from our solar rays deep beneath the desert sand. Below the numerous, sky-reaching triangles of Meroë, a multitude of subterranean burial chambers hid the bodies of the hibernating Ouroboros. The ancient Kushite's knew of the visitors, and to some they were deities to be worshiped. The hieroglyphics upon Meroe's mighty temple columns hinted as much, but few mortals understood their relevance.

However, now was their time. For just a few minutes, the sun would be shadowed by the moon, and so under cover of total darkness and with the Equinox looming, the Ouroboros would at long last exit planet Earth. Their exit could be visual and explosive. It was Soul's job to create a mystical, magical, colourful distraction. It was a job he accepted with a heavy heart. The strange aliens had become his friends.

***

As the moon started to drift across the path of the sun, the world held its breath. The air was ghostly still. Insects stopped crawling and birds had stopped singing. Nature was confused. The temperature suddenly started to drop. This was different tonight; this was daylight being exterminated. Our sweet, obedient moon – the very symbol of feminine energy – for once dominated the masculine power of the almighty sun. She now called the shots. Everything felt unnatural and a strange, and surreal atmosphere bathed the arena in anticipation. Darkness crept onto the podium like a shroud being slowly pulled over the face of the departed.

Soul stood centre stage. A great deal of time and trouble had gone into constructing this temporary theatre. Care had been taken to not overly disrupt the local ecology, and so the end result was quite primitive and yet blended in perfectly with the setting. With one single beam of light illuminating his frame in a golden shimmer, Soul addressed his audience and set the scene. 'Welcome to Abri. The name is most fitting as this is the first three letters of the word Abracadabra. Some believe that this is an Arabic word which translates to, "I create as I speak." Whatever its source or its meaning, it is a welcome coincidence and most appropriate for the beginning of my … of your magic show. Very soon you will take part in an unusual sensory experience. This will be conducted under the eerie darkness of a total lunar eclipse. Every one of your senses will be heightened, so be prepared for the unexpected.' He had set the scene. Manipulating the psychology of the audience was part of his skill set.

Soul paused a moment as he watched the moon slowly pass before the sun; little by little. His timing would need to be near perfect as totality would last but a few minutes. In that time, he would need to confuse his audience with his supposed presence and yet be 700km away at the exact same time. He pointed to the south and the distant mountains. Soul was building up the mystique and moving his audience into an altered state of mind. He was dressed in black with a long, purple cloak – looking both magical and yet sinister. Soul understood the importance of presentation and setting the scene.

He addressed his audience with a commanding tone. He told them, 'The pyramids and temples to the south are dedicated to the ancient deity of Amun-Ra. These are two gods combined into the one body. Ra was the mighty sun god – so it is fitting that we watch the sun fade in the land that worshipped him. Amun was the king of all gods. According to ancient scripts, when Amun was combined with the sun god Ra he became even more powerful. He was then called Amun-Ra and many of the Sudanese temples and pyramids are dedicated to him. Also to the south are the lands where Sudan meets with Ethiopia. It is told that this was the Garden of Eden and the beginning of mankind. What better setting to celebrate the return of the sun after it has been shadowed by the moon? Let us drink to Amun-Ra – the twined gods. Let us ask that our sun be returned. Let us raise a cup to shared bodies.' Soul held a large, golden goblet up to the sky. As much as he was saluting the ancient legend of Amun-Ra, he was also thinking about his own body – one that he had also shared with another strange being. Then … as though taking upon the role of an Egyptian high priest, he shouted, 'We drink to Amun-Ra.' Music began to trickle around the amphitheatre as the sound of Gustav Holst's 'The Planets – Mars, the Bringer of War' threatened the ears of those who dared to listen. Sinister, disturbing, unnatural – yet ultimately magical. Not an eye blinked, not a head turned.

The audience gasped as a bolt of lightning appeared from out of nowhere, igniting the goblet into blue and orange flames. The flames trickled down Soul's raised arm like liquid magma and enveloped his entire body in fire. The audience gasped. Each looked around at each other wondering if this was part of the stage act or some spite from God at Soul's alleged blasphemy. Should someone rush onto the stage with a fire extinguisher. The organisers did not seem to be panicking or taking any action. The alarmed guests felt some reassurance. This was surely part of the stage act, some impressive, well-rehearsed illusion.

Soul's body, still consumed by flames, rose into the air and levitated above the onlookers. As he floated above them, they could hear the spit of the blaze, feel the heat from the inferno and smell the smoky aroma of his flesh being burned. Totality was but a moment away. Soul threw a spear in the direction of the moon. Maybe the audience were in a state of mass hypnosis, but he had managed to create the illusion that the fiery spear had pierced the moon directly in its centre. It changed colour – first to blood red, then to purple, then to orange. It continued to change as it worked its way through the colour spectrum. At full totality, an amazing display of fireworks ignited the Sudanese horizon.

Then came blackness. Soul's burning body vanished, the music stopped. Everything became dark and still, like the inside of a coffin. The audience were left hanging in a state of alarm and anticipation. It was a psychosomatic technique. One that Soul had acquired over the years. He had learned to play his audience by over-stimulating all of their senses, followed by sudden withdrawal of all stimulus. Slightly cruel, maybe, as it left people feeling confused and disarmed. Yet it also pumped pure adrenaline into the bloodstream. As one feels elation after a roller-coaster ride, so it left his viewers after his show. Soul recognised that adrenaline was addictive, as indeed had many of his mystical forefathers. Adrenaline was the ultimate wonder drug used by the ultimate alchemist.

***

In the ancient kingdom of Kush, 700km away – in a place known as "the Island of Meroe" – over 200 Nubian pyramids lanced the horizon with their pointed skewers. Greater in number and structurally more pointed than their Egyptian equivalents, they were a sight to behold on the relatively flat desert vista.

Each sitting upon a camel, three European visitors were being led to the site by their tour guide. Saskia, Eve and her husband Gérard entered the Bedouin encampment just after breakfast and shortly before the moon started to make its passage before the sun. They each simultaneously gasped when they first beheld the surreal landscape which welcomed them. The smooth, rippled desert sand had been suffused by geometrical structures which did not look Earth-like. Forever the intellectual, Gérard had been doing some research into the area and mentioned the theory that some believed the island had inspired Plato's Atlántida Nesos.

Eve agreed with her husband, 'If ever there was a city lost in time, then this surely must be it. By the way, you cannot see them, but we are not alone.' With her clairvoyant eyes, Eve could spot thousands of spirits and energies from other realms. 'This is a major event,' she declared, 'and probably fitting that something ends where humanity began.'

As they dismounted from their camels, they were taken to the tent facing the largest pyramid. Soul was waiting for them. 'How the hell can you be in two places at once?' asked Gérard. 'I am a magician,' responded Soul with a cheeky smile. 'He is also an illusionist with a helicopter, a lookalike actor and has amazing technical skills with holographic technology … as learned from a certain place called Darwydden,' responded Saskia with a hint of sarcasm. Of course, she knew that Soul could have performed all of these tricks by using genuine magic, but constantly concerned with being labelled as a freak, he made each of his shows as plausible as possible … with maybe just a smidgen of authentic fairy dust.

'Do you have to do that "pulling out the energy thing"?' asked Gérard. 'By all accounts it killed you last time, and as many times as my dear wife has tried to explain the details, I still don't understand how you survived.' Soul shivered at both the memory and the plummeting temperature as the desert became darker. 'Not this time,' he responded. 'None of our desert ET friends are trapped behind collapsed rock – thankfully. The Ouroboros hiding here are all bubble-wrapped in their own skins and just waiting for a pulse of galactic energy to zap them up.

My only job for the day is to deliver George into the central chamber of the pyramid. Talking of which, it's now my turn to make tracks. I am looking forward to resuming singular residence of my own body again – sorry George.' 'No offence taken,' came the softly spoken reply of his resident alien spirit.

Saskia tried not to look concerned, but the memories of the Crank experience still weighed heavily on her mind. She felt unsure about her husband's safety. She shielded her true concerns by the guise of humour. It was one of many masks and something she had practised since childhood. 'Will you come back all old and wrinkled?' she asked of Soul. Her husband laughed. 'George has promised me that he has regenerated my cells, sorted out my irritable bowel issues and I should age naturally from now onwards. I doubt I will crumple into a heap, Saskia.' George chipped in, 'And let's not forget that I have cured you of gout.'

Over the years, Saskia had struggled with the fact that two souls had occupied her one and only beloved Soul. Normality sounded like a good option. Nonetheless, watching Soul walk towards the activated pyramid, she still felt deeply uneasy. Timing was everything. What if it all went terribly wrong? She was glad to have Eve and Gérard for support. She was also relieved that her teenage daughter wasn't here to pick up on her anxiety. She could hide many things from many people, but she was incapable of hiding anything from Candace.

A small group of humans had always known about the Ouroboros. Archaeologists, scientists and politicians alike were aware of their existence. Over the years, many advanced technologies had been shared with mortals in return for other favours. As such, a small, furtively selected team stood within the tent. As totality approached, a digital clock counted down the universal time. Four minutes was all they had – four small, very precious minutes to vacate planet Earth. A lilac beam emerged from the apex of the main pyramid as the inner cavity opened up. All around the camp, a strange, unearthly noise resonated as it bounced off the angled sides of the other pyramids. Eve commented that she had never heard such a sound before. Gérard commented that he had never seen such a light as this before. It seemed to move and swirl within tiny electrified bubbles within tiny radiant bubbles.

A panic had developed within the tent. The scientists seemed concerned. They each looked upon the digital clock as though something was going dreadfully wrong. 'What is it?' yelled Saskia. 'Should we be worried?' The scientists refused to answer. Of course, Eve could read their thoughts. She turned to her sister-in-law. 'They are running out of time. They should all be within the inner chamber by now and they are not. There is only one minute left of totality.' 'What then? What if they don't make it into the light?' Saskia's eyes glazed over as an uncomfortable feeling of dread hit the pit of her stomach. She felt a wave of nausea consume her body. 'I don't know,' replied Eve. 'I think it could be serious,' she added.

Thirty seconds and counting. The lilac light needed to change colour to indicate it was full and ready to propel its passengers into the ether. Twenty seconds were left on the clock and the colour hadn't yet changed. Gérard marched over to the scientists, demanding to know the situation. They merely shrugged. The lead technician was talking to the engineer in the main pyramid. Just ten seconds remained on the clock. 'Some kind of disruption in the energy flow,' he finally responded. 'We can fix it, but we simply don't have the time. Sorry, but it looks like we have lost the window.'

Nobody moved. Nobody spoke. Nobody really knew what any of this actually meant. Would another window occur in the future and, if so, when? Saskia dare not think about Soul and where he was, or what he was. The thought occurred to her that she would grow old and maybe even die before the next window was available. Yet her magician husband would be forever young. Maybe his own daughter would age beyond his own years? She needed George Smith out of her husband's body, so he could be a true human again, and like a true human, grow old … grow old with her.

Zero! Time had run out as time always did. The lilac streak of energy pierced a hole in the atmosphere with electrifying precisions, but alas it was empty. Nobody knew what to do or what to say. The scientists were nameless people, apparently void of all emotion – but even they looked drained and troubled. Eve wandered outside the tent, and walked towards a line of spiritual entities invisible to the human eye. She recognised some of them. They tried to communicate with her, but she visualised a psychic bubble around her head to shut out the noise. She didn't want to listen. She had no answers to their many questions. She sat beneath a clump of palm trees and listened to the silence. The desert encampment was veiled in a surreal, cool darkness. The sun was still blackened, with just the faintest hint of a silver halo. With the alien-like geometric shapes permeating the desert sands, this remote place faraway didn't even resemble planet Earth. This was a strange yet ancient place. It could tell stories that few could hear.

Eve looked at her watch. 'Hang on a second,' she thought, 'the sun is still obscured by the moon. Surely totality would have passed by now?' She heard garbled chatter coming from inside the tent. The chatter became louder. Eve ran back inside the tent to find a sea of bewildered faces. She ran up to her husband. 'Gérard, what is happening? Why is it still dark?' Gérard shrugged his shoulders. 'The moon hasn't moved,' he replied. 'What do you mean?' she asked. Saskia approached them both and added, 'He means exactly what he just said. The moon appears to have stopped dead in its tracks.' Eve was confused. 'But who or what could stop the moon from orbiting? Could this be Soul? Has he become that powerful?' Saskia was not sure what to say next, but she was certain that her husband hadn't become some sort of superhuman overnight.

She put her arm around the chilled, bony shoulders of her sister-in-law. She finally replied, 'I am sure that this isn't Soul's doing, or else why would he need a helicopter to get from Abri to Meroë. If he could grow wings and fly, then surely, he would. He cannot stop the orbit of the moon.'

At that moment, a supersonic-type blast echoed around the encampment. The lilac light was now bathed in an exquisite golden glow. Pearls of pure energy seemed to be emitting their radiance from within the beam. The scientists became animated. The only three words anyone could hear was, 'They are in – my God – they have done it.' All eyes were on the apex of the pyramid and the exquisite light being secreted from its zenith. Nobody looked elsewhere – aside from Eve. Her eyes were drawn to the small clump of palm trees from where she had just been sitting.

The silhouette of a female shape appeared. The feminine outline was totally engulfed in a radioactive-type glow. This was power – raw power in its purest form. Eve nudged Saskia and her husband. 'I think you both need to come with me,' she instructed. The trio walked pensively towards the fervent shape. Three demons also emerged from the shadows. Emmanuelle, Tobias and Arabella walked slowly in the same direction. Surrounded by a small crowd of six, the orange glow faded to reveal the presence of a young female.

'Candace,' exclaimed her mother. Everybody was shocked and momentarily speechless. 'Candace, did you do this? Did you just stop the moon in its tracks?' asked her aunt. The young woman smiled. 'Yes, of course. My father needed a bit more time,' came the cheeky, adolescent reply. Emmanuelle approached her and tenderly touched her cheek. 'But how could you have done this? You are a mere mortal.' Candace giggled as though slightly embarrassed. 'But you are wrong, Grandmother. I am far from a mere mortal. It has taken me quite a bit of time to figure it all out, but I now know exactly what I am.'

Soul rushed out of the pyramid and in the direction of his wife and daughter. 'What is going on? What has just happened? Candace, how the hell did you get here?' Saskia slipped her hand into his. She asked, 'Can I just confirm, Soul, am I talking to you or George or both of you?' 'Just me, Saskia. George has left now. They are all gone. The Ouroboros have vacated the planet.' Saskia looked deeply into her husband's face. His powerful, square jaw was still taut and youthful. His sparkling blue, Icelandic eyes still shone with life. His head was far from bald. With a proud mane of golden locks falling upon his shoulders, he had suffered no hair loss at all. He stood strong and tall, his back not even remotely hunched. Soul noticed her probing eyes. 'No, I have not disintegrated, Saskia. I may gain a few crow's feet from now on, but George promised that I would age slowly and naturally.'

For a moment, all eyes had diverted to Soul; however, now they were back on Candace and they had many questions. Candace had some explaining to do. She first addressed her grandmother – the cunningly evil demoness Emmanuelle. 'Gran, you just referred to me as a mere mortal and indeed part of me may be human; however, you must surely recognise the fact that as your granddaughter, I am also one-quarter demon. However, you have been hiding something else from me, haven't you, dearest Gran? Once upon a time, you were the mistress of a very wealthy Russian entrepreneur. I believe my grandfather was Sergei Beselovaya. I use the word "was" because he is no longer with us. By any chance, did you come here to say goodbye to him?' Her mother Saskia interrupted her, 'What do you mean by this, Candace?' She responded, 'Mother – your father Sergei Beselovaya went into that lilac beam. Have you never wondered why the Ouroboros employed you? Yes, you were bright and got top grades in your law degree, but so did many hundreds of others. You were chosen because your father Sergei was part of the Ouroboros – in fact, he was their main financier. Were you so unquestioning and subservient that you never even recognised this?' Saskia looked stunned. She addressed her mother, 'Is this true?' Emmanuelle hung her head down low. She gave a simple, monosyllabic answer – 'Yes.' Candace heaved an impatient sigh. 'At long last the truth is out. Mother, you are so slow on the uptake. Why did you think Granny became the mistress of a human? Answer, duhh … he wasn't a human. She was in league with the Ouroboros. So, let's take stock – from my maternal side I am one-quarter alien and one-quarter demon. Not quite such a mere mortal now, am I, folks?'

Candace then turned to face her father Soul. 'We haven't really discussed your parentage in detail, have we, Father? I have seen your birth certificate, Daddy, and it names you as Saul Leifsson. I do prefer your stage name, however. Soul really suits you. You once told me that your father Leif was a worker in an aluminium-smelting company. Part Icelandic and part Russian if my research serves me well. I believe he died when you were both quite young – something about a terribly tragic accident in the plant. Who knows; maybe that is why Aunt Eve became so obsessed with the afterlife and you became so connected to rock and metal. Just a theory ...' Soul grew impatient and seemed irritated by his teenage daughter's assumptions. 'Get to the point, Candace.' She continued, 'Your father Leif was the human component of my composition. At long last I acquire my one-quarter of my "mere mortal" bit – even though it was a human contribution which descended from the line of Tamar and her daughter Sheol. The infamous Tamar mutant gene, constantly prophesised and probably way oversold. However, I wouldn't be at all surprised if you had acquired your magical streak from your human father. After all, he was a carrier of the rogue chromosome.' Eve looked shocked. 'Are you sure about this, Candace?' Candace held her hands up in the air in despair. 'Which bit confuses you, Aunty? The fact that I am one-quarter human or the fact that you come from a long line of mutant ancestors? The witch of Endor was a psychic medium, just like you are, Aunty Eve. Yes, of course you both inherited your special traits from your father and his forebears. However, let us talk about your mother, Aunt Eve. My sweet darling grandmother Roserie – she with the

Spanish twang. I believe your father died insolvent and although there was some industrial compensation thingy, it didn't last very long. Your mother Roserie was multilingual and I understand she got some high-profile nanny jobs with an exclusive clientele. You have both told me how you spent your childhood travelling the world and living in a multitude of mansions. Did it ever occur to either of you that in fact your mother Roserie was an angel?' Soul looked shocked. 'No, no, not at all. I mean – she was a nice lady, but we hardly saw her after Dad died.' He looked to his sister Eve. 'Is this true? You can see such things?' 'I have suspected it from the minute I could string a thought together, however I didn't know for sure until we visited Ruby at Darwydden. The night we were taken into the secret prayer room – when you went to show Ruby where her sister's body lay – an angel appeared to me. It was our mother,' Eve replied. 'I think I even told you once, but you didn't believe me and poked fun at me, so I never told you again.'

Candace stood back to address the growing crowd, paying particular attention to her demoness grandmother, Emmanuelle. 'The Ledanite have had it wrong all this time. They misunderstood the original scripts. Hey, that happens – they won't be the first and won't be the last. Over time, you get this whole "Chinese Whispers" thing, and people read into stuff what they want to believe rather than what the author actually intended. Truth is, Tamar's sacred gene – the one she passed on from clone to clone – remained recessive. Talk about chasing one's own tail. Mongrels are always stronger than pedigrees. Himmler's racial purity theory was bullshit. A mixed genetic gene pool always wins the day, and mine is as mixed as it could possibly get. It took me a long time, but I finally figured it out – I am part-demon, part-angel, part-human and part-alien. I have a lot of interesting parts to me.'

The crowd fell silent. Nobody knew how to react. Eve looked at her watch and then at the moon. 'I hear what you are saying, dear niece; however, you have held the moon still for ten minutes and that could affect our calendar system or the tides or whatever. Any chance you could return it back to its orbit?'

The crowd stood back as heat started to emerge from Candace's body. A lime glow consumed her entire being. She raised both her hands towards the moon as though cradling it between her hands. It took less than a minute for the moon to continue along its path, casting a shadow upon the Earth as its journey continued.

***

Lunar experts, astrologers and other prominent scientists would debate this for many years to come. None would know the answer to this scientific conundrum aside from a select few. The world would continue to spin on the axis of its own ignorance, and the Ledanite would continue to give credence to their secret prophecy in equal ignorance. Yet beneath their feet, a young female with a perfect spiritual, racial and cosmic mix was gaining dominance. The general rule being, nature likes balance.

In the meantime, the queen of an ancient Kushite kingdom had returned to the Garden of Eden. Princess Candace, wife of Moses, had returned yet few had even noticed. This was a prophecy that even the bible had not foretold – unless she was the meek that was to inherit the

Earth. She came like a thief in the night – or more accurately, the dark totality of a solar eclipse.

***

Once the crowds had dispersed, a young gypsy woman approached Soul's daughter. She clapped loudly as her bare feet sunk into the dunes. 'Hi Candy, nice to meet you at long last,' the girl pronounced. She spoke with an unusual part Irish, part Yorkshire accent. Candace looked through her, as though her eyes were an MRI scanner; thus examining every cell and organ in her body. 'You are the same age as me,' Candance stated. 'Yet you are older. How can that be? Have you have travelled from the past to meet me? 'The young woman smiled as she replied, 'of course I have Candace. I wouldn't have missed this spectacle for anything in the world, or the moon for that matter.'

Candace was divinely powerful and exceptionally gifted, even when compared to universal standards of phenomenal brilliance, but she was not alone.

Mother nature would never put all its eggs in just the one basket…

THE SEQUEL

CLARAH

A bewitching tale of begrudgery and extraordinary consequence

Quotes to ponder ...

- 'I cannot confirm or deny this, but there is something inside the pyramid that is "not of this world."' – *Professor Dr Alaaeldin Shaheen, Dean of the Faculty of Archaeology, Cairo University.*

- 'Man, has gone out to explore other worlds and other civilisations without having explored his own labyrinth of dark passages and secret chambers, and without finding what lies behind doorways that he himself has sealed.' – *Stanisław Lem, Solaris*

- 'You're an interesting species. An interesting mix. You're capable of such beautiful dreams, and such horrible nightmares. You feel so lost, so cut off, so alone, only you're not. See, in all our searching, the only thing we've found that makes the emptiness bearable, is each other." – *Carl Sagan, Contact*

- 'The universe is full of magical things patiently waiting for our wits to grow sharper.' – *Eden Phillpotts, A Shadow Passes*

- 'Light and Darkness. One cannot exist without the other. There is no true Master, without the power of balance. ℱ' – *Luis Marques, Kemet – The Year of Revelation*

- 'Human beings are ultimately nothing but carriers – passageways – for genes. They ride us into the ground like racehorses from generation to generation. Genes don't think about what constitutes good or evil. They don't care whether we are happy or unhappy. We're just means to an end for them. The only thing they think about is what is most efficient for them.' — *Haruki Murakami, 1Q84*

- 'We do not need magic to change the world. We carry all the power we need inside ourselves already: we have the power to imagine better.' – *J. K. Rowling, speech to Harvard Alumni Association, 2000*

ABOUT THE AUTHOR

I was born in the Lancashire mining town of Leigh , back in the days of black & white TV and when children played out, climbed trees, scuffed their knees and made dens. Enid Blyton was my heroine, and I have often aspired to write an adult version of "the secret seven". Some of us never really grow up...

My father died when I was a baby, and so as a child I was raised by my Grandmother Florrie. She was a loving intelligent lady, and also an avid reader, who went through about 5 books a week. Every night she read to me, and so by the time I started school at 4 years old, I could already read, write and quote my 12 times tables off by heart. Thank you gran. With her encouragement, I have been writing books from about the age of 6. These were for my own entertainment and not for public consumption.

It has taken me a long time, (and life has a way of creating other priorities to distract us), but eventually I decided I should publish. With a love of history, mythology, theology, genealogy, the paranormal, gothic mansions and anything that involves secret tunnels – I was destined to be a science fiction writer. I like to add authenticity to my books, by using well researched chronicles, and then scattering a thimble full of fairy dust to magic the facts into a story.

I hope you enjoyed the Line of Tamar – book 1 of the Tamar prophesy series.

Please don't forget to leave a review if you like what you have read – your appraisal means everything.

THANK YOU

'If the doors of perception were cleansed everything would appear to man as it is; Infinite. For man has closed himself up, till he sees all things thro' narrow chinks of his cavern.' William Blake

Sheila Mughal